The HAUNTING of HERO'S BAY

Originally from Devon, Amanda Block moved to Edinburgh in 2007, where she attained a master's degree in creative writing. Her work is often inspired by myths and fairy tales, which she uses as starting points to tell new stories. Amanda's writing has been shortlisted in contests such as the Bridport Prize and the Mslexia Short Story competition. Her debut novel, *The Lost Storyteller*, was published in 2021 and was a Waterstones Scottish Book of the Month.

Also by Amanda Block

The Lost Storyteller

The HAUNTING of HERO'S BAY

AMANDA BLOCK

HODDER &
STOUGHTON

First published in Great Britain in 2025 by Hodder & Stoughton Limited
An Hachette UK company

The authorised representative in the EEA is Hachette Ireland, 8 Castlecourt Centre, Dublin 15, D15 XTP3, Ireland (email: info@hbgi.ie)

1

Copyright © Amanda Block 2025

The right of Amanda Block to be identified as the Author of the Work has been asserted by her in accordance with the Copyright, Designs and Patents Act 1988.

Map © Joanna Boyle 2025

All rights reserved. No part of this publication may be reproduced, stored in a retrieval system, or transmitted, in any form or by any means without the prior written permission of the publisher, nor be otherwise circulated in any form of binding or cover other than that in which it is published and without a similar condition being imposed on the subsequent purchaser.

All characters in this publication are fictitious and any resemblance to real persons, living or dead, is purely coincidental.

A CIP catalogue record for this title is available from the British Library

Hardback ISBN 978 1 529 36083 7
Trade Paperback ISBN 978 1 529 36085 1
ebook ISBN 978 1 529 36084 4

Typeset in Adobe Caslon Pro by Manipal Technologies Limited

Printed and bound in Great Britain by Clays Ltd, Elcograf S.p.A.

Hodder & Stoughton policy is to use papers that are natural, renewable and recyclable products and made from wood grown in sustainable forests. The logging and manufacturing processes are expected to conform to the environmental regulations of the country of origin.

Hodder & Stoughton Limited
Carmelite House
50 Victoria Embankment
London EC4Y 0DZ

www.hodder.co.uk

For Chaz,
Who scares easily,
And loves deeply.

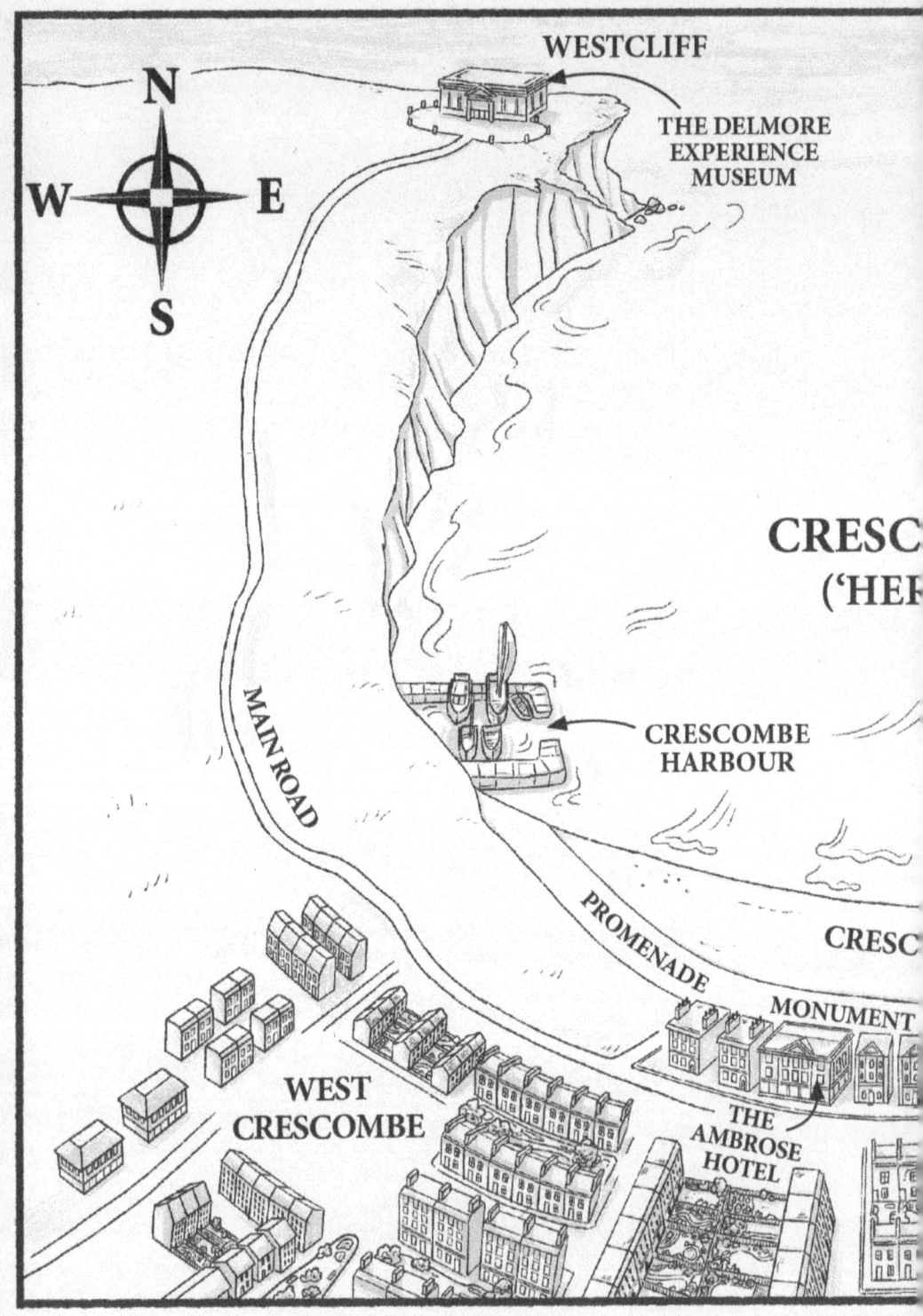

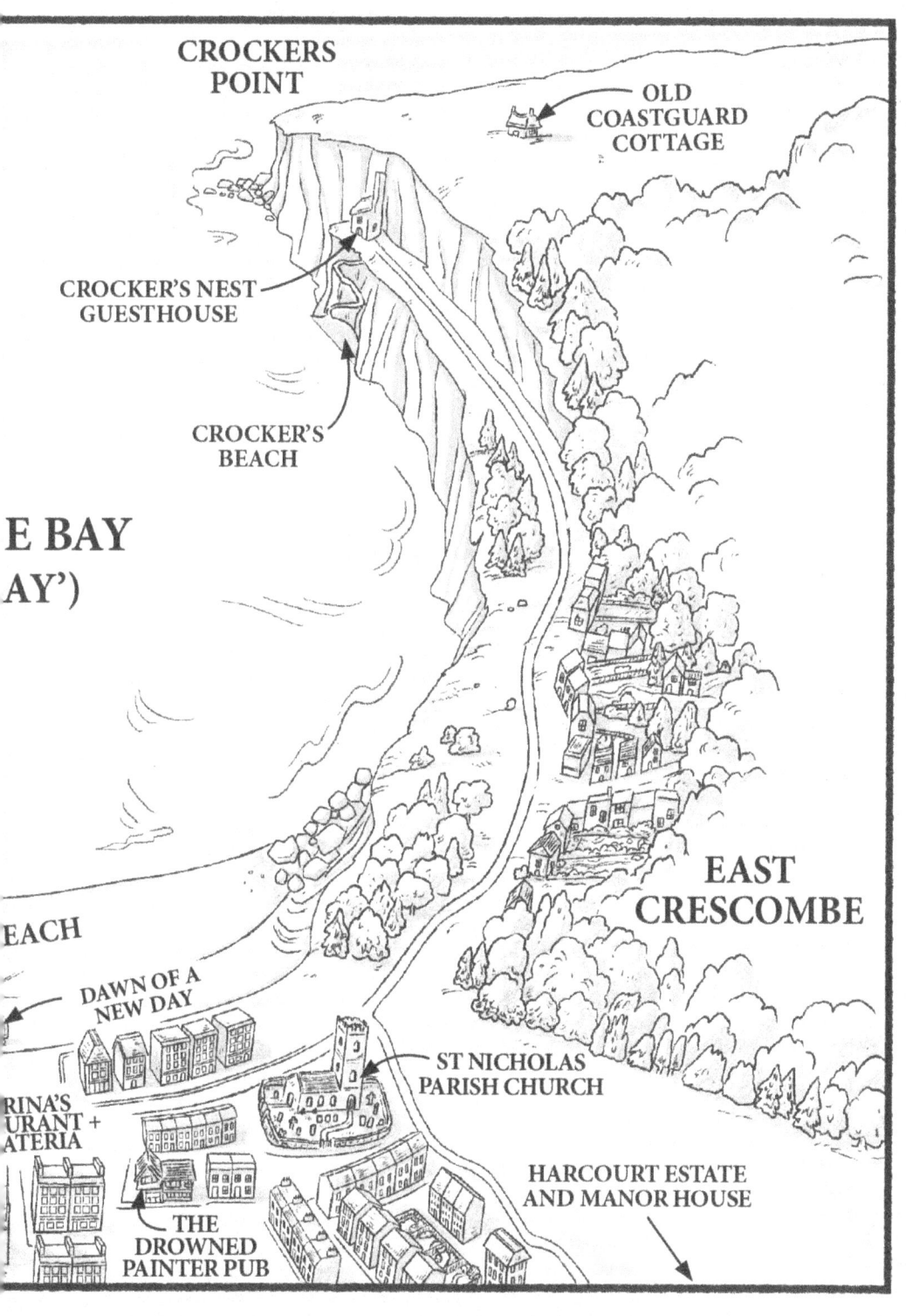

August, 1977

She's found before anyone realises she's missing.

It's just before dawn, and a photographer has puffed his way up the cliff path, hoping to capture the first glimpse of sunlight as it bleeds into the bay. He sets up his tripod in the dewy grass a few feet from the precipice, then can't resist shuffling past it to peer over the edge.

At first, in the grey-blue gloom, his mind still woolly from sleep, he can't work out what he's seeing. Something is snagged on the rocks below; a knot of driftwood, perhaps, or a clump of flotsam. Even as the photographer's eyes adjust, and understanding begins to writhe in his empty stomach, for a few more seconds he tries to convince himself it's something else down there: a seal; a mannequin; a mermaid.

Later, after two local constables have arrived, secretly thrilled by their unexpected summons, there is some debate over how to get to her. She is caught at the most easterly point of the bay, wedged between the rocks, though the hem of her nightdress is fluttering in the water, giving the impression she's still breathing. By both land and sea, the route to her is treacherous. But they don't deliberate for too long – they can't risk her being carried out into open water or, worse, any tourists stumbling across this scene – and, in the end, a pair of grizzled fishermen manage to navigate the rocky shoreline and drag her into their boat like a prize catch.

Later still, the constables are replaced by their superiors, who try to piece together what has happened. She was staying at the nearby hotel, they discover, where no one seems to remember her in any detail; why she was there, or when she was last seen, or even much about what she looked like. If it weren't for her name and address in the hotel register, her order for the breakfast she never ate tacked to the board behind the desk, she might not have been there at all. The only part of her that seems to have stuck in people's minds are her glasses. Lenses like jam jars, explains the receptionist, cupping her hands to demonstrate.

They don't find the glasses. It's one of a few inconvenient loose threads, though the police forge ahead with their enquiries. Foul play is ruled out – she doesn't seem to have made enough of an impression on anyone for that – and if she slipped from the cliff path by accident, why was she out there after dark, and in only a flimsy nightdress? No, suicide seems most likely, especially when the family in the room below report that they heard strange noises: scratching, banging, crying. The whys and wherefores seem to matter a little less after that; she obviously wasn't quite right in the head.

The hotel's manager, an agitated man at the best of times, frets it will be bad for business, a guest dying like that. But it's almost the end of summer. The other guests quickly disperse and, soon enough, most of the staff too – back to college, or university, or other brighter opportunities in bigger towns. The story goes with them, of course, but fades and shrinks as it travels, until it's just a half-remembered anecdote the manager needn't worry about. Not yet, anyway.

She lingers in the locals' memories a little longer. Her death might be a tragedy, a further blight on an already stormy and disappointing sort of summer, but, for some, it is not a shock. For there are those who have always distrusted that stretch of coast, that side of town. They know the tales about that place – most of them, at least – because they were told them by their grannies, who were told them by their own grannies before that.

Ultimately, though, it's the sea that remembers her the longest. It takes its time to wash her away; untangle the strands of her hair caught in seaweed, scrub the spots of her blood from the rocks. It holds on to her glasses, which sank to the depths when she fell, bumping them around the seabed until they are cracked and cloudy. There is no hurry to erase her – no point, even. The sea doesn't forget. Ever-present, it knows all of this has happened before.

And will happen again.

1

Crescombe

'You'll know all about that painting, then.'

Finley barely heard the taxi driver's pronouncement, because he was fairly sure he was about to die. Since the station, they'd barrelled down country lanes, narrowly avoiding collisions with other vehicles, alarmed-looking ramblers and, at one point, several sheep. As he gripped the rucksack on his lap, Finley pictured the taxi overturning in a ditch or perhaps simply plunging into the sea – though the thought of Mollie weeping regretfully over his picture on the news was not wholly unwelcome.

'*Hero's Bay*,' continued the driver, undeterred by Finley's silence. 'By that artist who drowned: George, Lord Delmore.' He attempted an affected tone, but in his broad West Country accent the name was mostly Rs. 'You'll know about him and all.'

'Erm, yeah,' Finley said, because it seemed to be more of a statement than a question. Besides, what else was there to know, beyond the drowning? Like Van Gogh's ear, Delmore's death was as famous as his paintings.

A pineapple-shaped air freshener was dangling from the rear-view mirror and watching it judder was almost as nauseating as its tropical stench. As the car lurched around a hairpin bend, Finley longed for a proper view of the sea. He kept catching sight of it between the trees, glinting in the early-evening light. If it would only stay put at the horizon, perhaps staring at it would curb some of his queasiness (or did that only work *at* sea?).

'Don't rate the painting myself,' the driver said a few minutes later, hurtling past a stop sign. 'It's a bit dark, a bit blotchy. Can't even tell it's Crescombe.'

'No,' agreed Finley, who wouldn't have been able to identify any image of Crescombe.

The sea glimmered again. It was toying with him, peekaboo-ing between branches. Ordinarily, Finley thought the sea too vast, too dangerous, but today – presumably because he was hot, and the water so close – its pull was undeniable. He imagined lying at the shoreline, sand shifting beneath his back as he was gently rocked by a cooling tide . . .

The taxi vaulted over a hidden dip. As Finley bounced in his seat, half the contents of his open rucksack – which he'd been hugging to himself like a lifebuoy – went tumbling to the floor, including several books and his just-in-case juice. Leaning down to collect them, a clump of dark hair fell into his eyes and his stomach gave a dangerous tremor.

'Here we are.' The driver took both hands off the steering wheel to gesture ahead.

Re-emerging from his knees, Finley found they were zooming towards a group of hikers gathered at the side of the road and, in their midst, a white sign that read:

Crescombe
('Hero's Bay')

The hikers, who were all women, were clutching at the sign like it was a friend – while their real friend was wobbling on the rungs of a nearby gate, her phone aloft, trying to fit everyone into a photo. In spite of their walking clothes and rucksacks, something about this group put Finley in mind of bridesmaids posing around their bride. Or maybe he just had weddings on the brain.

'Popular spot for photos, that,' remarked the taxi driver. 'They'd be better off taking it up at Westcliff, though, where he painted it. S'pose they'll go there later. S'pose you will too.'

Finley once again noted the statement, the *certainty*.

'You weren't wanting a picture yourself?' the driver continued.

'Oh – no, thanks,' said Finley, assuming this to be an empty offer, considering the sign and its bridal party were now specks beyond the rear windscreen.

Even so, he winced to imagine that photo; how clammy and awkward he'd look – and how overdressed, because it had been far chillier in Edinburgh that morning, and now he was too worried he'd sweated through his T-shirt to remove his jumper.

What would be the point of a picture, anyway? He never posted on social media, and it wasn't as though he had anyone to send it to, aside from his mum. Most of his closest friends – the ones from university – had now drifted exclusively into Mollie's orbit. In any case, the whole point of coming to Crescombe was to keep a low profile, so it seemed counterproductive to advertise his presence when, by and large, he just wanted people to forget about him. Assuming they hadn't already.

'It doesn't get the same attention as places like Woolacombe or Clovelly,' mused the taxi driver. 'If it wasn't for the painting, nobody would come here. But there's something about Crescombe, you'll see.'

This comment, which sounded slightly muffled due to the popping in Finley's ears, was intriguing enough to rouse him from self-pity. They had begun a sharp descent and, having emerged from their wooded surroundings, he now had a clear view of the bay below, where little houses and boats fringed an arc of yellow beach. At either end, the coastline curved, so its eastern and western points curled back towards its body, like the claws of a crab.

Beyond was all sea. It leaked between Crescombe's pincers, spilling out towards the sky. Perhaps it had been that talk of Delmore, and drowning, but it all looked far less welcoming than in Finley's imaginings of this moment: the water was greyer, rougher; even at this distance he could see it frothing against the shore.

He had been right before: the sea *was* too vast, too dangerous. But there was no turning back now. He was expected, and he'd come a long way to be here – or rather, to be anywhere but there. Better, then, to submerge himself in it all – the unfamiliar surroundings, the solitude, even this terrible taxi ride – and let the next month wash over him until he was ready to resurface.

Upon seeing Crockers Nest, Finley's first thought was that it looked lonely. Jutting from the end of a natural ledge that snaked around the middle of the cliff, the guesthouse felt far removed from the vibrant seafront that had just flashed by. Undoubtedly, it was the last building in Crescombe – though in the evening gloom, the tall stone structure hardly seemed like a building at all, more an extension of the jagged cliff face at its back.

Still, anything felt more inviting than getting back in that taxi, so Finley shouldered his rucksack and began to drag his suitcase along a precipitous driveway. Tucked into the guesthouse's weathered stonework, he found a teal front door that smelled freshly painted, and was just reaching for its whale-tail knocker when a family of four emerged from the other side. Eagerly, they eyed his taxi, but before Finley could warn them about the driver, another figure wafted over the threshold, her floaty multicoloured dress and stream of chatter putting him in mind of a talkative tropical fish.

'... Oh look, there's a taxi here already, that's a bit of luck! You take this one, then, my loves, and I'll cancel the—' She broke off as she spotted Finley. 'Oh, *here* he is!'

'Hi, Lorraine.'

He hadn't seen her for years, but she looked much the same as she did in the framed photograph at his parents' house, where she and his mum were perched on a pub wall with pints: her shoulder-length hair was still fluffy and blonde, her make-up still a little overdone, and she had retained that twinkle in her smiling eyes.

Waggling an admonishing finger at him, she announced, 'The last time I saw you, young man, you were piddling in a paddling pool!'

'So, quite a long time ago!' Finley spluttered, lest the assembled onlookers – who now included the taxi driver – thought him some twenty-eight-year-old pervert who lurked around kids' gardens.

Lorraine merely laughed. 'Come here – give your godmother a squeeze...'

She opened her arms so wide she might've meant to squeeze the whole driveway. Reluctantly, Finley allowed himself to be scooped into a tight embrace, acutely aware of how sweaty he was in his jumper, and that people were watching, and that he hardly even *knew* this woman...

Eventually, she released him, waved off her other guests, then took his arm and led him into Crockers Nest, breathlessly enquiring about everything from his journey to his family, before informing him that his accent was *ever so nice* – an impressive observation, Finley felt, considering he'd hardly said anything at all.

The guesthouse's entrance hall was brighter and more modern than he had anticipated, largely due to a new-looking skylight that illuminated its whitewashed walls and a mint-coloured carpet still as fuzzy as a show home's. Still, it contained nods to the building's history and proximity to the sea, such as the artful arrangements of shells and pebbles on the mantlepieces, and the reception desk whose top seemed to be propped up by three old and slightly pungent barrels.

'Now, your room's right at the top...'

At this, Finley expected them to head up the main staircase, but instead Lorraine beckoned him through a side door, where they emerged at the foot of a much narrower, spiralling set of steps. Clearly, this was part of the original building, and Finley experienced a little thrill as they began to ascend: it felt like they were exploring an old lighthouse.

'I was sorry to hear about your bookshop closing, love,' Lorraine called over her shoulder.

'Oh,' said Finley, immediately downcast again, 'thanks. Though it wasn't really *my*—'

'And about... *Mollie*, was it?' Lorraine looked around, forcing them both to stop. 'Your mum told me that and all. What a little cow.'

Finley presumed this last remark referred to Mollie, rather than his mum, and felt a deeply ingrained need to defend her: 'She's fine – it's all fine.' Though as he stared down at the handle of his suitcase, his despondency deepened. 'It was ages ago now...'

'Doesn't matter,' said Lorraine firmly. 'Doesn't mean it won't still hurt. Took me years to get over The Dickhead. *Years.*'

The Dickhead, Finley assumed, was Lorraine's ex-husband, an accountant who'd had an affair with his secretary – which suggested to Finley a lack of originality as well as moral fibre. In response to this infidelity, Lorraine had extracted vast sums from him in the divorce ('Not so good with money now, is he?' Finley's dad had chuckled) with which, just under a year ago, she'd moved to North Devon and bought the then dilapidated Crockers Nest.

'I *understand*, is what I'm saying,' she went on. 'And if you ever need to talk, I'm right here.' She jabbed a pink fingernail towards the step on which she'd stopped.

'Thanks,' muttered Finley, both embarrassed and a little clearer as to why she'd agreed to have him to stay for the summer. 'And thanks for all of this, for putting me up...'

Lorraine smiled and, to his relief, continued to climb the stairs, her brightly coloured dress rippling around her ankles. 'I'll be expecting you to pull your weight!' she trilled. 'I've plenty of jobs for you!'

'Of course,' said Finley, who had hoped for this: he wanted all the distractions this place had to offer.

'It's only admin, really,' admitted Lorraine. 'Although—' She stopped and spun around again. 'You're a historian, aren't you, Finley?'

'A classicist,' he said, before clarifying, 'I mean, I studied Classics at uni.'

'History, Classics . . .' Lorraine gave a sweep of her hand to denote *same thing*. 'Because I've been thinking, I could maybe use you for my little research project. I've been looking into the history of this place, you see, and especially into the Crockers themselves. They were *smugglers*, you know.'

'Really?' said Finley, recalling those barrels at reception, his interest piqued once more.

A few moments later, both a little out of breath, they reached the top of the spiralling stairs, where there was a lone arched door that wouldn't have looked out of place in a chapel. Producing a key dangling from a crocheted seagull, Lorraine explained, 'Now, the handle gets a bit sticky sometimes, so you might need to give it a rattle.' She duly demonstrated, then nudged open the door, saying, 'Here we are: home sweet—*Oh, for God's sake!*'

A cold blast rushed over the threshold. It ruffled Finley's hair and snuck beneath his jumper, irresistibly reminding him of books he had read about the discovery of ancient tombs, and the hiss of stale, trapped air escaping for the first time in centuries.

Lorraine, meanwhile, had dived into the room and thrown her weight against the round window on the far wall, which had blown open. 'Bloody thing,' she panted, pushing against the wind, 'always coming loose . . .'

While she resecured the latch, Finley stooped to pick up the local leaflets that the breeze had scattered across the floor and took in his new surroundings. It was a small, square room, its walls comprising either wooden panels or wooden cupboards. In addition to the window – which he now saw was fashioned like a large porthole – this gave the impression he had just walked into a ship's cabin.

'Here, come and look at the view,' said Lorraine. 'It's the best in the house – the best in Crescombe.'

Unlike the local taxi driver, who had barely bothered with the town's second syllable, Lorraine drew it out until it rhymed with *tomb*. Obediently, Finley joined her at the window, and suddenly the floor felt unsteady, as though he really were on a ship. After all those stairs, he had guessed they were high up – and he had already seen how precariously Crockers Nest was perched on the cliff ledge. Nevertheless, it was still a shock to peer beyond the round window's flimsy-looking safety bars; to see that there was very little between himself and the water.

'We're right at the eastern tip of the bay here,' explained Lorraine, oblivious to his discomfort. 'That's the beach, of course' – she tapped at the glass – 'and the main bit of town behind it. And up there, that's Westcliff, where Delmore painted *Hero's Bay*.'

Still feeling apathetic towards Crescombe's most famous export, Finley forced his gaze towards the long stretch of sand to his left, then up towards the darkening mass of land on the other side of the water.

'It's all a crescent, see?' continued Lorraine, tracing the shape on the window. 'They think that's why it's called Crescombe.'

Finley tried to make an interested noise, but had returned to staring at the encroaching sea below, mesmerised by the way its foam marbled after it had lashed against the rocks.

Lorraine, perhaps sensing his attention was elsewhere, asked, 'Are you hungry, love? I could heat you up some spag bol or something?'

'Oh, I'm okay, thanks,' said Finley, taking a step back from the window and almost tripping over his suitcase. 'I ate before, at the station,' he added, untruthfully.

'You sure?'

Lorraine looked surprised, even disappointed. There was a small pause, which was probably only noticeable because she was so talkative, but made Finley wonder whether she, like he, was weighing up what they were to one another. Now, was he principally her godson, guest or employee?

'Well, all the info you'll need about Crockers Nest and the town and whatnot is in the folder,' she continued, a touch more business-like than before. 'And let me know if you have any issues. We've just had this room done up and you're the first to stay here – my guinea pig, if you like.'

Finley, who hadn't known this, wondered what – if any – issues she was anticipating. Before he could ask, however, Lorraine had returned to the door, where she knocked at the neighbouring wooden panel saying, 'It's like a cave under here, the walls are that much of a mess. Must've been where the servants lived or something. I guess we'll find out, won't we?'

'Sorry?'

The twinkle returned to her eyes as she ducked out of the door. 'In our research . . .'

Finley waited until her footsteps on the stairs had faded, then tapped his phone to the sensor on his arm. He'd done a lot of snacking on the train, so was surprised to find his blood sugar wasn't too bad. After a brief search, he located a kitchenette inside what was essentially another cupboard, and with a heavy feeling he couldn't entirely attribute to tiredness or even heartache, he unloaded his insulin into the fridge. Between a pint of milk and what looked like a local ale, he then slotted his just-in-case juice; he would need more supplies tomorrow.

On closing the fridge door, Finley became aware of a faint floral smell, as if Lorraine had spritzed around some room fragrance before his arrival. Still, this was all a vast improvement on the last place he'd lived – a dingy flat off Leith Walk that had smelled of damp and his housemate's weed – so Finley strove to ignore the niggling feeling that coming here hadn't been his most rational decision, and began to unpack.

He got as far as laying out all the books he had brought – most of them vestiges of The Book Bothy's closing-down sale – before flopping back onto the striped covers of the single bed and reaching for his phone. More out of habit than any genuine interest, Finley began to scroll through various updates from people he wouldn't exactly call friends, until – with a jolt that rivalled what he'd felt on seeing that vertiginous view – he spotted a familiar profile and the words *HEN DO!!!*

Don't, Finley thought, even as he tapped on the first picture. Don't do it to yourself.

The party must have been organised by Mollie's screechy schoolfriends, because everyone was decked out in matching pink sashes and those stupid bobbing headbands. Still, Mollie looked happy enough – more than happy, Finley realised, an invisible weight pressing at his chest, emptying his lungs, as he drank in the sight of her freckles, her dimples, her shiny red hair . . .

In one picture, he spotted Fiona, which was another unpleasant surprise. His sister might have known Mollie just as long as he had, but her presence there felt highly disloyal. Still, Finley gleaned some satisfaction from the tight-lipped expression on Fiona's bony face – almost certainly a reaction to the penis-shaped straw poking out of her drink.

Eventually, Finley dropped the phone onto the bedcovers and stared up at the low wood-panelled ceiling (really, this room was almost reminiscent of a sauna), trying to distract himself from the images of Mollie and her friends still imprinted on his vision. He considered sneaking out to find some chips – maybe eating them on the beach, where he could make a start on one of his books. After all, coming to Crescombe was his chance to get back to things like reading; to get back to himself.

He must have fallen asleep, though, because the next thing he knew it was dark, and he was cold. Groggily, he pushed himself up, and it took him a moment to remember where he was. The porthole window had blown open again. He groped for the switch on the bedside lamp – it was darker here than it would be in Edinburgh right now – and then stumbled across the room, the cold air stinging his bleary eyes.

This time, he braced himself for the view when he peered beyond the spindly safety bars, and whereas before the sea had been advancing upon the cliff shelf, now the invasion seemed complete. Logically, Finley knew that there must still be something of the ledge left beyond the footprint of the guesthouse, yet at this hour – and with the tide as high as it was – Crockers Nest appeared entirely surrounded by dense, dark water.

Hastily, Finley pushed the window shut with a clunk, then examined the stiff latch for a moment, marvelling at how strong the wind must have been to dislodge it. But when he looked back at the window, his heart lurched: on the other side of the glass, a pale face was looming out of the night, staring straight at him.

With a grunt of shock, Finley staggered backwards, before his sleep-addled mind made sense of what he was really seeing: his own reflection, peering back at him from the dark glass.

Heart hammering, he forced his focus beyond his anxious face, towards the distant lights of Crescombe, but continued to feel strange: clammy, and a little lightheaded, as if he'd been climbing a misty mountainside. Presumably it was only tiredness or his blood sugar, because in reality he had never felt closer to sea level; he could still hear the water's endless churning. The sound followed him back to bed, where he lay awake for a long time, listening to the sea's deep, rhythmic breaths until, eventually, they merged with his own.

Oh, look – you're new.

2

The Drowned Painter

Finley awoke early, roused by the keening of seagulls and that steady pulse of the sea, which was quieter now, as though the beast that had spent the night thrashing against the rocks was now at slumber. The view from his room was also less unsettling this morning; the low sun was beaming straight into the bay, and Crescombe Beach was glittering at the collar of the land like a gold necklace. Experimentally, Finley prodded at the weighty latch of the large porthole window and, when it didn't budge, wondered whether he might have dreamed it blowing open.

Regardless, he felt brighter by the time he emerged through the teal front door of Crockers Nest, especially after pausing to glance back at the guesthouse. He identified his room, far above, by its round window – and the fact that it protruded from the top of the building like a princess's turret. It was, as he had suspected, the highest point of Crockers Nest, though it didn't look quite as perilous as it had felt last night, and he was reassured that it seemed firmly embedded in the cliff face behind.

He turned to stare out at the open expanse of the Bristol Channel, breathing in the fresh, briny air, and was just pondering where he might find breakfast this early when something caught his eye: carved into the rock beyond his feet were lumpy steps, zig-zagging right down to the water. The sea was a sculptor, Finley knew, but they looked too deliberate to be natural, and he wondered whether he was looking down on a fisherman's shortcut – or perhaps, he thought, recalling Lorraine's words about the Crocker family, this route had once been used by smugglers.

It was this intriguing idea that drew Finley down the uneven footholds, his fingertips digging into the rough stone at his side, for there was nothing in the way of a handrail. At one point, the rest of the rocky slope even seemed to fall away, and Finley was suddenly left sidling next to a sheer drop into the water. Gasping, he managed to scramble onwards, though only because, twenty metres or so below, the milky green water looked still and calm, almost *inviting*...

At the base of the steps, Finley discovered a small beach. Judging by its wet sand, it had been entirely underwater only hours ago, which made it feel secret, almost enchanted – as did the fact that perched between the humps of a rock just off its shore was a mermaid.

But no, of course she wasn't; she was just a girl – a *woman* – sitting there in a black swimming costume. She had her back to him, and was gathering up her long, tangled hair, which must have been dark blonde when dry, but now, dripping in the low sunlight, had an almost greenish hue. As she began scrunching it into a heap on the top of her head, Finley backed away – he didn't want her to think he was spying – but the crunch of tiny shells beneath his trainers made her pause, her hands still in her hair.

'There's no need to leave because of me.'

Unlike her words, her tone was not encouraging. So much so that Finley wondered whether he'd stumbled across a private beach – though if it *was* private, surely it belonged to Crockers Nest?

'Sorry,' he said, to be on the safe side. 'I didn't realise—I'm staying at the guesthouse.'

As she twisted to look at him, her hair fell back over her shoulders in soggy tendrils, like frayed rope. She was pale and lean, with a narrow face and wide-set eyes, which did not entirely dispel Finley's suspicion that he had disturbed some mythical water spirit – an encounter, he knew, that was unlikely to end well for him.

After a few moments passed in which she simply stared at him, he felt obliged to fill the silence: 'I only just arrived last night.'

'Yes,' she said, her gaze drifting down towards his trainers, which were already sandy and sodden.

In turn, he looked at her, suddenly noting she had nothing with her; no bag, no dry clothes, not even a pair of flip-flops.

'Did you *swim* here?' he asked.

'Yes.'

'From where?'

She gestured vaguely over the water, which could have meant the small harbour opposite, or the western tip of Crescombe, or perhaps the middle of the Atlantic. The sea rippled gently beneath her arm, like a silken sleeve, but Finley could still picture how it had seethed in the dark the previous night.

'Is it safe?' he asked doubtfully.

Her brow furrowed. 'It's the sea.'

'Right, yeah,' he said, feeling foolish. 'I just meant— I heard the weather's really changeable here.'

She neither confirmed nor denied this, instead asking, 'Are you going to be here a lot?' She glanced at the cliff behind him. 'No one ever comes down those steps.'

Finley wasn't sure how to respond: did she or didn't she mind him being here? Given her general demeanour was almost hostile, she might have been warning him and, once more, he thought of the water women in legends, like the selkies who shed their skins to come on land – and the misfortune that came with trying to catch one.

'Well, see you,' she said, apparently now bored with their conversation – if it could even be classed as that.

She stood up, revealing a figure more sinewy than skinny. Without a trace of self-consciousness, she stretched, her muscles visibly shifting around her shoulder blades, and, with a little leap, disappeared under the water.

He waited for her to re-emerge: five seconds, ten seconds . . . surely thirty seconds by now . . . As the small splash her dive had made subsided, he began to grow uneasy. Where was she? Had she banged her head on a rock, or become tangled in seaweed? Or what if – and this was ludicrous, but the whole encounter had been so strange – *what if he had simply imagined her?*

Then she bobbed up, further than where he'd been looking, her hair now plastered to her head, her profile as sleek as a seal's. He expected her to turn and smirk, acknowledge she'd been messing with him (*had* she been messing with him?). But she just kept swimming, her long arms carving through the smooth water, and she didn't look back.

After reascending the steps to Crockers Nest, Finley joined a section of coastal footpath snaking out from behind the guesthouse. For about ten minutes, he walked through an untended passage of greenery, until he arrived at the eastern edge of Crescombe Beach. It was already dotted with bright towels and windbreaks, a few families paddling and playing ball games at the shoreline, and a great number of dogs zooming around the expanse of wet sand.

Finley wished Mollie was here. Before he could stop himself, he was picturing how she might look; her fair skin shiny with sun cream, her toenails freshly painted. Maybe she'd even have brought that enormous hat from their holiday in Menorca, which he'd had to protect on his lap for most of the plane ride home.

In an attempt to escape these imaginings, Finley eschewed the beach and stuck instead to the paved promenade that ran parallel, where the owners of little shops and eateries were rolling up security shutters and setting out tables and chairs. Until, around the halfway point of this walkway, where the curved ends of eastern and western Crescombe looked equidistant, Finley encountered two, more unexpected sights. The first was a shed-like structure with large wooden wheels that looked like a cross between a beach hut and a traditional travellers' caravan. It was dark purple, with a border of hand-painted flowers garlanding each side, and a sign that read:

DAWN OF A NEW DAY

FORTUNE TELLER

CRYSTALLOMANCY, PALMISTRY, TAROMANCY, TASSEOMANCY

(FOR OTHER SPIRITUAL GUIDANCE, ENQUIRE WITHIN)

The idea of fortune telling intimidated Finley – experience had taught him that the future was rarely pleasanter than the past – so he turned his attention to the promenade's other incongruous sight. Lodged in a block of concrete was a bronze sculpture of an anchor and a paintbrush, entwined together like a coat of arms. Its scale was puzzling: either the anchor was extremely small, or the paintbrush much too big.

Nailed into the concrete was a plaque:

IN MEMORY OF THE CREW OF THE PERSEPHONE,

WHO PERISHED OFF THE COAST OF CRESCOMBE

ON 30 AUGUST 1840

AND OF GEORGE, LORD DELMORE,

WHO DROWNED SWIMMING TO THEIR AID

Finley's gaze drifted to the base of the monument, where two bouquets of flowers had been left – one of them some time ago, judging by its wilting petals. He was just wondering about the sort of person who left tributes for victims of a historical shipwreck when an arch voice in his ear said, 'If you think that's odd, sometimes they leave art supplies.'

Finley spun around to find a woman standing just behind him. She must have been in her fifties, though her sweep of short hair was very dark. Where had she come from? As far as he'd been aware, this part of the promenade had been deserted. He wondered whether she might have jogged here, because she was dressed in leggings, trainers and an overlarge sweatshirt. But, incongruously, she was also sipping from a dainty, gold-rimmed teacup, the kind he often saw in the windows of charity shops.

'Erm ... art supplies?' he repeated, nonplussed.

'Yes – pencils, paintbrushes, that sort of thing. Unhinged, isn't it? But that's the cult of Delmore for you.' She gestured at the monument with her teacup, before continuing, 'Of course, that eyesore's only really there for him.'

'Delmore, you mean?' asked Finley, unsure exactly how he'd been drawn into this conversation.

'Yes – because there were dozens of shipwrecks along this bit of coast,' she explained, before nodding towards the curve of West Crescombe. 'Morte Point, which is a few miles that way, was even named for them. But the only *monument* to a shipwreck is right here, and that's because of Delmore. It's for you tourists.'

'Oh, I'm not a tourist,' said Finley quickly.

'No?'

She raised an eyebrow, and he could almost hear her thinking, Then why are you here?

He wanted to ask the same of her. She sounded local and was clearly knowledgeable about the area, so perhaps she ran some sort of walking tour and was passing the time before her shift.

'I'm just helping out my godmother for the summer,' he said, in answer to her unasked question. 'She runs Crockers Nest, and I'm ...' He trailed off, because the woman had visibly tensed at the mention of the guesthouse. 'You know it?'

'I know *of* it.'

Her gaze flicked towards the way he had come, her expression guarded. Until that point, everything about her clothes to the way she had struck up this conversation had been casual, almost careless. The sudden change in her was disquieting.

Before Finley could discover the reason for it, however, she became chatty again: 'Well, tourist or not, if you need a little guidance while you're here, you know where to find me . . .' She took a few steps towards the fortune teller's hut, rapping her knuckles against its side, like she was knocking on wood for luck.

'Wait, you're . . . ?' Finley gaped between her and the sign that started DAWN OF A NEW DAY, whose owner he hadn't expected to look quite so like a PE teacher.

'Well, I haven't put all my gear on just yet,' she said, as though reading his mind (*was* she reading his mind?). 'But yes, that's me – Dawn.'

Finley re-examined the sign, as though it might have contained some kind of heads-up about her identity, then asked, 'What's tasseo—?'

'Tea leaves,' she said at once, and with a hint of impatience suggesting this was far from the first time she had been asked this. 'Tasseomancy is tea leaves.' She waggled her own cup. 'I can read yours if you like? Make us a fresh brew?'

Finley now suspected that this hadn't been a chance encounter, and that her shed or beach hut or whatever it was had been parked next to Delmore's monument deliberately, in order that she might ensnare the tourists who gravitated towards it.

'Erm, maybe another time,' he said, once again unenthused by the idea of being informed of a grim future – especially in a confined space by this mercurial person.

She gave an impassive sort of shrug, then seemed to lose interest in him, offering a few half-hearted pleasantries (How long was he staying? Had he visited The Delmore Experience yet?) before disappearing back into her hut. Finley could see her shadowy form beyond its beaded curtain, presumably where she was eyeing the promenade for impressionable tourists like a birdwatcher in a hide.

And with this thought, Finley wondered whether all of their conversation had been premeditated. There was nothing wrong with Crockers Nest. Her reaction – those amateur dramatics – must simply have been her attempt to unsettle him into having his fortune told. He shook his head as he continued along the promenade, trying to reframe their whole encounter, and striving to dislodge her words – *I know* of *it* – from his mind.

Aside from its name, The Drowned Painter appeared to be a fairly standard small-town pub. Tucked away in the sloped backstreets behind the beach, it was a warren of threadbare carpets, low beamed ceilings, and walls saturated with nautical paraphernalia: old buoys, fishing nets, historical prints of boat schedules.

After peeking into the pub's noisy dining room, where several young families had been penned, Finley opted for the quieter bar room. Its only occupants were a trio of men, and a blonde barmaid doodling by the till, none of whom paid him any attention as he settled himself at a wobbly table by the dormant fireplace.

This suited Finley, who laid his book on the sticky tabletop and began to study the laminated dinner menu. Almost immediately, however, his eye was drawn to a large framed print of *Hero's Bay* hanging opposite the bar. Finley had already spotted Delmore's painting all over Crescombe during his wanderings that day – on postcards and guidebooks, around chocolate bars and sticks of rock – but this was the biggest rendering he had seen so far, and it prompted him to consider the night-time seascape anew.

Now he had his bearings a little, he could appreciate that the painting's almost impressionistic view looked over the water towards East Crescombe, and so somewhere in its shadowy sliver of land Crockers Nest would be tucked – or whatever Crockers Nest had been back then. Like a vast, oily puddle, the sea swelled below it in a dark rainbow of blues, indigos and greys, a sight Finley found simultaneously beautiful and unnerving.

Yet his gaze was soon caught by the light. It blazed down from the top of the painting, though from no obvious source – at least, none that any art historians had ever agreed upon. So, despite its brightness against the murky night, Finley thought it was more the beam's incongruity, its *mystery*, that made it impossible to ignore . . .

'Megan, for the last time, will you keep this animal away from next door – he's just eaten four chicken goujons!'

Finley wrenched his gaze from the painting to see a large, red-faced man bustle into the room, trailed by a black cocker spaniel. The barmaid too looked up from her drawing towards this newcomer and, with a jolt, Finley realised she was the swimmer he'd met that morning, on the little beach beneath Crockers Nest.

'Oh,' she said, noticing him as well, 'it's you.'

She didn't sound particularly surprised, though Finley supposed Crescombe was so small it was normal to bump into the same people over and over. She was wearing a shapeless white T-shirt, which was half hanging off one shoulder, faded jeans, and had tied back her hair into a long straggly ponytail. All in all, she looked a lot more ordinary than she had earlier – or would have done, had it not been for those wide-set eyes, which still gave her the look of something amphibious.

A soft thump around Finley's knees alerted him to the fact that the dog was now nudging at him, wagging not only his tail but the entire back half of his body. Finley bent to pet him. He liked dogs; they were cheerful and loyal and uncomplicated. He and Mollie had sometimes talked of getting one, and he had loved those conversations because a dog would have been a precursor to marriage, and children. A dog would have meant forever.

'What's his name?' he asked the girl, Megan, who was peering over the bar at them.

'Skipper.'

'Is he yours?'

'Unfortunately,' she said, though without conviction.

'He's her familiar!' called her colleague and, judging by the way Megan rolled her eyes, it was not the first time this joke had been aired.

Still, as Finley continued to stroke the dog's glossy black fur – which was difficult, because the animal was practically bouncing with joy – he couldn't help but reflect that Skipper was almost the total opposite of his owner: dark, stumpy, *friendly*.

The large man, it soon emerged, was The Drowned Painter's landlord, Keith, and a far more efficient host than Megan, because before Finley knew it, there was a pint on his rickety table, and fish and chips were being prepared for him in the kitchen. Megan, meanwhile, had been tasked with loading glasses into a crate, and was doing so with frequent, furtive glances towards Finley's feet, upon which Skipper had finally settled.

The landlord was also a lot more interested in Finley than the other occupants of the bar had been, and within a few minutes had extracted from him his name, where he was from, and where he was staying.

'Crockers Nest, eh?' he mused, tucking his doughy hands into his apron pocket, while the men at the bar looked up from their pints. 'Didn't think we'd see that place open again ... Well, I'm sure she's done a good job with it – what's she called, Lorraine?'

'I heard she's opened up that top room,' piped up one of the drinkers, who was wiry and red-nosed.

'Yeah, that's where I'm staying,' Finley told him.

'Lucky you're not a female, then,' he muttered, before being elbowed by his sniggering neighbour.

Puzzled, Finley looked between them. 'What do you mean?'

'He doesn't mean anything,' Keith assured him. 'He's full of nonsense already. So, Finley,' he continued, before Finley could pursue the point, 'what do you think it is, then?'

'I'm sorry?'

'The light, in the painting,' said the landlord, nodding towards *Hero's Bay* on the opposite wall. 'I saw you looking at it – any ideas?'

'I thought nobody knew?' said Finley, who had the vague impression that it was this unknown quality, as much as any aesthetic merit, that had solidified the painting's status as an iconic work of British art.

'Doesn't mean there aren't *theories*,' said the landlord. 'There's no harm in guessing.'

Finley considered the golden light beaming from the top of the otherwise dark and hazy seascape. It put him in mind of a nativity book he'd had as a child, and the overlarge, overbright illustration of the star; it looked like a light to be followed.

'Is it some kind of signal light?' he suggested. 'I don't suppose there was a lighthouse anywhere around there?'

There were gentle guffaws from the bar stools.

'Only a coastguard's cottage,' said Keith, with an amused smile. 'And that's over the other side of the hill – you wouldn't have seen it from Westcliff, where he painted it.'

Finley thought that might be the end of the conversation, but then one of the occupants of the bar stools – who had a flat cap pulled low over his eyes – said, 'It's obviously the moon.'

'It's not the moon,' said the landlord at once. 'It's too yellow to be the moon.'

'The moon can be yellow,' insisted Flat Cap. 'You get harvest moons and that, don't you? It's the moon, gone fuzzy through cloud.'

'Looks more like the sun than the moon,' remarked the stringy man who had mentioned the top room of Crockers Nest. 'Those hazy lines around it – they're like sunbeams.'

'It's definitely not the sun,' said Keith firmly. 'It's night-time!'

Megan, Finley noticed, was wearing a glazed expression, and he wondered whether – like the comment about Skipper being her familiar – this was far from the first time this conversation had played out in this bar room. Perhaps Keith and his friends put on this performance for all the tourists.

'I reckon it's a spirit,' said the youngest of the trio, who was wearing paint-spattered overalls. 'It's probably that ghost that walks the cliff path . . .'

'Crescombe has a ghost?' broke in Finley, intrigued.

Keith chuckled. 'It has several, depending on how many of the stories you believe.'

'You might as well go the whole hog and say it's *heaven*!' cried Flat Cap. 'That's what I heard a tourist say once. She thought that the light was a glimpse of the afterlife – the pearly gates, you know – and that, when he was painting it, Delmore had had a premonition of his own death.'

Something about this suggestion caused a chill to seep down Finley's spine. The men at the bar, however, were chuckling more than ever.

'Sounds like something *Dawn* would say!' cried the red-nosed man, before turning to his neighbour in overalls. 'I s'pose you believe in the curse and all?'

'Maybe I do,' said the younger man, seriously. Then, in response to Finley's enquiring – or perhaps wary – expression, he explained, 'They say it's cursed, *Hero's Bay*. 'Cause of what happened to Delmore. They say that it brings bad luck, that it brings *death* . . .'

A crashing noise stopped him short, and almost sent Finley toppling off his chair: Megan had slammed down her crate of glasses.

In the silence that followed, she asked Keith, 'Where do you want these?'

This put paid to the discussion, and as the men swivelled back towards the bar, Finley gazed down at his unopened book, *Underworlds*. A leaving present from Duncan at The Book Bothy, it was a fiction anthology based on the bit-players of Greek mythology, and ordinarily Finley would have been keen to lose himself in its pages. But all that talk of ghosts and curses and unexplained lights was rooting him firmly – unusually – in the here and now.

'He likes you.'

He looked up to find Megan bearing a small caddy stuffed with napkins, a knife and fork, and sachets of sauces, peering under the table at a now-snoozing Skipper. Finley, who had become used to the warm soft weight of the dog on his feet and had almost forgotten he was there, said, 'I'm sure he likes everyone.'

Megan looked as though she were considering a smile as she deposited the cutlery and condiments. 'True.'

Encouraged by this more receptive expression, and the way her gaze had flicked towards *Hero's Bay* on the wall, Finley asked, 'What do *you* think that light is?'

Momentarily, Megan looked thrown. Maybe no one had ever asked her opinion on this before. A second later, however, she shrugged.

'I know what it is.' She nodded back at the bar, where Keith and his friends were complaining about Crescombe's imminent Art Festival. 'So do they – they're only messing with you. Everyone around here knows, they just don't like to tell.'

She turned to go and Finley assumed that this was the last she had to say on the matter; that she, like the others, was protective of Crescombe's secrets. But something – perhaps the sight of her dog's head on his feet – seemed to give her pause, because she said, 'You were almost right before: it's a smuggler's signal.'

'Really?' said Finley, though when he considered those steps he'd scrambled down earlier, the idea didn't seem too outlandish.

Megan nodded. 'They used to take lanterns out onto the top of the cliff to signal to ships coming up the Channel. That's what the light is.'

A sense of wonder began to steal through Finley: in this small pub, on this otherwise unremarkable Saturday evening, had he really just learned the answer to this centuries-old mystery? It seemed unbelievable – perhaps *too* unbelievable, and with a sinking feeling, Finley wondered whether Megan too was having a little fun at his expense.

Nevertheless, he asked, 'Do you think *Delmore* knew what the light was?'

'Maybe.' Megan shrugged again. 'He stayed here a whole summer, he could've heard what was going on.'

This interested Finley, who was about to ask her to elaborate when a distant bark caused Skipper to jump awake, sniffing the air. Megan moved to grab his collar, but too late: the dog had bolted, knocking over an old umbrella holder on his way out of the bar room.

'*Megan!*'

At Keith's strangled yell, she departed, though without any great haste. A little disappointed, Finley sat back in his seat, idly flipping over *Underworlds* to study the book's back cover. But he wasn't really seeing it; he was too aware of the painting still in the periphery of his vision, and in particular that enigmatic glow. Even out of the corner of his eye, it was so bright that it seemed to shine right out of the frame – right at *him* – making Finley feel a little exposed, as though he had strayed into an expectant spotlight.

What are you doing here?

I've been watching you for days, but I still don't understand how you've washed up on our shore. You're lonely, I think. Well, there are worse things to be.

You need to be careful. This place isn't safe, even for someone like you. Especially for someone like you. You have no idea what we do here, who we are here.

You must not find out.

3

The Delmore Experience

George, Lord Delmore
(1818–1840)

George Etienne Delmore, 3rd Baron Delmore, was an English Romantic and pre-Impressionist artist. During his short life, he produced an impressive body of work, though he is most famous for his iconic final painting, Hero's Bay.

In July 1840, Delmore came to Crescombe, where he stayed here, at Westcliff House, then the residence of town developer Ambrose Montgomery. Over the course of that summer, Delmore painted his masterpiece.

Shortly after completing Hero's Bay, Delmore died attempting to swim to the aid of a ship that had foundered on the area's notoriously perilous coastline. This tragedy cut short the career of an artist only just finding his style, and one who undoubtedly would have made an even greater contribution to English art.

After reading the printed panel, Finley blinked, a little surprised to find himself standing in the marble-clad entrance hall of The Delmore Experience. Unlike most, he hadn't come to Crescombe for the artist, so hadn't planned on visiting the town's premier tourist destination. But that conversation in the pub the previous night had made him a little curious – curious enough to walk from Crockers Nest to the opposite side of the bay, where the boxy mansion-turned-museum perched on the western cliff, its pillared façade and long narrow windows putting him in mind of a slightly shrunken Buckingham Palace.

Accompanying the introductory panel was a self-portrait of the artist. Delmore – in his own imagination, at least – had been very handsome, with russet-coloured hair, dark eyes and fine features. In fact, there was something a little too self-assured about his slumped posture and the upward curve of his mouth – though Finley couldn't pretend that if he'd been able to paint he wouldn't have immortalised himself as an Adonis, or at least a bit taller.

He made short work of the museum's first room, which related the artist's idyllic, uneventful childhood on his family's estate in Kent, and felt similarly unenthused as he moved into the neighbouring Royal Academy gallery. Delmore had attended the famous art school for just a year, and other than a few anatomical sketches he had submitted for his application, most of the displays consisted of letters the restless artist had written at the time, especially to his mother, the red wax on their accompanying envelopes imprinted with an insignia of two mermaids and a shield – the family crest, Finley presumed.

'Delmore was a Romantic,' said a loud voice, and Finley turned to find a squat, bustling woman leading a tour group into the room. 'And I mean Romantic with a capital R. He loved sweeping landscapes and epic stories. His style was naturally big and bold, but, unfortunately for him, Impressionism was still half a century away. Instead, the age of Realism was about to begin; the art of the everyday, the everyman ...'

Which Delmore certainly wasn't, thought Finley, drifting into the next room.

This was dedicated to Delmore's grand tour – that rite of passage he'd had in common with many other wealthy young men of the age. As Finley studied a map of Europe on which Delmore's route to and around Italy could be traced, he wondered – not for the first time – what would have happened if he'd taken up that opportunity to spend a year of his degree studying in Greece, rather than staying in St Andrews to protect his then new relationship with Mollie. Perhaps this was why it rankled slightly to see Delmore's Italian work turn classical; to be surrounded by images of mythical scenes – Romulus and Remus in the wolf's den, Aeneas's escape from Troy – reanimated in Delmore's confident brushstrokes.

During his time abroad, it seemed Delmore had developed another interest: women. Because at least half the Grand Tour Gallery was devoted to female nudes. Finley told himself to be a grown-up about this – it was *art*, after all – but it was difficult to look at these figures draped over chairs and chaises longues without feeling a little flustered. They were undeniably *sensual*, not just in their nakedness, but in their knowing, playful expressions (he was trying to focus on their faces).

The next room covered Delmore's return to England and, once again, it was divided between landscapes – dreamy, Turner-esque paintings of the Thames and London's parks – and figures. These portraits, however, could not have been more different from his work abroad, for they featured unsmiling, buttoned-up subjects swathed in furs and jewels. His interest waning, Finley was about to hurry past these greyish, sombre figures, when a voice disturbed the relative peace of the gallery.

'Now, we saw in the last room how Delmore developed a reputation for being a bit of a womaniser, a bit of a *rake*, and this is when it began to catch up with him ...'

The tour guide was back, her flock at her heels, and Finley – whose resentment of the handsome, privileged artist was only growing – couldn't help but listen in on the next part of her spiel.

'Lady Josephine here is Delmore's final completed portrait,' said the tour guide, gesturing at the image of a dark-haired woman with a rather heavy brow, 'and it has a colourful backstory. During the painting's creation, it's widely believed that Delmore and this woman had an affair, prompting a confrontation with her husband that almost led to a duel to the death.' The tour guide paused, either for effect or to let her audience take photos, before continuing, 'The scandal that followed, along with Delmore's already shaky reputation, forced him to retreat from society – and he made the fateful decision to lie low right here in Crescombe.'

Her audience *ooh*ed, and Finley almost joined in himself. He hadn't thought to question how Delmore had ended up here; what chain of events had led the worldly young aristocrat to this remote seaside town – and to his death, Finley reminded himself. He recalled the artist's dates from that first panel – 1818–1840 – and all of a sudden his own disdain seemed ridiculous: Delmore had been just twenty-two.

In order to get ahead of the tour group again, Finley slipped into the next room, where he stopped short. Unlike the previous galleries, whose walls had been busy, this space featured just one painting: *Hero's Bay*.

For a moment, pinned to where he was standing by the power of the dark seascape, Finley thought it was the real one. It was certainly a painting, rather than a print. Then he remembered, of course, that the original was in the National Gallery – he had once seen it there himself, on a school trip – and he tore his gaze from the murky, enigmatic image to its caption:

HERO'S BAY (REPRODUCTION)

For a few years after Delmore's death, the original Hero's Bay was displayed here at Westcliff House, where its fame began to grow. However, when the artist's mother, Lady Delphine Delmore, requested the painting for herself, this copy was commissioned, which used the same tools and techniques as the original.

Nevertheless, there was something very different about seeing *Hero's Bay* here, like this, to catching sight of it on T-shirts or coasters, or even opposite the bar in The Drowned Painter. Perhaps it was the brushstrokes, Finley thought, moving his weight from foot to foot, so the artificial light – there were no windows here – shifted across the surface of the canvas. The texture of the paint gave it movement, animation; it seemed to make the waves ripple, and that brilliant light – whatever it was – shine like a beacon, beckoning right out of the canvas: come closer, *closer*.

Finley wanted to. He had the strongest, most uncharacteristic urge to reach out and press a fingertip to that bloom of brightness. Obviously, it wouldn't be allowed – and in any case, it would be like touching the replica of Michelangelo's *David* in that piazza, rather than the real sculpture in its gallery. However, Finley thought it was only the memory of what he'd heard in The Drowned Painter the previous night that made him get a grip on himself: *they say that it brings bad luck, that it brings* death...

A little spooked, he wrenched himself away and, through the next doorway, was faced with a choice: continue straight on to learn about the shipwreck of *The Persephone* and Delmore's untimely demise, or head to the first floor to see the guest quarters where he'd stayed. Deciding his thoughts were macabre enough already, Finley opted for upstairs.

Until now, he had almost forgotten he was in an old mansion, but this part of Westcliff House had been restored to how it might have appeared during Delmore's time, complete with chandeliers, mahogany furniture and botanical wallpaper. However, the main focus of this floor – the eponymous *experience* the museum offered that nowhere else could – was the artist's studio. It was a small and comparatively modest corner room, but much brighter and warmer than elsewhere, because sunlight was spilling in through both its large windows. Dominating the space was a paint-splattered easel, upon which a blank canvas was perched – which struck Finley as a little sad, as it seemed to highlight all the masterpieces Delmore had never had the chance to paint.

Currently, the spot in front of the easel was vacant – unusually so, Finley suspected – and he found himself shuffling forward to fill it. He hadn't intended to linger here, but after half an hour of absorbing information about the artist, it felt wrong to pass through his studio without, at least for a moment, standing where Delmore had stood; seeing what he had seen.

As he peered through the nearest window, which was as hot as an oven door, Finley could appreciate what Lorraine had meant about the bay being a crescent. An exaggerated crescent, in fact, because the speck of Crockers Nest on the opposite cliff looked closer now than it had for much of his walk here, which had taken longer than he'd expected; if only there was some kind of ferry that ran between the two tips of land.

Finley's head thrummed. The reflection of sunlight on water was dazzling, and though he was trying to concentrate on the view across Crescombe – on the scene Delmore would have gazed upon, almost two centuries earlier – it looked nothing like *Hero's Bay*. Now, daylight was blanching everything that was shadowy in the painting, like the negative of a photograph.

'Were you wanting a picture?'

Finley spun around. That wretched tour guide was back, her charges clamouring behind her, impatient for their turn at the easel. Then he blinked: he had turned too fast and now he felt dizzy, and so hot. Suddenly, he wondered whether it wasn't the room, but *him*. He had thought he would be fine – his blood sugar control hadn't been too bad recently, especially during the day – but perhaps he had misjudged the effort the long walk here had cost him.

'I'm done, thanks,' Finley muttered, ducking away from the window.

His legs felt wobbly, and now came the sweat: it was prickling at his forehead, under his arms, seeping through the back of his T-shirt. With shaking hands, he fumbled through his bag for his just-in-case juice while looking wildly around for somewhere to sit down and recover. But the tour group were pressing in on him in their eagerness to get to the easel, and when someone accidentally knocked his elbow, a little of Finley's drink went slopping over the rim of his bottle.

'Excuse me,' said a soft voice to his left, 'I'm afraid you're not actually allowed any food or – are you okay?'

'Fine,' panted Finley, who was now staring into the bearded, bespectacled and concerned face of a man in a short-sleeved shirt and lanyard. He wiped his sweaty brow with the back of his hand. 'I just ... I need ...'

'Over here,' said the man, gently guiding Finley into a stairwell.

Finley sank onto a stone step, where he began to gulp down his juice, which was warm from its time in his bag. He was unwilling to check in front of this stranger, but was fairly certain his blood sugar had just plummeted; he was having a hypo.

A few minutes passed, during which his companion introduced himself as the museum's curator, Adrian Salter, then waited quietly nearby, occasionally offering to fetch a first aid kit, a bucket, a sandwich from the café (Del-moreish). Finley declined each suggestion, choosing instead to glug down all of his juice – this had felt like a bad one.

'I'm fine now, thanks,' he said, for the third or fourth time. Then, gesturing down the stairs, he asked, 'Can I get out this way?'

'Yes ... Actually, I'll show you a shortcut.'

Finley wished he wouldn't. The curator had been more than considerate, but his continuing presence was delaying the moment Finley could start pretending this had never happened.

'You're not the first and you won't be the last,' said Adrian seriously as they started down the steps, and Finley realised he had a North American accent – Canadian, perhaps? 'That room's like a greenhouse, and after all the anticipation of seeing Delmore's studio ...'

Clearly, he was trying to be reassuring but, if anything, Finley felt worse.

They reached the ground floor, emerging into a room that, like Delmore's quarters, appeared largely unchanged from the nineteenth century. It was a library, one that might once have been used for entertaining, for in addition to its ornate desk there were several luxurious armchairs and settees. Ordinarily, Finley would only have had eyes for the books, but here they competed with cabinets full of miscellaneous old objects: bottles and vases, snuff boxes and pocket watches, animal skins and bones – and, perhaps most striking of all, an ammonite the size of a hubcap.

In the corner of this new room was an unfinished portrait. Its background was mostly blank, but it seemed the artist – Delmore, presumably – had completed the vibrant figure at its centre, who was a portly middle-aged man with lots of fuzzy red hair and a round face that would have been extremely boyish, had it not been for his enormous moustache.

'Who's that?' Finley enquired, mostly to keep Adrian's attention from what had happened upstairs.

A small smile tweaked the curator's features; it looked slightly unnatural on him, as though it hadn't happened in a while. 'Ambrose Montgomery,' he said.

Though the name felt familiar, Finley was at a loss: 'Sorry, who?'

'Yes, exactly,' said Adrian, the smile disappearing. 'Montgomery was the owner of this place. In fact, he built it – or had it built, I should say. He was a businessman obsessed with turning Crescombe into a fashionable seaside resort, one that would rival places like Ilfracombe and Torquay. Most of West Crescombe – the more modern half – owes its existence to him.'

As Adrian spoke, Finley thought there was something familiar about him as well – though perhaps he simply reminded Finley of a few of his former teachers.

'He was a big character, and a crucial figure in Crescombe's history,' continued the curator, adjusting his browline glasses as he considered the portrait. 'But this room never gets much attention because, for all his achievements, Montgomery's not . . .' Adrian trailed off, weighing up his next words.

'He's not Lord Delmore?' suggested Finley.

'He's not Lord Delmore,' the curator agreed, a little sadly. 'Though of course if it weren't for Montgomery, Delmore wouldn't have come here in the first place. He wouldn't have painted *Hero's Bay*.'

And he wouldn't have drowned, thought Finley.

They left the library, talking a little more of the museum – for which, it turned out, Adrian had moved to the UK; apparently he even had an apartment on the top floor. To Finley's embarrassment, the curator seemed determined to escort him all the way out, even as far as the gift shop, where Delmore's final painting was emblazoned on some increasingly outlandish merchandise (brooches, travel cups – and was that a *shower curtain?*).

'Why's it called *Hero's Bay?*' Finley wondered aloud.

Before coming here, though he'd understood the painting had some connection to the town, he had assumed its title referred to a real place. But that dark view depicted Crescombe Bay itself, which – as far as Finley knew – had never gone by the name *Hero's Bay* before Delmore's arrival.

'Nobody knows for sure,' said Adrian, coming to a halt at the exit, next to a machine that produced *Hero's Bay* souvenir coins. 'According to Montgomery, Delmore had always called the painting that, from the moment he started it, so it's generally accepted to have been named by the artist himself.'

Finley, who hadn't thought to doubt this, asked, 'But what does it mean?'

'Your guess is as good as mine. Delmore set a lot of store by myths and legends, so most people think that he fancied himself a bit of a hero. He was a daring sort – always scaling mountains and throwing himself into rivers, you know? And at the time he painted it, his latest adventure was Crescombe.'

Finley, who found this explanation a little insufficient, asked, 'Are there other theories?'

'Personally, I believe Montgomery named it,' said Adrian. 'The original painting was displayed here for about a year after Delmore died, so I think that once Montgomery saw the attention it was getting, he decided to give it a catchy title.'

'One that did help make a legend of Delmore,' mused Finley. 'One that helped immortalise him.'

'Precisely.'

Though, as he said it, Adrian looked almost mournful, and Finley wasn't sure whether he was dwelling on Delmore's drowning, or Montgomery going unrecognised, or something else entirely.

All in all, it was a relief to thank him and finally escape the museum. Outside, Finley found some shade under one of the few trees in sight; unlike the eastern side of Crescombe, which was thick with woodland, Westcliff House topped a slope of elegant parkland. He was feeling better, and though he assumed this was a sign that his juice had taken effect, he thought he'd better check his blood sugar level.

However, when he tapped his phone to the sensor on his arm, he received a shock: it was high – much too high. Finley rummaged for his insulin pen, cursing himself for not checking his level inside, because it must have actually been fairly normal, and drinking all that juice had caused his blood sugar to skyrocket.

But did that mean, contrary to how it had felt, he hadn't experienced a hypo at all? Had he been absolutely fine? After a furtive glance around, Finley lifted the bottom of his T-shirt, pinched a section of his stomach, and pricked at his skin with the tiny needle of his insulin pen. There was a slight sting and a clicking noise as he injected the corrective dose, then he glanced back at the sea, still glittering innocuously in the sunshine, questioning what – if not plummeting blood sugar – had happened to him in there.

Finley felt rattled for the rest of the day, and long after he had returned to Crockers Nest. He had now unpacked his belongings and stocked up his fridge, but was yet to feel settled, despite it being his third evening here. Even if he ignored the fact that his lofty, wood-panelled room still reminded him of a floating ship, its window had blown open twice more last night and, tired and fed up, Finley was considering sleeping under an extra blanket to combat the chill, rather than getting up to resecure the latch.

Really, though, he hadn't felt at home anywhere since moving out of Mollie's flat: not here; not at his parents' house, where he had retreated directly after the break-up; and certainly not in that rented hovel he'd just escaped. Finley yearned to be back in the sunny two-bed he and Mollie had shared, and still found unexpected things to miss about it, like the garish tangerine colour she had painted the kitchen, or the hair ties she had left all over the bedroom floor. What, if anything, now remained there of him? Probably nothing – he doubted she even thought of him anymore.

With her wedding now under a fortnight away, Mollie McClaine had better things to do.

And so did Finley, now he was here – well, he had *things* to do, at least. Since that first evening, he had only seen Lorraine once – in the lounge, tidying the shelves of puzzles and board games – but they had arranged to meet tomorrow morning to discuss Finley's work for the summer. In the meantime, she had given him the password to her account on the travel site, Guidebook, so he could start liking and replying to any reviews of Crockers Nest.

Feeling he might as well make a start on this before bed, Finley logged in to Guidebook on his phone, squinting at how bright its neon branding was in the gloom of his room. However, his eyes soon glazed over after several minutes of scanning through the guesthouse's reviews, which – save for the odd grumble about persistent draughts and the quality of the gluten-free bread – seemed to be unanimously positive:

> Nice clean room with a spectacular view and a surprisingly good breakfast.
>
> Weather a bit iffy, but it didn't dampen our spirits!
>
> Crockers Nest is a great base for exploring Crescombe, which is so much more than just Hero's Bay. We loved the boat tour around the coast and saw loads of seals.
>
> DO NOT STAY HERE!!

Finley blinked, certain he must have misread that last post. But there it was, shouting from the screen: *DO NOT STAY HERE!!*

'Why not?' he muttered.

Of course, there was no reply, save for the distant, constant sighing of the sea. Still, a chill pitter-pattered across Finley's shoulders, especially when he remembered how Dawn and those men at the The Drowned Painter had reacted to the mention of Crockers Nest.

The reviewer was called *cross_my_hart* and when Finley clicked on their username he found, in addition to their having no profile picture or personal information, only that one review. Which made him feel better, even a little foolish: it was nothing, just a random troll, or someone who had taken exception to their eggs being overdone. Maybe it was even The Dickhead (what was his real name again?) or his secretary-turned-mistress trying to undermine Lorraine's new venture.

Deciding he would find a way to raise this during their meeting, Finley put down his phone and tried to get to sleep. But his mind seemed to be stuck in the museum. It was more labyrinthine in his dream than in real life, and all the portraits and sketches plastering the walls had only one subject: *Mollie*. Finley hurried past them, desperately searching for a way out, trying not to stare at Mollie in a classical scene, Mollie in furs, Mollie in nothing at all ... Ahead was a light, and a disorientated Finley followed it, assuming it must be Delmore's bright studio. Before he could reach the easel, however, the leader of the tour group had stepped into his path – only it wasn't really her hurrying him along, but his sister, Fiona. Finley tried to explain that he was lost, but Fiona was being absorbed by the light at her back, which Finley now saw wasn't coming from the windows at all, but from the painting on the easel, from *Hero's Bay* ...

Thunk!

The window had blown open again. Groaning, Finley pushed himself out of bed, realising he had left his light on – which explained that bright beam burrowing into his dream. Zombie-like, he shuffled towards the window, when suddenly the ground seemed to lurch beneath him. Limbs flailing, he just managed to keep his balance, but when the soles of his bare feet reconnected with the floor, he felt dampness seep between his toes: there was water all over the floor.

Finley crouched to examine the small puddles. Where had *they* come from? There was a glass of water on his bedside table and he supposed it was possible he had spilled a little earlier, on his way from the kitchenette. Otherwise, above its wooden panels, the ceiling must have sprung a leak (though it hadn't rained, had it?). Unless . . . Could it be the sea, extending a long, watery tentacle through his window while he slept? But no, that was impossible.

Still, as Finley began to dab at the damp floorboards with a tea towel, he couldn't shake the feeling that there was something wrong with this place. It wasn't just that review, or Dawn, or those men in the pub; Finley knew it with the same instinct that, at fourteen years old, had told him something disastrous was happening to his body and, more recently – and despite Mollie's assurances that everything was fine – to his relationship.

Though when he thought of it like that, and reflected on his queasiness at The Delmore Experience, perhaps it wasn't Crockers Nest at all; perhaps, Finley thought with mounting despair, there was only something wrong with *him*.

I'm locked in again.

I was watching you from the cliff, wriggling through the thicket to keep you in sight, and I stayed out too long. When I finally returned, my sleeves snagged and my boots dusty, Ma didn't even say anything, just seized me by the arm, bundled me up the steps and slammed shut the door.

In the day, it isn't so bad. I lay out my shells and stones, creating patterns on the floor. I turn my jar of petals, watching them float through the thickening, yellowing spirit. And I continue to work the knife into the wall, its blade scraping between the loosening stones.

But she's taken my lantern, and the moonless night is so dark I can't see my own body. Now, I could be nothing more than a mind; uncontained, untethered. The thought is curious, though not unpleasant.

I grip at my sea stone, smooth and solid between my fingers, and imagine its colour burning in the darkness, that near impossible blue. A living blue, the colour of dragonflies and jay feathers and robin eggs. The colour of my mother's eyes, though my memory of them – of her – is fading. Long ago, when my father first pressed this stone into my palm, he told me it was a drop of the sea from his homeland. He said he would show me the rest, when he returned for me.

I listen too. No ships are due, but along with snatches of conversation, and the odd shout or laugh or song from voices both familiar and not, I can hear the sound of work: the rolling and clunking of barrels; the clip-clop of hooves and trundle of wheels.

Sometimes I hear footsteps directly below, and I sit taller, waiting to be yanked back into the house. But then they quieten, and I slump against the door again. It seems I'm to stay here a little longer.

How long? Last time, it was over two days. I'm growing restless, and hungry, but I'm not worried. I know they won't forget me.

They need me.

4

Crockers Nest

As Lorraine talked, Finley's gaze wandered to the nearest window, where he followed the progress of several raindrops wriggling down the glass. They were sitting in part of the modern extension of Crockers Nest – the sunroom, Lorraine called it, though there was no sun to be seen that morning. Outside, beyond the drizzly window, a strip of sea was just visible, but the rest of Crescombe was entirely lost to mist. The effect was disorientating, isolating; it felt like they were perched at the edge not just of the bay, but of the world.

Lorraine paused to push her reading glasses to the top of her head and helped herself to another biscuit. She had just listed, at length, Finley's responsibilities for the summer, which included proofreading the website, posting from the social media accounts and sorting all the paperwork that had accumulated since the accommodation had opened.

'And remember,' she added, picking up the spotty teapot and topping up their matching cups, 'if anything has a whiff of finance, just chuck it in there for the accountant.'

The teapot's spout dribbled as she used it to indicate a purple box, which looked as though it should contain a present – though Finley doubted Lorraine's accountant would appreciate the collection of crumpled receipts, letters and unopened envelopes they were to be gifted. It was a little too reminiscent of Duncan's filing system, or lack of, at The Book Bothy, though the fact that

Lorraine even knew what social media was boded better for her business.

'But never mind all that,' continued Lorraine, who could perhaps tell Finley's attention was drifting. 'What I really want to talk to you about is my little research project . . .'

From beneath her wicker chair, she retrieved a box that, to Finley, looked slightly more interesting than the one holding her accounting. It was plain cardboard, held together by peeling parcel tape, and covered in scribbled-out labels, the clearest of which read, in spidery handwriting: For Lorraine/Crockers Nest.

'The vicar's already given me this, which is everything he can find on this place,' she continued, 'and he's got some parish records you can look at too.' Then, noticing Finley's puzzled look, Lorraine explained, 'Reverend Clay, from St Nick's – he's Crescombe's unofficial curator. He's been telling me all sorts about Crockers Nest . . . It'd been empty for decades when I bought it – you should've seen the state it was in – and before that it was a hotel: the *Bay View*,' she added, with mock snootiness. 'Apparently, some of the Navy moved in during the Second World War – or was it the First? – and back in the day it belonged to the Harcourt Estate. It doesn't really exist anymore, the estate, and Harcourt Manor's a National Trust property now. You should go, Finley, they do a lovely cream tea.'

This seemed to remind her of her own drink, which she paused to sip. Then, perhaps aware she had veered off-topic, Lorraine said, 'My point is, Crockers Nest has a lot of history. And while I'm sure the Navy being here and whatnot is all very interesting . . .' she waved a dismissive hand '. . . what *I'm* interested in is the Crockers themselves, and what they got up to.' Her eyes glittered. 'I want to know about this *smuggling*.'

Finley found himself nodding. It appeared they were on the same page – and, as far as he was concerned, that page was straight out of one of the many adventure books he had inhaled as a child.

'You want to make that the focus of this, erm, project?' he asked, still a little unclear on what exactly she was planning. 'The smuggling history of Crockers Nest?'

Lorraine leaned forward, and – in the haze, with the rain pattering around them – they might have been two conspirators themselves. 'I want to make that the focus of this whole guesthouse,' she said. 'Well, it worked for Jamaica Inn, didn't it? We've already found those barrels for the front desk and, I don't know, maybe we could do a permanent exhibition in the hallway? Not a museum, exactly, but *something* about the smuggling that went on in this place . . .' She hesitated, looking daunted by her own plans.

Finley, who feared any exhibition might look amateurish in comparison to The Delmore Experience, the first stop-off on most people's Crescombe itinerary, felt she should think a little smaller. 'How about we start with a booklet?' he suggested. 'That would be easier to produce, and then people could just look through it at their leisure.'

'A booklet . . .' Lorraine mused, before poking Finley with a pink fingernail. 'See, this is why I asked you down here, I knew you'd be full of ideas! How lucky am I, having a historian for a godson?'

'I'm not actually a—'

'A *booklet*!' she repeated, delighted. 'Oh yes, we can get them bound up all nice, maybe even have some for sale . . .'

Before she could elaborate, there was a knock on the glass door and, with a start, Finley saw that a dark figure had emerged from the mist. But it was just a man in waterproofs, setting down the handles of a wheelbarrow. He was quite short, with a ruddy face and greying curly hair poking out from under his hood, which gave him the look of a burrowing creature, or a damp hobbit.

'Hello, Lorraine?' His voice was muffled through the glass.

'Martin!' She opened the door but stood well back to avoid getting wet. 'You haven't met my godson, Finley – he's staying with me for the summer.'

'Nice to meet you, Finley,' mumbled Martin, in a thick West Country accent, and there was a deference to his manner that made Finley feel like a visiting member of the gentry.

'Any problems with your room, Finley, you just tell Martin,' continued Lorraine. 'He'll have it sorted in a jiffy.'

Briefly, Finley considered mentioning that his window was still blowing open, and that there must be a leak somewhere, considering those splashes of water across the floor. But Lorraine had deigned to edge towards the door, offering a spotty plate into the rain.

'Have a biscuit, Martin – go on, have *two*.'

'Very kind of you, Lorraine,' he muttered.

She bestowed on him a pink-lipped smile as he fumbled for a couple of custard creams with calloused, dirt-encrusted fingers, and his already reddish complexion darkened in a blush.

'Erm, I found these in the cellar,' he said, with a nod towards his wheelbarrow. 'I assume you don't want them?'

Finley followed his gaze, then almost recoiled: piled up in the wheelbarrow were what must have once been garden statues, only they were so weathered that their features were distorted, their bodies blurred. They reminded him of the human remains unearthed in Pompeii.

'Lord, no,' said Lorraine, grimacing. 'Just take them to the tip or something, Martin – it's not far, is it?' Then, with unconvincing nonchalance, she asked, 'Are you nearly finished sorting that cellar?'

'Hardly making a dent in it, to be honest,' he said, though cheerfully enough.

He reached for the dripping handles of the wheelbarrow, then seemed to realise he was still holding his biscuits, because after a moment's hesitation he crammed them into his mouth. Colouring again, he hurried away, the stone bodies wobbling as he disappeared into the mist.

'And Martin's your . . . ?' Finley had no idea how to finish his sentence; from what he'd just witnessed, the next word could have been anything from *boyfriend* to *serf*.

'My handyman, yes,' smiled Lorraine, closing the door so firmly the whole extension shook. 'He lives just over the cliff, in the old coastguard's cottage, so he's literally *on hand*!' She laughed at her own joke. 'Says I can call on him anytime, day or night!'

Privately, Finley felt this was a slightly rash offer. Between the purple box for the accountant, the cardboard box from the vicar, and his own list of tasks, he was beginning to suspect Lorraine had a talent for delegation.

'Now, where were we?' she said, taking another sip of tea.

'Smuggling,' Finley reminded her. 'But . . .' Somehow, Martin's appearance had returned him to reality. 'I mean, there definitely *was* smuggling around here? It's not just . . . local legend?' More specifically, he thought it might be the sort of thing those old guys in The Drowned Painter would make up to amuse outsiders like himself and Lorraine.

'Oh yes, the vicar's quite certain,' she said. 'Smuggling was big business around here, and the Crockers were definitely part of it – the ringleaders, he reckons.' There was a distinct note of pride in her voice. 'Actually, he says it's likely they used the cellar to store all the brandy and whatnot.'

'And these Crockers were around when, exactly?' asked Finley, realising he wasn't even sure what century they were talking about.

'Well, that's the thing, they were here for generations. A real old Crescombe family, you know? The vicar thinks they were fishermen originally – well, most around here were – and that this house started life as a fisherman's cottage, and got built up and out as they came into more money.'

Finley, supposing this explained the irregular appearance of Crockers Nest, said, 'Presumably they're not still around? There aren't any Crocker ancestors we can talk to?'

'Not on *this* side of the world,' said Lorraine. Then, in response to Finley's obvious confusion, she laughed. 'Hold on . . .'

Retrieving her winged reading glasses from the top of her head, she searched through the box's papers until she located a photocopy of a small newspaper article dated 1842. Finley had to squint to read it – the tiny print was faded and grainy – but soon learned that, after a much-anticipated trial, Crescombe's Agnes 'Ma' Crocker, along with her three sons, William, Thomas and Edwin Crocker, had been sentenced with transportation to Australia's penal colonies. Ostensibly, this punishment seemed to have been for highway robbery, but the article also mentioned burglary, assault and smuggling.

'There's a picture and all,' said Lorraine, passing Finley another photocopy.

It was a pen and ink drawing, one that reminded Finley of the illustrations found within the pages of nineteenth-century novels. Its subjects, too, wouldn't have looked out of place in something by Dickens: Agnes Crocker was a large, hard-faced woman with two burly, near identical sons, and a third leaner son who looked no less menacing, not least because he was missing an eye.

'The state of him!' Lorraine cried, pointing at the smallest brother – Edwin, according to the drawing's caption. 'Looks like some kind of pirate!'

Finley made a noise of acknowledgement, but found he couldn't quite share her enthusiasm. In his imagination – and again, no doubt this had been informed by the stories he'd read as a child – historical smugglers had been spirited, Robin Hood-like figures who had outwitted foolish customs officials to bring wealth to their impoverished communities. Obviously the artist behind this drawing might have been biased, but there was no escaping the fact that these Crockers looked *mean*.

'Excuse me, please, Lorraine?'

They turned to see a middle-aged couple hovering just over the threshold of the sunroom. Finley recognised them as fellow guests – he thought they might be Danish – and today they were wearing identical blue ponchos, the flimsy kind he had seen for sale by the beach.

'Where is the Delmore walking tour leaving from?' asked the man.

'The anchor monument on the promenade, my loves,' said Lorraine at once, perhaps having anticipated the question. 'Although' – she checked her dainty gold watch – 'it starts at eleven, so you'll have to hurry. Two ticks, I'll find you the timetable for the shuttlebus . . .'

A few minutes later, she returned to her wicker chair with a roll of her eyes. 'That's the other thing about this smuggling stuff,' she said to Finley in an undertone, 'it'll give my guests something other than *Delmore* to think about. Don't get me wrong, it's a nice enough painting – there's just so much more to Crescombe, you know?'

She was sounding like a local already, thought Finley, amused. Then he realised that most of the real locals he'd spoken to – Megan, Dawn, even that taxi driver – had been similarly dismissive of Delmore and his masterpiece. Did anyone who lived here actually like *Hero's Bay*?

'This was actually only a few years after Delmore was in Crescombe,' he said, tapping the date of the newspaper article, which was still on the table between them. 'Their smuggling could've been going on while he was here.'

'Oh, don't you start!'

Finley considered mentioning Megan's theory that the light in *Hero's Bay* was a smuggling signal, but decided against it, still suspecting she'd been messing with him. The thought made him feel unduly glum.

Predictably, Lorraine was keen to hand over as much of the work for her project as possible, and asked Finley whether he could start sorting through the box of papers from the vicar, extracting anything relating to smuggling and the Crockers – a task Finley was happy to take on, given he was much more at home with old documents than fiddling about on social media. There was also something heartening about the way she trusted him to get on with it. Again, he was reminded of The Book Bothy, and the free rein Duncan had given him over the fiction section – though when he tried to picture himself back there, all he could see was how it had looked at the end: the boxes of books waiting to be returned; the dismantled shelving stacked against the bare walls; the 'Everything Must Go!' posters scrunched up in bin bags.

After he and Lorraine had made plans to catch up over another tea at the end of the week, she asked, 'Oh, how did you get on with Guidebook?'

Inwardly, Finley winced, recalling the words of *cross_my_hart*: **DO NOT STAY HERE!!**

'Erm, okay,' he began, cautiously. 'There are loads of nice reviews. But there's this one that's a bit strange ...'

He found it on his phone and showed her.

'Eh?' She frowned through her reading glasses, then looked back at Finley. 'Who wrote that?'

'I don't know,' he said, for although he had messaged *cross_my_hart* on Guidebook, politely requesting that they delete or at least explain their review, he was yet to receive a reply. 'Although, I was actually wondering whether it might be ...' He faltered, not wanting to upset her. 'I mean, I was thinking, seeing as there's no name or anything, there's a chance it could be—'

'Spit it out, Finley.'

'Your ex-husband?'

To his surprise, Lorraine laughed. 'Oh, he wouldn't *dare!*' she scoffed. 'Seriously, he's terrified of me now – and so's that nasty little hussy he's shacked up with,' she added, intuiting Finley's next question. 'No, love, it's just a random whatsit – *troll*. Delete it, will you?'

Finley doubted this was possible – if it were, it would slightly defeat the purpose of Guidebook – and though he was relieved Lorraine didn't seem bothered by the review, the reminder of those words made him feel uneasy, just as he had on seeing that drawing of the Crockers.

'Erm, Lorraine?' he ventured.

'Yes, love?'

How should he put it? 'Over the past few days, around Crescombe . . . Well, I've been hearing some stuff about Crockers Nest.'

'Oh yes?' She raised an eyebrow, suddenly steely.

'Nothing bad about it *now*,' he said quickly. 'But it seems like it has – *had* – a bit of a . . . reputation?'

Lorraine made a disapproving clicking noise with her tongue, then muttered, 'That bloody woman.'

'Sorry?'

'Dawn!' Lorraine cried. 'The loony in the hut! That's who you've been speaking to, isn't it?'

'Well, it wasn't *just* her . . .'

But Lorraine wasn't listening: 'She's obsessed, says Crockers Nest has *bad energy*. Warned me off buying it when I first came here.'

'Really?' said Finley, who was not finding this conversation as reassuring as he had hoped.

Lorraine, however, let out a dramatic gasp. 'Here, you don't think *she* wrote that review?'

'Erm ...' Finley knew next to nothing about Dawn, but couldn't quite picture her sitting in that tiny hut posting venomous reviews online. Then, proceeding carefully, he asked, 'So, there's nothing ... *off* about Crockers Nest?'

'There's a lot off about Crockers Nest! Did you see those statues?' Then, perhaps because the memory of the eroded figures had failed to rouse a smile in him, she continued, 'Look, Finley, don't let people like that get under your skin. It's an old house. It has a lot of history, not all of it very nice.' She prodded the cardboard box towards him and, once again, he thought of the Crockers and the list of their misdeeds. 'And this is a small town, so naturally there are going to be all sorts of rumours and stories about this place,' Lorraine continued. 'But that doesn't mean it has *bad energy*, does it? It's just an old house,' she said again, with a shrug.

Her tone was matter-of-fact, almost firm. She believed what she was saying – or wanted to, at least. Because although she seemed to be a pragmatic sort of person, it wasn't lost on Finley that this guesthouse was Lorraine's new start, her second act. And as he bade her goodbye, his fingers curling around the soft cardboard of the box he now had to lug up to his room, a part of him wondered whether it was in Lorraine's own interests – for her own self-preservation, even – to close her ears to whatever rumours persisted about Crockers Nest.

Thunk!

Finley gasped, jerked from a dream full of dark, churning waters. It took him a moment to remember where he was, before, with a grunt of annoyance, he detangled himself from the duvet, stumbled towards the porthole window, and slammed it shut.

There was water on the floor again. He skirted around it on his way back to bed, too tired and irritated to mop it up now. He would do it tomorrow, and report the leak to Martin the handyman. Maybe he'd ask him to look at the window too.

Finley sank back against his pillow, and as he tried to slow his breathing, he became aware of an intermittent grating noise in the opposite wall – the wind nudging between the old stones, perhaps (no wonder the place was leaking). Distracted, he switched on the bedside lamp, deeply inhaling the floral and slightly soapy scent of the plug-in air freshener he had yet to locate, and looked from the framed pictures of seaside scenes on the walls to the sprigs of dried flowers on the mantlepiece.

'It's just an old house,' he reminded himself.

His gaze then moved to the cardboard box from the vicar. Following his meeting with Lorraine, he had spent much of the afternoon setting aside dozens of old parish newsletters and tourist information leaflets – most containing only a passing reference to the guesthouse – in his hunt for anything related to the Crockers. But, aside from that piece Lorraine had already showed him about the deportation of their last members, he'd only spotted the name *Crocker* on an old title deed and a marriage announcement. Which, while frustrating, was probably to be expected; if the family had been as unsavoury as Lorraine seemed to think, it was likely they had kept a low profile.

Still, he was awake now, so to distract himself from the uneasiness of being shocked from sleep, he leaned out of bed to grab another handful of papers from the box: a faded brochure for the original Bay View Hotel, a floorplan of the property, a list of recommended reading in the reverend's untidy handwriting . . .

'Ouch.'

There was a pricking sensation in his side, not unlike the nick of his insulin pen: a corner of paper was poking him. Finley picked it up, seeing it was a photocopy of another newspaper article. This one was dated October 1993, and when Finley read its bold headline his stomach dropped:

North Devon Hotel to Close After Second Drowning

A hotel in Crescombe, the North Devon town made famous by Delmore's *Hero's Bay*, is to close just a few months after the drowning of a young backpacker. American art student Michelle Lei, 22, was a week into her stay at The Bay View Hotel last August when her body was recovered from the sea. She had been missing since the previous evening.

Over two decades ago, Londoner Jacqueline Fairchild, 24, died in similar circumstances, leading police to consider that Lei's death might be a 'copycat' suicide. This claim is strongly refuted by the victim's family, who insist she had been looking forward to further travels around Europe.

The manager of the hotel, who does not wish to be named, insists its closure is unrelated to Lei's death and he is merely seeking hospitality opportunities elsewhere.

Finley stared at the page, his heart drumming once again. Suddenly, the attitude of the locals towards Crockers Nest made a lot more sense – and was *this* what Lorraine had been referencing, when she'd spoken of the guesthouse's history? *Not all of it very nice . . .*

He read the article a second time, then a third, trying to take it all in, but was left with more questions than answers. Were these drownings – whether accidents or not – the reason the property had been abandoned for so long? And what, specifically, were the *similar circumstances* that had led police to consider the second death a copycat suicide?

Finley snatched at the papers scattered around him on the duvet, the Crockers now forgotten as he searched for anything else on these drownings. When all he found were yet more letters and leaflets, he grabbed the whole box, so impatient to see all it contained that he knelt up on the bed, preparing to tip it out; never mind if it spilled everywhere, never mind if half of it ended up in that water ...

Finley's eyes flicked towards the floor, and his skin erupted into gooseflesh. He had thought the splashes random, but now – at this angle, in this light – he saw an unmistakeable pattern: they were long, curved, and formed two staggered lines that snaked from the window towards the bed – towards *him*. Only now, they didn't look like splashes at all, Finley realised, the box dropping from his hands; they looked like footprints.

The rain has forced us together. It beats against the house, seeping between its stones, so we are huddled in the kitchen, where Old William has let us keep the fire burning low. I'd rather be outside, though. I want to watch the sea strike against the rocks, straining and straining to reach us.

My hands are already blistering as I work the rope, which is stiff from salt and stinks of damp and sweat. I was let out for this – my eyes are the keenest at checking for wear, my fingers the deftest at knotting – though if a tub falls from anyone's back or chest, I will suffer worse than being locked up again.

Most of us are occupied with something. Old William is squinting over his accounting book, his pipe clenched between his lips. Bill and Tom are smacking battered playing cards onto the tabletop. Ma is slicing fish after fish from belly to head, then throwing fistfuls of entrails into a bucket.

Only Edwin is empty-handed, pacing while we work, consumed, as always, by news of the gentleman from Westcliff: that he's poaching our men to build his new houses, that guests from his hotel are straying onto the beach at night, that all the fashionable people he's inviting to the town will only attract yet more visitors ... And the more he rants, the more Bill and Tom snigger: we have all heard this before.

'You sound like Harcourt,' Old William tells his youngest son, smoke leaking between his remaining teeth. 'You think we can't change, but we can. We have.'

'Moving the signal, keeping the coastguard in drink – it's not enough,' says Edwin. His scowl stretches the scar running from his left brow, marking the place where his eye once was, before that ancient squabble with his older, stronger brothers. 'And if it's true, what they're saying in London about import duties—'

But Old William interrupts with a grunt. To him, to all of us, London might as well be Havana or Kingston: it is far, far from Crescombe. 'We have always been free traders,' he says.

That should be the end of it, but Ma flicks another spool of guts into the bucket with her knife and says, 'Let the boy finish.'

Bill and Tom look up from their game. The whole town shrinks from them, but even they wouldn't dare give orders to their father.

'I am finished,' says Edwin, ungrateful as always. 'This whole family will be finished if we continue like this. One of you must see it!'

His remaining eye bulges as he glares around at them all: his stony father, his stupid brothers, his ruthless mother, who is still busy with her knife and so must be avoiding his gaze on purpose, because she could carve up a fish in her sleep.

Last, Edwin looks to me. The others have forgotten I'm here, but not him. He knows I watch all, hear all. And he knows that, even if my opinion was worth anything at all, I'd rather side with the Devil himself than with Edwin Crocker.

A rasping cough draws his attention back to Old William.

'Father, you are weakening . . .' he begins, with more scorn than sympathy.

'You mind your mouth!'

There's a flash of silver as Ma jabs at the air between them with her knife. Edwin glowers at her, but I saw him wince.

'Get out, boy,' says Old William, his voice quiet, but as sharp as the edge of Ma's blade. 'You're not in—'

But the rest of his sentence is lost to more coughing. Ma rushes to his side, while Edwin begins to stalk from the kitchen. As he passes me, the only one smaller than him, he aims a kick in my direction. I hop backwards, managing to avoid the toe of his boot but my head crunches against the wall behind, and the coil of rope drops from my hands. Bill and Tom laugh, noticing me at last, but Edwin looks sourer than ever: he would have preferred to inflict the hurt himself.

'You!' Ma turns her knife towards me. 'What are you staggering about for? Get rid of this.'

She gestures towards the bucket of guts. The back of my head is still throbbing and as I bend for the handle I almost retch. But despite Ma's knife, I hang back, unwilling to follow too closely behind Edwin, fearing worse than a kick if we find ourselves alone together.

He's lingering by the door, searching for the final word. 'Crescombe is changing whether we want it to or not,' he mutters. 'We can't just sit down in the sand, waiting for the tide to take us.'

I hope it does, I think. I hope it takes you all.

Even though, when the water comes, they will grab me by the wrist or ankle, any part of me they can reach. They will find a way to drag me down with them.

5

The Bathing Machine

Finley had finally given up on sleep around sunrise and headed down to the little beach below Crockers Nest. The tide was retreating, leaving intricate, undulating patterns in the sand and gradually exposing more of the rock where Megan had been sitting, its partially submerged humps putting Finley in mind of the Loch Ness Monster. Boats were bustling out to sea, and he watched them for a long time, still ruminating on that article about the Bay View drownings, which he had now read so many times he could have recited it by heart.

At some point after the sky had turned steely blue, Finley spotted a small vessel heading straight towards him, and recognised the straight-backed figure at its helm, who was rowing with as much ease as she had swum. With the hazy water at her back, and her long hair loose, there was something of the Lady of Shalott about her – or there would have been, had it not been for the black cocker spaniel at the bow, quivering with excitement at the prospect of disembarking.

Megan guided the boat right up to the little beach, where Skipper splashed through the shallow water and threw himself at Finley's legs. Bending to pat this dark blur of enthusiasm, Finley managed a smile: it was difficult to feel too gloomy when a dog was this pleased to see you.

Drawing her oars into the boat, Megan asked, 'Are you better now?'

'What?'

'After almost fainting at the museum.'

'I didn't almost faint!' Finley spluttered. 'How do you even know about that?'

'My dad told me.'

'How does *he* know?' Suddenly, Finley was concerned that the whole of Crescombe was talking about him.

'You met him?' said Megan, her manner suggesting that Finley was being slow. Then, when he still looked blank, she added, 'He's curator there.'

'That was your *dad*?' said Finley, reflecting on the serious, scholarly figure of Adrian Salter. 'Wait – do you live at The Delmore Experience too?'

'Yes.'

Again, her tone implied he ought to have known this already, and Finley supposed, in Crescombe, everyone knew everything about everyone else.

Skipper, perhaps disappointed that Finley's attention was elsewhere, trotted off to burrow in the sand. Megan, however, remained in her boat, which was pale blue and white, and had a motor attached to the back. On the side, in loopy dark blue letters, a name had been painted: *Sandy Bottom*.

'Is that your boat?' Finley asked.

'Not really.'

Was she joking? It was difficult to tell. 'I like the name,' he persevered.

'Hmm.'

What was she doing here? It seemed unlikely she'd rowed all this way to enquire after his health. He thought about asking why she wasn't swimming this morning, or when she would next be back at The Drowned Painter. But instead, reasoning that their conversations were a little out of the ordinary anyway, he asked, 'Do you believe in ghosts?'

'No,' she replied at once, apparently unsurprised by the question. Finley thought this might be the end of it, but she went on, 'We'd see them all the time, wouldn't we? If they were real?'

'What do you mean?'

She began to pick at the peeling paintwork on the side of her boat. 'If they could, the dead would come back for the living, for those they'd loved and left behind. They wouldn't be able to stay away.'

This was surprisingly sentimental for someone who, so far, Finley had found curt and a little cold. It made him want to draw her out, because although she was inscrutable, and quite intimidating, she was *interesting*.

Before he could ask her anything else, however, Megan flicked a piece of dried paint into the boat and said, 'Do you?'

'Believe in ghosts? I'm not sure.'

She shot him a shrewd look. 'Is this about what they were saying in the pub the other night? About East Crescombe's ghosts?'

'No . . .'

But as he said it, Finley wondered whether that comment had been playing on his mind more than he'd realised; perhaps it was the reason he was seeing things that weren't really there, like footprints.

'There *are* stories, though?' he ventured.

'Loads,' said Megan, before counting them off on her fingers. 'There's the fisherman's widow who walks up and down the beach, waiting for her drowned husband to return. There's the man who knocks on your door – some say he's a pedlar, some say he's a smuggler – only when you open it, there's no one there. Oh, and there's the little boy who waits at the roadside by the church, where he was trampled by a horse. That's the best one, I reckon – apparently, you know when he's going to appear because you can hear the sound of galloping hooves . . .'

Perhaps Finley's disquiet was obvious, because Megan said, 'None of it's true, obviously. Stories like that were just put about by smugglers to stop people sniffing around that part of town.'

'Really?'

Megan nodded. 'All those so-called sightings were probably reported just before a big shipment of brandy or lace or whatever came up the Channel.'

Finley felt both reassured and a little distracted by this anecdote, which was potentially useful for his project with Lorraine. Then, reasoning they had come this far in the conversation, he admitted, 'I found out about those women, the ones who stayed at Crockers Nest back in the day. The ones who—I mean, I read an article that suggested they might've—'

'Killed themselves?'

'Well – yeah,' said Finley, a little taken aback by her bluntness. Then, remembering the drinkers in The Drowned Painter thinking it significant that Lorraine had opened up the top room, and particularly that comment – *lucky you're not a female, then* – Finley said, 'Those women were staying in my room, weren't they? The one up there.'

Megan gazed up at the porthole window. 'That's what I heard,' she said.

Again, Finley thought of the footprints – no, *not* footprints, just patches of water from a leak.

'You should go and talk to Dawn,' Megan told him.

'Dawn?' he repeated, surprised.

'The fortune teller. She has a hut on the—'

'Yeah, I know,' he cut in. 'I just—Why, exactly?'

'*She* believes in ghosts,' said Megan pointedly. 'Plus, she's been in Crescombe forever. So, you're probably better off talking to her about this stuff than me.'

When she put it like that, it sounded logical, and Finley didn't know how to explain that psychics and fortune telling unnerved him almost as much as the idea of ghosts.

'We can go now,' decided Megan, throwing her flip-flops onto the sand and hopping out of the boat after them.

'Erm...'

'It'll be fine, tide's still going out,' she said, misinterpreting Finley's reluctance for concern over *Sandy Bottom*. 'Skip? A walk?'

They started along the footpath towards the beach, where the flower-speckled hedgerows hummed with bees. Megan seemed content to walk without saying much, but Finley didn't like silences, and after a couple of false starts landed upon a topic that elicited from her more than a few syllables: Skipper.

'I don't know if he's even mine, really,' she said. 'He just started following me one day and never stopped.' She gestured at Skipper, who, technically, was leading their little group, his fluffy black tail beating against bracken and nettles as though to say, *Come on!*

After some prompting, Finley learned that Megan had found Skipper as a puppy, huddled under an upturned *Sandy Bottom* on the beach. The way she told it, she had tried everything to get rid of him – knocking on doors for his owner, taking him to the local animal shelter – though Finley wasn't sure he believed her nonchalance, especially after a cyclist came haring down the footpath and Megan bolted towards the dog to drag him out of harm's way.

At the edge of the beach, they stopped at a kiosk for tea and bacon rolls, plus a few extra rashers for Skipper. As Finley's left hand grew hot from the polystyrene cup, his right greasy from leaking butter, he began to feel brighter than he had in a while, perhaps since his arrival in Crescombe. But as they ventured along the promenade, and Dawn's dark purple hut became visible, Finley found his good mood disappearing as quickly as his breakfast: what exactly was he going to say to her?

Dawn was perched on the low wall between her hut and the beach, though it took Finley a moment to recognise her. He had been looking for a short-haired sporty-looking person, whereas today Dawn was wearing a midnight blue dress with lots of velvet and lace embellishments and a curly copper-coloured wig. The overall effect was less PE teacher and more sorceress in a fantasy film.

She watched Finley and Megan approach with apparent interest, remarking in a far dreamier voice than before, 'You're an unlikely pair.'

Finley wasn't sure how to respond to this greeting, though he felt he should explain he and Megan weren't any kind of *pair*. Before he could say anything, however, Megan announced, 'Finley wants to ask you about ghosts.'

'Yes,' said Dawn, before taking a leisurely sip from the same chintzy teacup as before, 'I thought he might.'

Embarrassed, Finley was reminded of those miserable meetings where his mum and various headteachers had talked about him as though he wasn't there. 'Well, not *ghosts*, exactly,' he insisted, now regretting that question to Megan, 'more Crockers Nest, and what might've happened there . . .'

Dawn, however, was nodding. 'Come on, then – step into my office.' She drained the rest of her tea, then beckoned him towards her hut, her ring-laden fingers glinting in the morning sun.

Finley hesitated: he had hoped they could just discuss this outside.

'I'll have to charge you,' she continued, sounding more like the Dawn he'd met the other day. 'How about we say a fiver, which is the rate of a single-card pull? That's the cheapest reading I offer, by the way.'

'Right – thanks,' said Finley, who had no idea what a 'single-card pull' meant, and couldn't help but feel he'd been tricked.

Megan, he noticed, had begun to wander down the beach with Skipper, and Finley was fairly certain he wouldn't see her again today. She didn't seem big on goodbyes – or hellos, for that matter. He felt a little abandoned – and like he had even less of a choice now other than to follow Dawn through the beaded curtain into her hut.

A surprising amount had been packed into its small interior. The galaxy of fairy lights on the ceiling illuminated two long benches, each lining a wall dotted with prints and photographs of everything from herbs to crystals. It smelled of wood, and tea – there was a small kettle and a collection of tins on some corner shelving – and had a general air of mustiness, probably due to all the cushions and blankets scattered about the seating.

'Do make yourself comfortable,' said Dawn, indicating the bench opposite the one she had just occupied. 'Feel free to stretch out, even lie down ...'

The seat creaked as Finley pointedly sat: nothing would have compelled him to recline here. He was very aware of how close they were sitting, and that his denim-clad knees were almost touching her velvet-covered ones. He tried to edge along the bench without her noticing, and the back of his head knocked against one of the framed photographs. Turning to straighten it again, he noticed it was a black and white image of the very structure in which they were sitting, only its large wheels were half submerged in the sea.

'Is that *this* hut?' he asked.

'Oh – yes. Back in its bathing machine days.' Then, in answer to Finley's curious expression, she explained, 'If you were a woman staying in Crescombe in Georgian or even Victorian times and you wanted to go sea-bathing for your health – because obviously you'd never go for pleasure – you had to hire one of these contraptions.' She knocked on the wooden wall. 'And then a horse, or sometimes a great big local woman, would drag you down the beach in it, and from the door you'd dunk yourself in the water, fully clothed.'

'So, women couldn't just ... *walk* into the sea?' asked Finley, whose mind then conjured the not unwelcome image of Megan in her black swimming costume, and the ease with which she had slid through the water.

'Oh no,' said Dawn, 'it wasn't *proper*. Men could, of course. Some beaches were segregated by sex, but mostly men swam wherever they liked, and completely starkers.' She smiled. 'All right for some, eh?'

Finley wasn't sure what the right reaction to this was, so said nothing – though, if he were to be given the choice today, he thought he'd much rather head into the water fully clothed than fully naked.

'Anyway,' said Dawn, with a shake of her long fake hair. 'I don't believe you came here to ask me about historical swimming habits.'

'No,' agreed Finley, who still wasn't entirely sure why he *was* here. Perhaps he should just make some excuse, go back to his room, make a proper start on that smuggling research.

Dawn, however, leaned forward, suddenly intense. 'You've felt something, haven't you? At Crockers Nest?' Then, before he could respond, she said, 'You *have*. You must be very intuitive, Finley – very sensitive.'

He thought she meant this as a compliment, but, to him, it didn't sound too different from all the other things he'd been called over the years: *wimp, sissy, poof.*

In an attempt to regain control of the conversation, he asked, 'When you said you knew *of* Crockers Nest, was it because of those women who stayed there and then drowned?'

'Yes – and no,' said Dawn. Then, after a moment's deliberation, she continued, 'Before we start, I should be clear that I'm not a medium, or any kind of . . .' she cast around for the right words '. . . *paranormal investigator*. I'm concerned with the future of the living, not the past and those long gone.'

'Okay . . .' Finley was confused: was she trying to tell him she couldn't help after all?

'Having said that, I'm not *uninformed* on the subject,' Dawn went on, with a little smile. 'Plus, I've been in Crescombe long enough to know that there have always been stories about Crockers Nest, and that part of town.'

'Megan said those stories were spread by smugglers,' Finley jumped in, 'to keep people *away* from that part of town.'

'Stories have to start somewhere.'

Finley had no response to this. He was beginning to feel a little trapped, not only by the cramped interior of the hut, but by her expectant expression.

'Say there was some truth to those stories, then,' he began, carefully. 'Say I really had felt something. What might it actually *be*?'

'Well, that would depend on what exactly you'd felt,' Dawn reasoned, and Finley was once again reminded of those headteachers, who must have had a pretty good idea why he'd turned up with a soaking wet school bag, or lines scored into his arm by a maths compass. But, apparently deciding to respect his desire to speak hypothetically, Dawn continued, 'There are different kinds of haunting, of course: poltergeists, possession, residual . . .'

'Sorry, *residual?*' repeated Finley, whose insides were already squirming with discomfort.

'Yes, that's probably the most common type,' mused Dawn, 'and perhaps, in this case, the most likely . . .' Then, appearing to realise she had already lost him, she explained, 'A residual haunting is the sort of phenomena people report experiencing in castles and old houses: sounds like footsteps or crying that seem to come from nowhere; figures walking down the same corridor or appearing at a particular window. Essentially, it's the *memory* of what was once there, repeating itself over and over.'

'Why?' asked Finley, before he could help himself. 'How?'

'Nobody knows, not really. But there are theories . . .' She seemed to consider Finley a moment, as though sizing him up. 'Many believe a residual haunting is the result of a particularly traumatic event – or series of events – that somehow becomes imprinted on a place, like a recording. Then, under certain conditions, that recording is replayed.'

'So, it's specific to location?' asked Finley, picturing that box of research about Crockers Nest – all that potentially traumatic history.

'Generally, yes,' said Dawn, 'and my feeling is that Crescombe is especially susceptible to this kind of thing. Partly because it's a place associated with death; as I told you before, this stretch of coast was once plagued by shipwrecks – they even used to call it "the sailors' grave".' She shot Finley another searching look, then said, 'And partly, I think, it's because Crescombe is surrounded by water.'

'What difference does that make?'

Dawn gave her wig a tweak. 'It might sound a bit hokey, but some people believe water has a kind of memory, meaning that recording process I just mentioned would be even easier. And when you consider the shape of Crescombe' – in the air, she traced a crescent on its side – 'it's almost trapping that energy, isn't it? Like a simmering cauldron.'

She was right, thought Finley: this did sound hokey.

Perhaps Dawn could sense his scepticism, because she swiftly moved on, saying, 'The key thing to remember about a residual haunting is that it's not *intelligent*. You can't really interact with it – or it with you. As I said, it's like listening to a recording, or watching a film. If you were to see a spirit of this kind in Crockers Nest, you wouldn't be able to communicate with it. They'd be stuck in this loop of memory, they wouldn't even know you were there.'

Finley, though still striving to remain dispassionate, wasn't wholly reassured by this: the idea of seeing any spirit in Crockers Nest was unnerving, regardless of intelligence.

'That's one of the reasons we often think of ghosts as walking through walls,' Dawn went on. 'It's likely that, consciously, they exist in a time before that wall was built – as far as they're concerned, it isn't there. And it's why a lot of residual hauntings go unnoticed. Yes, you probably wouldn't miss an apparition drifting through a wall, but hearing a bit of unexplained noise? Most people wouldn't think to question it.'

In spite of himself, Finley thought of Lorraine's assumption that a heavy, securely fastened window must be regularly blowing open.

'So, a residual haunting,' he said, keen to stay in hypothetical territory, 'if it is just a part of the past repeating itself, regardless of what's happening in the present, it's ... harmless?'

He expected Dawn to agree at once, maybe remind him of what she'd said about not being able to interact with these phenomena. However, she took her time in answering: 'In theory, yes. In practice ...' She sighed, smoothing out a section of dark lace at her sleeve. 'Look, Finley, we're talking about forces that nobody really understands here – forces that nobody *should* understand, perhaps. There aren't any rules. Energy like that, it's powerful, unpredictable – and it can be really bloody dangerous. It's one of the reasons I'm here, reading palms, not there' – she gestured at the wall of her hut, presumably indicating Crockers Nest far beyond – 'with a ouija board. Unless you're very confident in what you're doing, you don't mess around with the dead.'

Finley felt as though a sudden chill had rushed through the beaded curtain of the fortune teller's stuffy hut; the idea that Dawn herself might be afraid of Crockers Nest disturbed him more than anything she had said so far.

He shouldn't have let Megan bring him here. It was mad, all this talk of forces and spirits and hauntings – yet, at the same time, it was feeding his paranoia about Crockers Nest.

'Going back to those women, the two who drowned ...' he said, eager to return to less speculative territory.

'You know, I met Michelle,' Dawn broke in.

'You—*Really?*'

'I was just starting out back then, but I read her tea leaves . . .' Dawn's gaze moved to somewhere above Finley's head. 'She'd been travelling around Italy on an art tour and had come all the way to Crescombe just to see where Delmore had painted *Hero's Bay*. She was a sweet girl. From California, I think – very bright-eyed and peppy, you know the type.'

Finley, who thought he could see where Dawn was going with this, said, 'Not the type about to take her own life?'

'Obviously you can never really tell, but . . .' Dawn shook her head. 'She told me she'd overcome some kind of serious illness as a child – leukaemia, perhaps? – so was all about *seizing the day*. She did mention her room, said it was a bit creepy – she was especially bothered by some sort of scratching . . .'

Finley wondered whether Michelle had meant in the room or on herself. His right palm felt suddenly itchy at the thought.

'I didn't pay it much attention at the time,' Dawn continued, before he could ask. 'Again, Crockers Nest has always had a reputation. I knew about the other woman – Jacqueline someone – but I was a child when that happened, so I didn't put two and two together until after Michelle died.'

Now, Finley couldn't help but shudder, yet forced himself to ask, 'She was staying in the top room too?'

'They both were,' confirmed Dawn. 'That's the reason the police decided Michelle's was a copycat suicide: two women, same room, same cause of death. Their bodies even washed up in practically the same place – around the most easterly point of the bay, just beyond the guesthouse.'

Finley, who was fighting the childish urge to press his hands against his ears – he didn't want to think about this too closely, didn't want to *picture* it – said, 'But you think the police were wrong?'

Dawn took a moment to consider her next words: 'If you ask me, something bad happened at Crockers Nest long before those so-called suicides; they're the symptom, not the cause. As I said, the stories about that place are far older than the 70s. So if you're wanting to look into this, Finley, I'd go back further.'

Am I wanting to look into it? he wondered.

'But if I were you, I'd get out of there,' Dawn told him, suddenly severe. 'It shouldn't be open – that whole building should be razed to the ground. I tried to warn that silly woman last year, before she bought it . . .' Dawn gave a jerk of her shoulders. 'There's a reason it was so cheap, and had been on the market for so long: no one around here would go near it.'

Evidently she had forgotten that Finley was staying with his godmother and, to curb further slander, he asked, 'What did Michelle's tea leaves say?'

'Oh . . .' Perhaps for the first time that morning, Dawn seemed surprised by his question. 'Well, as it happens, I saw a very clear cross at the bottom of her cup.'

'Which isn't a good sign?' Finley guessed.

'At the very least, a cross can signify trouble and suffering,' she explained. 'But, as I said, Michelle had had this terrible illness as a child, so I thought it might be in reference to that. I was only just starting out back then,' Dawn added, with a touch of defensiveness.

Her gaze drifted towards the beaded curtain, though this time it seemed she was less lost in wistful reflection and more preoccupied by the teenage girls reading the signage of her hut.

'Is that everything you wanted to know, Finley?' she asked, her eyes still fixed on these potential customers.

'Erm, yeah – thanks,' he said, now eager to depart the stale hut, even if it meant returning to Crockers Nest. And with this thought, the words DO NOT STAY HERE!! entered his mind. 'Wait, actually there was something: you're not on Guidebook, are you?'

Dawn frowned. 'On what?'

'Never mind,' said Finley, who still hadn't received a reply from *cross_my_hart*, and now wondered if they might be someone who had known about the deaths. 'It's just a travel review site.'

'Oh, I don't bother with all that,' said Dawn airily. 'If people need me, they tend to find me, one way or the other ...'

She chivvied him out of the hut, though as they squinted through the now bright sunshine they saw the teenage girls had wandered off towards the arcade. To Finley's surprise, however, Megan and Skipper were still on the beach, playing with a tennis ball near the shore: they weren't waiting for him, were they?

A little buoyed by the idea, he glanced over towards the distant shape of Crockers Nest on its rocky ledge, nestled into the largely wooded cliff of East Crescombe. Now, bathed in sunlight, the guesthouse seemed more eccentric than ominous – and, away from the airless interior of her hut, his discussion with Dawn a little ridiculous.

'I never did your reading,' she said, scrutinising the Scottish five-pound note Finley then handed her.

'Oh, that's all right,' he said, now keen to get away – and keen to dispel the image of a cross of tea leaves that had just re-entered his mind.

'A deal's a deal.' Now she'd lost her next customers, Dawn seemed keen to keep him. 'Here, shuffle these.'

From a pocket, she produced a deck of tarot cards. Finley eyed them warily.

'Go on,' she urged, 'they won't bite. Shuffle them and think of a question.'

'What kind of question?'

'Whatever question you like. Maybe something that's been playing on your mind? Is there anything in which you'd like a little guidance?'

Tentatively, Finley took the sky-blue deck, which was larger and more cumbersome than a pack of playing cards. He shuffled slowly, partly because he was worried about dropping them (what would *that* mean?) and partly because his head was suddenly teeming with questions. The first that had sprung to mind – *Am I safe at Crockers Nest?* – was quickly followed by dozens more: *Was coming to Crescombe a mistake? Did Mollie ever love me? What am I doing with my life?*

'Got it?' asked Dawn.

'Erm ...'

'Now, with that question in your head, just pick a card, any card.'

Still anxious they were going to tumble from his hands, Finley fanned out the deck. He wasn't sure he wanted to do this (wasn't the *Devil* in here?) but Dawn was watching him expectantly, so he chose an innocuous-looking card nestled in the middle of the pack and offered it to her.

'Turn it over.'

He did so, revealing a bright illustration of a young man standing on a precipice, gazing up at the sky. A small bag was propped over his shoulder on a stick, he was holding a white rose, and a white dog gambolled at his feet. At the base of the card were two words: THE FOOL.

A familiar rush of self-contempt flooded Finley: of course he was the Fool.

'Now, don't look like that, the Fool's often a very positive card,' said Dawn. 'He's a man at the beginning of his journey, stepping out into the unknown. In relation to your question, Finley, the Fool encourages you to set aside your worries, trust your instincts, and *go*. Now is the time for an adventure! See how few possessions he has? You have everything you need in *yourself*. The Fool is full of energy, setting out with a hopeful heart and—'

'Looking like he's about to wander off a cliff?'

Megan had rejoined them on the promenade, and was peering at the card with a mixture of amusement and disdain. Finley thought she had a point: the youth in the picture did appear to be on the verge of plunging to his doom.

'The cards aren't meant to be interpreted literally,' huffed Dawn, clearly resentful of being interrupted mid-flow. 'Though perhaps *you'd* like to choose one, Megan? I've always wanted to do a reading for you . . .'

Finley, eager to get rid of the cards, passed them to Megan. She, however, was shaking her head.

'I'm all right,' she said, automatically straightening the deck between her slender fingers. 'You know I don't believe in any of—'

A card sprang from her grasp and fell to the ground, where it landed face down. Dawn gave a little gasp.

'*The deck has chosen for you!* Quick – pick it up, pick it up!'

Rolling her eyes, Megan retrieved the card and turned it over. Finley's heart lurched: it depicted a skeleton in black armour riding a white horse, carrying a banner bearing a white rose. Under a setting sun, various figures seemed to be pleading with this ominous figure, while one had already expired. Beneath the picture was just one word: DEATH.

'I suppose that's not to be interpreted literally either?' said Megan lightly.

'Actually, it isn't,' said Dawn. 'Often, the Death card is – if you'll pardon the pun – gravely misunderstood. It's about *change*. It doesn't so much signal the end of your life, but the end of a phase or aspect of your life that is no longer serving you. It may be, Megan, that you're being held back by a negative experience, or perhaps simply negative feelings, and it's time to let them go. It is time to put the past behind you.'

Finley, his heart still thumping, wondered whether this was the sort of spin that, years ago, Dawn had given Michelle. He watched as, for a moment, Megan blinked at the sinister image in her hand, before thrusting the whole deck back towards him and turning on her heel, announcing, 'What a load of crap.'

She hopped over the low wall onto the beach again, striding towards Skipper, who was digging an enormous hole and only visible by his relentlessly wagging tail. Finley glanced at Dawn, wondering whether she was insulted by Megan's abrupt departure, but the fortune teller merely smiled to herself and beckoned for Finley to return the tarot deck.

The Death card was still on top of the pile as he handed it back, and the image of that skeleton on horseback remained with him long after Dawn had returned to her hut with the deck. He knew Megan was probably right – most likely, it *was* a load of a crap – but after everything Finley had learned over the past few days, it didn't feel like the best of omens.

'*Ouch!*'

He staggered as something struck his chest, temporarily winding him. When the shock had subsided, he cast around for what had hit him, and spotted a tatty old tennis ball rolling down the promenade.

'You were meant to catch that!' Megan yelled.

As Finley bent to pick up the soggy, smelly ball, the ache in his chest was replaced by something warmer. Megan was watching him expectantly, her hand shielding her eyes from the dazzling sun, and Skipper was bounding straight towards him, ears and tongue flapping.

'Well?' Megan called. 'Are you going to throw it back for him or what?'

I snuck out at first light, while the family were still sleeping. Though I should be sleeping too: a ship came in last night, and even when my part is done I'm kept awake by the shouts and crashes from below – and by the fear that, at any moment, men more powerful than even the Crockers might discover us.

I've already wandered up through the woods, and down to Crockers Beach, and along beside the promenade. I've found a tuft of sheep's fleece clinging to a gate, a limpet shell with a hole the size of my eye, and a bush of fat dark blackberries, ones that burst on my tongue in sharp juices. And I've ended up here, as I always do, where only the humming of insects and the whispering of leaves disturb the silence of the dead.

I like it best here in the spring, when violets froth around the gravestones like seafoam, making the air smell so sweet I could almost gulp it down like those blackberries. Still, today I can stretch out in the sun, letting it warm me after all that time spent indoors.

My mother is here, and has been since I was a child. Soon, they will put Old William in the ground, then one day Ma and the rest of them. Not me, though. Even if they cared enough to bury me, to give me a stone, I will be long gone.

I remember them lowering my mother's coffin, and how Ma couldn't bear to watch; she was wailing in a way I had never heard from her before and have never heard since. But I don't believe my mother exists in this dark, cold earth, not really. She is in the woods, at the shoreline, in the fields; she lives in tufts of sheep fleece, in the holes of limpet shells and the juices of blackberries. She blooms, over and over, in the violets.

I come here to talk to her, though. She used to tell me stories about pixies and mermaids and even a beast that prowls the moors. I don't know any stories like that – I don't know anything beyond Crescombe – but I still speak to her because she is the only one who ever listened to me. Because I still miss her.

Today, I tell her of the first people on the promenade this morning: the elderly and the sick being wheeled along in their bath chairs; the boy delivering a stack of newspapers to the hotel; even a group of young women with frilly sleeves and ruffled skirts, out early with their parasols and hoping, perhaps, for a glimpse of you.

Nobody noticed me, slipping along the beach, which still bore the lines of boats and the footprints of the fishermen who left at dawn. Occasionally, when I stray too close to the new houses, people will stare – once, a gentleman even tried to shoo me from his path with a handkerchief. But usually it is like today, and I can creep beside the promenade unobserved. After all, the visitors are there not to see, but be seen.

Edwin is right: Crescombe is changing, and too fast for us.

I feel for the sea stone in my pocket and hold it above my head, where it looks unusually faded against the deep blue of the sky. My father told me just one story. He knelt down, placed this stone into my palm, and in his deep, strange voice explained that he had scooped this drop of sea from the faraway shore where he was born.

'I have carried it across oceans,' he said, 'and now it is yours, until I come back. Until we go home, and you can swim in those clear, warm waters ... They are waiting for you – and for this,' he added, folding my small hand around the stone. 'So, will you promise to keep it safe, and we can return it there together?'

I was just a child, and knew even less about the world than I do now, yet it was so easy to say, 'Yes – I promise.'

It was just a story. This is just a stone. Our meeting lasted a matter of minutes, and then he was gone. Yet even after all this time, I remember him: how his dark hands were calloused and scarred yet so gentle in mine; how he looked tired, and sad, yet more pleased to talk to me than anyone has been since. And although it was just a story, I believe there was truth in it, because above all I remember not knowing how to tell him that I couldn't swim.

6

St Nicholas Parish Church

The church looked half forgotten. Surrounded by a large, overgrown graveyard, the woodland of East Crescombe pressing at its back, only a square belltower rose defiantly above the greenery, its toothed walls more resemblant of a fortress than a place of worship.

'Hello?'

Finley peered through the open door, breathing in the smell of old stone and dusty prayer cushions. Between the altar and a vaulted ceiling, a stained-glass window glinted in the gloom, depicting a vivid red-robed figure – Saint Nicholas, presumably – against a backdrop of rolling sea. Otherwise, the church was deserted.

'Hello?' Finley called again.

'Up here ...'

It struck Finley that a church was quite the place to be hearing a faint, disembodied voice from on high – but even *his* imagination was not that overactive and, moments later, he spotted a series of steep wooden steps, more like a ladder than a staircase.

He soon emerged into a square high-ceilinged space that must have formed part of the belltower, only it looked more like a dingy storeroom. The rickety floor was littered with boxes like the one lent to Lorraine, while trestle tables sagged beneath stacks of ring binders and loose paperwork. An assortment of random objects had been propped up against the stone walls, including display boards still advertising old harvest festivals and charity bake sales, and several model farmyard animals that might have belonged to a nativity scene.

Stooped over the nearest table of papers was an elderly man in a dark shirt and trousers, a wooden cross hanging from a string looped around his clerical collar. He was lean, with a slightly sallow complexion and wispy white hair, which put Finley in mind of a recently extinguished candle.

'Excuse me, Vicar?' he ventured, unsure of the correct form of address. 'Reverend Clay . . . ?'

'Seymour is fine,' said the man in a reedy voice, without looking up from his reading. 'You'll be wanting to see the book, I suppose?'

Finley hesitated: did he mean the Bible? 'Sorry, which book?'

'The book, the Delmore book!' said the vicar, displacing clumps of dust as he rearranged some papers.

'Oh – no,' said Finley, realising he must be expecting someone else. 'I'm Finley, from Crockers Nest. I think Lorraine phoned ahead to ask whether I could look at some parish records?'

'Ah, you're the *historian*.' At last, the vicar – Seymour – looked up.

'Well, not exactly,' said Finley, who wished Lorraine would stop telling people this. 'I studied Classics at uni, but—'

'Mm-hmm, mm-hmm,' said Seymour, now advancing upon Finley, his pale eyes intense. 'And what did you specialise in? The ancient languages? The history?'

'Erm, the culture mostly,' said Finley, a little unnerved by the vicar's sudden attention. 'The myths.'

'Yes . . .' Seymour nodded. 'All those shining heroes and fearsome beasts; all that wretched, unavoidable tragedy . . .'

Finley wasn't sure what to make of this. The vicar was standing very close now; Finley could see the mottled skin of his scalp beneath his fine hair. He wanted to step back, but at the same time he had the impression he was being tested, so he held the other man's gaze.

Sure enough, a moment later, Seymour said, 'So, interested in the Crockers, are you?'

'Yes,' said Finley, pleased they were on the same page at last.

Although he had been dispatched here by Lorraine, to investigate whether the parish records contained anything that might be useful for their smuggling booklet, Finley found he was glad of the task: after that obscure and unnerving conversation with Dawn, it was a relief to be back in the realm of facts.

'You know, some locals can be a bit funny about that family, even now,' remarked Seymour.

'How come?'

Finally, the vicar drew back from Finley and began to shuffle between the tables, every so often pausing to examine a piece of text or straighten a pile of books. The silence felt as palpable as all the dust, but Finley forced himself to wait, sensing his companion couldn't be rushed.

'Well, in the early nineteenth century, a rather foolish man called Ambrose Montgomery tried to turn this town into a seaside resort,' Seymour began at last, while Finley winced inwardly at the thought of Adrian Salter's reaction to Montgomery being described as *rather foolish*. 'Obviously, he couldn't have the great and good of London society realising there was a family of thugs running the place, so the Crockers and their activities were hushed up – though, naturally, that only made them more feared.'

'By "their activities", you mean their smuggling?'

Finley hadn't come here unprepared. Having done a little research of his own, he had discovered that smuggling – or 'free-trading' – genuinely had been rife in Devon and Cornwall from the seventeenth century onwards, following the introduction of huge taxes on imported goods. Even so, he was still getting his head around the reality of something that, until now, had only existed for him in childhood stories.

'Yes, of course,' said Seymour, with a touch of impatience. 'Until the mid-nineteenth century, when slashed import taxes made smuggling virtually pointless, Crescombe would have been an extremely well-positioned stop-off for ships sailing up the Bristol Channel.'

'Even though the North Devon coast was notoriously dangerous for ships?' said Finley, recalling Dawn's comment about the 'sailors' grave' and wondering how many ships would have dared sail closer than necessary to the rocky shoreline.

'True,' allowed the vicar. 'But don't forget Crescombe has a wide sandy beach – that's unusual around here – and it would have provided a relatively safe point for smaller vessels to approach or even drop anchor. Plus, the surrounding cliffs would have given good cover from any customs officials.'

While Finley recalled his first glimpse of Crescombe from the taxi, and how concealed it had been in the valley, Seymour continued, 'That's not to say landing here was entirely without risk. There were still shipwrecks in the area, as you just implied. Some believe *The Persephone* – the very vessel Delmore died trying to swim out to – was attempting to steer into Crescombe to unload contraband and overshot the beach.'

'*Really?*'

'It's possible,' said Seymour, a little dismissively. 'Of course, it's equally possible *The Persephone* was simply blown off course on her way to Bristol. There's no evidence either way.'

As much as Finley wanted to dwell on this – again, it sounded like something from a classic novel – the mention of *evidence* had awoken a more academic part of his brain, which was beginning to feel this was all a little unfounded.

'And is there any proof of the smuggling?' he asked.

'Not much,' said the vicar, though the question seemed to please him. 'Because of course they were hardly going to shout what they were up to from the rooftops. But there are pieces of circumstantial evidence. Up at Harcourt Manor, the National Trust property in the valley, there are entries in an accounting book suggesting the Crockers used to keep the old lord of the manor in bootlegged brandy. And somewhere around here there's a letter from a London botanist who, during his stay in Crescombe, took a moonlit stroll and ran into one Thomas Crocker. Described him as a "savage West Country brute", if I remember correctly. I think it's safe to assume this botanist strayed a little too close to something nefarious and Crocker had to scare him off. I can try and track that down for you?'

'Only if it's no trouble,' murmured Finley, casting a doubtful eye over the belltower's clutter.

'But the truth is,' continued the vicar, 'that around here, people just *know* about the Crockers and their smuggling. And that's because, at the time, almost everyone was in on it.'

He said this with a little smile, as though he had been looking forward to revealing this particular detail. Happy to indulge him, Finley asked, 'How do you mean?'

'Well, it's generally believed that the Crockers were in charge of what was known as the "landing crew", who were responsible for unloading the contraband from the boats and transporting it inland. But they couldn't have done this on their own. In order to shift the barrels and so on, they would have needed labourers, or even horses and ponies from nearby farms, while other local fishermen might have provided smaller boats to ferry out to the ships. I can't speak for Crescombe, but elsewhere there are reports of town doctors treating those injured in the line of duty, local jurors refusing to condemn their neighbours, and vicars providing character references to anyone who got caught – in return for a barrel of brandy, of course.'

He smiled again, perhaps silently challenging Finley to wonder whether he could have been similarly swayed.

'Even the coastguard service – which was started in the early nineteenth century to clamp down on smuggling – was full of men who'd turn a blind eye for the right price,' continued Seymour. 'So, there was bribery, certainly, but also a lot of intimidation. The Crockers were known for their big builds and violent tempers, and there are all sorts of tales about what they did to, say, farmers who objected to their horses being returned too exhausted for ploughing. Barns would mysteriously catch fire, sheep would inexplicably fall ill . . .'

Finley thought back to that illustration of the Crockers who had been deported; that mean-looking woman and her three ferocious sons. Perhaps his impression of them hadn't been far wrong.

'A town doesn't forget a family like that too quickly,' went on Seymour, 'not when they had such a dastardly, Doone-like reputation. Even in my own school days, which admittedly weren't too recent, we were still saying, "Don't stay out too late or the Crockers will get you".'

Consciously or not, Seymour had begun to fiddle with the wooden cross dangling from his neck. Finley, meanwhile, was reminded of what Dawn had said about Crockers Nest – *stories have to start somewhere* – though taking things on faith wasn't an approach he'd grown up with; he belonged to a family of doctors, a family of *science*.

'However, if you're looking for something a little more . . . *tangible*,' said the vicar, suddenly changing tack, 'I suggest you take a look at the graveyard on your way out. At the back, on the right, that's the Crockers' plot. It's dreadfully overgrown, though – you'll have to fight your way through . . .'

Perhaps Finley, whose thoughts were straying back to the supernatural, looked dubious, because Seymour then continued, 'Otherwise, I've dug out those parish records for you.' He beckoned Finley towards a trestle table groaning under a stack of volumes bound in worn brown leather. 'These contain every baptism, marriage and death recorded in Crescombe – including those of the Crockers, of course.'

He opened the topmost tome, which cracked in protest, and which Finley now saw had been bookmarked with torn strips of what had once been a hymn sheet; the stark printer ink detailing snippets of 'Thine Be the Glory' seemed to reduce the looping handwritten records to whispers.

'This volume goes up to the 1840s, around the time the last Crockers were deported,' said Seymour, 'so maybe you could work backwards? Unfortunately, it's suffered some water damage, but it's more legible than some of the older records and, as you can see, I've taken the liberty of starting you off.' He tweaked one of the scraps of hymn sheet poking from the pages. 'Actually, I even began to draw you the end of the family tree ...'

He rifled through the clutter on the table until he retrieved an intact hymn sheet, the back of which featured the same spidery handwriting as Lorraine's box of research.

'These are the last of the Crockers,' said Finley, recognising the names from the article that had accompanied that illustration.

William Crocker	m.	Agnes Crocker (Née Babbage)	
(1776 – 1841)		(1796 – ?)	

William Crocker II	Thomas Crocker	Edwin Crocker
(1818 – ?)	(1820 – ?)	(1822 – ?)

'Presumably you've put question marks because we don't know when they died?' said Finley. 'Because there's no record of them after they were shipped off to Australia?'

'Precisely,' said Seymour. 'Agnes and her sons could well have lived out long and happy lives terrorising koalas and so on – we have no idea. Though, as you can see, William Senior died here in Crescombe.'

Finley continued to stare at the beginning – or rather, the end – of the family tree, feeling suddenly deflated: he wasn't sure how useful this would be for Lorraine's project. Would visitors to Crockers Nest today really be interested in a list of old names? Perhaps the vicar was right, and he should be paying more attention to the folklore surrounding this infamous family.

'It's easy enough once you get your eye in,' said Seymour, who seemed to think Finley daunted rather than dispirited by the task. 'Here's the death of William Crocker Senior, see?' he said, of the page marked by the last scrap of hymn sheet. Then, flipping back towards the beginning of the volume, he continued, 'And, almost twenty years earlier, here's the birth of his youngest son, Edwin. Then, this one's his middle son, Thomas—'

'Wait, you missed a few . . .'

'Ah, yes.' Seymour turned back to the first fragment of hymn sheet he had bypassed. 'I wasn't sure how detailed you'd want to go, who exactly you'd consider a Crocker. But this *is* interesting . . .'

He pointed at a baptism record from October 1822:

_____ bastard baby of Ellen Babbage

'Ellen Babbage was the younger sister of Agnes Crocker,' explained the vicar, 'and died a few years after her baby's birth here – that's the other place I've marked. Funny how they used the word *bastard*, isn't it? Obviously the father wasn't around, or he would have been named.'

Finley, who wasn't sure he would have used the word *funny* – *backward*, maybe – asked, 'What about the baby?' He was very struck by the blank space at the beginning of the entry. 'Was it normal for illegitimate children to be left nameless like that?'

'Not really,' admitted the vicar. 'I wonder whether it might have died in infancy – though this is obviously a baptism record, so it would have been given a name at some point. I suppose it's possible that the vicar at the time didn't think the child worthy of being recorded, because of it being born out of wedlock,' he mused. 'Though it's just as likely this was simply poor record-keeping.'

Maybe a little more than likely, thought Finley, with a glance at the debris scattered around the belltower.

When he looked back at the volume, he noticed another page had been marked, not too far from the death record of William Crocker Senior. Only, there was no scrap of hymn sheet here, and instead the top of a dark blue leather bookmark was visible between the pages.

'What's that?' he asked.

'Pah.' For some reason, the vicar looked irritated. 'That's nothing to do with the Crockers – but go ahead and look if you must. It's most of the reason I keep this place open to the public. Though I warn you, water's definitely got into these records . . .'

Intrigued, Finley leaned forward as Seymour turned to the place indicated by the bookmark. But there was nothing there: just a watery stain that clouded almost the whole page.

'Note the date,' said Seymour.

This was easier said than done, but after a great deal of squinting, Finley was just able to make out a little of the smudged writing: August 1840.

He drew back. 'This is Delmore's death record,' he said, before correcting himself: 'Or, it *was*.'

He felt suddenly cold, though he wasn't sure why. Was it simply because this was proof of a young man's untimely demise? Or was it the feeling that, wherever he went in this town, Delmore was there? The artist had been in Crescombe for just one summer, yet his influence seemed to creep into its every corner.

'We assume he's under there,' muttered the vicar.

'What do you mean?'

'Well, Delmore wasn't a member of the parish, was he? And ...' Seymour frowned. 'It's a bit *convenient*, this water damage. I almost wonder whether, at some point, someone might have splashed a little water over 1840, either for theatrical effect or to disguise the fact that Delmore's not actually there, on the page – though it would be in rather poor taste, considering how the man died.'

Finley thought of Montgomery, and Adrian Salter's theory that the developer had named *Hero's Bay*. Seymour seemed to be suggesting that this was a similar example of early publicity for the artist, and Finley realised that this must be the 'Delmore book' the vicar had assumed he had come to see. He wondered what sort of person came to gaze upon a largely blank page – the same sort of person, he supposed, who left flowers and art equipment at the Delmore monument.

At the same time, the longer he stared at the water-damaged page, the more intriguing it became. *Had* Delmore's name been there? What about the names of the other men who had drowned that night, the crew of *The Persephone*? Whatever water had dripped or been spilled on this paper had caused the ink to bloom outwards, and it took Finley a moment to realise what the bright core of this dark flower reminded him of: *Hero's Bay*. Unbidden, the words of that man in The Drowned Painter returned to him, and the theory he had related: *that the light was a glimpse of the afterlife ... and that, when he was painting it, Delmore had had a premonition of his own death.*

As he had with the painting in the museum, Finley felt a compulsion to reach out and touch that brightness. Reasoning that he already had permission to look through these records – and noting that the vicar's attention was wandering towards a stack of old maps – this time Finley surrendered to the urge, and pressed two fingers to the page. Nothing happened, of course – except, when he withdrew his hand, he was surprised to find his fingertips coated in something fine and gritty, like sand. Or salt.

After that, he felt he had little choice but to pore over the old records for a while, though it was more out of politeness than any real confidence in what he was doing. Initially, there was a certain novelty to turning back through the yellowed pages and trying to decipher the ancient handwriting, but the task quickly grew tedious. As he noted down the dates of yet another William or Thomas Crocker – the family seemed to be especially skilled at producing sons – Finley reflected he wasn't assiduous enough for this kind of work; he could never have been a real historian.

Once about an hour had passed, he thanked the vicar, feeling it acceptable to call it a morning. The day had turned bright and breezy, but Finley felt gloomy as he stepped outside the church. As much as he had enjoyed hearing about the Crockers, the only thing he had gleaned from going through those records was quite how many of them there had been.

He thought of his room at the guesthouse, wondering how likely it was that it had been inhabited by a series of burly Crocker sons. Lorraine might have done a good job at sprucing it up, but he suspected under all those wooden boards was a fairly dismal attic space. Maybe their smuggling had made the Crockers wealthy or influential enough to employ some kind of lackey? Or perhaps, Finley thought with a shudder, they had kept *prisoners* up there . . .

Rather than leaving through the front gate, Finley wandered past the church building until he reached the section of the graveyard the vicar had referred to as the Crockers' plot. It was, as he had warned, extremely overgrown; among the unmown grass, nettles and other weeds had thrived, and the mossy gravestones poked through this tangle at odd angles, like crooked teeth.

Wary of being stung and scratched – and of what lay deeper than the vegetation – Finley trod carefully through the gravestones, reading what he could of their names; the size of the plot seemed to emphasise the resilience of this infamous Crescombe family. As he then paused to shake off a thorny tendril that had snagged at his T-shirt, he couldn't help but consider the possibility that, somewhere beneath his feet, lay someone not quite at rest.

At the very back of the graveyard, squeezed next to a low wall that had all but crumbled away, Finley found the last few Crockers, for the dates on *this* William's gravestone matched those of the one whose wife and sons had been deported. To the left, with a noticeably plainer stone, lay *Ellen Babbage, beloved sister* – who must truly have been cherished, Finley thought, to have earned her place here. And to the right ...

Finley frowned. If he hadn't been standing right in front of William Crocker's grave, he might not have noticed it at all, or mistaken it for a grassy tuffet. But, beneath coils of ivy and blots of moss, a small stone was just visible, more resemblant of something that might mark a moorland trail than a grave. Why was it so small? Did it belong to a pet? A *child*?

With this last thought, a chill dropped down Finley's spine, and suddenly his brain seemed to catch up with where he was, what he was doing. He should go – let the dead keep their secrets. But curiosity was rooting him to this place quite as tightly as the greenery was clinging to the graves, so after casting around for a stick, he crouched down and began to poke at the surface of the stone.

The dates were revealed first: *1822–1840*. Not a child, then – although barely an adult, either. And there it was again, that date he kept seeing, over and over: *1840*. Without bothering to wipe his earthy hands, Finley consulted the family tree he'd tucked into the back pocket of his jeans, discovering that, as he had thought, 1822 was the year of Edwin Crocker's birth. But if the youngest Crocker son had died in 1840, how could he have been deported a few years later? Had that newspaper got it wrong?

Impatient to find out, Finley continued to work at the gravestone with his stick and, when that proved too slow, resorted to picking at it with his bare hands. The moss was clammy, and ordinarily he would have cringed to feel it wedging itself beneath his fingernails, which themselves kept scraping against stone, but now he hardly noticed, far more intent on this task than the one he'd undertaken in the belltower.

Eventually, a name appeared – though not the one he'd expected, or even one he recognised. His heart thumping, Finley leaned back on his heels, now oblivious to the nettles pressing in around him as he tried to take in what he'd uncovered.

'Who,' he asked the empty graveyard, 'is *Cora* Crocker?'

At the shoreline, I hunt for treasure. My skirts bunched up in one hand, I step barefoot between pungent loops of seaweed, then crouch to search the churned-up sand. I find a rusty button, a fragment of blue pottery and a long shell that spirals into a point, like the horn of a unicorn.

I can hear a distant sloshing, though at first I pay it no attention. It'll be a large wave, or a fish, or a gull. But as the noise grows nearer, I turn and stand, sensing movement beyond the humps of rock just off the little beach, and my treasures tumble from my fingers as I see a figure wading from the water.

You.

You are naked, and though the sight doesn't shock me – my cousins don't always trouble to cover up in my presence – I'm surprised, and a little afraid, and something else I cannot name that it is *you* I am seeing like this; that the man I have watched and watched has crept up on me.

Not on purpose, I realise, as your eyes widen and your hands fumble to conceal your nakedness. When you then shuffle back into the water, you turn from impressive and a little intimidating to vulnerable, even ridiculous.

'My apologies, miss.' Your voice is smooth and sweet, like honey. 'I didn't realise anyone was here.'

I don't speak, don't move, though the damp hems of my skirts nudge against my bare ankles, urging me to go.

As you sink into the shallows you relax a little, stretching out as though enjoying a hot bath, and ask, 'Who are you?'

I don't answer. I need to leave. The family, I know, will still be snoring in their beds, though not for much longer.

You don't seem offended by my silence, nor do you introduce yourself, though perhaps you assume I already know your name. Instead, you say, 'Whoever you are, you are very beautiful. In spite of . . .'

You make a lazy gesture towards me, and I think you mean my skin, which begins to smart with shame. Then I realise you're tracing the outline of my tatty apron, or perhaps the holey shawl I threw across my shoulders to guard against the chill of the morning. It's my clothes you dislike – though at least I am wearing some.

'A great beauty,' you continue, thoughtfully. 'Indeed, I should like to sketch you.'

Still, I say nothing, torn between scorn and something softer, warmer: nobody has ever called me beautiful before.

'Maybe I'll even paint you – should you like that?'

I try to imagine it. Should I, who have spent my whole life striving to go unnoticed, like to be captured on a canvas and sneered at by strangers?

'No,' I say.

You blink several times, until I think I've insulted you. Then you let out a great bark of laughter. Your teeth are very white, and some rather pointed. You look, I decide, like a fox.

'Where are you from?' you ask.

'Here.'

'Truly?'

'Truly.'

You cock your head to one side, still smiling. 'I wonder if you are toying with me?'

I leave you to wonder. It would be a humiliation to admit to someone like you that I have never left Crescombe.

'What's your name?'

I stand up: enough. I shouldn't have spoken to you. I shouldn't even be here.

'I hope to see you again!' you call, as I retrieve my boots and begin to scramble up the beach.

I ignore you and quicken my pace, hopping from rock to rock. I'm furious with you for coming here, and furious with myself for putting us both in danger. I won't let it happen again.

Midway up the cliff ledge, though, I pause, right at the point where, at high tide, the steps overhang a great drop into foam-flecked water. There, I dare to turn, half expecting you to still be lounging below, smirking at me from the shallows. But you are already swimming away. For a long time, I watch your lithe body slipping and dipping through the waves, my own filled with that strange new emotion, which feels like fear and fascination all at once – and an envy so strong it rises through me like bile, until I think I may choke.

7

Marina's

'How's your ghost?'

A shadow fell over Finley's notebook, and he glanced up to find Megan standing at his table outside Marina's, the Italian restaurant and gelateria on the promenade. He had taken to working here in the afternoons to escape his oppressive room at Crockers Nest – though today it felt impossible to concentrate anywhere, and instead of drafting the introduction to Lorraine's booklet he had been staring at the sea, thinking about Mollie.

Until now, the novelty of Crescombe, his research into the Crockers and even the eeriness of his room had been starting to drive his ex-girlfriend from his mind – so much so that he thought it might have been worth coming here after all. But last night she had left him a voice message beseeching him to come to her wedding, and now Finley felt just as confused and miserable as he had back in Edinburgh.

So, he was grateful for the distraction of Megan. She was Skipper-less this afternoon, and her dark blonde hair and patches of her baggy T-shirt were damp, suggesting she had recently been for a swim.

'Very funny,' he said, because although he wasn't sure she was joking about the ghost, he had decided, for the moment, that it was bad enough being tormented by the very much alive Mollie McClaine. Nevertheless, in an attempt to keep Megan there, he said, 'Hey, can I ask you something?'

She made a non-committal noise, but settled into the seat opposite.

'Have you ever heard of Cora Crocker?' he asked.

'Who?'

Finley picked up his phone and showed her the last photo he had taken: a small, overgrown grave in a forgotten corner of the churchyard.

Megan frowned as she studied it. 'I've heard of the family, obviously. I thought they mostly had sons?'

'I'm not actually sure she *was* a Crocker, officially . . .'

Megan, however, was still peering at the photo. 'Died in 1840,' she remarked.

'Yeah,' said Finley, 'the same year Delmore was here – the same year Delmore died.'

Following the discovery of the gravestone, Finley had returned to St Nicholas's belltower and looked back through the parish records of 1840 to see if he could find any mention of Cora Crocker. But there had been nothing, leading him to conclude that, like Delmore, either she wasn't there, or she was under that watermark.

'How did you even come across this?' asked Megan, handing back the phone, which was still displaying the photo of Cora's grave.

As succinctly as he could, Finley filled her in on his visit to the church, before adding, 'And that nameless, illegitimate baby of Ellen Babbage was born in 1822, just like Cora here, so I've been wondering whether they're actually one and the same person.'

'Wait, who was Ellen Babbage again?'

'The younger sister of Agnes Crocker, the last Crocker matriarch.'

'Oh, yeah,' said Megan, with a slight smile, as though remembering a detail from a childhood story.

'There's no father listed for Ellen's baby,' said Finley. 'After I found the gravestone, I went back to the church to have another look at the parish records, and I spoke to the vicar again too. He thought Agnes's husband, William Crocker, might have been Cora's father. She's buried next to him in the graveyard.'

'You think he had a baby with his wife's little sister?' Megan grimaced. 'Ouch.'

'It might explain why his name's not in the book. The vicar said usually the church was pretty keen to identify the father of an illegitimate baby, otherwise the parish might end up financially responsible for the child. But someone like William Crocker might have been powerful enough to keep his name out of it.'

Megan tweaked the handle of Finley's coffee cup, which contained dregs that had long since turned cold. 'This is all very interesting,' she said, though her expression suggested her own interest was waning, 'but I don't understand why you're investigating this person, this Cora Crocker.'

'I wouldn't say I'm *investigating* her . . .' began Finley, with a touch of defensiveness.

Then, realising he hadn't actually told Megan about his work for Lorraine, he explained that, for the month he was here, he was looking into the Crockers and their smuggling. 'And I just think Cora's a bit of an anomaly, a mystery,' he said. 'A female-born Crocker who doesn't seem to have been a Crocker at all, unless the vicar's right about her paternity. At best, there's only a partial record of her birth, and no record at all of her death, not officially. She has a gravestone, but one that looks totally different from the rest of the family plot. And above all,' Finley concluded, his gaze resting on the photo once more, and the dates carved into the old stone, 'she died at eighteen, during the most notable year of Crescombe's history.'

Megan blinked at him a few times, and something about the intensity of her wide-set eyes told Finley he had recaptured her interest. Before he could continue, however, a lanky teenage boy came over to clear away his cup and offer him the menu for dinner. Finley, who hadn't realised the time, suddenly became aware of buttery, garlicky aromas drifting through the open doors of Marina's; it smelled a lot better than the ready meals he'd been microwaving himself at Crockers Nest.

'I'll have a look,' he said, of the proffered menu.

The waiter handed it over, then automatically placed another menu in front of Megan. Feeling a little panicked, Finley wondered what to do. They had only spoken a handful of times, and – save for that morning they'd spent throwing a ball for Skipper – never for much longer than a few minutes. As aloof as she was, though, he enjoyed her company – and if nothing else, her appearance at his table this afternoon had once again expelled Mollie from his mind.

'Do you want to grab something here as well?' he asked, trying to make it sound as casual as possible.

'All right,' she said, equally as nonchalant.

However, as soon as she spoke a fat raindrop splashed onto the end of Finley's nose. As he wiped it away, several more followed, drumming against the largely blank page of his notebook like impatient fingertips. He looked up, discovering that, as with the time, he hadn't noticed the weather; the sky was now bruised with cloud.

'Indoors?' he suggested, closing his notebook.

Megan seemed to consider the restaurant a moment, until Finley wondered – or perhaps hoped – she was going to change her mind. But then she clutched at her bare arms, which were rough with goosepimples, and nodded.

Inside, Marina's couldn't have been more Italian if it had tried – and Finley suspected it *had* tried, very hard indeed: cascading over the exposed brickwork of the walls were sprigs of dried herbs and flowers, while the small square tables sported red and white checked tablecloths, and candles dripping wax over repurposed bottles.

They were shown to a booth by a pretty waitress with dark hair and a toothy smile, who introduced herself as Giulia. As the cooking smells intensified, Finley was reminded of Delmore's grand tour around Italy – and once more lamented the year in Greece he had given up to remain with Mollie. Reflexively, he checked his phone: no new messages.

'Are you expecting a call?' asked Megan, picking up a menu again.

'What? Oh – no.' Then, because it looked odd, the way he had placed his phone directly in front of him on the table, like his doctor parents when they were on call, he tried to explain: 'My ex-girlfriend got in touch last night, but it isn't—It's not important.'

Megan glanced up. 'No?'

'No,' said Finley, pocketing his phone.

Megan gave him one of her long looks. 'Right,' she said, returning to the starters.

Finley stared at her a moment longer, noticing there was sand in the parting of her hair. Then his gaze strayed towards the canopy of their booth, which was positively straining with foliage and fairy lights: this wasn't a *date*, was it? He hadn't meant it to be, he didn't fancy her (did he?). Not that she wasn't attractive – she was, in an athletic, ethereal sort of way. But she wasn't Mollie.

'Have you been here before?' he asked, attempting to change the subject.

'A few times with Dad, for my birthday,' said Megan, still perusing the menu.

Finley wondered whether her mum was around – and whether Megan had any friends. Save for Skipper, and that one interaction with Dawn, she always seemed to be on her own.

Shortly afterwards, Giulia the waitress returned, and Finley – who had balked at some of the menu's more sensual descriptions (*juicy, creamy, luscious*) – ordered a lasagne. Lasagne felt like a safe, wholesome choice. He was further reassured when Megan ordered the seafood linguine, which, according to its description, was full of garlic: this definitely wasn't a date.

Nevertheless, once Giulia and the menus had gone, and with their wine yet to arrive, silence swelled between Finley and Megan. He tried to fill it with questions: *How's work? Have you been for a swim? Where's Skipper?* But even the subject of her dog failed to elicit more than a few words from her. Glumly, Finley wondered why he had asked her to join him – and why she had agreed. Now, the thought of this being romantic seemed laughable; they weren't even friends.

Eons later, when Giulia came back with their wine, Finley willed her to pour it as slowly as possible, then cast around for something – anything – that might keep the waitress at their table for a few extra minutes. His attention landed on a small still life hanging over their booth depicting a white jug, a bunch of grapes and half a loaf of crusty bread.

'That's, erm, striking,' he commented, not disingenuously, for certain details of the painting looked so real he might have been looking at a photograph: the glint of the jug's glaze, the cloudy coating of the fruit, the feathery crumbs spilling from the cut loaf.

Giulia looked pleased. 'It was painted by my great, great . . .' she counted a few more *great*s on her fingers '. . . grandmother. That's her over there, in the self-portrait: Marina Vitali.'

Finley turned to where she was pointing. Positioned above the bar, in a spot that might have been reserved for the portrait of a reigning monarch, was a painting of a small, dark-haired woman in a plain black dress. She would have been fairly unremarkable had it not been for her owlish eyes, which seemed to rove the room, and gave her the look of someone all-knowing, like an oracle.

'So, this place is named after her?' he asked.

Giulia nodded. 'She was its first owner, along with her husband, Luciano.'

'It's old, then,' said Finley, surprised.

'It dates back to just after Delmore's time,' said Giulia, causing Finley to question whether everyone in Crescombe used the artist to mark the years like this. 'Marina and Luciano emigrated from Italy after I think the Napoleonic Wars? They had plans to start a restaurant in London, but because Marina's true passion was art, they ended up here.'

This puzzled Finley, who couldn't see the connection.

'Because of *Hero's Bay*,' supplied Megan, speaking for the first time since Giulia had reappeared. 'After Delmore died, the painting went on display at Westcliff House – you know, where the museum is now. For the next few years, before *Hero's Bay* was reclaimed by Delmore's mother, Crescombe became this artistic hotspot, attracting all sorts of street artists hoping to make a name for themselves.'

'Marina Vitali was no street artist,' broke in Giulia, with sudden haughtiness. 'She was born to paint. She could turn her hand to all sorts of styles, so some of her work is very modern, even more so than Delmore's. But . . .' Giulia seemed to deflate. 'She was a woman, wasn't she? And an immigrant. So she never got any glory, not like him up the hill – the one-hit wonder.'

At this, Megan snorted, and a brief look passed between her and Giulia that suggested she was forgiven for her street artist comment.

'Still, thanks to *Hero's Bay*, Crescombe was thriving back then,' continued the waitress, 'which is why Marina and Luciano decided to open their restaurant here . . . and here we are still.'

'So, she and Delmore would never have met?' said Finley, who had been vaguely trying to fit this Italian artist into the developing picture he had of Delmore's time in Crescombe.

Giulia shook her head. 'She arrived after his death – *because* of his death, really.'

A clicking noise made her turn towards the bar, where a short, elderly man was snapping his fingers at her, then gesturing to the other diners. Tucking the bottle opener back into the pocket of her apron, Giulia began to back away from the table, saying to Finley, 'If you're interested in her work, we always put on an exhibition at the Art Festival. It's the week after next – you should come and take a look.'

'Erm—'

But before he could respond properly, she had scurried away.

Megan watched her go, her lips slightly pursed. 'The Vitalis are another old Crescombe family,' she said, in a lowered voice. 'They basically replaced the Crockers here – it's probably not a coincidence that one came in as the other went out. I'm not sure this restaurant has always been *just* a restaurant, you know?'

'Really?' said Finley, looking doubtfully at his genial surroundings, before meeting the *Mona Lisa* gaze of Marina Vitali's portrait once again.

'These days they're mostly harmless,' Megan continued, taking a sip of wine, 'and in spite of stuff like this' – she plucked at the red and white checked tablecloth – 'about as Italian as I am.'

This struck Finley as catty, and in that moment he would have quite liked to swap friendly Giulia Vitali for the largely monosyllabic dining companion he'd ended up with. Fortunately, though, it wasn't long before the teenage waiter they'd met outside arrived with their food, and Finley was presented with a delicious-smelling slab of lasagne roughly the size and density of a brick.

'Do you want some?' he asked Megan, poised to slice off a portion for her.

Over her own tangle of pasta, she shot him a mystified expression. 'No, thank you.'

Feeling foolish, Finley helped himself to a forkful of the lasagne, which was rich and piquant, then felt the need to explain again: 'My ex, Mollie, was really indecisive in restaurants. She never knew what she wanted, and always ended up having half of whatever I ordered.'

Now he said it out loud, it sounded a little annoying. He half expected Megan to comment as much, but she just chewed on her mouthful of linguine until, just as Finley thought she was going to ignore his comment completely, she asked, 'How long were you together?'

'Five years.' Then, because this sounded insufficient, he added, 'But I've known her forever. Our parents have been friends since university, so we kind of grew up together, me and Mollie – and my sister, my twin.'

'You have a twin?' Megan asked, distracted by this – as everyone always was.

'Yeah, Fiona. We're nothing alike, though.'

Megan looked as though she wanted him to elaborate, and because Finley felt any description of Fiona – in which he would have to explain that she was a doctor, and use words like *successful, forceful, fearless* – would make him sound lacking in comparison, he asked, 'More wine?'

Megan still had a little in her glass, but she shrugged and pushed it towards him for a top-up.

'Five years is a long time,' she remarked. 'What happened?'

Finley readied himself to use all the phrases he usually wheeled out: *we grew apart, we lost our spark, we were better as friends* – all the things that were true but, at the same time, had not sounded the death knell for their relationship. Suspecting Megan would sense this, he took a gulp of wine and, for the first time, admitted, 'She cheated on me.'

Megan's impassive expression didn't change, but Finley noticed her fork, with which she had been scooping up a knot of linguine, had fallen still.

'Ouch,' she said.

This, he remembered, was exactly how she had reacted to the theory that William Crocker had had a baby with his wife's sister, Ellen Babbage. It was a good reaction – succinct, validating – and far better than the shock, disbelief and pity he imagined he would receive from his family and the friends he had once shared with Mollie.

Perhaps this was why the whole story then came spilling out, and Finley found himself explaining that, after graduating, he and Mollie had quickly fallen into an overly comfortable existence that had largely consisted of cooking together and slumping on the sofa in front of trashy TV. But then Mollie had grown restless and, in a bid to lose some imaginary Christmas weight, joined a running club led by one Blair Langley. And though something had begun to feel off, Finley had never dreamed she would do what she did. He had trusted her completely. He had known her all of his life, and been in love with her for as long as he could remember.

'They're getting married on Saturday,' he concluded dully. 'And Mollie wants me to come to the wedding, as her *friend*.'

He thought of her voice message, which he had initially put off playing for a few hours, so he could pretend she'd called him to say that she had made a terrible mistake, that she had cancelled the wedding, that she wanted him back... He had known she wouldn't really say all that, of course – that, instead, it had been her final attempt to convince him to come to the wedding – but even now, after listening to the message half a dozen times, he was still searching her words for some hidden meaning, some speck of hope to cling to.

'Do you want to go?' Megan asked, speaking for the first time in a few minutes.

As he had so many times before, Finley pictured Mollie in a big white dress, and *Blair* in a kilt, and all of the friends who had abandoned him for his more vivacious ex throwing one another around a dancefloor to the strains of a ceilidh band.

His stomach shrivelled. 'No,' he said.

'Then don't.'

When she put it like that, it sounded very simple.

'Everyone else thinks I should go,' he said. 'Mollie, Fiona, our families . . .'

'Everyone else wasn't cheated on,' Megan pointed out. 'Why does she want you there, anyway?'

'Because I was her friend for much longer than I was her boyfriend, and she wants us to be friends again. She's nice like that, she really—'

But Megan had made a small but unmistakeable noise of contempt.

'What?' said Finley.

'Nothing.'

'*What?*'

Megan sighed, resigned. 'If you really want to know, she sounds like a bit of a dick.'

Finley might have been offended by this, but he was so surprised that someone had called sweet, caring *Mollie McClaine* a dick that he started to laugh.

'She's not!' he insisted, trying to recover himself. 'You don't understand . . . I'm not explaining it properly . . .'

'Do you think it's possible she's invited you because she's trying to make herself feel better about how it all ended?' asked Megan, suddenly adopting the manner of a police interrogator.

'I don't—'

'Trying to make herself *look* better, even, in front of your families and friends?'

'No, she's not like—'

'But she hasn't really considered you in all of this, and how it'll make *you* look and feel when she marries someone else?'

Once again, Finley pictured himself surrounded by pitying friends and family members and his objection died in his throat.

'See?' Megan concluded, before sharing the rest of the wine between their glasses. 'Definitely a dick.'

Finley couldn't help it: he laughed again.

By now, they had both made significant progress on their food, and Finley was feeling pleasantly full and slightly drunk. He was also aware that he had been speaking for most of the meal. He wondered what Megan's love life was like. Again, she seemed so solitary, it was difficult to picture her with a partner, but she was about the same age as him; there must have been *someone*.

'What about you, then?' he dared himself to ask. 'Any romantic horror stories?'

'A few.'

She began to prod a prawn around her plate with her fork, and Finley had the impression she was weighing up her next words. He forced himself not to speak, to ignore his instinct to fill silence with banality.

Eventually, Megan said, 'I don't think most men view me as someone they need to treat particularly well.'

Finley wasn't sure what he'd expected her to say, but his full stomach felt suddenly cold, like a rockpool flooded with seawater. But then, Megan was different, *odd*. She was blunt to the point of rudeness, and so independent that he couldn't imagine her needing anyone, or going out of her way to make them feel needed in return. So perhaps it made sense that, at best, most men wouldn't know what to make of her, and at worst ... For far from the first time, Finley felt ashamed of his sex.

Megan, meanwhile, seemed to be steeling herself to say something. As she inhaled, however, her gaze drifted beyond his head. '*Shit.*'

'What?'

'No, don't look—'

But Finley had already turned in his seat, already spotted the woman in the tight black dress gabbling with their waitress. When she saw them looking over, she gave a little gasp.

'Shit,' Megan muttered again, as the woman then began to sashay towards them, her bulky handbag knocking into the backs of several chairs.

Her scent arrived before she did; a haze that was somehow sharp as well as syrupy. Her shiny, highlighted hair fell beyond her shoulders in loose waves, and she was wearing a lot of make-up, which Finley imagined might look good in a photo, but in real life was slightly unnerving.

'Well,' she purred, bearing down on them, *'Megan Salter.'*

'Gabriella,' said Megan, sounding resigned.

'Still in Crescombe, then, *bella*?'

'You seem to be here too,' Megan pointed out.

'Yes, but I'm just visiting, seeing my *nonna.*' She gestured towards the ceiling, presumably indicating another floor of Marina's. 'I live in Bristol now,' she said, in a tone that suggested the city was as far-flung as New York or Tokyo. 'With my fiancé – you remember Mike?'

'No,' said Megan, and Finley thought it likely this was a lie – and likely she was deliberately ignoring the enormous diamond sparkling on Gabriella's ring finger.

'So funny you're still here!' continued the other woman. 'We always thought your swimming would take you to the Olympics or whatever! You were so obsessed . . . But I guess it was just, like, *therapy* for you?'

As she smiled, and in spite of all her make-up, Finley thought she looked a bit like a toad. She was waiting, he was sure, for some sort of reaction, but Megan continued to look totally blank.

'Who's this, then?' Gabriella asked, and Finley had to work not to recoil as she turned her long-lashed gaze on him, presumably because Megan was being so unresponsive. 'You're new – *ciao, bello.*' Then, before either of them could respond, she said, 'If he's single, my little cousin's always desperate for a man. *Aren't you, Giu Giu?*' she called, raising her voice above the hum of the restaurant.

Now standing at the bar, Giulia shouted something back in Italian that Finley was fairly sure was a friendly *fuck you.*

'Well, *so* good to see you, Megan,' said Gabriella, turning back to their booth. 'I'll tell everyone you said hi.'

'Bye, then,' said Megan, forcefully.

But rather than leaving, Gabriella reached towards a tendril of Megan's long, straw-like hair. For one odd moment, Finley thought she meant to tug on it, and perhaps Megan did too, because her impassive expression faltered. Instead, though, Gabriella picked at the blonde lock with her dark red nails, until she extracted what appeared to be a tiny strand of seaweed.

'So funny,' she said again, flicking it to the floor and then swanning away.

Finley looked to Megan, anticipating some cutting remark, but now Gabriella had gone she seemed to have lost all her bravado: her usually pale face was flushed, and she had gathered all of her hair over one shoulder, as though afraid the other woman might suddenly reappear and grab it again.

Concerned, Finley wondered what to say to rescue what had already been a thoroughly strange dinner. He was loath to embarrass Megan further, but at the same time wanted her to know that he understood – that perhaps they were very similar, she and him. He tested out a few phrases in his head: *I know how you feel, I've been there, I hated school too . . .*

In the end, however, he simply nudged the gelato menu across the table, saying, 'Now *she* seems like a dick.'

Finally, Megan grinned. There was a gap between her top front teeth, Finley noticed, which suited her: it was unusual, striking. For some reason, the sight of that little gap had taken him by surprise, and it was a moment before he worked out why. He had never really seen her teeth; he had never really seen her smile.

Scrape.

Finley lurched upright, his body pulsing. He was soaked with sweat — as were his rumpled sheets — and his heart was beating so hard and fast it seemed to rattle at his ribs. Hands trembling, he groped for his phone on the bedside table and managed to bump it against the sensor on his upper arm.

'Shit.'

After gulping down some just-in-case juice, he turned on the bedside lamp and wrestled open a packet of biscuits, spraying crumbs all over the book of Greek myths he was still yet to start. When he finally managed to cram a biscuit between his lips he found no joy in the eating of it; he might as well have been trying to swallow a mouthful of sawdust.

He now regretted that gelato, and the complimentary limoncello shots Giulia had pressed upon them with the bill and an old-fashioned matchbook — and that he had eaten so much of that block of lasagne in the first place. And he regretted being so unwilling to take insulin in front of Megan that he'd done it quickly and — as it turned out — excessively in the bathroom of Marina's. Because in addition to feeling a little drunk and more than a little sick, Finley's blood sugar had crashed.

After two more biscuits — which were hardly helping the nausea — Finley hunched on the edge of the bed, feeling as saturated in self-pity as he was in sweat. The hypo had woken him, of course, but he had an odd feeling it had coincided with something else. A dream? Unexpected warmth rippled through Finley's body as he recalled that in his sleeping mind he'd been here, in this bed, but not alone. His companion must have been Mollie, though when he tried to remember any details – he'd settle for anything of her at this point – he could only summon a jumbled impression of entwined limbs and hitched breaths, of skin that tasted like salt...

Scrape.

Finley froze. His body was still tingling – as much from the recollection of that dream as the hypo – so he was too alert to dismiss the noise as a figment of his imagination. He waited, pinching biscuit crumbs between his fingers, and Dawn's words about Michelle came back to him: *she was especially bothered by some sort of scratching...*

Scrape.

What *was* it? It was coming from the opposite wall, beyond the wooden panelling. On unsteady legs, Finley rose from the bed and began to walk across the room, pausing only to shudder at a sudden wetness between his toes: there was water on the floor again.

Trying to ignore the trail those puddles made from the window – which was, of course, open again – Finley pressed his ear against the wooden wall.

Scrape.

He jumped back, convinced something was about to burst out at him. When it didn't, he began to feel stupid: it was just a mouse, or a draught knocking against something behind there. It was nothing.

'Stop,' he muttered, smacking at the wooden panel with the heel of his hand.

Scrape, scrape.

'I said, *stop!*'

Frustrated, Finley struck the wall again. He'd had enough: he was tired, and sick, and he couldn't stop shivering. He needed to sleep.

Ping.

He'd dislodged a screw, which was now rolling across the floor. Crouching, he inspected where it had come loose, and discovered he could squeeze the tips of his fingers between the bottom of the wood and the laminate floor. He gave the panel an experimental tweak from below, and was surprised by how easily another screw dropped out – and how readily the wood bent away from whatever lay behind.

He hesitated. What was he doing? This wasn't his room – this wasn't his house.

Scrape.

Instantly, Finley's reservations vanished, and he wrenched at the wood, harder than before. He tugged and tugged, silently apologising to Lorraine, until the whole panel clattered to the floor.

Finley stumbled backwards, suddenly feeling vulnerable in just his boxers. But there was only an old wall back there, a centimetre or so beyond where the wood had been – which at least assuaged his fear that something large had been trapped in the gap.

He dared to step forward again and extended a hand towards the old stonework. It seemed to belong to a totally different room to the cosy, cabin-like interior where he was standing. Finley began to trail his fingers down the cold, rough-cut stones, wondering how many people had touched this wall before him.

Around waist height, something trembled beneath his hand, and with a thumping heart Finley realised one of the uneven bricks had shifted in its spot. He bent to examine it, discovering that, unlike its neighbours, this stone was loose in the wall. He wobbled it again before digging his fingertips into its edges and – against his own instinct, which was screaming at him to stop – began to slide it out.

Scrape, scrape, scrape.

This time, it was him making the sound and, as he withdrew a lumpy stone roughly the size of a bag of sugar, he braced himself, imagining a nest of rats or spiders pouring from the hole, or perhaps a skeletal hand snatching for his own. But all was still, and after setting down the stone, he summoned the nerve to peer into the gap it had left.

He was half expecting to catch a glimpse of night sky, but it seemed there was more wall behind and, in removing that stone, Finley had revealed a dark hidey hole. For a moment, he thought it empty, but then, right at the back, he saw it: a circular metal box.

Don't touch that, Finley thought. Leave it alone, put the stone back.

But his hands seemed to be moving independently from the rest of him, because before he knew it his fingers were closing around the container – which was colder than even the surrounding stone – and he was withdrawing it into the soft lamplight of his bedroom.

The box, which he guessed was made of thin iron, was grimy, scratched and dented. There was a handle on its side, and a little chimney-like tube protruding from its round top. Finley had the feeling he'd seen something like it before, possibly in a museum, but couldn't think what it was. The lid was loose, and vibrated in his shaking hands, like chattering teeth.

Don't open it, he told himself.

But there was no going back now. His curiosity was stronger than his apprehension, his sense of self-preservation. So, after a steadying breath, Finley adjusted the tin in his fingers, and lifted its lid.

'Tonight, you're a shadow,' Ma hisses over her shoulder. 'You don't speak, you don't move unless I tell you to – and you keep your eyes and ears open, understand?'

I nod, though she's already turned back to hurry after the elderly butler leading us through Westcliff House's entrance hall. It's as big as the church and smells of wood and polish and something citrusy; it smells nothing like the damp, fishy reek of Crockers Nest, which I fear has followed us here.

I try to tread lightly, but my footsteps are still loud against the hard floor, making me feel like an intruder. Ma, too, seems to be carrying herself differently – more upright, more ladylike – and I wonder if even she is nervous. As we start down a corridor lined with cabinets, she doesn't so much as turn her head, whereas I can't help but stare at all the objects propped up behind the glass: coins and jewellery; weapons and bones; a large stony spiral that could almost be a carving of a vast snail shell; a stuffed fox with pure white fur, poised to pounce.

It makes my collection of pebbles and feathers look like nothing at all, and I want to linger in this corridor all evening, examining every treasure. But the butler is knocking at a door, beyond which we can hear the murmur of male voices, and after he announces Ma to the room, I've no choice but to slip in after her.

We've entered a library, with bookcases stretching to the ceiling and a half-finished portrait of a large, red-haired man propped up on an easel in the corner. This must be the developer, because the same man is leaning against a desk, beckoning us into the room. A dozen or so others are arranged on chairs and settees: I recognise the stooped figure of the vicar, and a few more by sight, but my gaze is immediately drawn to a younger man stretched out on a dark blue chaise longue: *you*.

'Mrs Crocker, we were expecting your husband.'

A wizened figure is leaning out of his high-backed chair to peer at us. I assume this is Lord Harcourt, though I've never seen him. He looks even older and sicklier than my uncle; his skin is yellowed and shrivelled, like the core of a discarded apple.

'My husband is unwell and sends his apologies.' Ma's tone dares Harcourt to ask why one of her sons is not here instead, and I wonder how she would explain that Bill and Tom are too brainless, Edwin too volatile.

As it is, Harcourt makes an impatient gesture towards an empty chair, as though he, not the developer, is our host. I follow Ma towards it, realising we're the only women in the room. Out of the corner of my eye, I can see Harcourt watching me the way men often do: half horrified, half hungry.

'Perhaps your girl should wait in the kitchen?' suggests the developer, more doubtful than unkind.

'She's my ward,' says Ma, and even though she's no fonder of me than I am of her, I'm pleased to hear the warning in her voice. 'My poor sister's child. She won't be any bother.'

She makes a shooing motion and I slink behind her chair. Several pairs of eyes follow me as I back against a bookcase, but I make myself small and still until all but yours look away.

'Shall we proceed?' Harcourt snaps, sitting back in his seat. 'Mr Montgomery, if you please.'

The doughy, red-haired man pushes himself away from his desk. An emerald green waistcoat is stretched tight over his paunch, and a puffy red cravat is obscuring most of his collar. Along with his vivid hair, which sticks up in tufts, it gives him the look of a chubby rooster.

'Gentlemen,' he begins, before making a flourishing bow towards Ma and adding, 'lady. Allow me to introduce myself for the benefit of those I have not yet had the pleasure of meeting. My name is Ambrose Montgomery and for almost a decade I have had but one aim: to transform your hidden gem of a town into the country's most splendid seaside resort!'

He pauses, perhaps expecting applause, but none comes. Aside from your smirk, the faces around the library are stony. They hate him, I think. They hate his mansion on the hill, they hate his promenade and his hotel and all those houses he's built. And they will hate anything else he tries to do to this town.

It's hardly surprising; his plans threaten the very enterprise that keeps this town going. Of course, Harcourt and the Crockers have the most to lose – and Ma's well-known involvement in the landings must be the reason she's tolerated here tonight – but I doubt there's anyone in this room who hasn't benefitted from free-trading.

Montgomery seems undaunted by the chilly silence, for he continues to beam around the room. 'I am most grateful to Lord Harcourt for suggesting – in the spirit of being neighbourly – that I outline to you my latest plans for Crescombe,' he says, with a more deferential bow in Harcourt's direction. 'In particular, my chief proposal for the resort's development, which is . . .' he raises both hands, tracing a long line in mid-air '. . . a pier.'

Alarm fizzes around the table like a wave frothing into sand.

'You cannot be serious!' someone cries.

Harcourt leans forward again, and there is an instant hush. 'Mr Montgomery, this is not Southend. We will not have Crescombe's seafront reduced to puppet booths and minstrel shows.' His gaze flicks towards me with this last remark.

'A pier for landing, not pleasure,' Montgomery quickly clarifies. 'Simply a means for more boats to dock. One of the drawbacks of this town is its remoteness, its—'

'I thought that was one of its benefits?' Harcourt may be ancient, but he's still sharp. 'Previously, you assured us Crescombe's location would keep away the riff-raff.'

Montgomery looks uncomfortable, and despite his showy clothes I wonder where he ranks in comparison to someone like Harcourt. According to Edwin, he's a self-made man.

'It is true, Crescombe's isolation means it is unlikely to see any . . . day-trippers,' Montgomery explains carefully. 'And when the railway finally arrives in Devon, I sincerely doubt there will be a branch line any closer than Ilfracombe. So, rest assured, gentlemen – lady – I am still envisioning a small, peaceful resort aimed at the well-to-do; at those nostalgic for the more exclusive seasides of years past. Yet even respectable tourists must arrive somehow, and with Crescombe's roads in such a poor state, we risk losing visitors to more accessible resorts. Hence, a landing pier.'

The other men seem reassured by Montgomery's words, because their scoffing has ceased. The developer begins to drift across the room, describing exactly where and how his pier would be built, and I notice on his desk something large and fairly flat concealed by a cover. It reminds me of the tatty old sheet they pulled over my mother after she breathed her last, but I suppose it's more likely to be another painting under there. At the thought, I glance towards you, and my chest tightens as I see you are already looking at me. For a moment, or a minute, or perhaps an hour, we stare at one another – though I'm not really seeing you slumped in that elegant chair in your sleek dark tailcoat; I'm remembering you lazing, naked, in the shallows of the early-morning sea.

I look away first, staring instead into the flame of the nearest candle, trying to focus on Montgomery's voice. The conversation has moved on from the pier, and he's now describing the kind of activities wealthy visitors to Crescombe might enjoy: sea-fishing, stag-hunting on Exmoor, appreciation of local flora and fauna ...

'We saw an upsurge of visitors after I invited several eminent doctors to write about Crescombe's healthy air and seawater – now, I am hoping we might repeat that success by encouraging some leading biologists to come and explore its beautiful surroundings.'

Several of Montgomery's guests are nodding now, though Harcourt looks unconvinced. 'To what end?' he demands. 'I thought we were trying to attract members of the aristocracy, not a pack of eccentrics with butterfly nets and dirty fingernails.'

'Ah, I am glad you mentioned the aristocracy,' Montgomery tells him, 'for you will notice I have a guest with me this evening – for the whole summer, in fact. I am sure he requires no introduction, but for civility's sake, allow me to present my esteemed friend: George, Lord Delmore, 3rd Baron Delmore.'

He pauses, and while there's still no applause, I have the impression his guests are more interested in you than they are in him, despite – or perhaps because of – the superior way you are looking around at them all.

'George,' Montgomery murmurs, 'perhaps you would be kind enough to outline for these gentlemen why Crescombe is such a draw for someone of your age, rank and disposition?'

'It is as you have already said, Ambrose ...' You make a careless gesture with your hand, where a ring glints in the candlelight. 'With the railway snaking its way across the country, across Europe, travel is becoming increasingly accessible to the masses. So, us fortunate few who have always had the means are now seeking leisure opportunities both further afield and off the beaten track.'

You speak softly, slowly, confident that nobody will interrupt. Again, I'm struck by the honey-smoothness of your voice. In comparison, even Harcourt sounds like a fisherman.

'Crescombe is exactly that,' you continue, before turning your languid gaze on Harcourt. 'And, forgive me, but being a member of the aristocracy and – how did you put it? – an eccentric with a butterfly net, are not mutually exclusive, at least not anymore. We *young* men of means have a wide range of interests: sea-bathing and fishing and hunting, yes – even biology and geology, too – but in particular we seek the picturesque. In order to inspire our pens and paintbrushes, we strive to exchange the familiar for the spectacular. And in this modest little place, I do believe I have discovered the most unexpected, astonishing beauty.'

Appreciative murmurs and even a few 'hear, hears' ripple around the library. But I don't make a sound, can't even breathe; with your last remark, you are once more looking straight at me.

Only Harcourt remains sour-faced. Perhaps he's heard the rumours – relayed to Crockers Nest by Edwin – that Lord Delmore is an artist of little talent, and has come to Crescombe not to paint or appreciate the picturesque, but to lie low after one too many scandals.

Despite this, your input seems to have turned the tide of opinion in the room. Though nothing has been agreed upon by the time Harcourt pulls himself up with his stick, signifying the meeting is at an end, I have the impression that most of the other men are now at least willing to listen to the developer's ideas.

Outside, Westcliff's driveway is illuminated by lanterns and a glow above the front door, where a semi-circular window unfurls like a lady's fan. Yet the path down the hill is unlit, and Ma and I prepare to start down it on foot, following the majority of Montgomery's guests, who are already melting into the darkness.

'Mrs Crocker? A word, if you please.' Harcourt is hobbling towards the driveway's only carriage. 'In private,' he adds, his gaze sliding towards me.

Ma shoos me away, but her look says, *stay close.*

While she joins him beside his carriage, I slip around the corner of the house. Here, only weak streams of light escape the curtains of the tall windows, and though I can hear the sea rumbling below I can't tell where the land drops to become water. Pressing myself against the wall of the house quite as firmly as I did against that bookcase, I try to make out Crockers Nest on the other side of the bay. But even I, who am practised at this, can see nothing but thick, endless darkness.

'... The man is obviously an imbecile,' I hear Harcourt say, 'yet if it wasn't him prattling on about promenades and piers, it would be someone else. What he is trying to do here is no different to what is happening at Lynton, even at Woody Bay ...'

I peer back around the corner of the house. Harcourt has now clambered into his carriage and is speaking through the window to Ma, whose large hands are clasped in front of her skirts. She looks almost demure.

'I really was hoping I might discuss this with your husband,' he grumbles.

'As I said, he's—'

'Yes, yes, he's ill. You know, one of your sons paid me a visit last week.'

Ma looks up. 'Which one?'

'I hope you are not expecting me to keep track of all your offspring, Mrs Crocker?'

'Of course not, my Lord.'

Nevertheless, Harcourt says, 'The one missing an eye. The runt.'

Ma's hands unclasp, and I wonder what she's thinking. Edwin isn't supposed to go to Harcourt Manor. Every once in a while, Lord Harcourt has been known to invite Old William to share in some of the brandy we deliver to his door, but he's never extended the courtesy to any of his sons.

'The boy told me what you have been planning,' Harcourt continues.

'Forgive me – what *he* has been planning,' Ma murmurs.

'He wanted my support. But I will tell you what I told him: it is far, far too risky. You might have placated the coastguard but, as you heard tonight, that preening halfwit is inviting most of London here for sea-bathing and God knows what else ... All eyes are on Crescombe, Mrs Crocker, so you and your family need to stick to what you know!'

Harcourt's raspy voice is now raised to a shout and, though I cannot see it, I imagine his thin, bloodless lips flecked with spittle. Ma's knuckles are clasped again, though when she speaks her voice is level.

'Edwin – my youngest – he shouldn't have come to you. He shouldn't have gone behind his father's back. But it's his belief that free-trading is already too risky, and though his ideas are rash, I don't think we should dismiss them entirely.'

Intrigued, I inch a little closer to Ma and Harcourt, as far out of the shadows as I dare ...

'So – you're a Crocker.'

My heart leaps and I spin around. You are leaning against the wall a little further along the house, a smile tweaking the corners of your mouth. How long have you been there? It is, I realise, the second time you've crept up on me.

'I heard the Crockers were big ugly brutes who jump out at you in the night,' you continue. 'You do not seem to fit that description – though, with you, I would not mind an after-dark encounter ...'

You laugh at your own remark, and I know I should stay silent – I am a shadow, I am a shadow – but I can't stop my next words spilling out: 'I am not a Crocker.'

'No?' You look uncertain, then your smile returns. 'No, I think you are even more dangerous.'

I don't know what to say to this – I don't know what to make of you at all – and perhaps you feel the same, because for a moment we just stare at one another again. You are the handsomest man I've ever seen. I think I could look at you all night: your tall, broad-shouldered frame, your prominent cheekbones, and your eyes, which are like Crescombe's grey-green waters on a stormy day; deep and dark and unknowable.

'Oh, do let me sketch you!' you suddenly cry. 'Everyone else in this town is horribly plain. I feel so uninspired here, so dreadfully bored!'

You lounge against the wall with such a heavy sigh that I glance around the corner, fearful we'll be overheard.

'But you . . .' You look sideways at me. 'Do you even know what you are, how you gleam like a pearl among all . . . this?' You wave a dismissive hand at the darkness of Crescombe. 'Say you will sit for me, Miss . . .' You smile, peel yourself from the wall and take a step towards me. 'Miss not-a-Crocker. Please. Say I may draw you.'

I'm tempted. You are charming, and exciting – and, like you, I am so bored. But you're also dangerous – this whole conversation is dangerous – so I shake my head.

You clutch at your heart in exaggerated distress, and any amusement I feel vanishes: this is all just a game to you.

'How can you be so unfeeling?' you groan. 'You are determined to torment me! What will it take to convince you? Tell me, and I will do it. I am perfectly serious – what is it you want?'

If I were a true Crocker, I'd say money. But what use is money to me here? Instead, I want to escape this wretched town, to sail far away and never see this place and these people again. For that – for freedom – one sketch would be nothing at all.

But then my hand closes around my father's sea stone in my pocket, and I remind myself: freedom is coming; I just need to wait a little longer.

'Think on it,' you say, twisting your ring around your little finger. 'I am sure we can come to some kind of mutually beneficial arrangement.'

Your fox-like smile is back. Perhaps you are anticipating how little money I would ask for. You take another step towards me, then another. I can feel your breath on my face, warm and slightly sour from the wine, though not unpleasant. I need to move away but something about you is holding me here. Your title? Your maleness? Whatever it is, it is something I am not. You are everything I am not.

'George?'

We jump apart. Montgomery, his vivid hair even tuftier from being outside, is emerging from a doorway further along the side of the house – the same doorway from which you too must have appeared.

'I thought we were going to discuss the meeting?' The developer's bushy eyebrows knit together as he looks between us. 'You should at least come inside,' he tells you, his gaze coming to rest on me. 'It is not advisable to stay out too late in this town.'

With another sigh, you back towards the door, though your pace is leisurely. Montgomery extends a hand towards your elbow to turn you around, hurry you along, muttering something I can't hear.

But you aren't listening. You're looking over your shoulder, at me, your expression surprisingly serious. Your dark eyes seem to be saying something, asking something, and though I can't explain how, I know exactly what it is. I can hear the echo of your earlier question:

What is it you want?

8

Crockers Beach

'What,' said Megan, staring at the grimy tin Finley had placed between them on the bar top, 'is *that?*'

She looked wary, as though afraid it contained something that might jump out at her, like a jack-in-the-box.

'I found it behind a wall in my room,' said Finley, deciding, for now, to omit mentioning the unexplained scraping noise that had led him to this discovery – and that he'd destroyed part of the wall in question.

Megan gave the metal cylinder a cautious prod. 'It looks like old camping equipment or something,' she said. 'Maybe it dates back to when the Navy was there?'

Finley had hoped she would be interested. Less than twenty-four hours had passed since their dinner at Marina's, but when he had found and then opened this tin – when he had seen what was inside – it was Megan he'd wanted to talk to.

Only, he had never sought her out before, she'd always just *appeared*. That morning, Finley had climbed down to the little beach beneath Crockers Nest, where he had settled himself on the Nessie-shaped rock and scanned the sea for a lone swimmer. He had even considered going all the way to The Delmore Experience after finishing his work for Lorraine – given the tin's contents, he might have to head there anyway. Instead, though, he had called in here, at The Drowned Painter, which was hosting a raucous pub quiz in the dining room, and had finally found Megan idling in the near empty bar room.

'Actually, I think it's older than that,' he said, in response to her theory about the Navy. 'I've looked it up, and I'm pretty sure it's a tinderbox.'

'You mean, for lighting fires?'

Finley nodded. 'The candle goes there,' he said, indicating the metal tube protruding from the tin's lid, 'and there's a bit of steel inside, and what I think must be flint.'

'But what was it doing in your wall?' Megan asked.

'Well, they were fairly common back in the day, before matches,' said Finley. 'I guess whoever lived there needed it for candles, or the fireplace . . .' Though as he said this, he realised there wasn't anything resembling a chimney on the roof of his room. 'Anyway, I don't think it matters what it is, I'm more interested in what it contains – aside from the flint and stuff.' Then, after steeling himself to say it, he continued, 'And the fact that I'm fairly sure it belonged to Cora Crocker.'

Megan, who had been looping a finger through the tinderbox's little handle, looked up. 'You and Cora Crocker . . .' she murmured, though half-heartedly, for her curiosity was obvious.

Before Finley could elaborate, however, a distraction appeared in the form of Keith the landlord, who squeezed himself behind the bar and began to haphazardly grab at packets of crisps and peanuts.

'Don't mind me, Megan, I'll just cope with all the customers next door by myself, shall I?'

Megan fixed Finley with a long-suffering expression and began to pull a pint. 'I'm with customers *here*,' she told Keith.

Over his pile of snacks, the landlord took in the sight of the bar room's other occupants: two women having a hushed conversation over gin and tonics, and an elderly man who appeared to have fallen asleep. Finally, Keith's gaze rested on Finley.

'He's a customer, is he?' said the landlord, who must have seen the way their heads had been bent together over the tinderbox, which Finley had now shielded with his hand.

In response, Megan plonked the fresh pint in front of Finley. Looking torn between annoyance and amusement, Keith said, 'You can at least keep that animal of yours in here – he keeps begging for chips.'

'Does he?' said Megan, feigning surprise. Then, barely raising her voice, she called, '*Skip?*'

Immediately, and with a great deal of snuffling, Skipper bounded into the bar room. When he saw Finley, he gave a yelp of joy and jumped at his stool, presenting his glossy head for petting.

'Cosy,' noted Keith, as Finley began to scratch at the dog's ears. 'Well, let me know if you feel like doing any work tonight, won't you, Megan?'

In response, she tossed a packet of crisps towards Finley, saying, 'It was salt and vinegar you wanted, right?'

'Erm – yeah, thanks.'

Keith gave them an *I-wasn't-born-yesterday* sort of look, adjusted his rustling armful, and departed.

'It's on the house,' Megan told Finley, after – with difficulty, for Skipper was still pawing at his legs – he had retrieved his wallet from his jeans pocket.

As Finley thanked her again, they held one another's gaze. Unexpected happiness was fizzing through him like the bubbles in his unasked-for pint, due not just to Skipper's enthusiasm for him (did dogs truly never get tired of you?) but the fact that, in Megan, he had found a co-conspirator.

Cheers rose from the quiz next door, and Finley thought he could hear Lorraine's whoop (apparently, she and her team, The Hero's Babes, were regulars). In another life, he could have been sitting through there with Mollie, on a team with the friends they'd once shared – as part of a university reunion trip, perhaps. But even when Finley tried to imagine it, he wondered whether he'd rather be here, with this new friend (*was* that what she was to him now?) and the world's happiest dog, huddled in a virtually empty bar room, trying to unpick a centuries-old puzzle.

Megan looked away first. 'Come on, then,' she said, turning her attention back to the tinderbox. 'Can I open this or what?'

Pausing his stroking of Skipper to gesture for her to go ahead, Finley watched as Megan carefully lifted the lid. He was tingly with anticipation, which felt like an echo of the stronger lurch of nervous excitement he had experienced the night before, when, in the lamplight of his room, he had first opened this tinderbox himself.

Inside, in addition to a stub of candle and the steel and flint, a collection of keepsakes was crammed: a few tiny pebbles and shells, a feather and a piece of sea glass, a small scroll of paper and some scraps of what once might have been pressed purple flowers ... But, just as Finley had the previous night, Megan first reached, magpie-like, for the chunky gold ring.

It was a signet ring, the kind a wealthy, influential man might wear on his little finger. Megan turned it over a few times before examining the engraving on its flattened side, which featured a pair of mermaids flanking a shield.

'Isn't that—' She drew back. 'Isn't that the Delmore family crest?'

Finley nodded, feeling pleased: having thought it looked vaguely familiar, he had already double-checked this online. 'It certainly is,' he said. 'So, I think we can assume it was Delmore's ring, given there were no other Delmores wandering around Crescombe at the time of Cora Crocker. The question is, how did *she* get it?'

Megan rolled the ring around her palm a few times before slipping it onto her middle finger, where it hung loose. Like the rest of her, Megan's fingers were long and slender and, once again, reminded Finley of something amphibious. He had, of course, been tempted to try it on himself, but something like awe had held him back: that ring had belonged to the person – to the *hand* – that had painted *Hero's Bay*.

'I've been thinking about it,' he said, deciding to focus on his own question, 'and I reckon there are three ways Cora could've got hold of that ring.'

'And they are?' said Megan, who was still twirling the gold band around her finger and only seemed to be half listening.

'She could have found it,' said Finley, undeterred. 'Let's say it slipped off while Delmore was walking or swimming, and washed up at the shoreline. We can see Cora was a bit of a beachcomber' – he indicated the shells and other natural trinkets in the tin – 'so perhaps she spotted the ring and decided to keep it.'

'Hmm,' said Megan, her tone non-committal.

Deciding to plough on, Finley said, 'Or maybe Cora stole it. We know the Crockers were crooks, we know there was tension between old Crescombe and the posh holidaymakers coming into the town. So maybe Delmore took off the ring to do a spot of outdoor painting or something, and Cora seized her chance to swipe it.'

Megan made a fist with her hand a few times, watching the space this created between her finger and the inside of the gold band. 'And your third theory?'

'He gave it to her,' said Finley, who couldn't decide whether this was the most or least likely explanation. 'Though that calls into question what on earth someone like Delmore – a baron – was doing, giving a precious heirloom to the illegitimate daughter of a fishing family with an extremely dubious reputation.'

Finally, Megan took off the ring, but instead of replacing it in the tinderbox, she slipped it onto the fourth finger of her left hand. 'I'd say it was pretty obvious what he was doing, wouldn't you?' She waggled her fingers to show off the glint of gold.

'I—'

Finley broke off, having lost his train of thought, for this universal gesture had immediately put him in mind of Mollie: her wedding was now exactly a week away. Suddenly, his joy of a few minutes before seemed ludicrous. Of course he'd rather be here – he'd rather be anywhere – with Mollie.

Perhaps because he was being so unresponsive, Megan continued, 'What's *not* obvious is why you're so convinced that this tinderbox belonged to Cora Crocker. Surely anyone could have hidden it in the wall?'

'Erm, bear with me on that,' said Finley and, in an attempt to pull himself together, he nudged the container back towards her. 'Meanwhile, does anything else in here jump out at you?'

More thoughtfully this time, Megan considered the contents of the tinderbox. While he watched her, Finley absently scratched at the palm of his right hand, which had been itching since . . . yesterday? The day before? There was no mark, but he wondered whether he'd done himself an injury ripping off that panel the previous night, or whether he was having a reaction to the vegetation he'd yanked off Cora Crocker's grave. He hoped he wasn't allergic to Skipper, who was now stretched out beneath Finley's bar stool, working his jaws around a bone-shaped chew toy.

'This isn't from around here,' said Megan, reaching among the pebbles and sea glass for something that wasn't quite either.

It was a gemstone about the size and shape of a date, though hard and perfectly smooth. Its pale turquoise colour was both warm and dazzling, and threaded with strands of brightness reminiscent of an electric charge.

'I'm not sure what that is,' Finley admitted, for with this stone his online research skills had failed him. 'Obviously, it's too pale and opaque to be a sapphire . . .'

'Topaz?' Megan suggested, uncertainly. 'Or isn't there something called aquamarine?'

'Actually, I believe that's larimar.'

They both turned. The two women who had been chatting in the corner had now put on their jackets and moved to the doorway, where the one who had spoken was holding out her hand for a closer look at the stone – and, with a jolt, Finley realised it was Dawn. Since their meeting in her hut, he had grown used to seeing her around Crescombe in her long dresses and wig, but tonight she was short-haired and in jeans, and he hadn't recognised her.

'Yes, this is larimar,' said Dawn, after Megan had passed the gemstone over the bar. 'It comes from somewhere in the Caribbean, if I remember rightly, and is often associated with the element of water because of its resemblance to tropical seas.'

As soon as she said this, Finley could see it: the white webbed pattern over the cyan-coloured stone looked exactly like light rippling on crystal clear waters.

'Is it yours?' Dawn asked Megan, before examining the stone under one of the fringed wall lamps.

'His,' Megan said, nodding towards Finley. 'Sort of.'

'I'll have to consult my books to be sure, but I believe larimar is said to bring clarity and wisdom,' Dawn told Finley. 'If you pop back to my hut sometime, I can give you a full consultation on how to get the most from this crystal?'

'Erm, yeah, maybe . . .'

Undaunted by this lukewarm response, Dawn began to smooth the gemstone between her finger and thumb. 'It's not quite the right shape, but you could even use it as a worry stone.'

Finley tensed: did he look like the sort of person who needed a worry stone?

For a few moments, Dawn continued to turn the gemstone between her fingers, before handing it back to Finley. He received it eagerly, clasping it in his right hand, where it seemed to soothe his itchy palm. He felt oddly possessive of it – though, as Megan had implied, it wasn't even really his.

Meanwhile, Dawn's gaze had strayed towards the open tinderbox and Finley willed her not to ask about it. He liked this being between just him and Megan, not only because – he might as well admit it – he liked Megan herself, but because her cynicism was a good counterbalance to his overactive imagination. He didn't need Dawn filling his head with more talk of *bad energy* and *residual hauntings*. For the moment, he was trying to focus on Lorraine's project, on facts – because this tinderbox was positively brimming with tangible evidence about the past of Crockers Nest (if only he could forget how he had found it . . .).

Finley needn't have worried, though, for Dawn made no comment about the incongruous object resting on the bar between him and Megan, and instead bade them both goodnight. Perhaps she wasn't interested – or perhaps she was simply aware that she had abandoned her friend, who had drifted into the corridor, where she was now being subjected to the noise of the quiz next door.

After their departure, Finley looked back to Megan, fully expecting her to start scoffing about *healing properties* and *crystal consultations*, but instead found her scrolling through an old, sand-encrusted mobile phone. Though it made perfect sense that Megan would have a phone (who *didn't* have one?) Finley was still surprised to see something so ordinary, so contemporary, in her long fingers. If he'd known about it, he might have located her a lot more quickly today – assuming he'd have had the guts to ask for her number.

'She's right, larimar's from the Dominican Republic,' said Megan, reading from a cracked screen. 'It was first discovered in 1916, but properly named later, partly after someone's daughter, and—'

'Wait a minute,' broke in Finley. 'If it was only discovered in 1916, how did Cora Crocker get hold of it in 1840?'

'Assuming it even belonged to Cora Crocker . . .' Megan muttered. 'Well, larimar must have *existed* back then,' she reasoned. 'Local people would have known about it, even if it hadn't been officially discovered.'

'Yes, but how did it end up in Devon?' Then, in an attempt to answer his own question, Finley ventured, 'Delmore again?'

'Even he didn't travel that far.'

Stumped, they lapsed into silence. Megan continued to play with Delmore's ring, discovering it fitted snugly on her thumb, while Finley began to sip his pint and, unable to resist the lure of the crisps any longer, examined the packet's nutritional information; after the severity of the previous night's hypo, he was trying to be more vigilant about his blood sugar.

'Are you calorie-counting or something?' Megan asked.

Clearly, this was a joke, but she was almost right – though carb-counting would have been more accurate.

'Erm . . .' Finley looked back at the packet for inspiration. 'Just seeing where these were made, whether they're local . . .' Then, because Megan appeared thoroughly unconvinced by this, he tried to distract her by opening the crisps and asking, 'Want some?'

'I'm not really allowed to eat at work . . .' Nevertheless, she helped herself to a few, then through a mouthful asked, 'Was this everything you were going to show me?'

She dragged a fingertip over the shells and pebbles, which clinked against the edges of the tinderbox, before tweaking at one end of the rolled-up paper. Finley's heart gave another leap of anticipation as he then watched Megan unfurl the little scroll: this was what he had really wanted her to see.

It was a sketch – done in graphite, he presumed, though portions of the small, detailed drawing were so dark they might have been etched in ink. It depicted a young, black-haired woman crouched on a rock surrounded by sea. The image, of course, was still, yet somehow it seemed to breathe: wind was tugging the surface of the water into peaks, and pulling strands of the woman's hair loose from her long thick plait.

The subject's clothes were those of a working woman; there was a patch on her apron, holes in her shawl, and the damp hem of her dress was frayed. Her hunched posture, too, was modest, as though she was trying to make her slight frame even smaller. Yet her jaw was set, her dark eyebrows drawn, and her faraway expression had a hint of something like pride. She gave the impression of a creature wild and watchful; a cat, perhaps, waiting at the water's edge to unsheathe its claws and spear a fish.

Megan inhaled sharply. 'This is by Delmore,' she said at once.

'Really?'

Finley had suspected this was the case, but had needed someone who knew more about the artist to confirm it.

'It must be, unless it's a very clever fake,' said Megan. 'See that *GD*?' She pointed to the bottom corner of the sketch and a small squiggle that Finley had barely registered. 'It's on all his work – it's on *Hero's Bay*,' she added, nodding at the copy of the painting hanging opposite the bar. 'Even without those initials, though, you can kind of just *tell* . . . Delmore was all about contrast – it's what made him so unique for the time. It's obvious in *Hero's Bay*, with that light blazing through the gloom, but even in his sketches he liked to play up the shadows and any darkness, see?' Her finger hovered over the deeper patches of sea, and the woman's untameable hair, before she looked up to meet Finley's amused gaze. '*What?*'

'Nothing,' he said quickly. 'It's just . . . I had the impression you weren't that bothered about Delmore?'

'I'm not,' she assured him, tossing the sketch onto the sticky bar top, which caused Finley to wince (how much was it worth?). 'But you can't live where I do and not ...'

Her voice petered away. Maybe because the drawing was now at arm's length, she seemed to be seeing it anew, focusing not on its style, but on its subject and setting. Finley watched her green eyes widen as she registered what he had noticed straight away: the rock on which the woman was perched, though half concealed by her skirts and frothing seafoam, was unmistakeably Nessie-shaped.

'This is Crockers Beach,' said Megan.

'Is that what it's called?' asked Finley, who hadn't known it had a name.

Megan shrugged. 'That's what everyone around here calls it.'

They looked at one another over the drawing, and Finley wondered whether she, like he, was remembering that Crockers Beach was where they had first met – where Megan had been sitting, mermaid-like, upon that very rock.

Once again, she dropped her gaze first, helping herself to another handful of his crisps. Then she nodded at the sketch, saying, 'And I reckon I can guess who you think she is.'

Finley picked up the piece of paper, rescuing it from the condensation ring that was threatening to seep from his beer mat. 'Actually,' he said, 'I *know* who she is ...'

He flipped the sketch over, and the image of the woman on the rock disappeared. Instead, they were left looking at a crumpled, slightly ripped and largely blank scrap of paper, one that kept trying to curl up on itself again, almost like the subject of the sketch. At its centre, scribbled in the same hand that had signed *GD*, were three faded words:

Cora, August 1840

Finley decided to return to Crockers Nest via East Crescombe's backstreets. He wanted a change from the beach and the promenade – from the town's polished façade, perhaps. The narrow, sloping streets just behind the picturesque rows of galleries and gift shops were where Crescombe began to lose some of its chocolate-box sheen; within a few minutes, Finley had passed two bookies and several boarded-up shops, while, up ahead, music was blaring from The Crown, a far seedier-looking pub than the one he'd just left.

From what Finley had read, there were pockets of real deprivation throughout the area – yet, on the whole, Crescombe remained a thriving tourist town. Of course, this was due in no small part to Delmore, and Finley reflected that however much the locals liked to disregard the artist, it was undoubtedly his legacy that kept their little town afloat.

Suddenly, a moaning shadow loomed into his path, causing Finley to jump backwards, heart hammering. But it was just a man pitching out of the pub. He mumbled incoherently for a few seconds before clapping Finley on the back and stumbling off down the darkening street, trailed by an odour of whisky.

Watching him go, Finley waited for his heart rate to return to normal, recalling what the vicar had told him about the Crockers scaring off anyone from West Crescombe who strayed into their territory. How, then, had Delmore got close enough to sketch Cora on that rock?

Finley continued past the church and along the overgrown coastal footpath that wound around the eastern edge of Crescombe. Just as he was having to squint into the gloom, the security light of Crockers Nest switched on, illuminating the guesthouse's driveway, where a 'Vacancies' sign was hanging from an old fence post. Gazing up towards his room, which stuck up like that candle holder in the tinderbox, Finley found he was reluctant to return just yet, and instead began to inch carefully down the steps carved into the cliff, to finish the day – as he had begun it – at Crockers Beach.

Having taken the back route, Finley hadn't realised until now that the tide was coming in, so he settled himself on the small strip of sand just below the steps, withdrawing from his pocket the lump of larimar. He had stuffed the tinderbox and its contents back into his rucksack before leaving the pub – including the ring, which he had managed to extract from Megan. Yet something – maybe Dawn's comment about it being a worry stone – had made him hold on to the larimar, which he now began to work between his fingers.

He didn't think it unreasonable to speculate that Delmore had at least tried to seduce Cora – it was, perhaps, a plausible explanation as to why the famously womanising artist would risk this side of town. But had their connection, whatever form it had taken, had greater repercussions for Cora? Because that sketch was dated August 1840, which – if Finley's theory about the watermarked parish records was correct – was not only the last month of Delmore's life, but of Cora's too.

A loud sloshing noise startled him, and the larimar stone threatened to jump out of his hand. Finley clutched at it, experiencing that same sense of possessiveness he had felt after Dawn had examined it at the pub, and looked up – just in time to see, a few metres from the beach, a pale figure diving back into the dark water.

Finley stared as the ripples of their splash subsided. His first thought was it must be Megan, but she was back at the pub, dealing with the quiz crowd who'd come spilling into the bar room as he was leaving. So, it was someone else – or some*thing* else. Maybe it had been a seal, or were there dolphins around here? But then, there had been a diaphanous quality to the figure's outline, like they'd been *clothed* ...

They had seemed to be swimming towards the beach – towards *him* – and, heart pounding, Finley waited for whoever or whatever it was to resurface. When they didn't, he stood up, edging to the shoreline and peering into the black water.

'Hello?'

Before he knew what he was doing, Finley had kicked off his shoes and was wading into the shallows. It was colder than he'd expected, but not deep. He crouched to drag his fingers through the water, now searching for a large plastic bag or bottle – anything that might have been nudged up by a wave – but there was nothing.

Then, all at once, the sand shifted under his toes, and he dropped into deeper water, right up to his waist. Here, he could feel the pull of the tide, urging him further out, and as Finley leaned against it, something coiled around his legs, grasping him in place.

With a cry, he bent down, half submerging himself to claw at the slippery limbs of whatever it was, while the sea drew him deeper. Until, throwing his whole weight towards the shore, Finley managed to untangle himself and stumble back to the beach, trailing behind him great curls of seaweed.

Panting, soaking, he threw off the slimy tendrils, grabbed his rucksack, then began to scramble back up the old steps, torn between embarrassment and unease. In his haste to escape the sea, he climbed quickly, and when he tripped on one of the uneven footholds – which were difficult to see in the dark – he had to press himself right against the cliff to keep his balance; to avoid plunging straight back into the murky water.

Finley remained there for a minute, willing himself to calm down, though from this vantage point it was even more obvious that whatever that pale outline had been, it had now completely disappeared. In vain, he continued to search the sea below, which was emitting a faint hissing noise as it stalked over what was left of the sand, like a predator whose quarry had managed, for the moment, to escape.

Water is slopping at the cliff steps. I stare down at the shadowy outline of the submerged beach and rockpools – the scenery of my mornings – feeling stranded by the sea's advance and waiting, once again, for you.

Why haven't you come back here? Perhaps you were only toying with me at Westcliff, amusing yourself after the tedium of that meeting. I doubt you've given our conversation a second thought – whereas I have thought of little else.

Then suddenly – finally – you are there, your golden body gleaming against the deep, and I'm gripped once again by a surge of envy as I watch you glide closer. But when you surface, gulping for breath and shaking wet hair from your eyes, you become ungainly and imperfect and human, and I have the strongest urge to smile.

'You have changed your mind,' you say, and it's not a question.

I nod, feeling there's no point pretending otherwise: we both knew I would.

'You will allow me to draw you, then?'

'Yes.'

You tilt your head to one side. 'And in return?'

I grip at the sea stone in my apron pocket, daring myself to say it aloud at last: 'In return, you will teach me to swim.'

In your surprise, you forget the rhythmic, circular motions you've been making with your arms and drop deeper into the water.

Somehow – with a kick, perhaps – you right yourself, but your eyes remain wide as you gaze up at me.

'You cannot swim?' It's as though I've just revealed I cannot walk, cannot breathe.

I have to bite my cheeks to stop myself from snapping, *When would I have learned? Who would have taught me?* Oblivious, you drift closer to the cliffside, to me. It's shallower here, and when you set down your feet, the water falls to just below your broad, bare shoulders.

'Perhaps you are not aware, but there is a ladies' beach just beyond Westcliff.' You indicate across the water with a dripping arm. 'It's a small, discreet bay where you could hire a bathing machine and sea-bathe among your own sex without fear of impropriety.'

Rage is now writhing in my stomach. You stand there talking of discretion and impropriety while wearing nothing at all. Even if I had the time and money to hire a bathing machine on the other side of town, how would those genteel visitors react to someone like me appearing in their haven of respectability? When I was younger, I used to sneak out to the main beach and try to play in the shallows with the other girls and boys, and even the young children of farmers and fishermen snubbed me.

But I can't explain all of this to someone like you, so instead I say, 'I don't want to bathe, I want to swim.'

This, too, is true, for when the visitors first came, I walked beyond Westcliff and picked my way down the grassy slope to that ladies' beach. There were three of those bathing machines, those little wooden houses on wheels, and as I crouched in the sand dunes, the stiff beachgrass prickling at my arms and legs, I watched those fine ladies being dunked in the water like old dishcloths, gasping and squealing as their woollen bathing gowns billowed around them.

That's not what I want; I want what you can do.

Your expression has turned thoughtful. Perhaps the need to swim is something you can easily understand. 'Is there not a woman, perhaps, who can teach you?' you ask. 'Someone of your . . . ?'

I wonder what you're trying to say. Your class? Your colour? Your side of town?

'There's no one,' I tell you, tempted to add, *Why do you think I'm asking you?*

Frowning, you rub the palm of your right hand against the back of your head, dislodging more water from your hair. For a moment, you seem self-conscious, and it looks wrong on you. I want to brush it away, just as I have the sudden, senseless urge to reach down and push back the strand of hair that has fallen over your forehead.

'I've never taught anyone to swim before – I'm not sure I'd know where to begin.' Your eyes are serious, genuine. 'What makes you think I'm the right person for this?'

I weigh up my response. Because you already want something from me? Because you're the only one around here bored and wild and mad enough to agree? But I sense, in this instance, flattery will get me further.

'Because I've watched you since you arrived, and I've never seen anyone swim like you. When you're in the water, you look . . . free.'

You continue to blink up at me and, conscious this is the most I've ever said to you, I can't meet your eye. Even without looking at you, though, I can sense your self-assurance return; the doubt is dripping off you as easily as the water from your skin.

'Very well, I agree!' you cry. 'I will teach you to swim – if you tell me your name.'

'You would like my name instead of a sketch?'

'Ha!' You throw back your head as you laugh, that loud bark of joy. 'I have lost track of all my bargains! So be it, my nameless pupil. When shall we begin? And where?'

I've been thinking on this: the ladies' bathing beach isn't the only secluded sandy bay beyond Westcliff, but it takes almost an hour to walk there, and I can't be gone that long. Crescombe's main beach is far too public, and the coastline on this side, beyond Crockers Nest, too rocky. So, really, there's only one place.

'Here,' I say. 'We'll do it here, on the days when the weather's good and the tide's low. And it'll have to be the morning – first thing, like now.'

You raise your eyebrows, then glance back at Westcliff, a speck on the other side of the bay. 'You do not ask for much, do you?'

I open my mouth to respond, but how to explain it? How to explain *them*? Here, we are right in the shadow of Crockers Nest, but they rarely come down here, and never this early. In meeting here, we will be hiding in plain sight.

'Is it too far?' I ask.

But you are laughing again. 'It is fine.'

'And you must . . .' Again, how can I make you understand? 'People can't know about this.'

Now, your gaze travels up the cliff behind me. 'Oh, I know all about your—' You stop yourself, perhaps remembering my reaction to being called a Crocker at Westcliff. 'I know all about them.'

You don't look worried, though, so you can't know much.

Maybe it's this realisation that I'm drawing you into our world, or that I'm asking much more of you than you are of me, but something makes me crouch down on the cliffside step, until our eyes are almost level, and say, 'My name is Cora.'

'*Cora.*'

It sounds strange in your honeyed voice, just as it feels strange to say it myself. I can't remember the last time anyone used my name. To the family, I'm just 'you', or 'girl'. I wonder how I even know what I'm called, and suppose I must remember my mother saying it, all that time ago.

We're almost as close now as we were at Westcliff. I'm suddenly aware you could seize me by the waist and pull me into the water. A small part of me wants you to do it, just to see what would happen next.

Instead, you sink back, kick against the rock, and begin to float away from me. 'Until tomorrow morning, then ...'

As you bob away on your back, I think you've forgotten you're naked, but from where I'm crouched it's difficult to ignore. I need to call you back, but I've no idea how.

'And ... Sir? My Lord?'

You smile. 'George!' you cry, tapping at your bare chest.

I'll never call you that, I wouldn't have the nerve. But now I need to find the courage to say something else: 'And, for our lessons, I must insist you ... wear something.'

You laugh. 'You must *insist*?'

The air around me seems to chill. Deliberately or not, you've reminded me that you're a wealthy, titled gentleman, and I'm nobody.

'Of course,' you say quickly. 'Naturally, I will be the epitome of modesty ...' At last, you seem to realise you're currently anything but, and allow the lower half of your body to drop in the water.

'As will I,' I say, for the avoidance of doubt.

You nod, then ask, 'For the swimming or the sketch?'

'For both.'

Your lips twitch as you try to keep a straight face.

'What a pity,' you say, and before I can react – before I can decide whether I'm amused or affronted or any of the other jumbled feelings you inspire in me – you dip below the water, and are gone.

9

The Montgomery Gallery

If the Crockers had wanted to keep Cora's existence a secret, they had done a fairly thorough job, and after the excitement of discovering the tinderbox had worn off, Finley wondered how much more he'd be able to uncover about the young woman who had, he was *sure*, once inhabited his room. Perhaps his only option was to pursue the link with Delmore. The tinderbox's sketch suggested Cora had at least encountered the artist, and so Finley felt a renewed interest in Crescombe's most famous visitor.

Between his work for Lorraine, he started to do a little research online, which quickly sent him down a rabbit hole of what Dawn had called 'the cult of Delmore'. Within a few short hours, Finley had learned the exact location of Delmore's grave in Paris, seen a plethora of Delmore-inspired artwork, costumes and even tattoos, and read several outlandish theories about the artist's death (faked, apparently, so he could run off with Lady Josephine from his final completed portrait) and the light in *Hero's Bay* (an extra-terrestrial laser). Yet, as far as Finley could tell, none of these Delmore enthusiasts had any new insights into the artist's time in Crescombe, let alone any relationships he might have formed here.

Soon enough, Finley decided his time would be better spent at The Delmore Experience. He hadn't been back since the day he had felt suddenly ill in the artist's studio, and the museum had become embarrassing by association. But revisiting it had to be more productive than trawling unverified nonsense online, so – checking and double-checking his blood sugar – Finley made the journey to the other side of Crescombe and stepped into the entrance hall of the mansion-turned-museum, where, once again, he found himself face to face with Lord Delmore.

The last time Finley had gazed upon the artist's lounging, smirking self-portrait, he had felt irrationally resentful of Delmore's youth, good looks and talent. Perhaps this was why, until now, he'd been only too happy to believe what everyone around here said about Delmore: that he was a cad, a layabout, a one-hit wonder. Today, though, Finley paused in front of the image, trying to reconcile it with everything he knew – or thought he knew – about the artist. Because was it really possible that someone of so little substance could have painted *Hero's Bay*?

The self-portrait, he now saw, was dated 1839 – the year before Delmore had come to Crescombe. Finley hadn't noticed before, but a corner of canvas was visible at one side of the scene, depicting a sliver of green landscape. So maybe the artist wasn't loafing around after all, but had flopped, exhausted, into that chair after a day's painting. Now Finley looked closer, he could even see what appeared to be paint stains on Delmore's right hand, while on his left . . .

Squinting, Finley stepped forward, his nose almost pressed against the printed panel. Delmore's left hand was dangling over the arm of the chair, and just discernible on his little finger was a glint of gold: *the ring*. At least, Finley assumed it was the same ring as the one he had found in the tinderbox. On this scale, and in Delmore's pre-Impressionist style, it was merely a smudge of colour – still, the observation didn't feel insignificant.

The small but unmistakeable noise of a throat being cleared alerted Finley to the fact that he was now blocking several people's view of the museum's introductory signage. At once, he sidled out of the way, hastening through the crowds milling just inside the first gallery, trying to work their audio guides, and into the Royal Academy room, where he briefly paused to re-examine the artist's letters, and specifically the image of those mermaids and their shield stamped into the scarlet sealing wax.

Next, Finley headed through to the Grand Tour Gallery, which was perhaps the chief reason for his return to The Delmore Experience. The last time he had contemplated the wall of female nudes Delmore had sketched in Italy, he had felt self-conscious, but today he tried to be dispassionate about the soft curves and languid gazes of all these female figures, and try – as Megan had the other day – to focus on the style rather than the subjects of Delmore's drawings.

It wasn't that he doubted Megan's near certainty that the sketch in the tinderbox had been by the artist, more that he wanted to appreciate it for himself. So, after noting the messy, faded *GD* scribbled into the corner of every sketch, he began to study the darkness and light in the images before him, remembering what Megan had said about Delmore's tendency to play up the contrast between the two.

Finley hadn't brought the sketch of Cora to the museum – it felt too valuable to be stuffed into his jeans or a bag – but over the past few days he had pored over that image so often he could recall it with ease; he could recognise, as Megan had, that the sketch from the tinderbox had been drawn by the same hand responsible for these others – yet at the same time it didn't feel the same at all.

Granted, there were superficial differences: unlike most of the women on the wall, Cora was clothed, and outside, and staring not towards the artist, but at something or someone far away. Conversely, though, her portrait felt more intimate. It had more character, Finley supposed, so seemed richer, deeper.

Had they been lovers? For some reason, Finley found it disappointing, the thought of Cora Crocker being just another of

Delmore's many romantic conquests. Though, if it had been just a fling, how had she acquired from him that family ring, and perhaps the larimar stone too? Unless Finley had it the wrong way round: what if *she* had used *him*?

The other difference between Cora and the women in these portraits was her ethnicity. It was difficult to tell from a sketch, but Finley was becoming increasingly convinced that Cora had been mixed race; the shape of her lips and especially her coiling hair set her apart from even the darker-haired of the Mediterranean sitters. But if Cora had had Black ancestry, it seemed unlikely she was the illegitimate daughter of William Crocker Senior, as the vicar had speculated. Assuming Cora's mother, Ellen, had been white, it had to be her father – the man whose name was missing from the parish records – who had been Black. Only, exactly how diverse had remote, old-fashioned Crescombe been at the beginning of the nineteenth century? It was hardly cosmopolitan now.

Then again, Cora's father hadn't necessarily been a local man, Finley thought, now withdrawing the larimar stone from his pocket and contemplating the light threaded through its pale turquoise surface, like the sun's reflection on tropical waters. *Even he didn't travel that far*, Megan had said of Delmore and the Dominican Republic, and now Finley thought about it, was it beyond the realm of possibility that someone else had brought the larimar stone to Crescombe? The town was remote by land, yes, but not by sea; plenty of ships from all sorts of far-flung places would have been travelling up the Bristol Channel at the time – and many of them had stopped off here to unload contraband . . .

'Hello – feeling better now?'

Finley turned to see Adrian Salter, the museum's curator, peering around at him. With his browline glasses and short-sleeved checked shirt, he looked much the same as last time, only today he was encumbered by an enormous electric fan.

'Yeah, much better, thanks,' muttered Finley, for that near faint had been almost a fortnight ago. Then his embarrassment increased tenfold as he remembered two things almost simultaneously: that he was standing in front of a wall of naked women – and that Adrian Salter was Megan's dad.

'I was just . . .' Finley tried to think how to explain his presence here. 'I was just wondering whether Delmore did any sketches like this while he was in Crescombe? Portraits, I mean.'

'It's a good question,' said Adrian seriously. 'Because of course Delmore was known for his portraits at the time—' The curator broke off for a moment as he struggled to hold on to the spindly legs of his fan, looking a little like he was wrestling an emu, then continued, 'As far as we know, most of the sketches he did here were landscapes, studies for *Hero's Bay*. He did, however, start one rather significant portrait . . .'

'Really?'

'Of his host, Ambrose Montgomery,' said the curator. 'You saw it yourself last time, in the Montgomery Gallery?'

'Oh – yeah,' said Finley, realising he meant the library, and trying not to sound disappointed.

At that moment, the neck of the electric fan suddenly collapsed, as though the emu had lunged towards something tasty on the floor. Adrian gave a heavy sigh as it folded over his arm, and stumbled backwards, entangling himself in the fan's wire.

'I'm heading there now,' he said, sounding daunted by the task as he tried to free his elbow. 'The aircon's stopped working and it's stifling.'

'Let me help,' said Finley, stooping to pick up the end of the lead before the curator tripped over it.

But by that point, Adrian had regained control over the body of the fan, so all Finley could do was trail after him holding its plug, feeling completely ineffective – and a little like a bridesmaid holding the end of a lacy train (Mollie's wedding was now just *three days* away . . .).

'We were lucky to hold on to those sketches,' Adrian said over his shoulder, as they wove through the crowd in the next gallery. 'Montgomery had to fight long and hard to keep any artwork Delmore left behind here. He had a bitter and rather public squabble with Delmore's bereaved mother over *Hero's Bay* in particular.'

On cue, they entered the gallery where the reproduction of Delmore's most famous painting hung. As on his previous visit, Finley was surprised by how arresting it was in comparison to its many other versions he regularly saw around Crescombe, on postcards, T-shirts and coasters. Here, he felt as though the murky water and dazzling light – again, that contrast Megan had described – might spill out of the frame at any moment. His pace slowed as he drew level with the painting, and perhaps he would have stopped walking altogether had the fan wire he was holding not tautened like a dog lead, alerting him to the fact that an oblivious Adrian was continuing through the museum.

Trotting to catch up with him, Finley asked, 'Montgomery lost that squabble over *Hero's Bay*, then?'

'Well, yes,' said the curator. 'It's rather sad, actually, because he and Delmore's mother, Lady Delphine, had once been great friends – that's why she entrusted him to keep an eye on her wayward son in the first place. And if you look through their correspondence – which you can, we have the letters – it all points towards a bit of a misunderstanding. Montgomery appears to be under the impression that Lady Delphine wants the painting for herself, as part of her private collection.'

'But she donated it to the National Gallery, right?' said Finley, remembering his school art trip to London – though his recollection of the painting itself was hazy in comparison to the various humiliations of that excursion: having to sit with the teachers at the front of the coach to avoid being travel-sick; going hungry for an afternoon because Oliver Johnson-Bruce had thrown his lunch in the Thames.

'Yes – presumably, Lady Delphine wanted to secure her son's legacy,' said Adrian. 'I always wonder whether Montgomery might have been a little more willing to part with *Hero's Bay* had he known it would still be on public display, albeit it away from Crescombe. Though I think by that point their friendship was completely broken. It wasn't just the painting she wanted – there was a whole business over a missing ring . . .'

'A *ring*?' repeated Finley, his voice a little higher than usual.

'Yes, Delmore had had a family ring he wore all the time, but it didn't show up with his body, and it wasn't found among his things here, either. Lady Delphine got it into her head that Montgomery had taken it, especially later, when his money troubles became public knowledge.'

Finley was pleased Adrian was walking a little ahead of him and therefore couldn't see his face, which had reddened. 'What do you think happened to it?' he asked.

'I've no idea,' said Adrian, his shrug causing the troublesome fan to wobble dangerously in his arms. 'But I'm not sure I believe Montgomery took it. If I remember rightly, this ring had huge sentimental value to Delmore's mother because it had belonged to her late husband, and his father before him, etcetera etcetera . . . But I doubt it would've been worth an enormous amount to someone like Montgomery. Personally, I think it's much more likely it was lost in the water – or whoever first found Delmore's body prised it off his finger.'

Finley's skin prickled. In all his theorising about how the ring had ended up in that tinderbox, he hadn't considered this last possibility. But it was plausible. After all, a ring like that wouldn't have been worth much to someone like Ambrose

Montgomery – but it would have been worth a lot to someone like Cora Crocker.

He wondered what to do. Obviously, Megan hadn't told her dad about the tinderbox and its contents – though why not? Perhaps she didn't know that The Delmore Estate was missing a ring, but what about the sketch, which she had seemed convinced was genuine?

Whatever her reasoning, it meant the responsibility of deciding what to do with these items fell solely to Finley – and, really, he should at least hand over the ring and the sketch. Someone like the curator could presumably get them verified – perhaps Adrian could even use his knowledge and connections to further investigate the link between Delmore and Cora Crocker ... In sharing what he had found, the whole matter could be out of Finley's hands.

Was that what he wanted, though? Finley thought it likely he was the first person in almost two centuries to have held that tinderbox – and the *last* person who had slid that tin of trinkets into its hiding place in the wall might well have been Cora herself. The thought made him feel protective, not only of the artefact, but of Cora's secrets – and above all of this strange form of contact between them, this touch across time.

They had now reached the stairs where, last time, Finley had chosen to head up to Delmore's quarters and suffered that embarrassing fuzzy spell. Today, though, the curator was leading them further along the ground floor, towards a room whose arrowed sign prompted a little shiver in Finley: 'The Sinking of *The Persephone*'.

The space beyond was dimmer than the more traditional gallery rooms they'd just left, and Finley didn't think he was imagining that it had a particular smell too; a salty, woody scent which, along with a soundtrack of creaking masts, crashing waves and shouting men playing on a loop, immediately evoked the feel of a ship in peril. Once again, his pace slowed, and this time, when Adrian kept walking, Finley allowed the fan's lead to slip from his hand.

Half the room was dedicated to *The Persephone* itself. Dominated by a detailed wooden model of a merchant ship from the same era, it contained panels detailing a typical day in the life of a sailor, lists of rations, and artists' impressions of scenes aboard a tall ship. There was even a map of *The Persephone*'s last, doomed journey, which marked out its route from Kingston, Jamaica, all the way to the rocks of East Crescombe.

The other – and, in Finley's opinion, more interesting – half of the gallery was devoted to the fateful night itself. According to another panel, the sailors of the day had been expert navigators, even in the dark, but the combination of an unexpected mist and Crescombe's treacherous coastline had proved to be fatal for *The Persephone*. The signage even made mention of the theory that the ship had been attempting to steer into Crescombe Bay to unload contraband, but was at pains to point out that this rumour was entirely without evidence.

Still, the mere allusion to smuggling was enough for Finley to spend several more minutes reading about what had happened that night, mentally filing away anything that piqued his interest. The first was that Delmore had not, as Finley would've assumed, been here at Westcliff House that evening, but down in the town, playing cards in the newly opened Ambrose Hotel on the promenade. Finley wasn't sure why this stood out to him, except that it made Delmore seem both more relatable and more tragic, unknowingly frittering away the last hours of his life.

It wasn't known how the alarm had been raised, or even at what stage Delmore had entered the water, but another point that surprised Finley was that the commonly accepted idea that Delmore had drowned was, in all likelihood, false. Instead, according to letters his mother had sent, the artist had been pulled ashore with a grievous head wound, making it far more likely that he had been killed in a watery collision with a rock or debris from the ship, despite the myth of his drowning later capturing the public's collective imagination.

Delmore's mother had quickly claimed his body, Finley read, but the remains of *The Persephone*'s crew had proved problematic for Crescombe. The graveyard at St Nicholas's could not accommodate the sheer number of men who had died that night, yet the parish was obligated by law to bury them on consecrated ground. In the end, the local squire at Harcourt Manor stepped up, and every man who had been pulled from the water was buried at the estate's chapel. Finley thought of the ruined, watermarked parish records from that summer, and it struck him as doubly unfair that these men's names and bodies had been lost to Crescombe, especially when their deaths were just a footnote in the story of George, Lord Delmore.

The final detail that caught Finley's attention was that, by first light, the townspeople of East Crescombe were down at the beach plundering anything of the wreck that had been washed ashore. Apparently, they had been trying to gather up what they could before a customs officer appeared on the scene, but the sight had apparently horrified the genteel holidaymakers of West Crescombe, one of whom had described them as being '*like carrion crows, picking the flesh from the ship's broken ribs*'. Personally, Finley felt this a little judgemental, considering any visitors to Crescombe would have been a lot wealthier than its locals, but he wondered how – if the disaster truly had been a smuggling run gone awry – the Crockers had felt at the sight of all and sundry claiming their lost bounty.

When Finley finally emerged from *The Persephone* room, he was taken aback to find himself in the library again. But of course this was the Montgomery Gallery and, as Adrian had said, it was stiflingly hot – though a lukewarm breeze was now blowing from the volatile fan. Aside from the curator and a young attendant fanning herself with a museum map, the space was empty and, like last time, Finley's gaze sought out the cabinet of curiosities – though today, one appeared to be missing.

'What happened to the ammonite?' he asked.

Adrian frowned. 'The what?'

'Last time there was an ammonite there,' said Finley, nodding at the cabinet. Then, suddenly doubting that was what it was called, he added, 'A big fossil thing?'

'Was there?' Adrian looked to the attendant, who seemed equally perplexed.

'I thought there was . . .' murmured Finley, disconcerted. It seemed a strange thing to have misremembered, even when suffering the effects of a hypo – what else could he have been looking at?

He glanced over at Delmore's unfinished portrait of the gallery's namesake, checking he really was where he thought he was. Montgomery was trussed up in so many layers of lavish fabric that he looked more like a Tudor monarch than an early Victorian businessman – or perhaps a child playing at dressing-up. His moustache was so enormous, his face so cherubic, that Finley couldn't help but wonder whether the portrait was an authentic likeness, or whether Delmore had been having a little fun at the expense of his host.

'Were they close, Delmore and Montgomery?' Finley asked Adrian, keen to move on from his ammonite question.

'Difficult to know for sure,' admitted the curator. 'According to various letters Montgomery sent, he and Delmore were great friends, but . . .' Adrian shot the unfinished portrait an apologetic expression. 'Well, Montgomery was prone to exaggeration, especially when trying to convince people to come to Crescombe. There was a class difference too, of course; Montgomery was a self-made man.'

Still studying the slightly absurd figure in the painting, Finley thought of the languid handsomeness Delmore had evoked in his own self-portrait and, despite all he had read in the previous gallery, his dislike of the artist flared once again.

'In these letters,' he continued, 'does Montgomery give much insight into what Delmore got up to in Crescombe, besides painting?' Then, because this sounded like a random question, he added, 'It must've been quite a change of pace for him after London.'

'Yes, it must,' Adrian agreed, thoughtfully. 'But no, not much. He and Delmore's mother wrote to one another frequently before their falling-out – she wanted to know her son was keeping out of trouble, I suppose – and in those letters Montgomery makes Delmore sound rather reclusive, and absolutely obsessed with swimming: *I am beginning to suspect that your son is half-fish . . .*' After affecting a deep voice for this quote, Adrian attempted a chuckle. 'You know, people say very similar things to me about my daughter.'

At this, Finley felt himself redden, something he couldn't entirely attribute to the temperature of the room. He didn't think it had been a pointed comment, but it suddenly felt awkward that he hadn't acknowledged that he and Megan were . . . *friends*, he supposed – though it was unlike any friendship he'd ever had before, considering most of their interactions were unplanned, and their conversations largely revolved around the dead.

He wasn't about to get into this with her dad, though, so instead he asked, 'I don't suppose you know whether Montgomery had any links to the Crockers? I'm doing a bit of research into the family for my godmother.'

'I couldn't tell you off the top of my head,' said the curator, 'but it's perfectly possible. Oh, yes,' he added, noting Finley's surprise, 'Montgomery had a finger in every pie in Crescombe, and the Crockers had substantial influence, from what I've heard.'

As though struck by an idea, he beckoned Finley towards a glass cabinet, where a large leather-bound book lay open, its pages scrawled with almost indecipherable dates, names and sums.

'These are some of Montgomery's accounts,' said Adrian. 'It might be worth having a look through to see if the name *Crocker* appears – as I said, Montgomery was involved in all sorts of business around Crescombe, and ended up owing money to all sorts of people: numerous builders, of course, but also the parish, the Vitalis . . .'

'The *Vitalis*? As in, the family who owns that restaurant?'

'Yes, goodness knows what that was about,' mused Adrian, with a frown. 'Especially as the Vitalis had something of a reputation themselves back then . . . Anyway,' he said, gesturing back at the accounting book, 'you'd be welcome to have a look through for the Crockers. I wouldn't be surprised if they appeared.'

But Finley had just noted the date on this particular volume: 1842. Two years after Cora and Delmore had died, and probably around the time the remaining Crockers had been deported. Unwilling to linger in this stuffy room while the curator hunted out a more relevant volume, he muttered vaguely about returning to look at accounts on another day.

'They do tell a rather sorry story,' said the curator, apparently picking up on Finley's lack of enthusiasm. 'If you study them at any length, you're really just following a man spiralling more and more into debt.'

'Really?'

'Yes, Montgomery's plans for Crescombe were far too ambitious. He didn't have the finances for everything he wanted to build, for everything he *started* to build. And the town was simply too remote to attract the visitors he needed, especially after he lost *Hero's Bay*.'

Finley turned back to the portrait of the foolish-looking businessman and found his gaze straying outwards, to the empty backdrop that Delmore had never filled. This blankness was not, as Finley had first thought, bare canvas, but pale smears of what was presumably underpaint. The more he stared at it, the more eerie it looked, like Montgomery was standing before the window of a closed-down shop.

'What happened to him?' asked Finley, with some trepidation.

Adrian twisted his lanyard around his index finger a few times. 'First, he was forced to sell everything – not just this place, and the properties he'd built in Crescombe, but his other, more successful investments elsewhere. But it wasn't enough. He spent some time in a debtor's prison, then—' The words seemed to catch in the curator's throat. 'Then he took his life a few years later.' In answer to Finley's unasked question, he added softly, 'Hanged himself, I believe.'

Finley's eyes darted back towards Montgomery's glowing face: it was almost impossible to imagine this cheerful figure looping a rope around his neck.

'It's one of the reasons they say *Hero's Bay* is cursed,' continued the curator, a little mournfully. 'Its first two owners – if Delmore and Montgomery can be called that – met very unfortunate ends. It's superstitious nonsense, of course, but when all's said and done it's probably for the best that the painting ended up where it did.'

It might have been superstitious nonsense, but the idea that *Hero's Bay* brought misfortune remained at the forefront of Finley's mind long after he had bid Adrian goodbye. He barely noticed he had almost drifted out of the museum until he found himself outside the gift shop, where an open *Hero's Bay* umbrella was propped up in the window (was that double bad luck?). As he stared at it, Finley's fingers found the larimar stone in his pocket again, which he began to rub with his thumb like Aladdin at the lamp, his thoughts returning to Cora.

Here he was, obsessing about a potential connection between her and Delmore, and it had only just occurred to him that Cora might have had a connection to *Hero's Bay* too. If she had known Delmore, had she known he was working on the painting that would turn out to be his masterpiece? If she had lived, would she have been able to reveal whether that light was a smugglers' signal, or an extra-terrestrial laser, or even a premonition of the artist's death ...

Finley shuddered, though it was hardly cooler here than it had been in the Montgomery Gallery, and his vision blurred a little as he continued to gaze at that patch of brightness rippling from the umbrella's tip. Because Cora *hadn't* lived, had she? Delmore and Ambrose Montgomery weren't the only ones whose lives had been cut short either in or because of Crescombe. Somehow, Cora Crocker had also died young, at just eighteen years old – so if *Hero's Bay* was cursed, was it possible she had been another of its victims?

We begin with play, like children.

You want to watch me in the water, I think, to see how fearful I am. So, for the first few mornings we remain in the shallows: paddling, flinging pebbles, jumping over the waves that bump at our legs. Even here, the water is constantly pushing and pulling, wrapping my wet chemise around my ankles and shifting the sand beneath my toes. Its coldness, too, is unnerving, and though I know this is the warmest the sea will be this year, it's hard not to wince as I step into the foam.

'You'll get used to it,' you assure me.

These first few days give you time to consider how to teach me. You are taking our bargain more seriously than I imagined, yet sometimes you forget how helpless I am. When an unexpected wave knocks me off my feet, your instinct is to laugh, and it's only when I begin to flail and gasp in a tangle of water and fabric that you finally dart forward to hoist me upright again.

Slowly, we venture deeper. Under your gaze, I wade further than I have ever dared, my pace becoming plodding as the sea needles at more of my body. I bend my knees where I stand, lowering myself until the water is covering my shoulders, my neck, my chin, my mouth. Aware of your scrutiny, I keep my gaze and breathing steady, but this submersion is a little like allowing a serpent to gradually swallow me whole.

You are surprised by how readily I will press my face into the water, blowing streams of bubbles from my nose or mouth.

I don't tell you it is a lot easier than having my head forced into a bucket of slop by one of my cousins. Nevertheless, you tell me to practise in my washbasin – as though I have such a thing – and during our mornings you encourage me to sink under the surface and dwell for a while in that cold, blurry world beneath the waves.

'Sometimes, I sing down there,' you tell me, with a grin. 'After all, nobody can hear. You should try it.'

I consider this as I slip back under. But instead of singing, I screw my eyes shut, open my mouth wide, and I scream.

You tell me you learned to swim in the lake on your family's estate. Your expression turns wistful as you describe how your late father taught you in that still, silver water, while your mother and infant sisters watched and cheered from the bank. I can picture it, just as I can picture how, soon, I will be able to swim with my own father, far away from here. Only, in my imaginings, I too am still a child – that same little girl he said he would come back for – as though the shimmering sea of his homeland is enchanted, and has washed away all the years together we have lost.

You have swum everywhere – in England and abroad, in ponds, rivers, even a lido – but the sea is the most exhilarating, you say; the most unpredictable. Frequently, you bemoan that I must learn here, at the mercy of the weather and the tides and the sea's many moods, yet there are advantages too. A person floats more easily in salt water than in fresh, you explain.

Strangely, floating is harder than anything I have done so far.

'Relax,' you tell me, as I lie back and stare at the sky, the water gently rocking me.

But it isn't possible, not when your hands are supporting me under my back and shoulders. When we made this arrangement, I didn't envision how close we would have to be. Perhaps I imagined you standing on the cliff steps, calling instructions into the dawn.

And, until now, save for pulling me up after my stumble and one or two moments when you've steadied or guided me, you haven't touched me at all.

To float, though, I must swoon into your arms, languishing there while you lightly press at my back and remind me to raise my chin. But I don't want to lift my head, I don't want to see you gleaming above me, strong and steady – and only half dressed, for at some point you abandoned the shirt you wore for our first few lessons. Even if I close my eyes, though, I can still feel you, hear you; I can still sense your body responding to mine.

Floating on my front is easier. It's better having my face in the water, having you out of my eyes and ears and nose, and I barely need your carefully positioned hand hovering under my stomach. If I breathe out slowly through my mouth – if I imagine the bubbles streaming from my lips as tiny as pinpricks – I can lie there for a long time, until my thoughts begin to turn fluid and obscure.

One time, while I'm in this state, you seize me by the shoulders and set me back on my feet, and it's like being wrenched from a dream.

'I'm sorry,' you stammer, and I notice you have turned pale. 'I thought—I feared you might stay down there.'

We can't meet every day. One morning, Ma intercepts me on the stairs; on another, you are obliged to remain at Westcliff, where Montgomery wishes to show you off to some visitors. Mostly, though, it's the sea that stops us, either because the tide is too low or bad weather has churned up the water. And it is crushing, those mornings when I peel myself from my bed, often after just a few hours of sleep, to discover the sky and sea in turmoil and the beach deserted, knowing my day will be long and lonely.

When we do meet, I spend the rest of the day exhausted, insensible and counting the hours until I can collapse into bed. Do the family notice that I now move between my chores half asleep, or that, no matter how much I douse myself with fresh water, my skin remains dry, my salt-encrusted hair stiff and spiralling? Ordinarily, I think Edwin might suspect something – he watches me more closely than the others – but these days he is so consumed by his schemes that even he has forgotten about me.

When I practise on my own, you will sometimes float or swim or jump into the water nearby, and on sunny mornings you like to stretch between the humps of the rock and bask bare-chested in the fine weather. I feel envy to see you lolling there so contentedly, eyes closed, arms and legs dangling in the water, a smile still tweaking at your mouth – envy, and that curious craving feeling that swoops through my body, warming me in spite of the cold water.

You sketch, too, in the sand with a stick, or on the side of a rock with a sharp stone: figures, animals, objects you find in rockpools or on the beach. Even in these crude drawings your skill is plain to see – and your compulsion, for once you start it's difficult to convince you to return to the lesson. For the first time, I find myself wondering how you will depict me.

When you talk – which you do, frequently – it's with the confidence of someone who has no secrets, no shame, and no doubt in his mind that everything he says is of interest. Which, to my irritation, it is, because none of it concerns Crescombe. I begin collecting up the fragments of yourself you reveal in your chatter, trying to piece you together, like a mosaic: a cossetted childhood, an overbearing mother, a directionless wander through Europe, a banishment to Crescombe . . . And though you continually insist that you have been misjudged and underestimated, it's difficult for me to look upon this picture you've created in my head without giving it a name: *spoiled*.

At the same time, though, you are much more than that. You are generous with your time and attention. You are mischievous, and make me laugh, though I try not to show it. You have boundless enthusiasm for the things that interest you: art and swimming, of course, but also history, and travel, and in particular old stories from the ancient world – some of which I dimly remember, so my mother must have told me them years ago. Above all, you have more energy, more fervour, more *life* than anyone I have ever met.

Once I've mastered floating, you teach me to glide, showing me how to kick off from the side of the rock. With my arms outstretched, I bend my knees and propel myself through the water; on my back, on my front, on my sides. It only lasts a few moments, this miraculous motion, then I lose momentum and must surrender to the rhythms of the sea once again. But every time I dart through the water, my heart seems to race ahead, pulling me along in its wake: this feels, as I knew it would, like flying.

I'm close now, I can sense it – and though I've had no choice but to trust you from the start, I'm able to see how all the things you've taught me will fit together. After all these years, swimming in those warm, clear waters half a world away might just be possible . . . Yet any excitement I feel is tempered by the thought that our time together is almost done. There's the sketch, of course, but when I can swim – when you've fulfilled your side of our bargain – you will have no cause to come here.

So, I try to make the most of you, and in doing so the defences I've put up against your easy charm begin to falter. When you look me in the eye, I hold your gaze. When you make a joke, I laugh. When you ask me a question about myself, I try to answer. And when you take my elbow to adjust how my arm cleaves through the water, or take my hand to help me back onto dry land, I don't pull away, but allow the connection between us to linger.

I think you sense a change in me, because your restraint begins to waver too. You start to find more little ways to touch me: brushing your fingers against mine under the water, or dusting sand from my arm as we sit, side by side, on the beach. But you are you, and I am me, so I try to convince myself these small caresses are accidental, or meaningless, and strive to ignore the way each one seems to sizzle on my skin long afterwards, like an untreated burn.

10

The Cellar

The lone bulb flared to life, its sudden brightness making Finley squint, then yawn. As his vision adjusted, he stared around at the cluttered cellar of Crockers Nest, inhaling a damp, earthy smell that seemed to confirm they were underground. The uneven ceiling wasn't particularly high, but the space extended far beyond the glow cast by the dangling bulb, perhaps covering the entire footprint of the guesthouse.

'Well, here we are,' said Martin, releasing the light's cord pull.

Finley and the handyman had been dispatched down here by Lorraine, who was currently in a state of high anxiety over the Crescombe Art Festival, which started the following week and would bring extra visitors to Crockers Nest. For the past few days, in addition to his usual admin work and smuggling research, Finley had washed the windows of the sunroom, alphabetised the books in the lounge, and rearranged the tables in the dining room no fewer than three times. Which he wouldn't have minded, exactly, only Lorraine never allowed him enough time to finish one job before finding him a far more pressing task to tackle.

Following her vague directive to dig out objects she might use for a smuggling display, Finley had felt almost enthused about coming down here this evening – after all, he had wanted a look at the cellar ever since Lorraine had mentioned it was likely where the Crockers had stored their contraband. Now he was here, however – now he was faced with piles and piles of boxes that looked like they might disintegrate if picked up – the job felt daunting, and Finley weary.

Because it wasn't just boxes; the cellar was crammed with stacks of objects that appeared to have been loosely grouped by type. To Finley's left, a jumble of old electrical appliances including an L-shaped hoover and a chunky brown TV. In a corner, a collection of signs and decorations, including a faded 'For Sale' placard, a banner reading 'Happy Christmas from The Bay View Hotel!' and a grubby-looking Union Jack. There was even a heap of what seemed to be damaged and broken objects, which included some paisley-patterned curtains marked with the outline of an iron, an old lantern whose glass was smashed, and a chair with only three legs.

'I'll start over here, shall I?'

As Martin moved away, Finley blinked a few times, trying to wake himself up. Almost two weeks of interrupted sleep was beginning to take its toll, and no amount of coffee could ease the groggy, grumpy fog that seemed to be clouding his mind. If only he could go just one night without being startled awake by the thunk of that window, or the scraping in the wall. Almost worse were his dreams, which were either obliquely sensual – full of sighs and shivers, damp skin and trembling caresses – or downright odd. Last night, he had been staring down at what, in his dream, he had known to be a blanched model of Crescombe, an unpainted miniature toy town. But when he'd tried to recall it upon waking, all he could picture was something stony and spiralling, like that ammonite he thought he'd seen at The Delmore Experience.

'This could be something?'

From behind a box, Martin reappeared, a pair of small, ornate binoculars pressed to his weather-beaten face. 'Maybe they used them to keep a lookout from the cliffs?'

Finley hesitated, wondering how to tell Martin that he was holding a pair of opera glasses. 'They look a bit ... *fancy?*'

'S'pose,' the handyman agreed, discarding the binoculars.

'I think it's probably more likely the Crockers had some kind of nautical telescope to watch out for ships,' Finley mused. 'Or just very sharp eyes.'

Having spent the last few days paired on increasingly pointless tasks, Finley and Martin had long ago exhausted the topic of Crescombe's unpredictable weather, but the subject of smuggling was still providing ample material for small talk.

Now, moving behind a pile of boxes, the handyman called, 'What I don't understand is how they could've been doing their signalling up at Crockers Point without the coastguard seeing them. *I'd* see them, if people were waving lights around outside my window.'

Martin, Finley remembered, lived in the old coastguard's cottage just over the other side of the cliff from Crockers Nest.

'Any coastguard was probably in on the smuggling,' said Finley, parroting what the vicar had told him during his visit to the belltower.

Martin popped back into view, eyes wide. 'But I was told that's why my cottage was built up there, to keep an eye on Crockers Nest!' Guiltily, he glanced around, as though suddenly unsure he should be here.

Finley said nothing, but reflected it couldn't have been a popular job, coming into a small, rural community to essentially spy on your neighbours – especially when those neighbours were people like the Crockers.

'Maybe, after the coastguard arrived in Crescombe, the Crockers just moved their signal somewhere else, like the beach?' suggested Martin.

'Maybe,' Finley allowed, though without conviction.

He was thinking of *Hero's Bay*, where the light seemed to come from the top of the cliff. If it was a smugglers' signal depicted in the painting, as the locals thought, the coastguard at the time had likely known what the Crockers were up to and, willingly or otherwise, looked the other way.

'Find anything?'

Lorraine's voice was coming from somewhere above their heads, and Finley felt a prickle of irritation: they couldn't have been down here for longer than five minutes.

'Not yet, no!' Martin called back, benignly.

A few seconds later, Lorraine's blonde head appeared in the cellar's hatchway, which opened to an overgrown spot outside, not far from the sunroom extension. 'Well, can you come back up here, Martin?' she said. 'I need you to hang those lights around the garden before it gets dark.'

'Righto . . .'

Finley watched Martin and his bulky toolbelt disappearing through the hatchway, still feeling annoyed by Lorraine's interfering – and by the fact that he had now been left to this meaningless task alone. Reminding himself he was just tired, he tried to banish his bad mood by yawning widely.

What was he even looking for? He'd been doing more reading up on smuggling since talking to the vicar, and it sounded as though most of the contraband had been perishable: brandy, wine, tea – plus, because ships sailing up the Bristol Channel were often heading back from the New World, sugar, rum and tobacco. Any goods that had been left behind – which in itself seemed unlikely – wouldn't have survived almost two centuries.

Finley supposed he might have more luck finding some of the smugglers' distinctive barrels, which, he'd read, had been made with flattened sides, so they could be worn. Or perhaps there were wooden clubs or even pistols down here, because the half of the landing crew not lugging the contraband from the beach would have been armed against customs officials, coastguards or even rival smuggling gangs.

Finley wondered how much Cora Crocker had known about this dangerous endeavour. Had she been involved? If that Dickensian drawing he had studied with Lorraine had depicted Agnes Crocker faithfully, he could well imagine the large, tough-looking matriarch wielding a wooden bat, but *Cora* ... ?

A chipped vase, a pile of faded deckchairs, a rusty weathervane ... As Finley moved deeper into the cellar, which was certainly big enough to have stored a shipment of contraband, these random objects laid out like a garage sale seemed to emphasise the scope of Crockers Nest's history. Muddled and mouldering though it was, this place contained evidence not just of its smuggling days, but of all the house's past lives. So perhaps it was natural that, ducking past the weathervane, Finley's thoughts turned to the people who had populated each era. Had Jacqueline Fairchild walked over that stripy rug? Had Michelle Lei checked the time on that now-dormant clock? He shivered: like the larimar stone in his pocket, these objects made the past – and those who inhabited it – feel far more tangible, almost close enough to touch ...

Pop!

All at once, everything went dark. For one odd moment, Finley thought he might have blacked out. Then he noticed dusky light was still coming from the now-distant hatchway, and realised the cellar's lone bulb must have blown.

He stood there for a few seconds, too irritated to do anything but listen to his own breathing, which was a little uneven from the shock of being suddenly plunged into darkness. Now he couldn't see, his other senses seemed heightened. There was a tightness to his throat, and that itchiness in his right palm was back – *was* he allergic to something? Maybe it was that stupid air freshener or whatever it was from his room. There must be one down here too, because its soapy floral scent was competing with the pervasive aroma of damp.

Wearily, Finley reached into his pocket for his phone and switched on its torch. Guided by its beam, he took a few, tentative steps back towards the hatchway, then noticed another, fainter light ahead, somewhere at ground level. Whatever it was had a flickering quality, like a candle – though Finley thought it more likely a torch at the end of its battery life had slipped from Martin's overstuffed toolbelt.

Still, there was something disquieting about that unplaceable glow, and the way it sent shadows dancing across the low ceiling. Or perhaps Finley was just unsettled by the cellar's jumble, which, by torchlight, looked stranger and – he might as well admit it – *creepier* than ever. As he edged forward, his mind conjured the unhelpful image of those weathered garden statues from Martin's wheelbarrow, the ones that had looked like remains from Pompeii. He hoped the handyman had disposed of all of them; he didn't want to see one of those distorted faces leering out at him from the gloom.

Then, out of nowhere, pain pierced Finley's skull.

'*Shit!*'

Clutching his head, he staggered backwards, hardly hearing the ruckus as he sent a pile of objects crashing to the floor, because *someone or something had struck him*. But then, a moment later, the cellar's dangling lightbulb glimmered again, reilluminating his surroundings – including that rusty weathervane which, in the dark, Finley had forgotten to duck under.

Swearing again, he strode towards the exit and up the steps, then relieved some of his anger and embarrassment by slamming shut one of the hatchway doors. The evening sky had turned mauve and mottled, and as Finley stared up at it, he took a deep breath of fresh air, trying to get a grip on himself.

'Oh, there you are, my love, did it go dark for you too?'

Summoned, no doubt, by all the noise he'd been making, Lorraine was sidling through the sunroom door. Finley tensed: he wished she'd just leave him alone.

'I think Martin tripped a whatsit – fuse,' she continued, undeterred by his silence. 'You couldn't go and help him with the garden lights, could you? He's got himself in a right tangle.'

'I'll do it later,' muttered Finley, gingerly prodding at the side of his head, which was still throbbing.

'Oh, go on, love, it won't take a—'

'*I said, I'll do it later!*'

It came out harsher than he intended; even out of the corner of his eye, he could see Lorraine draw back in surprise. He knew immediately he ought to apologise – and ought to be more understanding, because she was on her own, and didn't mean any harm, and was obviously anxious about the busy week ahead. But instead Finley found himself muttering, 'I'm going for a walk,' and stalking away.

He didn't really know where he was going – though, after making quick work of the coastal footpath into town, it occurred to him he didn't have a lot of options, not unless he wanted to go scrambling up the wooded cliff in the dark. For the first time, Crescombe's smallness felt more claustrophobic than comforting. He supposed he was hoping he might bump into Megan, but at some point between devouring a fish supper on a bench and the sun going down, Finley concluded she must be at the pub or the museum, and didn't have the energy to seek her out in either.

In the end, he headed to the town's main beach, where the slabs of rock that jutted from either side of the bay were cast in silhouette, like ghoulish sentries standing guard over Crescombe. The tide was right out, having left behind it a vast stretch of creased sand. It made the beach feel barren and strange, and if it hadn't been for the familiar rhythm of the sea, Finley might have been treading the surface of a distant planet – an impression not helped by the small, translucent creatures that kept skittering over his feet (crabs, he hoped).

When he reached the shoreline, where the water snuck towards a point just shy of his toes, Finley was uncomfortably reminded of the last time he'd been this close to the sea at night, and tensed at the thought of seeing – or rather, imagining – another pale figure diving towards him. He tried to focus on the handful of lights flickering at the dark horizon: some buoys or far-off ships, perhaps. At his back, it was brighter: from the houses and bars and arcade; from the lampposts lining the promenade and the odd car heading down the hill; even from the phones of the last people he'd passed, a group of teenagers surreptitiously sharing a bottle of cider at the edge of the beach.

It would have been very different a few centuries ago, Finley thought, gazing up to the cliff above Crockers Nest – Crockers Point, Martin had called it – and imagining how bright a single light up there would have looked against almost total darkness. A slight breeze ruffled his hair, and suddenly Finley could picture it all: the tall ship slowly slipping off course and into the bay; the men wading out into cold inky water to receive the goods being tossed overboard; the return party stealing back across the beach, laden with barrels or brandishing bats, then disappearing through that tunnel of greenery and, eventually, into the bowels of Crockers Nest.

Something was needling at him, scuttling around the murky recesses of his mind like the crabs across the sand, almost too fast to grasp. Up at Crockers Point, a light *had* now appeared on the cliff, as though Finley had just imagined it into being. But of course it was probably just Martin going home; perhaps even the handyman had had enough of Lorraine – perhaps he had found his torch too.

Finley's mind circled back to their conversation in the cellar: *Maybe, after the coastguard arrived in Crescombe, the Crockers just moved their signal somewhere else, like the beach?* At the time, Finley had inwardly dismissed Martin's theory, but as his gaze roved over the dark tip of East Crescombe, and the cluster of lights at its heart that was Crockers Nest, he realised: the Crockers *had* moved the signal from the cliffs, but not to the beach. They had moved it somewhere more elevated, somewhere that faced the ships coming in from the west, yet was a blind spot for anyone patrolling the clifftop above. And they had entrusted the signal to someone too slight to do any of the dangerous grunt work of a smuggling run, but perfectly positioned to hold up a lantern at her window ...

A sudden coldness at his feet alerted Finley to the small wave that had just washed over his trainers, but he hardly cared. He was too consumed by excitement – plus a rush of validation, because hadn't he known there was something different, something *important* about Cora Crocker? This must be why she'd had a tinderbox squirrelled away in her wall; to spark the light that guided great ships towards this very beach. She had been the *signalwoman*, marvelled Finley, the water still nipping at his toes – which meant that, for a time, that whole illicit scheme, that conspiracy spanning an ocean, had depended on *her*.

'Thanks so much for leaving feedback about your time at Crockers Nest, though unfortunately there's nothing we can do about the seagulls ...'

Finley groaned, throwing his phone down onto the bed. He didn't really know why, at almost midnight, he was trying to reply to the guesthouse's earliest reviews on Guidebook – the ones Lorraine had never acknowledged – though he suspected it might be connected to the guilt he was beginning to feel over how he had spoken to his godmother.

In any case, he'd needed to do *something*. Because in spite of how tired he was – and in spite of knowing he needed to get some sleep before the window and the scraping and those dreams started up again – when he'd returned from the dark beach a few hours earlier he'd still been buzzing about his theory, his *certainty*, that Cora had been the Crockers' signalwoman.

Now, for the third or fourth time that night, Finley picked up Delmore's sketch, studying the poised, proud figure of Cora through bleary eyes. Was he expecting her to look different? Was there some clue in this drawing that here was a woman who had regularly risked her life for her family's shady enterprise? Because the punishment for smuggling, Finley had read, was usually death – meaning Ma Crocker and her sons had actually been lucky to be transported.

Finley then contemplated the faded *GD* at the bottom of the sketch, pondering how much the artist had known about all of this. Because if the light in *Hero's Bay* truly was the Crockers' smuggling signal, had Delmore been aware that the person responsible for that now iconic beam was the very woman in this drawing?

Unable to answer any of these questions, Finley resumed his contemplation of Cora. Regardless of what he didn't know about her, she was beginning to feel like a real person. One who had collected shells and pebbles, one who had sewn that patch onto her apron. Cora Crocker had woken and walked, she'd breathed and dreamed; she had *lived*.

A faint rattling noise made Finley look up: the door to his room was quivering in its frame. From a draught, he supposed, returning his attention to the sketch. But a moment later the door shook again, louder, harder – almost as though someone was on the other side.

'Hello?' Finley called, his pulse quickening.

Maybe it was Lorraine. On his return to Crockers Nest, Finley had sneaked straight up here to avoid her. Now, he feared she – or perhaps Martin, on her behalf – had come to talk to him about earlier, and he felt sullen again.

'*Hello?*' he snapped, as the door rattled once more, wondering why they were doing this so late – and why they couldn't just knock.

With a sigh, he put down the sketch, pushed himself from the bed and strode over.

'Just a minute,' he muttered, tugging at the handle – but the door didn't open.

Frowning, he tried again, the door now quaking from his own efforts. He definitely hadn't locked it; he rarely did, since no one else ever came up here.

Trying to quell his growing unease (why wasn't whoever it was *saying* anything?), he recalled Lorraine talking about the door when first showing him around. Hadn't she called it *sticky*? Probably the wood had warped from all the damp coming in from that window. With a grunt, Finley wrenched the handle a third time, so hard it sent a bolt of pain through his already itchy palm, and, finally, the door swung open.

There was no one on the other side. Unsure whether or not to feel relieved, Finley peered down the stairs, straining his ears for the sound of retreating footsteps. But all was quiet, so after testing the door's stickiness by closing and opening it a few more times, he decided it must have just been one of the guesthouse's powerful draughts making it sound like someone was trying to get in . . .

Ding.

At this new noise, Finley whirled around. But it was just his phone, alerting him to a message on Guidebook. He picked it up, intending to log out of the Crockers Nest account – it really was far too late to be replying to anything – when he noticed the name of the sender: *cross_my_hart*.

There was no ignoring that. Given Finley had heard nothing in the week or so since he had messaged the reviewer, he had all but given up on learning why they had written *DO NOT STAY HERE!!* Finally, however, it seemed he had a reply:

> I wrote that because that place ISN'T SAFE, it should NOT be open.

Finley winced – and not just from *cross_my_hart*'s shouty capitals: this didn't sound like a random troll, or even someone with a personal vendetta against Lorraine. Reasoning that there was a chance the sender was still logged in, he wrote a hasty response, once again imploring them to elaborate. To his surprise, three dots immediately appeared, suggesting *cross_my_hart* was indeed writing a reply. Then the dots vanished, popped up again, and disappeared once more.

An anxious texter himself, Finley was fairly certain *cross_my_hart* was drafting and redrafting their response – perhaps, then, they weren't as sure of themselves as all their capitals implied. Plus, they would have no idea who they were speaking to, he realised. A little guiltily, Finley decided to emulate an assertive, professional person catching up on emails after a busy day, not the owner's jumpy godson working late on his bed because he had nothing better to do:

> May I ask when you stayed at Crockers Nest? Because this is a review site for guests only.

The reply came immediately:

> 1989

Finley frowned: he hadn't expected that. The guesthouse would have been The Bay View Hotel back then, and he offered some generic assurance that it was now under new management, more to keep *cross_my_hart* talking than anything else.

> Doesn't matter who owns it, won't change anything
>> What needs to change?

Finley dispensed with the semi-formal tone, beginning to suspect *cross_my_hart* was as keen to impart something as he was to learn it. And, sure enough, after the dots had appeared and disappeared a few more times, another message came through:

> You must know its history!! Women have DIED

Finley exhaled, though hardly with relief: so that was what this was about? After casting another uncertain look around his room, he braced himself to return to the conversation, to try to ascertain whether *cross_my_hart* was just some crackpot conspiracy theorist, or whether ...

The three dots were back, there was more:

> I almost died

'Swim to me.'

I've crept down the cliff steps to find the beach submerged again, and you a little further out than usual. For a moment, I think you're balanced on the glassy surface of the sea itself, then I recognise the humps of rock just visible beneath your bare feet. Standing there, your naked torso burnished copper by the early sun, you could be a statue on a plinth.

I laugh, assuming your suggestion to swim out to you a joke, and when you don't join in, I shake my head. 'I can't.'

'You can,' you tell me. 'Cora, it is time.'

The sound of my name on your lips makes my skin tingle. You haven't used it since we first made this arrangement – being just the two of us, you've never needed to.

I consider the distance between us, which on land I could cross in a few strides. The sea is calm and clear, and not even very deep – here and there, I could probably place my feet on rock or sand – so I understand why you've decided that it must be today.

'Swim to me,' you urge again, softer now, as though I'm a little bird that might flit away.

I certainly feel like a little bird as I shuffle towards the edge of my step; one preparing to take that first, fateful tumble from the nest. When I finally drop into the sea it's with a clumsy plop. The sudden cold makes me gasp, and as my chemise begins to twist around my body like a tentacled creature, I grope behind me for the slippery cliff face, for that last chunk of land.

'Swim!' you cry, and you don't sound worried, but excited.

Heartened, I face you again, trying to ignore the fact that, from my new vantage point in the water, you look even further away. I'm trembling, and though I try to remember all you have taught me, my mind seems to have jammed, like an overstuffed mangle. But it doesn't matter, because my body – my small, skinny body that's growing stronger by the day – knows what to do. Without my even realising, my torso has unfolded in the water.

When I push off from the rock, I glide for a few soaring seconds, then quickly unravel in a tangle of wiggling limbs. Everything I've learned has deserted me: my body is dipping in the water, my breaths are ragged, my arms and legs are thrashing out in all directions... And yet, I am moving. You are getting closer, and a quick glance over my shoulder confirms the cliff face is now a few feet behind me. Elation fills my chest like air, raising me in the water: *I am doing it.*

Whack! A wave slaps me in the side of the face. I reel, struggling to stay afloat with my nose stinging, my mouth full of salt and my vision half obscured by my own hair. My body is tipping, and I want to stretch out a toe to see if I'm in my depth... But I won't – I *won't*. I spit the water from my mouth, rub the hair from my eyes and, with a grunt, throw myself forward.

As my body and breath find an erratic new rhythm, I screw up my face against the glare of the rising sun and the increasingly choppy waves, to see you jumping from foot to foot, like a jester.

'Swim!' you urge. 'Swim!'

Am I encouraged or annoyed that you dance while I struggle? I can't decide and, either way, I want to shove you off that rock.

There is so little between us now. But everything feels heavy – my body, my clothes – while my limbs and lungs are burning.

Even over the sounds of the sea, I can hear my own heartbeat crashing in my chest and throat.

You cease your jigging and crouch down, your hands outstretched. With a final, agonising kick, I launch myself forward, into your arms. You lift me from the water, up and up, and as I rise, I feel suddenly light, like I may just float away. But then your arms curve around me, solid and reassuring, and I collapse, panting, over your shoulder.

You begin to whoop, revolving on the slippery rock as though it's a stage and we are taking our bows. I should shush you – someone will hear, or we will both tumble back into the water – but all I can do is bury my face into the side of your neck and beam. You should enjoy our victory, for it's yours as much as mine.

When at last I have the strength to lift my head, I realise I'm still bundled up in your arms. Your face is raised to mine, your broad grin showing off your white teeth. It should feel wrong to be this close to you, but it doesn't. Nothing is the same anymore; everything has turned upside down.

With a boldness I can barely believe, I place my hands on either side of your face, my thumbs tracing the lines of mirth in your cheeks. At once, your smile disappears, replaced by an expression I've never seen on you before, something half wary, half pleading. You've been waiting for me, I realise, all this time – and in this world turned topsy-turvy, it's the easiest decision I have ever made, lowering my face, pressing my lips to yours.

11

The Cove

At the foot of the cliff, where the last of the smugglers' steps became a blur under the water, *Sandy Bottom* was being gently buffeted by the high tide. Warily, Finley eyed the little blue and white vessel, which contained Megan, Skipper and a cool box. The last time he'd been out in a boat – a miserable snorkelling trip in Menorca during his final holiday with Mollie – he'd been horribly seasick.

With her arms around Skipper, who was trying to launch himself overboard, Megan nodded towards Finley's rucksack and asked, 'How long do you think we're going for?'

Finley didn't know how to answer this without revealing that half the contents of the bag were to keep him alive, so he decided to ignore the question and ask, in reference to the short, unexpected text that had summoned him here, 'How did you get my number?'

'Lorraine,' Megan replied, 'at the pub, yesterday evening – karaoke night,' she added, with a shudder.

It definitely hadn't been his godmother rattling at his door, then. Unwilling to dwell on this thought, Finley instead chose to feel put out by Lorraine's disregard for his personal privacy – though this was secondary to how pleased he was that Megan had asked for his number in the first place.

Today, Megan was wearing a pair of tatty denim shorts and a holey khaki jumper, which was currently hanging off one shoulder, revealing the strap of her black swimming costume underneath. Her dark blonde hair was scrunched on top of her head, and she was peering at him over a pair of circular plastic sunglasses that might have been designed for a child. Striving to ignore that slight thrum of desire she seemed to inspire in him, Finley tried to decide – not for the first time – whether she was a complete oddball or the coolest person he'd ever met.

'Where are we going?' he asked.

'That way,' she said, now nodding towards the other side of the bay. 'There are some little beaches beyond Westcliff you can only really reach by sea.' Her hands still occupied with Skipper, she pointed at the boat's other seat with a flip-flop-clad foot. 'Come on, get in.'

The boat lurched as Finley stepped into its hull, though fortunately he kept his balance. The wooden seat must have been splashed on the way, because as he sat down, an unpleasant dampness began to seep through the navy-blue swimming shorts he'd had the foresight to change into.

Megan released her grip on Skipper, who bounded over to greet Finley, and turned to the black contraption behind her, announcing, 'Engine's a bit temperamental. It's been okay so far today, but sometimes I have to row.'

Though he hoped she was joking, Finley noted the two oars lying in the boat – and that there were lifejackets and a lifebuoy stuffed beneath her seat. Megan then pulled something on the engine, and in a splutter of noise they shot away from the rock and began to chug out to sea.

It took Finley a few minutes to accept that he didn't feel sick, and that there were, in fact, worse ways to spend a sunny Saturday morning. The sea was relatively calm, so the boat was cutting a smooth course, and, to their left, Crescombe unfurled like a smile, its beach and promenade freckled with holidaymakers. The noise of the engine meant it was almost impossible to hold a conversation, so Finley didn't feel rude turning his back on Megan to face the horizon. He even made a start on one of the cereal bars he'd packed, while Skipper propped himself up at the front of the boat, his ever-wagging tail swishing against Finley's knees, his silky ears flapping in the wind.

Finley also found the breeze invigorating – which was fortunate, because he'd stayed up late the previous night, trying to elicit more from *cross_my_hart* – or Cynthia Hart, as she was apparently known in real life. But she had seemed reticent to go into too much detail over Guidebook and, frustrated, Finley had ended up making the rash suggestion to meet in person. He hadn't expected her to agree – to hash out with a stranger something that had apparently almost resulted in her death – but, to his astonishment, she had told him he could come and see her in Surrey, where she presumably lived.

Should he go? Surrey wasn't exactly close – for some reason, Finley had foolishly imagined any meeting taking place in Crescombe. He was also aware that 'Cynthia Hart' could be anyone: a crackpot, a con artist – on the internet, you never really knew who you were talking to. It was one of the reasons his mum's gentle suggestions that he try online dating to get over Mollie had filled him with such dread.

On the other hand, he was desperately curious. As far as he could tell from her short, shouty messages, Cynthia Hart was claiming to have survived whatever it was that had resulted in the deaths of Jacqueline Fairchild and Michelle Lei. Finley had been trying not to think about Dawn's belief that those women had been caught up in something supernatural, but there was no denying that the list of unsettling and largely inexplicable incidents he himself was experiencing at Crockers Nest was growing ever longer. *That place ISN'T SAFE*, Cynthia Hart had written – and Finley wanted to know why.

At least, this was how he was justifying the expense and upheaval of this potential trip – and, while he was there, he could go on to

London and see Fiona, who kept threatening to descend on him in Devon. The prospect of a visit from his sister made Finley feel fiercely territorial: Crescombe, for all its faults, was *his*.

As *Sandy Bottom* approached the other side of the bay, Finley became aware of a lot more seabirds wheeling and keening overhead; they had come from the cliffs, he realised, and looked set to divebomb the boat if it came too close. It almost seemed as though they were guarding The Delmore Experience, which was looming high above the water. Finley wondered how it must have felt for Crescombe's fishermen to stare up at Ambrose Montgomery's imposing residence as they set out to sea in their little boats, just as their fathers had before them, and their fathers before that.

Once they had rounded Westcliff, Finley saw, for the first time, what was beyond Crescombe's most westerly point: beaches. Not wide stretches of sand, like the town's main beach, but a series of little enclaves among the cliffs, which gave the landscape the look of a viaduct. The first of these bays seemed to be the biggest and most accessible, and as *Sandy Bottom* skimmed past, Finley couldn't help but notice that the people populating it all had one thing in common: none of them were wearing any clothes.

'Don't worry, we're not stopping there!' called Megan, who could apparently sense Finley's unease. 'You know, back in the day that beach used to be for women only, so they could bathe *discreetly*. What a difference a few centuries makes, huh?'

After they had passed a few more bays, some of which were almost empty of people, Megan seemed to find what she was looking for and steered *Sandy Bottom* around a sheet of rock jutting from the water at an angle, like a wafer in an ice cream. Beyond was a small deserted cove, where the milky blue water splashed gently at a beach dimpled with shells and stones.

They both jumped into the shallows to push *Sandy Bottom* towards the shore, then Megan produced a mask and snorkel from its hull, threw her clothes onto the sand, and began to stride back towards the water in her swimming costume. Only when she was in ankle-deep did she turn back to Finley, as though just remembering he was there.

'Coming for a swim?' she asked, before holding up the mask and snorkel. 'We can share these.'

'Erm, I might wait for a bit ...'

For Finley, the memory of stumbling about off Crockers Beach the other night was still very fresh. Now, in the sunshine, it wasn't so much that he feared seeing another inexplicable figure diving into the water, but more that he was wary of returning to the cat-and-mouse game the sea had seemed to play with him in the dark.

He thought Megan might object, or at least ask him why, but she simply shrugged and continued to wade into the water, Skipper splashing around her legs. Finley then began to explore the little beach, clambering between the jagged rocks that seemed characteristic of this stretch of coast. Their counterparts on Crescombe Beach had looked so sinister the other night, but here, in the sunshine, there was something whimsical about the random way they seemed to have been dropped into the sand, like a giant's game of knucklebones.

Megan had not reappeared by the time he returned to their belongings, but a damp Skipper was now sniffing around the boat, leaving Finley reasonably confident that, at some point, she *would* come back. So he found a patch of speckled shade under a tree overhanging the cliff and laid out the towel he'd brought from Crockers Nest. Digging through his rucksack – through all the bananas and cereal bars and his just-in-case juice – he located *Underworlds*, the book of retold Greek myths Duncan had bundled into his hands as they had departed The Book Bothy for the final time, and contemplated it without enthusiasm.

At the bookshop, he had read widely, devouring anything and everything, and for all sorts of reasons: because a publisher had sent an advance copy, because a customer had made a recommendation, or simply because his eye had been caught by something on the shelves, which had been as colourful and tantalising as those of a sweet shop. But his appetite had been gone for some time. Reading – something he had always cherished, not least because it had been his refuge growing up – felt like an effort, a chore.

Now, though, there was little else to do – even if his phone hadn't been data-less, it was too bright to see the screen properly. So he flicked through the pages of the book a few times, as though revving an engine, until something caught his eye: handwriting. Finley opened the book properly, revealing that, on the title page, a short note had been scrawled in blue fountain pen, which had bled a little into the thin paper. The handwriting was neat and old-fashioned, slightly shaky, and instantly recognisable:

> Dear Finley,
>
> To a new chapter! And a reminder, perhaps, that if one shifts around the story a little, anyone can be the hero.
>
> With very best wishes,
> Duncan

Finley frowned, surprised to find a slight lump in his throat. Now feeling it would be churlish not to read at least some of the book, he scanned its contents page, his attention lingering on one title in particular: 'The Ferryman'. On this hot, bright day there was something irresistible about the idea of Charon, the ferryman of the dead, who – for a coin – would carry recently deceased souls across the River Styx to the underworld.

Within minutes, Finley was transported. Gone were the beach, his belongings, the dog now digging in the sand nearby... Instead, he was entirely in the realm of the dead, and in the mind of the strange, sinister boatman who had no shining narrative of his own, but who appeared in the darkest moments of the stories of so many others: Orpheus, Heracles, Theseus...

'That looks good.'

A shadow had passed over Finley and his feet were getting wet. A little confused as to whether he really was in the underworld, he lowered his book and discovered a dripping Megan standing above him. He propped himself up on his elbows and, careful not to lose his place, set the book down beside him.

'It's really good,' he said. Then, as Megan wrapped herself in a green beach towel and plonked down beside him on the sand, he asked, 'How was your swim?'

'All right,' she said, wringing out her hair, which had come loose, then searching in the sand for something. 'Quite clear. There's a spot for snorkelling and diving just a bit further on; you can see all sorts: cuttlefish, spider crabs, sometimes even seals. My mum was a diving instructor, and this was one of her favourite places to bring the dive boat.'

Though surprised she had volunteered this snippet of personal information, the notion of Megan's mother having been a diving instructor made perfect sense to Finley – much more sense, in fact, than her father being a bookish curator.

'What does she do now?' he asked.

'She's dead now.'

Though he knew it wasn't in Megan's nature to sugarcoat anything, Finley was still thrown by her matter-of-fact tone. 'Shit, I'm really sorry...'

She gave a jerk of her shoulders. 'It was a long time ago. Cancer,' she added.

Finley didn't know what to say. What *was* there to say? He thought of his own mum – his cosseting, well-meaning mum – and something squeezed his heart. He missed her. He missed all of them, even Fiona.

As it had at Marina's, Finley's silence seemed to draw Megan out: 'Mum was also an artist. She made these pieces out of things that washed up on the beach – stuff that shouldn't be there, I guess, like sea glass and bits of pottery. It was rubbish, but it was beautiful. She was always out and about, with this little collecting basket, and people used to say stuff like, *You haven't been outside 'til you've seen Sandy Salter*. She lived in Crescombe all her life, and everyone thought she'd be around forever.'

Finley could practically hear Megan's next thought – *I thought she'd be around forever* – and his heart clenched again. Her mum sounded very like her, and he was about to tell Megan so when his gaze fell upon the boat by the shoreline and something else occurred to him: 'Did you say her name was Sandy?'

'Yeah – well, Sandra.' Then, seeing where he was looking, Megan said, 'That was her boat originally. Dad bought it for one of their anniversaries, named it *Sandy*. She thought that was a bit much, a bit soppy, so added the *Bottom*.' A little laugh escaped Megan, an unfamiliar sound.

As she hugged her towel-clad knees to her chest, Finley had the impression she was finished, at least for the moment. Again, he tried to think of something to say that wouldn't sound trite or insufficient, fiddling in the sand between them, when his fingertips came into contact with something thin and black. Thinking it a stringy bit of dried seaweed, he almost buried it again, then realised it was a hair tie and that this was what Megan had been searching for earlier. Wordlessly, he offered it back to her, and when she took it from his hand he squeezed her fingers in his own, just for a moment. It was the first time he had ever touched her, and though he was half expecting something akin to an electric shock, the moment of contact felt warmer, less fleeting.

If Megan was surprised, she didn't let on, though Finley thought she might have been wrestling with a smile as she bundled up her hair. Then, as impassive as ever, she declared, 'I'm hungry. Let's have lunch.'

As she went to fetch the cool box from the boat, Finley wondered how he was going to take insulin without her noticing. He supposed it depended on what she'd brought – which, it turned out, were several sandwiches and cakes with wrappers reading *Del-moreish*.

'We often get the unsold stuff from the café for free,' Megan explained, unpacking a few bottles of fancy-looking lemonade.

While they ate, she laid her damp towel on the sand and sat cross-legged in just her swimming costume, her body slightly angled towards the sun. There was something refreshingly unselfconscious about her, Finley thought, especially for a girl – though he himself had remained in his T-shirt in spite of the heat, reluctant to reveal both his skinny, pasty torso and the blood glucose sensor on his arm. He wanted to look at her. Not to admire her (not entirely, anyway) but because everything about her fascinated him: the freckles on her shoulders, her well-trimmed fingernails, the fine, blonde hairs above her knees, even the rough skin on the soles of her feet.

They talked about Finley's project with Lorraine, and Megan's work at the pub, and especially about Skipper, who, unsurprisingly, had been drawn away from his digging by the arrival of the cool box. Around the time they started on Del-moreish's cakes, a pair of kayakers paddled by. Megan raised her free hand to them, but Finley was too surprised by the sudden appearance of their sleek red boats to react until they were almost out of sight.

'It kind of feels as though we're the only people in the world here,' he remarked.

As he said it, he reflected that it was a nice feeling, and that Megan wouldn't be the worst person to be stuck in a kind of modern Eden with. Then he wondered where these strange thoughts came from – perhaps it had been that book – before Megan surprised him by saying, 'This is where I'd come if there was some sort of invasion or disaster. It feels safe. Though it might be submerged by then,' she added, explaining, 'I'm hoping for a watery apocalypse.'

Finley laughed. 'Makes sense.'

'What about you?' she asked. 'Zombies? Plague?'

'Oh, I wouldn't survive any kind of apocalypse,' he assured her.

Megan rolled her eyes.

'I wouldn't,' he insisted. 'Whatever it was, I'd be a goner almost straight away.'

'How come?' she challenged.

Finley hesitated: why not just tell her? After all, she'd confided in him about her mum. 'Because . . .' He took a breath, steeling himself to do it: 'Because I'd run out of insulin,' he said. 'I have type 1 diabetes.'

Initially, Megan reacted to this with silence and, as it stretched on, Finley became acutely aware of other noises: the snuffling of Skipper, who was now nudging at a piece of driftwood; the buzzing of insects in the greenery behind them; the persistent murmuring of the sea. He couldn't remember the last person, other than a medical professional, he'd talked to about his diabetes. It must have been Mollie.

'Is that what that thing on your arm is?' Megan asked, eventually.

'Yeah . . .' Finley made a mental note to try and position it further up his sleeve in future. 'It's a kind of sensor – it measures my blood glucose levels and feeds them back to my phone.'

'How long have you had it?' asked Megan.

Presuming she meant the diabetes, rather than the sensor, Finley said, 'Since I was fourteen.'

Then, perhaps because his resolution never to mention any of this unless absolutely necessary had already faltered, Finley found himself telling her more, until suddenly the whole story was spilling out of him, like water from a burst dam: how he had started to lose weight, crave sugar, how his coordination had suddenly been all over the place...

'But I was fourteen,' he said, with a shrug. 'It didn't feel any more random than everything else happening to my body.'

After his vision had started to blur, an optician had advised he see a doctor. Obviously, he hadn't gone to his parents – again, he had been fourteen – so another GP had taken his blood and sent him home to wait a week or so for the results. Only, he had been called up that afternoon and told to go straight to A&E.

'I knew then it was really serious,' said Finley. 'There were loads of people waiting to be seen, but I was rushed straight through...'

He closed his eyes, the details of that night returning to him in fragments: the endless parade of doctors and nurses; the number of times they had poked and pricked at his skin to take his blood; his mum's high, anxious voice; his dad making endless trips to the vending machine. Most of all, he remembered clutching a giant bottle of water, because he hadn't been able to stop drinking; unbeknownst to him, his body had been trying to flush out the sugar. He could still remember the crackle of the thin plastic beneath his fingers. Now, the sound made him feel a little sick.

When Megan next spoke, he was surprised: he had almost forgotten she was there.

'Does anyone else in your family have it?' she asked. 'You have a twin, right?'

'Yeah,' said Finley, 'but no. It's just me.'

He knew the bitterness in his voice was obvious, but he couldn't help it. Of course he wouldn't wish diabetes on Fiona – he wouldn't wish it on anyone – but he had never quite got over the fact that he had it and his sister didn't. It didn't feel *fair*. They had so much in common: genetics, upbringing, they even looked irritatingly alike. Why couldn't he be like her in this?

'It's fine,' he said, in an attempt to bolster himself. 'I've got used to it.'

This was true, but there was much it didn't convey that Finley couldn't explain. The months – *years* – it had taken him to understand the intricacies of carb-counting, blood glucose levels, how many units of insulin to take, even with the distinct advantage of having two doctors for parents. The intense bullying his condition had indirectly caused, because practically overnight he had gone from an easy target (skinny, awkward, nerdy) to a downright unmissable one (withdrawn, feeble, prone to taking inexplicable breaks during PE). His derailed career prospects, because on his first day of work experience – just two years after his diagnosis at the same hospital – it had all come thundering back to him, and the resulting panic attack had ended his ambitions of following his parents into medicine. Not that he ever escaped the hospital, because there were so many appointments he now had to attend, all those check-ups, all those examinations of his eyes and feet . . . He could never escape full stop; even if he got blind drunk, even during *sex*, it was a consideration, somewhere at the back of his mind. And, of course, his life expectancy, in comparison to that of the average man, was now ten years shorter.

But yes, he'd got used to it.

Megan, perhaps sensing, as he had with her, that he had talked himself out, remarked, 'This trip got deep.'

Finley smiled. 'Right?'

'I only meant us to come here for a bit of a swim and some sandwiches.'

'Speaking of . . .'

Finley retrieved the wrapper he'd discarded in the cool box and studied the nutritional contents. Then he retrieved the bright orange insulin pen from his rucksack and lifted the hem of his T-shirt. He could feel Megan's eyes on him as he inserted the needle into his stomach. Half an hour ago, this would have been excruciating – again, the last person to see this must have been Mollie – but now he felt oddly grateful for Megan's attention; after everything he'd told her, it would have been worse if she'd pretended not to notice.

'It's pretty brave,' she remarked, as he capped the insulin pen.

'What is?'

'That – you. I wouldn't want to do it.'

'I don't really have a choice,' said Finley, though he was reluctant to dismiss the compliment entirely; never before had he been called *brave*.

After lunch, Megan returned to the water and Finley to his book. However, he only had time for one story – about Cassandra, the princess of Troy cursed to see the future but never be believed – before Megan reappeared, drenched again and scowling down at him.

'Can't you swim or something?' she demanded.

'Of course I can!' he spluttered, a little indignant. 'I mean, I'm not an expert, but—'

'Come on, then!' she interrupted, now grasping his arm and pulling him to his feet. 'Let's go!'

As he followed her down the beach, Finley tugged his T-shirt over his head. Somehow, this felt less exposing after the conversation about his diabetes – and Megan wasn't even looking, but bounding back down the beach quite as eagerly as Skipper, who was at her heels. Finley followed at a less enthusiastic pace, stepping gingerly over the small shells at the shoreline before wincing as the chilly water washed over his ankles.

'Shit, this is cold!'

'This is *warm*!' corrected Megan, who was already waist-deep.

Finley clutched his arms, noting his sensor felt very smooth in comparison to the goosepimpled skin around it. What was wrong with her? How could she do this for *fun*?

'Oh God . . .' He took a few more steps, then whimpered as the seabed suddenly dipped and he was submerged to his genitals, which seemed to want to jump up into the rest of his body. 'Ah, *fuck*!'

'Come on!' Megan called. 'Try and catch me!'

Finley knew there was absolutely no chance of that happening, but she looked so full of glee and so absurdly beautiful that, like a foolish fisherman pursuing some unobtainable sea spirit, he launched himself into the water after her.

The cold seized him by the throat, shocking the breath from his body. He made a *neeeurgh* noise, and forced himself to move his limbs, trusting that at some point they would stop feeling like they were about to snap off. Sure enough, after he had cajoled his body into a shivery but passable breaststroke, satisfaction began to hum in his chest as he stretched and pushed and kicked. He had forgotten it could be like this. It didn't feel like battling against the water, as he always feared; it felt like being held.

Megan slowed her pace to swim alongside him, until they could have been two pensioners trundling up and down a public pool.

'How deep is it here?' Finley asked, for he had lost sight of the sandy seabed.

'Not deep at all.'

Clearly, this was a lie, but Finley decided not to worry about it, especially because he thought he had spotted their destination:

ahead, a rocky outcrop rose from the water in four lumpy peaks, like a larger version of the Nessie rock at Crockers Beach.

'I want to show you something,' said Megan, darting forward in the water.

With difficulty, Finley tried to keep up with her as she swam to the rock, before – with less difficulty – he watched her pull herself out of the water, her long limbs glistening. The elements had rendered the outcrop relatively smooth and, had it not been for the barnacles and seaweed clinging to its surface, it might have resembled the kind of artificial formations that decorated fancy hotel pools.

'Come and look at this,' said Megan, pointing at something in the water.

As Finley heaved himself up onto the rock, which was surprisingly warm beneath his feet, he remembered what she had said about spider crabs and ... What else had there been?

'What is it?' he asked, cautiously.

'Go on,' she urged, prodding him towards the edge. 'Just there.'

Finley squinted into the water below, which was such a deep shade of teal it had a dense, soupy quality. 'What am I—?'

'*Look!*'

And suddenly, he was falling – flailing – through the air. With an almighty *splash*, he broke through the surface of the water, then continued to flap about for a few seconds in a blurry confusion of bubbles. Until, like a cork, he bobbed up again, tugging at the waistband of his swimming shorts, which were threatening to ride down.

'You—' he gulped, blinking up at Megan, realising what she'd just done. 'You *knob!*'

She was wheezing with laughter; he had never seen her look so delighted.

'*Right*,' he said, shaking his dripping dark hair from his eyes. 'You'll pay for that, Salter ...'

He hoisted himself back onto the rock but, before he could reach her and return the shove, Megan had thrown herself off the edge, twisting mid-air into an elegant dive.

So began several minutes of hurling themselves into the water. They jumped, they dived, they bombed – at one point Megan attempted a cartwheel. And as he clambered up the rock for the umpteenth time, Finley wondered when he had last done something so pointlessly pleasurable. He felt like a child again.

Then he and Megan met, unexpectedly, at the ledge, for she had found another way up the rock. Teetering together on the jumping-off point, they made a grab for one another's arms, either to keep their balance or to try and jostle the other into the water, Finley wasn't sure. They remained there for a moment, breathless, laughing, and, locked in this strange stalemate, Finley became acutely aware of their bodies: their closeness; their near nakedness; their similarities, pale and dripping and goosepimpled as they were – and their differences, too.

It was Megan who ended their impasse: 'Hey, Finley?'

'Yeah?'

'We'll storm all the hospitals and pharmacies.'

Finley wondered if he had water in his ears. 'Erm – what?'

'When the apocalypse hits. We'll do raids for insulin and needles and stuff, gather you a lifetime supply.'

His first, fatalistic thought was that even if they found enough, it was unlikely, in this hypothetical scenario, they'd be able to store it at the right temperature, or that it would last more than a few years. But the idea that she'd been mulling this over was touching, amusing – a little encouraging, too. Somehow, Finley wanted to tell her this, *show* her this; he had a sudden impulse to reach for her damp face and brush back the wisps of hair sticking to her skin. Only, she had already released him, already given a little smile and leaped away, and he was left staring at the glittering spray that arced through the air as she slipped, once again, into the deep.

By the time they finally left the little cove, a thick canopy of cloud had descended, rendering the dwindling day grey and murky. As they journeyed back across the bay, Megan switched on what looked to be a glorified bike light roped around the bow of *Sandy Bottom*, which cast a pearly beam across their darkening route.

Sitting just behind this light, Skipper snoozing on his feet, Finley realised his own spirits remained bright, in spite of the warm tightness in his face and shoulders, which suggested he'd stayed too long in the sun. He'd had a good, active day, and now the quiet hum of *Sandy Bottom*'s engine – which Megan had switched to the lowest setting after the boat's coughing fit upon their departure – was making him feel pleasantly sleepy.

Influenced, no doubt, by that book he was now keen to get back to, Finley kept slipping into imaginings he'd not entertained since childhood. Back then, before teenage self-consciousness had set in, he'd found it comforting to picture himself in the stories of the ancient world; against all the real-world bullying, it had helped to swing a ruler around and pretend he could behead a gorgon. *Anyone can be the hero,* Duncan had written, and as the boat continued to carve through the water, the lights of Crescombe twinkling in the dusky distance, Finley allowed himself to pretend: he was Odysseus returning from Troy, Jason commanding the Argonauts; perhaps he was even Leander swimming to—

Finley gave such a start that *Sandy Bottom* bucked beneath them.

'Hero,' he breathed.

'What?' called Megan, from behind him.

'Hero. *Hero's Bay.*'

Finley spun around on the seat to face her, Skipper snuffling in protest as he was dislodged from his sleeping spot.

'I know what it means, why he called it that,' Finley continued, his heart thumping. 'It wasn't after himself, it was after her – Cora.'

Megan looked completely nonplussed. 'What are you talking about?'

Finley ran his hands through his unruly hair, which was crusty with salt, and tried to separate his racing thoughts. 'Have you ever heard the story of Hero and Leander?' he asked.

Megan shook her head.

'It's a Greek myth. They were famous lovers, like Orpheus and Eurydice, Cupid and Psyche. She, Hero, was a priestess of Aphrodite who lived in a tower at the edge of the water. And he, Leander, lived on the other side of this water, this strait called the Hellespont. They fell in love and, in order to be together, Leander would swim across the Hellespont at night, guided by the light of a lamp from Hero's window.'

Finley paused, mostly because he was too excited to get any more words out, but also to give Megan the chance to react. She, however, was still looking at him with bafflement.

'Okay . . .' she said, slowly. 'And you're telling me this story because . . . ?'

'The *light*!' Finley burst out, gesticulating wildly towards the far-off glow of Crockers Nest, frustrated not with Megan but with himself for being so slow: how could it have taken him so long to see something so *obvious*? 'That's what the light in the painting is!'

'The smugglers' light?'

'Well – yes, it *is* a smugglers' light,' Finley allowed. 'But the person holding it was Cora, up at her window – she was the Crockers' signalwoman.' Then, before he became distracted explaining to Megan the ins and outs of that particular theory, Finley continued, 'What I'm saying is, it's not *only* a smugglers' light. While all the Crockers were heading to the main beach to unload contraband,

Delmore would've seen that light and known it was safe to swim across the bay to Cora, just like Leander to Hero.'

Megan leaned forward, her elbows resting on her knees. 'So you think Cora and Delmore were, like . . . *re-enacting* this myth?'

'Yes!' said Finley, choosing to ignore the doubt in her voice.

'You think Delmore swam across this whole bay, in the dark, guided by one little light, so he and Cora could – how did you put it? – *be together?*'

'Yes,' said Finley again, flushing at his own prudish turn of phrase.

'Couldn't he have just, you know, *walked?*'

'With the Crockers and their men prowling about, scaring off anyone from West Crescombe? And Delmore wasn't exactly unknown, even then . . . Besides, wouldn't it be almost quicker to swim?' Finley asked, reflecting, once again, that it was a much shorter distance between Crescombe's pincers than around its body.

'In the day, maybe,' Megan admitted. 'But at night . . . ?' She wrinkled her nose. 'I suppose if conditions were good, and the tide was right, and you were a really strong swimmer—'

'Which Delmore was,' Finley broke in eagerly. 'And wasn't he a keen classicist too? Casting himself as a mythical figure like Leander is exactly the sort of thing someone like him would have done. And the *painting!*' he cried. 'Of course that's what it shows! It's him looking over to her; it's *his* Hero's Bay.'

Finley twisted back on his seat to face that same darkening view. Now, it was still possible to see the outline of Crockers Nest and, further along, the row of fishermen's cottages that lined Crescombe's eastern shore. But the pinpricks of light from each building gave some indication of what it must have been like to journey through this shadowy water at night, following a lantern's beam towards Cora's room – *his* room.

'What happened to them?' Megan asked. 'To Hero and Leander?'

This time, Finley didn't turn, but remained staring at the view, hardly paying attention as the end of the story tripped easily off his tongue: 'One night, there was a storm, which blew out the flame in Hero's lamp. With nothing to guide him, Leander lost sight of the shore and drowned. Hero discovered his body the next day, washed up on the rocks, and, unwilling to live without him, threw herself into the water ...'

Absently, Finley began to scratch at the palm of his right hand, the excitement that had been fizzing through him beginning to dissolve, like a tablet in water.

A little later, Megan brought *Sandy Bottom* to a stop on the now-exposed beach beneath Crockers Nest. Finley jumped into the shallow water, and was about to thank her for the trip, when his phone started to buzz and buzz, as though trapped in the pocket of his now-dry swimming shorts was a particularly irate bee. He had signal again – and a surprising number of texts. Going by the preview screen, most seemed to be from his mum (*let me know if you want to talk at any point*) and Fiona (*people keep asking about you*) and it took Finley a few seconds to work out why: it was Mollie's wedding day.

For weeks – months – he had been fixated on this date, and today he had just ... *forgotten*? Somehow, this was more shocking than the knowledge that Mollie was now married, which didn't feel quite as painful as he'd imagined. It ached a little, certainly – but only in the way a scar might, more from the memory of the injury than anything else.

Finley looked up from his phone, intending to tell Megan – though perhaps she knew already, because hadn't he mentioned Mollie's wedding day to her that evening they'd had dinner? Unnoticed by him, though, she had eased *Sandy Bottom* from the beach, and as Finley watched the boat drift away, he experienced a twinge of disappointment – of *guilt*, even – though he tried to reassure himself that Megan never really said goodbye.

By the time he had let himself into Crockers Nest, his thoughts had returned to Hero and Leander. Finley began to bounce up to his room two steps at a time, feeling invigorated, because, for him, myths were familiar territory. He understood this aspect of Delmore's personality – hadn't he just imagined himself in those ancient stories? And, if he'd been a stronger swimmer, would he not have dared to do the same?

Delmore must have been truly daring, Finley thought, as he arrived at his door and searched his rucksack for the seagull key ring; Crockers Nest wouldn't have been totally deserted on those nights a ship had come in – at least, not for long. The contraband might have arrived at Crescombe Beach, but its destination had, after all, been the cellar. As Finley pictured that fearsome-looking family from the illustration, his conviction began to waver: would Delmore really have risked running into them in their own house?

The answer came to him as soon as he stepped into his room – as soon as he saw the window, which, as usual, had swung open. Finley approached it, peering down between the thin safety bars. It would just about be possible to clamber up here from the roof of the floor below. And before that? Finley pressed his face against the bars, the cool metal biting at his cheeks. Before that, a person could sneak up the cliff steps, and then up the side of the house. Again, if they were particularly foolhardy, and motivated by love – or, more likely, lust.

He drew back, leaning against the rounded window frame, thinking now of Cora, who must have stood in this exact spot, her lantern raised . . . Then without warning, pain shot through his right hand, like a slice from a knife. With a yelp, Finley stared at his skin and saw a faint but unmistakeable pink line among the natural creases of his palm.

'What the . . . ?'

He studied the window for a loose nail or large splinter, and, finding nothing, then wondered whether he'd cut himself earlier without noticing, maybe on that rocky outcrop. Though it didn't look like a cut; no skin was broken – plus, this was the same hand that had been itching for, what, a week now?

Frowning, Finley massaged his palm with his other thumb, trying to rub away the mark like he would a line of pen. But it remained, as did a throb of discomfort. Until eventually, he simply stared out at the bay instead, and the retreating form of *Sandy Bottom*, whose watery trail made the little boat look like an arrow, pointing to something that, in the darkness, Finley could not see.

'How much longer?'

You don't reply, perhaps haven't even heard. A deep line divides your brow as your hand sweeps across the paper, and it's strange to see you so solemn.

I dare to shift my weight between my tingling feet. I must look like an old fisherman bent over his net. But when you arrived at our beach this morning – by foot, for the wind is up – and saw me here, staring into the water, you immediately began to sketch.

'It's no use!'

You throw down your graphite and collapse backwards, glaring at the mottled sky. Trying not to laugh, I judge it safe to move, stretching out my stiff knees and then bunching up my skirts to wade back to the beach.

The little sketch is lying abandoned in the sand. I dust it clean and decide it's my favourite so far. Somehow, you've made me look so much more than just a girl in a tatty dress and holey shawl. It's my expression, I think; I'm staring at the sea as though I have command over it.

'Is this really what I look like?'

'No.' You sound as sullen as a child. 'You are far more beautiful.'

Sitting up, you frown at the drawing like it has insulted you, then reach out to crumple the nearest corner.

'I'd like to keep this one,' I say, catching your graphite-smudged fingers.

I tap at the page and, with a scowl, you scribble your initials. 'You are doing it on purpose,' you grumble, flipping over the paper and adding my name and the date. 'I've done dozens of portraits – hundreds! Why is it so difficult to capture you? It's yet another way you torture me ...'

Your own words seem to make you aware of our proximity and, as I roll up the sketch and tuck it away in my apron, you curve an arm around my waist. I let you pull me closer, and as our mouths bump together, I feel the grin at your lips. The drawing is already forgotten.

We are easily distracted now. We meet at our beach with every intention of swimming – or, if conditions are bad, sketching – but, inevitably, our attention soon turns to one another. I'm learning new lessons now. Once again, you're guiding me through the shallows and, once again, I grow bolder and more trusting by the day.

'Cora ...?' you murmur, planting little kisses down my neck.

'It isn't possible,' I say, because I know what you're asking, and I can't leave Crockers Nest after dark, not for Westcliff, not for anywhere.

You moan into my skin. It makes me shiver, but I mustn't change my mind. I wonder how much you truly know about what happens in this town. You've asked about the light before, and perhaps you've guessed its purpose, and even that it keeps me here.

'Then I will come to you.'

I shake my head. 'It's too dangerous.'

You draw back, and I realise I've hurt you. I feel suddenly cold, as though a shawl, rather than your arms, has slipped from my body.

Yet how can I explain it? To someone as carefree and careless as you, they probably aren't so frightening. You don't fully understand why you must stay away. If you stray from your side of town, you won't just be stumbling into their territory but disturbing something far bigger than just you and me.

I'm ashamed, too. I told you I wasn't one of them, but what else am I, if not a Crocker? I'm part of them, I'm part of everything they do here. Maybe I have less blood on my hands, but if we're caught I'll be hanged just the same. Deep down, then, it's not just them I wish to protect you from, but myself.

When I look back at you, though, your demeanour has changed. You no longer appear wounded, but energised. You are staring not at me, but between Westcliff and Crockers Nest, that fox-like smile returned to your lips. With a thrill of foreboding, I realise that, in seeming to question your nerve, I have only spurred you on.

'You can't.' I grip your hand, wanting to shake you until you see I am not worth the risk. 'Their men are everywhere. If you walk into East Crescombe at night, they will know.'

'Well, then . . .' Your smile widens. 'Why don't I swim?'

12

Bonlo Superstore

Finley thought there were few experiences that could have returned him to real life more effectively than a trip to a twenty-four-hour Bonlo Superstore. On the outskirts of Staines-upon-Thames, the vast, two-storey supermarket, with its glaring lights and blaring music, felt far further than the five-hour train ride he'd just taken from quiet, quaint North Devon. As he contemplated the surge of customers pushing trolleys through the automatic front doors, Finley felt he'd not only been propelled into another world, but another time too.

He headed for the supermarket's in-store café, where the illuminated board above the counter made reference to sandwiches, salads and kids' meals – though Finley doubted many people went to Bonlo's eatery for anything but their famous all-day breakfast. Even now, there was a lingering smell of bacon and eggs which, though not unpleasant, was a little incongruous for eight o'clock in the evening.

But then, everything about this evening felt a little off. Finley assumed the Guidebook reviewer Cynthia Hart had asked him here because it was a very public meeting space for two strangers from the internet – though why she'd asked to see him so late, he had no idea. Regardless, Finley was grateful for his busy, brightly lit surroundings; he couldn't pretend that he wasn't slightly nervous to see what this woman, with her tendency to yell in all-caps online, would be like in person.

He glanced around the café, taking in the occupants of its white plastic tables – an old man squinting down at his phone, an exhausted-looking young mother pushing a pram backwards and forwards – before he spotted a small woman bent over a magazine. Her brown hair was threaded with grey and twisted up in a tortoiseshell clip, and she seemed entirely dwarfed by the shapeless cream blouse she was wearing, the sleeves of which almost entirely covered her hands, perhaps to combat the effects of the air conditioning. As Finley approached, she looked up at him from beneath a thick fringe, her dark eyes very round, and he was put in mind of a mouse-like creature peeping from the undergrowth.

'Erm, Cynthia?' he ventured. 'Cynthia Hart?' Then, when she gave an almost imperceptible nod, he continued, 'I'm Finley, from Crockers Nest – The Bay View Hotel, as it was.'

He might have imagined it, but he thought he saw something spasm in her right cheek. He offered his hand across the table, but she didn't take it – in fact, she practically recoiled from it.

'You look very young to be running a hotel,' she said instead, her voice barely louder than a whisper.

Finley, who was frequently told he looked young for everything, said, 'Oh, I don't run it, it belongs to my godmother. I'm just helping out for the summer.'

Cynthia processed this in silence before murmuring, 'Don't sound like you're from Devon either.'

She seemed to be reassessing some preconceived idea of him – as he was of her, he supposed. Unsure how to respond to the accent comment, he gestured towards the chair opposite her, wordlessly seeking permission to sit down.

'You've come a long way to get me to take down that review,' she said, when he was settled.

There was a certain bravado to her words – a challenge, even – that didn't match her tone or manner. Her voice was still very soft, and she was hunched over her magazine – which was open at an article headlined 'My Lover Came Back from the Dead!' – as though she wanted to disappear into its pages.

'That's not exactly why I'm here,' admitted Finley. 'I mean, I'd like it if you took down the review, but I'm more interested in hearing about what happened to you at the hotel.'

'Why?' she asked at once.

Again, Finley thought of her words on Guidebook – *that place ISN'T SAFE* – but hesitated before answering, unwilling to admit that he didn't feel entirely safe there either.

'Because this is a new era for Crockers Nest,' he said, deciding, once again, to pretend he was there in a semi-professional capacity. 'Over the past year, my godmother's put a lot of work into renovating and reopening it, and we want to have a fresh start.' Then, because he knew this sounded insufficient, Finley leaned forward a little and, in reference to Cynthia's messages on Guidebook, added, 'Because I *do* know its history. I realise that, like most old buildings, it has a chequered past. So, I suppose I just want to understand what happened there – to you, to others – so we can all move on.'

Finley thought this sounded fairly convincing, though as Cynthia blinked at him from beneath her fringe, he had the distinct impression she was waiting for more. But then a blonde woman in a sky-blue Bonlo apron, who had been wiping down the neighbouring table, approached them, causing Cynthia to give a little start of surprise.

'Sorry, Cyn,' said the newcomer. 'I was just wondering whether you wanted another?'

'Oh!' Cynthia stared at her empty coffee cup and seemed to retreat further into her blouse. 'Yeah, double-shot Americano, please, splash of milk. And whatever he's having.' She gestured towards Finley with a floppy sleeve.

'Erm . . . Just some water, please,' he said, encouraged that Cynthia seemed to be staying, yet feeling it was a little late for quite so much caffeine.

As the other woman departed, Cynthia called, 'It's on him! Don't put it on my tab!'

This interested rather than affronted Finley: how often did she come here?

When Cynthia returned her attention to the table, her gaze fell upon Finley's hands, and he realised he was picking at a crack in the laminate. Promptly stopping, he asked, 'Do you think you could tell me about your time at The Bay View Hotel?'

'All right . . .' she said, guardedly.

'When were you there?'

'August '89.' She tweaked at the handle of her empty coffee cup. 'I didn't even want to be there, not really, but the sarge needed me out the way for a while . . .' Then, in response to Finley's obvious confusion, she explained, 'At the time, I was training to be a police officer.'

Finley could not have been more stunned if she had revealed she'd been training to be a lion-tamer. A *police officer*?

'I was nearly qualified,' continued Cynthia, who seemed unaware of his surprise. 'I'd gone through all this intense training, and 'cause it was still a man's game back then, I'd had to be twice as good, you know? They had height restrictions and all sorts – didn't let in women under five four. Somehow, I snuck in – I'm five three.'

This was the most she'd said so far and, keen to keep her talking, Finley asked, 'What kind of training did you have to do?'

'All sorts. Classroom stuff, driving stuff, first aid . . . And you have to be really fit, so I did a lot of swimming. It wasn't part of the official tests or anything, but I was always good at swimming, so it seemed the easiest way to keep up with the guys. Plus, HQ had this big training pool we could use – the most chlorinated pool I've ever swum in. Played havoc with my eczema...' She scratched her hand beneath her sleeve, then continued, 'So, I was almost there, almost qualified. And then I got stabbed.'

'You—*What?*'

'It was nothing,' said Cynthia dismissively. 'We were called to a robbery at a factory, it got out of hand. I took a knife to the shoulder.'

While Finley gaped at her, she pressed a spot just below her collarbone.

'It was nothing,' she said again. 'Some doctors patched me up, told me I was lucky. I could've been back at work in a few weeks. Thing is, the sarge didn't want me there. He was in trouble, 'cause only experienced officers should've been at that factory. He wanted me to disappear while it all blew over. Told me to take myself on holiday for a bit.' She gave a humourless little laugh. 'Some holiday.'

Finley continued to stare at her, unable to reconcile the little person sitting in front of him with what she was saying. Was she making it up? It seemed unlikely – what would be the point?

'I saw the pictures on your website,' said Cynthia, presumably in reference to Crockers Nest. 'You've done it up nice. Back in the day, it was grotty. Faded carpets, peeling paint, that sort of thing. 'Course I didn't realise that until after I'd arrived.'

Despite now having dozens of questions totally unrelated to Crockers Nest, Finley forced himself to ask, 'What about your room?'

She hadn't said as much in their messages, but he thought he could make an educated guess as to where she had stayed.

Sure enough, Cynthia said, 'It was the one at the top. The girl on the phone said it was a budget room, perfect for backpackers, but when I got there it was obvious that was bullshit because it was basically just an attic. It was so damp, so cold...' Her shoulders hunched. 'But what could I do? I was young and poor and on my own – I tried to convince myself it would be an adventure.

An *adventure*.' She laughed at her own word choice. 'Staying in that place, in that room ... It was the biggest mistake of my life.'

Finley's skin began to prickle, and perhaps Cynthia's had too, because she was scratching her arm. He pictured that room in Crockers Nest – which, somehow, was both the one he knew and the one Cynthia had described – and, suddenly, he wasn't sure he wanted to hear this after all. But then the blonde woman reappeared with their drinks, returning him to the comforting mundanity of clinking crockery, wafts of coffee, and an announcement in the main store requesting that someone move their car from the loading bay.

Feeling a little less unnerved, Finley asked, 'How was it a mistake?'

'Because there's something wrong with that room,' said Cynthia, before taking a gulp of her coffee. 'Actually, there's a lot wrong with it ...'

And as she began to outline how it had all started – the opening window, the water on the floor, the incessant scratching – Finley felt no surprise at what she was saying, only that she was saying anything at all. It was like she was describing a TV show they were both watching, except she was a few episodes ahead.

'Then there were the dreams,' Cynthia went on. 'I had these really vivid dreams, which were like nothing I'd ever had before. *Erotic dreams*,' she whispered, avoiding Finley's eye as patches of colour appeared in her cheeks. 'And I know, I know, who doesn't have dreams like that every so often? But it was almost every night and it wasn't like I was especially ...' She tried and failed to find the right word. 'At the time, I was sick to the back teeth of men.'

Trying to ignore his discomfort that she was sharing this with him, Finley thought of his own dreams, which he'd assumed stemmed from his feelings for Mollie. But given what he now thought he knew about Cora and Delmore, perhaps they weren't about him at all . . .

'It wasn't just the dreams,' said Cynthia, perhaps eager to move on from this awkward subject. 'I became obsessed with the window – *obsessed* – and I'd wake up standing beside it, staring out into the night. And during the day, too, I would have these . . . *blackouts*, I suppose.' Suddenly, she scratched so hard at her neck that three pink lines appeared, as though some animal had taken a swipe at her throat. 'Like when you've been really drunk, and can't remember what you've done. I'd find myself down at this little beach by the hotel, or up on the cliff path, and I'd have no idea how I got there.'

An ominous feeling began to creep through Finley. Assuming she was telling the truth – and assuming she wasn't a little mad – what Cynthia was describing didn't even sound like the kind of residual energy Dawn had described, which had no influence on the present. It sounded like . . . *more*.

'I should've left earlier,' continued Cynthia. 'I should've left as soon as it started. But it's easy to say that now. I didn't know what was happening, how bad it was going to get. And I didn't believe in ghosts, never had done. If anything, I thought I was going a bit, you know, *loopy*. Maybe the stabbing had affected me more than I'd thought.'

Finley thought this a reasonable conjecture, though he was distracted by the fact that, for the first time, she had used the g-word: *ghosts*.

'And how bad *did* things get?' he asked.

'Pretty bad.' Cynthia smiled grimly. 'Like I said, I almost died.'

Somehow, Finley had forgotten this, and though Cynthia's voice was still quiet, her words struck him with such force that his hand gave an involuntary jerk, and a little of the water from his glass slopped over his fingers.

'How?' he asked.

'I don't really know,' said Cynthia, her own sleeve-covered hand unsteady as she passed him the paper napkin that had come with her coffee. 'One night, I just—' She took a steadying breath. 'It's like, I woke up in the sea.'

Finley tried to swallow, but his throat had turned dry. 'You mean . . . ?' he began, before realising he had no idea what she meant.

'I don't really know,' she said again, her expression stricken. 'It was like waking into a nightmare, I don't even know how long I'd been there – not long, I shouldn't think – but suddenly I was myself again. So I swam.'

'And you survived,' said Finley, partly to bolster her, because she had turned very pale.

Cynthia glanced at the garish surroundings of the Bonlo Superstore, as though to double-check. 'Well, I'd done all that swimming, hadn't I? I was trained, I was at my peak – and I swam for my life that night. Clawed my way out of the water, packed my bags, got a taxi to the station first thing. Never went back.'

She picked up her coffee cup and took a long glug. Finley, under the impression she needed a moment, reflected on how casually she had spoken of being stabbed, in comparison to how shaken she seemed by this. But then, when he tried to imagine what it would be like to wake up in the dark, cold embrace of the sea, it was almost impossible. As she had said, it was the stuff of nightmares.

'You mentioned ghosts,' he said cautiously. 'Is that what you think this was? Some kind of haunting?'

'Don't you?'

'I—' Surprised that she had batted this back to him, Finley faltered. 'Well, it definitely sounds *strange* . . .'

She gave him a look that was almost disappointed. 'You know, this hasn't just happened to me,' she said, a little pointedly. 'After I left, I started looking into the history of that place, and the first thing I discovered was the alleged suicide of a woman called Jacqueline Fairchild. You know about her, I assume?'

Finley nodded. He had been wondering if – or rather, *when* – that name would come up.

'I did a bit of digging after that, spoke to the receptionist on the phone, pretended I was part of an official, follow-up investigation. She confirmed that nobody liked that room, hardly anyone ever stayed there – and, if they did, there were usually complaints. But when I started looking earlier – to when it had been a bunkhouse, or taken over by the Navy in the war – nothing very strange emerged, no unexplained deaths as far as I could find. So I think this started with Jacqueline,' said Cynthia, her magazine creasing beneath her elbows as she leaned forward. 'Somehow, she lost her life at that hotel – and for some reason her spirit's still there.'

Finley tried to keep his face blank – he was striving to remain sceptical – but he couldn't help but feel that Cynthia had it *wrong*. What was it Dawn had said? *The stories about that place are far older than the 70s . . .*

'And perhaps that would've been it,' Cynthia said, scratching her arm again. 'Perhaps it would've been enough, knowing about Jacqueline. But just a few years after I'd been there, the body of a young woman called Michelle Lei, who had also been staying in that room, washed up in East Crescombe, not far from where Jacqueline had been found. Not far from where I had been.'

Again, Finley had been anticipating the mention of Michelle, but hearing it all laid out like this made him feel like someone had turned up the air conditioning to full blast.

'That messed me up a bit,' said Cynthia, shaking her head. 'First, because it could've been me, couldn't it? Almost *was* me. Then those papers would've said *I* was the copycat suicide – my poor mum would've had to read that! But also . . .' Cynthia's scratching intensified. 'I could've stopped it, couldn't I?'

'How?' asked Finley, with such vehemence that the young mother at the neighbouring table gave him a resentful look – apparently, her baby was finally asleep. 'I mean,' he went on, more quietly, 'what could you have done?'

'I don't know,' muttered Cynthia, into her sleeves, 'but I should've done *something*. Warned someone, maybe even tried to get the place closed down. But I wasn't thinking beyond my own escape, it hadn't occurred to me it might happen again. That poor girl ...' She shook her head, unable to continue.

Finley thought he was beginning to understand why Cynthia had written that review on Guidebook, why she had agreed to meet him this evening, and why she was being so open with him. Clearly, she was carrying a lot of guilt, but he suspected her motivation was altruistic too.

'Are you still in the police?' he asked, though he thought he already knew the answer.

Sure enough, Cynthia shot him an incredulous expression, before saying, 'No, I left years ago. Around the time Michelle died, actually. But even before that, I hadn't been all there. That summer, it changed me. I came back jumpy, paranoid. I couldn't sleep, and I'd still get those blackouts when I lost track of where I was, what I was doing—'

'Wait,' broke in Finley. 'You mean, that didn't stop when you left?'

Cynthia shook her head. 'It's not as bad now,' she said. 'It's only once in a while ... But yeah, it still happens.'

Finley wondered whether this was the most alarming thing she had said so far. He had assumed that whatever Cynthia had experienced had been restricted to Crockers Nest, yet here she was implying its influence extended well beyond Crescombe – and well into the future.

'The sarge said it was because of the stabbing. Well, that was convenient for him, wasn't it? Suddenly I was all jittery and confused, so he could get rid of me permanently.'

'God, I'm sorry . . .'

'Thing is,' went on Cynthia, without acknowledging Finley's sympathy, 'I didn't really care, not at the time. All the work I was doing – the job I'd been dreaming of since I was a little girl – it didn't matter anymore. Not in comparison to this new theory I had, about what was going on in that place.'

'Which was?' prompted Finley, wondering whether she was about to mention Cora Crocker.

Instead, though, Cynthia said, 'I don't think Jacqueline Fairchild jumped into that water. I think she was pushed.'

'*Pushed?*'

'It's not that unbelievable, is it?' asked Cynthia. 'I'd tracked down some of Jacqueline's family, you see, and all those years later they were still in shock that she'd done such a thing. She'd had a bit of a year, they said; a bad break-up, and someone had crashed into her car. So she hadn't been swinging from the chandeliers, exactly, but she was all right. Crescombe was just a bit of a break for her, a change of scenery. Her diary was full of plans for when she got back home – her brother was going to take her to buy a used car, stuff like that.'

Finley wondered whether Cynthia was clutching at straws here. 'It could've been an accident?' he suggested, thinking of the treacherous coastline around Crescombe. 'Maybe she went for a walk and slipped?'

'On her own? In the middle of the night? Nah.' Cynthia made a clicking noise with her tongue. 'That ghost or spirit, whatever it is, it's angry. I could feel it, in here.' She kneaded a knuckle against her chest. 'That's why she's hanging around, I reckon. Someone did that to her.'

'Who?' asked Finley, feeling shivery again at the words *her, she*.

'Well, that's the question, isn't it?' said Cynthia. 'Personally, I reckon Jacqueline had a lover, going by all those dreams . . . He could have lured her out there.'

'You mean, someone she met in Crescombe?'

'I don't know!' cried Cynthia, throwing up her sleeves. 'That's as far as I got. I couldn't do any more, not without police resources, and not without going back there.' She grimaced again. 'Not without the Fairchilds, either, and they were—Well, they were getting a bit fed up with me by that point.'

She seemed to retreat beneath her fringe, and Finley wondered how much of an understatement 'a bit fed up' was.

'Around that time, I heard the hotel was closing anyway,' Cynthia went on. 'It was a couple of months after Michelle's death. And I decided – well, some doctors decided for me – it was better if I stopped going over and over it all. I mean, what was I hoping to achieve? What was going to happen if no one was there?'

Her voice, which had grown stronger and louder as she had spoken of her theories and investigations, had faded once more, and she had begun to scratch and fidget again.

'Was that why you wrote that review on Guidebook?' Finley asked. 'Because the hotel reopened, became Crockers Nest?'

She nodded, somehow looking both sheepish and defiant. 'I check, every so often.'

They looked at one another, and Finley wondered what, if anything, she wanted from him. Did she think he had more intel on Jacqueline Fairchild's death? Was that another reason she was here?

Because he could tell her, couldn't he? As much as he was trying to repress his own theories, he had more confidence in them than her speculations. *You should have looked earlier*, he could say, just as Dawn had advised him. He could tell Cynthia about Cora, about Delmore, about all of it. He could tell her about himself.

But what good would it do? It wasn't difficult to read between the lines of her story: *that messed me up a bit . . . some doctors decided for me . . .* The woman before him had been deeply damaged by what had happened to her in Crescombe. Would it really be helpful, opening it all up for her again?

Possibly, Cynthia would say yes – at the very least, she might want some choice in the matter. Before Finley could find out, though, he became aware of a faint chiming noise, one that was reminiscent of church bells, and Cynthia withdrew a clunky old phone from her bag, which she jabbed at with a fingertip.

'That's me,' she said. 'Got to get ready for my shift.'

'Your shift?' repeated Finley, though, as he said it, he saw she was pulling on a sky-blue fleece that – unnoticed by him until now – had been draped over the back of her chair. 'Wait, do you *work* here?'

'No need to sound so surprised,' muttered Cynthia, adjusting the plastic name badge now pinned to her chest.

'I didn't mean . . .' Finley floundered. 'I just . . .'

'I've always felt there's something very grounding about supermarkets,' she said, with a fond glance around Bonlo. 'They're like the opposite of haunted houses, aren't they? Very bright and public, even at night. This is the first job I've been able to hold down since . . . Well, since all of that stuff. And it suits me, working through the night, only being by myself during the day . . .' She attempted a laugh. 'I mean, what's going to happen here – something's going to jump out at me from behind the frozen veg?'

Finley tried to smile, but could find little humour in her reasoning. True, he too had found Bonlo's familiarity a comfort when he had walked through its automatic doors this evening – but Cynthia had stayed in Crescombe in *1989*. It was staggering that, thirty years later, her entire existence was still shaped around her experiences there.

'You won't go back, will you?'

They had both stood up, and though Finley was not particularly tall, he felt he was towering over her. Nevertheless, and in spite of the tremble in her voice, what Cynthia had said sounded more like a command than a question.

'To Crockers Nest?'

'You mustn't,' she hissed, 'you *mustn't*. Call your ... godmother, was it? Call her, get her to board up that room – get her to board up the whole building. But you – *you* can't go back there, you'll only make it worse!'

Finley glanced around, aware that people were starting to stare. It wasn't that he didn't believe Cynthia – obviously, there was overlap in some of their experiences – but he was beginning to suspect she wasn't entirely stable, and perhaps hadn't been even before she'd gone to Crescombe. After all, *he* hadn't experienced any blackouts, had he?

'I'll certainly talk to her about boarding up that room ...' he began, probably untruthfully.

But Cynthia was shaking her head. 'It's not enough,' she said, her voice almost a wail.

'But if whatever it is can be contained ...'

'You still don't understand,' she said and, before he knew what was happening, she had made a grab for his wrist.

Finley almost cried out in surprise. Her grip was surprisingly strong; now, she was less like a mouse and more like a stoat, small and vicious. He had no idea what she was doing – trying to shake some sense into him, perhaps – until she flipped over his hand, revealing the faint pink line that now marked his palm.

'It doesn't just live there, in Crockers Nest – or whatever you want to call it,' she hissed. 'Now, it lives here, in *you*.' She pressed a fingertip to the line and Finley winced, both from the unasked-for touch and the unexpected twinge it prompted.

She knows, he thought, and with a mixture of guilt and dismay he recalled how she had flinched when he'd offered her his hand to shake. She'd known all along, from the moment she'd seen his palm. *That* was why she'd told him so much; she'd been warning him.

To his relief, Cynthia then dropped his wrist, but when she pulled up her sleeve to reveal her own right hand, Finley's stomach seemed to flip over: her palm was bound up in a bandage marked with a brownish line of dried blood.

'Everyone says it's just my eczema,' she told him, 'but I didn't have it before, and it never goes away, no matter how many creams and whatnot I try. It just bleeds and bleeds, every day . . . It never goes away,' she repeated.

Finley, who was starting to feel a little sick, tried to think of something to say, but a second alarm on Cynthia's phone had begun to chime, and she shouldered her bag.

'Don't go back,' she told him. 'Don't become another Jacqueline Fairchild, another Michelle Lei . . .'

Her tone suggested she hadn't quite finished, but she pressed her lips together and without another word, turned and departed the café, dropping her magazine into a bin as she passed.

Finley watched her go – watched her small figure duck between a tower of disposable barbecues and a display of children's jelly shoes before she disappeared between Bonlo's aisles – and, through his growing nausea, he wondered whether he could guess what she had been unwilling or unable to articulate: *Don't become another Cynthia Hart.*

I strike flint against steel and sparks shower onto my tinderbox, like falling stars. Squinting against the sudden glare, I blow gently at the charcloth. It used to take me so long to coax a flame to life; now, it's a matter of moments.

When the candle is lit, I secure it back in the lantern, a little wax dribbling over my knuckles. Instantly, the room brightens. The lantern is an old sailor's light and mostly made of glass, though its brass back reflects the glow of any candle tenfold. My flame will be seen for miles.

I savour the short walk to the window, for the lantern hanging steady from my hand heralds a kind of inverted dawn, and the town will now awaken. I can already hear it happening below; the rousing calls and whistles, the clunk of the cellar doors being thrown open, even the swish of someone cleaving their club through the air, practising. Soon, men will move further along the lane, knocking on doors and tapping at windows, positioning themselves from here to the beach. They will swarm this dark land like bees from a hive, all because of me – or, because of my light.

It would be so easy to snuff it out and throw all their plans into chaos. Some nights, I'm even tempted to let the lantern fall from my fingers. I imagine the crash of shattered glass, the flames leaping free of their casing and roaring across the floorboards, the smoke consuming the room, and me, and everything . . .

Tonight is not one of those nights.

I secure the lantern's handle to the top of the window, where it squeaks as it settles into place, and slide down to sit beneath it, gazing into the gloom. Have you, too, been looking out for my light? Will you really come? Earlier, on the beach, I was certain you would, but now ... It is a long way in the dark.

I lean back against the rotten, rounded window frame and extend a bare foot over the edge, a slight breeze rippling the hem of my nightdress. Perhaps, if you have changed your mind, it will be a relief to pass this evening like any other. I won't have lured you into perilous waters, or towards a confrontation with my cousins. I won't have set in motion something I cannot undo.

The lantern creaks above my head. The window frame digs into my spine. I grow cold. Yet I continue to wait there, crouched in that opening to the sky until I spy another light, just beyond the bay. I wait a little, just to be sure, then I reach up to reclaim the lantern and slide its screen across the glass, dimming the light within. I do this once, twice, three times, in order that that near invisible ship advancing upon the bay knows: we are ready.

Am I ready? I'm not a fool, I understand at least a little of what will happen if you swim to me tonight. My cousins like to boast about the women they've bedded – crudely, cruelly. So, in spite of your pretty words, I know you won't be here for love, or anything like it. I'm a diversion, one that won't last beyond the summer. After that, you will leave and never look back.

And I? I'll be ruined, I suppose. Only, who would know? Who would care? I've been ruined since before I drew breath; since a spirited sailor strayed into the path of a sweet fisherman's daughter, half a world away from where he was born. That was love, or so she said. I have no such hopes for my own heart, only the knowledge that, as long as I stay in this room, guarding this light, it makes no difference what I do.

The candle is half gone by the time I see you. I've been staring out at the sea, trying to follow your progress, but of course you have no light of your own. At last, though, you emerge from the dark water below, your outline pale, insubstantial. It puts me in mind of a jellyfish, or even some kind of phantom rising from the deep, and this feels like a warning. As much as I want this – as much as I want *you* – I'm tempted to smother my light and slam the window shut. Go back. Before it's too late, go back.

Instead, I watch you steal across the little beach where we have spent so many of our mornings, and begin to climb the side of the cliff. I glimpse your fine features, your bright eyes, and my alarm dissolves, washed away in a surge of desire. Perhaps I should be more afraid for you, navigating that perilous slope in the dark, but you are athletic and sure-footed and, above all, a charmed man. As long as you avoid them, nothing bad will happen to you.

For a few moments, I lose sight of you, but I know you're close. I can hear the rustle of your movements and your short, sharp exhalations. I draw back from the window, my body tensing. Suddenly, it seems so futile, all the time I spent teasing the knots from my hair this evening, or that I thought to sprinkle some of the perfumed oil from my jar of petals not just on my skin, but around the room too. It cannot disguise or distract from what you will find here: a desperate little place containing a desperate little person. You have swum all this way – and for what?

When, panting, you finally spill through the window, there's a wildness to you, like the crossing has transformed you into something not quite human. Your face is shiny with moisture, your hair is dripping into your eyes, your clothes are sodden; I've seen you wear less, yet there's something indecent about the way your shirt is sticking to your torso, revealing glimpses of skin. In this shadowy little hovel, where nobody ventures but me, you seem much bigger than I remember.

We stare at one another, both stunned that you are really here, that you really did it. Then you stagger towards me and, to my astonishment, drop to your knees. Still breathing hard, you lower your head, almost bowing, and I move my hands to your wet hair, smoothing it back from your face. My body is reverberating with the same sense of power I'm granted by the lantern: this is not how I expected to feel.

But I am the flame now, hot and bright and trembling – though not with fear. I have summoned you here. I have drawn you to me. Sliding my hands down your face, I cup your jaw, nudging you up. You rise, suddenly large again but, for once, I do not feel small.

When you dip your face to kiss me, I stand on my tiptoes to meet you, pressing my lips to yours with a fierceness that surprises us both. You respond readily, hungrily, your hands roaming over and then under the thin fabric of my nightdress, though it's not enough – not nearly enough. I grip at your damp shirt, urging you from the window, away from the little puddle you and your wet clothes have made on the floor, and, together, we stumble to the bed, our route marked out in watery footprints.

13

The National Gallery

'You look quite tanned.'

From most people, this would have been a compliment, yet Fiona's tone was accusing, as though she felt Finley had been squandering his time in Devon. He decided to ignore her – what was there to say anyway, when her appearance was the same as always? Looking at his twin was like seeing himself through one of those phone filters that changed your appearance to that of the opposite sex; it reinforced that their shared features – their pale, narrow faces, their big blue eyes, their untidy dark hair – were much better suited to a woman.

Finley had just arrived at Fiona's Clapham flat, which was small, warm and full of homely little touches: framed prints of Celtic knots, a crocheted rainbow blanket that looked hand-knitted, a mantlepiece strewn with greetings cards. Fiona, Finley knew, would have been responsible for very little of this décor and, for the first time, he was relieved to be away from all of Mollie's knickknacks.

'How's Lorraine?' Fiona asked. Then, before Finley had a chance to answer, she said, 'So odd, her opening up that guesthouse. What was she in before, recruitment or something?'

Finley had no idea, but was spared having to say so by the arrival of Fiona's partner, Maeve, who was bearing a tray laden with tea and flapjacks. Maeve was freckled and curvy, with long strawberry blonde hair, which today she had arranged into a complicated-looking plait. Having met her a few times before, Finley knew

Maeve to be calm and kind, with a gentleness that softened some of Fiona's pointier moments.

'We're talking about Finley's godmother, Lorraine,' Fiona explained, even though Finley hadn't said a word. 'She's Mum's daffy friend from school or something.'

Despite Lorraine still having been a little cool with him before his departure, Finley felt a stab of annoyance on her behalf. But then, Fiona's godfather was Dominic McClaine, an indomitable surgeon, who also happened to be Mollie's dad. Finley had always been deeply envious of the way Dominic and Fiona had holed up together discussing her medical career, and had often wondered whether Dominic might have warmed to him a little more had he been his own godparent.

Perhaps sensing that he was needled, Maeve said, 'Tell us about Crescombe, Finley. We were looking at photos – it's gorgeous!'

His mood lifting, Finley began to describe the town, its beach, and his work for Lorraine, quickly becoming aware that Fiona seemed completely uninterested in how he had spent the last few weeks.

'Don't you want to hear about the wedding?' she asked, as soon as Maeve had run out of Crescombe-related questions. 'I took loads of pictures – I can show you if you like?'

'I'm all right, actually, Fiona . . .'

She showed him anyway. Mollie was wearing a very lacy dress with a long train, while her red hair was pinned up in ringlets, not unlike a Jane Austen character. She looked extremely pretty – and extremely happy, gazing up at her handsome, be-kilted new husband – but Finley was surprised to find that it wasn't too much of a wrench to see these pictures. They were no worse than what he had imagined, a thousand times before.

Even the sight of old friends from university, or his mum in one of those miniature feathery hats, failed to rouse much regret in him.

Had he been there, Finley knew he would have felt lonely and deeply uncomfortable, and had it been his own wedding ... Was this the sort of day he'd had in mind when he'd imagined marrying Mollie? Now he saw it all laid out like this – the speeches, the first dance, the ceilidh band – he wasn't sure.

'It looks nice,' he said, handing the tablet back to Fiona when he had reached the final picture (Maeve, her make-up smudged, triumphantly brandishing a burger).

He meant it genuinely, but at the same time, *nice* was the only word he could think of to describe it all: nothing less, nothing more.

Once they had finished their tea, Fiona sent Finley to the spare room while she and Maeve made dinner. After his meeting with Cynthia the previous night, Finley had been reluctant to deal with his sister so late, and had booked a last-minute room near the supermarket. Its grey speckled carpet, bright white walls and functional furniture had felt clinical, and not entirely unwelcome after Crockers Nest.

This room was only slightly less minimalist – obviously, it was Fiona's domain – with just a large desk and a sofa bed competing for floor space. Finley studied the prints on the wall, which included an old railway poster of Edinburgh and a gruesome diagram of human anatomy, before his eye moved to the framed photographs propped at the back of the desk.

It surprised him Fiona had bothered with something so sentimental, and while most of the pictures were of her and Maeve, Finley was interested that he made two appearances himself. The first was in a family shot from their parents' thirtieth wedding anniversary party, but the second was of just him and Fiona, eating ice creams at Leith Shore. Finley had hated this picture when it had been taken – by Mollie, who'd been delighted that they were both sitting cross-legged and slightly turned towards one another, and that they had independently chosen the same ice cream (mint choc chip); not since childhood had they looked more like twins. Now, though, Finley found he quite liked it – or perhaps he just liked that Fiona had kept it.

The bookshelves above Fiona's desk were stacked with thick, dog-eared medical textbooks, plus a few biographies and one or two popular science books that looked completely inaccessible to Finley. After pulling a face – he didn't trust people who didn't read fiction – he retrieved *Underworlds* from his bag, which he had almost finished on the train from Devon. Idly, he flicked through it a few times, and a little sand sprinkled from its pages, like sparks after a magic spell.

Smoothing a few grains between his fingers, Finley thought of Crescombe, wondering whether it really had worked some kind of enchantment on him – for how else could he explain his near apathy towards those wedding photos? He certainly felt different after a few weeks of being away, and outside, and properly by himself for the first time since the break-up, without The Book Bothy or his parents to fall back on. And, he had to admit, he felt different after a few weeks of *Megan*.

But then, dusting the last of the sand from his hands, Finley found himself staring down at that thin line on his palm, which was growing more livid by the day. *It just bleeds and bleeds*, Cynthia had said. Until now, as unnerving as that room could be, he'd never considered that his time in it might have a lasting impact on his life *beyond* Crescombe.

When he was called through to the kitchen, Finley discovered a feast laid out by the open window: a vast risotto, crusty bread and an extravagant-looking salad all jostled for space on the little tiled table. His stomach growled: when was the last time he'd had proper, home-cooked food?

'This looks amazing,' he said, adjusting his chair so that the potted herbs lining the length of the wall weren't tickling the back of his neck.

'It's all Maeve's doing,' said Fiona, which Finley knew was unlikely to be false modesty.

Once they had praised the risotto, which tasted as rich as it smelled, and performed a perfunctory toast, there was a natural lull in the conversation while they ate, during which Finley glanced sideways at Fiona. The size of the table meant they were sitting very close – their bony elbows kept threatening to knock together – and perhaps it was this proximity to his twin that made Finley absolutely certain that she was about to bring up Mollie's wedding again.

'Okay, I have a question,' he said, to prepare them for the seemingly random topic he had decided to introduce as an alternative. 'Do you believe in ghosts?'

Fiona's response was instantaneous, as he knew it would be: 'Of course not,' she snorted. 'What a weird thing to ask, Finley.'

'Why?' he wondered.

'Why is it weird or why do I not believe in them?'

'The second one.'

'Because – where do I start? – because there's absolutely no scientific evidence for the existence of a soul or spirit or whatever bit of you allegedly gets left behind. We're just *animals*: we live, we die, we decay, we're eaten by worms.'

'So glad we're talking about worms and decay over dinner,' murmured Maeve, with a mournful glance at her risotto.

'Is that what you think too?' Finley asked her.

Maeve took a sip of wine, considering her response. 'I don't have especially strong feelings on the matter,' she admitted. 'But I'm not sure you can definitively say there's no such thing as ghosts, or that there's no proof: plenty of people swear they've seen them, sensed them, caught them on camera . . .'

'Plenty of frauds,' broke in Fiona. 'Plenty of nutjobs.'

'Plus, ghosts are so *universal*,' Maeve continued, with a patient look at her partner, 'and that's interesting, isn't it? They're a shared belief, they probably appear in every culture throughout history...'

'So do dragons,' said Fiona bluntly. 'Are you saying they exist too?'

Finley had never considered this before, and found the idea irresistible. His sister, however, was radiating disapproval, and he suspected that if anyone but Maeve had put forward these points, Fiona's responses would have been even less restrained.

'Why are you asking this, anyway?' she demanded of Finley.

In truth, he suspected it was because he had known Fiona would react exactly like this; her logical, scientific mind, plus her inability to entertain anything farfetched or fanciful, could always be relied on. And perhaps, for once, this was exactly what Finley wanted to hear, especially after that unsettling discussion with Cynthia.

'There are rumours that East Crescombe – the oldest part of town, where I'm staying – is haunted,' he said.

Now, Fiona rolled her eyes. 'Of course it is.'

'Some say there's a fisherman's widow, waiting for her drowned husband to return,' continued Finley, deciding to relate what Megan had told him, rather than try to explain whatever was going on with his room (where would he even start?). 'And there's a story about a smuggler who knocks on your door, only when you open it—'

'Is it possible,' Fiona interrupted, 'that if there were dodgy activities like smuggling going on, these rumours were spread deliberately? To scare people away?'

'Well ... yes,' Finley admitted, recalling Megan had made this very same point. 'One of the locals said pretty much the same thing.'

'There you go, then,' said Fiona. 'A *rational* explanation.'

She looked unbearably smug – so much so that Finley regretted instigating this conversation. He tried to think how to change the subject, but it seemed Fiona was just warming up.

'But you *want* to believe it, don't you?' she said. 'For you, the more impossible something is, the more it appeals. When Finley was younger,' she went on, to Maeve, 'he was obsessed with myths. You know, like Hercules and Achilles and that idiot who flew too close to the sun and . . .' Clearly, Fiona was reaching the extent of her classical knowledge. 'And *Spartacus*!'

'Spartacus was a historical figure, not a myth,' snapped Finley.

Fiona ignored him. 'And now it's *ghosts*!' she cried, with an infuriating little laugh. 'Is that really what you've been doing this summer, ghost-hunting—'

'I haven't been *ghost-hunting*—'

'With some bored, lonely divorcee?'

'She's not—'

'Is that why you didn't go to Mollie's wedding?'

'*Oh, fuck off about that stupid wedding!*'

Fiona pulled back her neck, looking, for a moment, like a startled chicken. Finley had to press his lips together to block an instinctive apology. He would never speak to anyone else like this – but then, no one else wound him up like this.

'Give it a rest,' he told Fiona, in a quieter voice.

Fiona, however, wasn't done yet: 'She was your friend . . .'

'And now she's my ex,' said Finley, firmly.

'But—' his sister began, and this time he interrupted her.

'Fiona, she *cheated* on me.'

He said it for emphasis, but as Fiona's eyes bulged, he remembered: she didn't know. Nobody did – apart from, weirdly, Megan. The break-up had already been so miserable, so painful, and Mollie's unfaithfulness had felt like a reflection on him; he hadn't been enough.

'What?' Fiona gasped.

'Yeah.'

She continued to stare at him. '*What?*'

Finley knew she wouldn't argue anymore, but he was still annoyed. Maybe he should have told her earlier, but she should have been on his side regardless. It felt good to stand up to her – though now he had started, it was difficult to stop.

'And, by the way,' he continued, because this was still bothering him from earlier, 'Lorraine isn't *daffy* – or bored, or lonely. She's warm, and funny, and she's actually doing really well after all that shit her ex-husband put her through.' With a surge of affection, Finley vowed to properly patch things up with his godmother. 'She might not be your idea of the perfect godparent, Fiona – she might not be *Doctor Dominic McClaine* – but *I* think she's great.'

Another silence followed this outburst, one that Finley hardly registered because blood was now pulsing in his ears. Maeve picked up her wine glass and took a very long sip.

At last, Fiona spoke, her voice small: 'To be honest, I don't think Dominic is that perfect.'

'What?' snapped Finley, annoyed that this was the part of his rant on which she'd chosen to focus.

'He hasn't really talked to me for years, not properly. He's been very distant with me since—Well, since I came out, I think.'

She lowered her gaze, and Maeve extended a hand around the salad bowl to interlace their fingers.

'Well, he's a dickhead,' said Finley, because as maddening as he found Fiona, he now had an uncharacteristic urge to punch something – preferably Doctor Dominic McClaine.

'I shouldn't have said all that about Lorraine,' Fiona continued, still unnervingly contrite. 'I'm sure she *is* great. I guess I was just a bit jealous – Dominic didn't even bother to say hello on Saturday.'

Finley gave a grunt of disapproval, though he was a little distracted: *Fiona* had been jealous of *him*.

Maeve, meanwhile, began to top up their wine glasses with her free hand. 'Ah, feck him,' she said, in a resigned tone that suggested this was far from the first time she'd heard about Fiona's godfather. 'Feck the lot of these McClaines, don't let them ruin our evening. Now, come on – eat up.'

Finley and Fiona did as they were told, and for the rest of the meal let Maeve lead the conversation towards safer topics. After a dessert of pavlova passed without further incident, Maeve went to call a cousin in America, and the twins returned to the cosy living room armed with some cheap whisky Finley had picked up before arriving.

'Dad would be horrified by this,' he said, tilting his hand so the whisky sloshed around his tumbler.

'Ach, the stuff Dad likes is undrinkable,' said Fiona.

They spoke for a while of a Highland trip in which their dad had got them horribly lost searching for an obscure distillery, before their reminiscing turned to other childhood holidays, many of which had featured the McClaines.

'You, me and Mollie were best friends back then,' Fiona mused. 'We were equals.'

Finley didn't say so, but he couldn't recall much equality; those holidays had largely involved Fiona bossing him and Mollie into playing doctor (her) and patients (them).

'When you both went off to St Andrews, it was bad enough,' continued Fiona, 'but then you *got together*...' She winced. 'I knew then that I'd lost Mollie for good. She would always prefer you – unless you broke up, and then she wouldn't be able to stand either of us.'

'But that's not happened, has it?' said Finley, marvelling that Fiona seemed to care so much about Mollie's opinion of her. 'You two are still friends, aren't you?'

'It's not the same...'

Again, it was staggering for Finley to contemplate the idea that Fiona might be envious of him, and that *he* had taken something away from *her*. It felt like a grown-up version of the squabbles they had once had over toys and trading cards.

'I guess that's why I kept going on about the wedding,' said Fiona, contemplating the remains of her whisky. 'I thought if I could fast-track you back to friendship, things could go back to the way they were.'

'I don't think it works like that.'

'No . . .' agreed Fiona sadly. She downed the rest of her drink, which seemed to restore her, because she then leaned forward conspiratorially. 'You know, between us, I think Blair's a bit . . . *dim*.'

'Yeah?'

She pulled back her chin in scorn. 'He kept calling the canapés *canopies*.'

Finley smiled. 'I think that's allowed when you're that handsome,' he said, though he gleaned a certain satisfaction from this intel nevertheless.

In spite of swearing at her over dinner, this was the best they had got on for as long as Finley could remember, which was perhaps why he then said, 'Hey, Fiona? Can I ask you something? As a doctor?'

'Of course,' she said, looking startled but pleased.

He could understand her surprise: he had never, ever sought medical advice from her before. Her being a successful doctor was still a source of bitterness for him, and she probably knew it. For the moment, however, Finley forced himself to push aside his pride.

'What's this?' he asked, showing her his right palm.

'What, that scar?'

'It's not a scar,' he said, though he could see why she had thought this. 'I haven't cut myself or anything – at least, I don't think I have.'

Fiona frowned, then took his hand. 'And you haven't just been leaning on something?' she asked, scrutinising the mark.

'No, it's been there a while – a few days, maybe?'

'Does it hurt?'

'Not really.' Though as he said it, he remembered that stab of pain he'd experienced after returning from the cove, and even the twinge Cynthia had prompted yesterday evening when pressing her finger to his skin.

'Is it itchy?'

'A little.'

'Could be a rash,' Fiona allowed. 'Sometimes you get ones made of wee bumps that kind of join together . . .' She sounded unconvinced. 'But this isn't really my area of expertise – you should probably see a dermatologist if it doesn't go away.' She folded up his palm and returned his hand, adding, 'I think you'll live, though.'

Finley tried to smile. 'Thanks.'

He had been hoping Fiona would diagnose something mundane and treatable, so he could dismiss it from his mind, along with that image of Cynthia's bloody bandage. Now, he wished he hadn't brought it up at all. The fact that it had stumped Fiona made it seem even worse.

'You are looking after yourself, aren't you?'

Finley grimaced: this was *exactly* why he never asked her advice.

'I know you know this, but you need to take extra care of your extremities,' she continued, apparently unable to help herself.

'*Fiona* . . .'

'I'm just saying,' she told him. 'If they have to cut off your feet, I'll be raging.'

Wavering between annoyance and amusement, Finley was plunged into a memory, one from half a lifetime ago. He was lying in the hospital bed, listening to the bleeping of machinery, staring up at the large square ceiling tiles, breathing in that same sterile scent he now smelled every time he injected himself. It was late, but Fiona had been there, curled up in a plastic chair beside him.

He wasn't sure why she'd been allowed to stay – she too had been just fourteen at the time, a child. But it had been a comfort to have her there, more so than finally knowing what was wrong with him, and more, even, than the fresh, foreign insulin coursing through his blood. Fiona, he had known, wouldn't let anything happen to him. She had practised for this – faced down his tormentors on the bus – and, like Orpheus, she would fetch him from the underworld if she had to.

He looked at her now, trying to brush an unruly curl of hair from her eyes, as he so often did himself. They weren't identical twins, of course, but sometimes it felt like they were – and that they had split in two not as an egg, but that night in the hospital. Most people had no way of knowing how their life might have turned out had it not been derailed by something huge, but Finley did. He'd always been able to track exactly who he should have become, had diabetes not rendered him self-conscious and directionless, just by watching Fiona.

At least, that's how it had always felt. But as Finley topped up their tumblers, he wondered, for the first time, whether he actually wanted Fiona's life. Aside from her disappointing book collection and horrible godfather, it was a nice life, but it wasn't *his*. Maybe his diabetes hadn't caused a derailing, then, more a diversion – and though Finley still couldn't see where he was heading, one thing he was better equipped to deal with than his sister was the unknown.

Before leaving Clapham the following morning, Finley dipped into a small, maze-like bookshop. It had a cheerfully disordered air, with handwritten signs hanging at odd angles and books piled up on threadbare pouffes and spindly chairs, waiting to be shelved. Somehow, though, Finley found exactly what he was looking for: an earlier collection of stories by the author of *Underworlds* and

Ovid's *Heroides*, through which he intended to reacquaint himself with the story of Hero and Leander.

The Book Bothy had been lighter and neater, yet Finley was irresistibly transported back to his old bookshop as he walked between the crammed shelves of this unfamiliar one, the wooden floor creaking beneath his feet. It was the smell, he decided. As fond as he was of the musty and slightly sweet scent of old books, he thought he preferred the crisp, papery aroma of new ones; of all those fresh words waiting to be read.

His train back to Devon wasn't until after lunch and, while he was passing through London, Finley had decided there was something he wanted to see. Around half an hour later, he emerged from one of Charing Cross's many exits – the wrong one, it turned out – and began to negotiate his way across gridlocked roads and through the flocks of pigeons and tourists in Trafalgar Square. He was always surprised to find he quite liked London. Obviously, it paled in comparison to his native Edinburgh – a far friendlier and more manageable city – but London's size and bustle made it easy to feel anonymous. Right now, as he headed towards the imposing outline of the National Gallery, with its domed roof and pillared portico, he could have been anyone.

Even Delmore seemed reduced here. The National Gallery housed just one of Delmore's works – *the* work – while everything else had either remained at The Delmore Experience or been distributed to smaller galleries and private collections. Over the past few weeks, Finley must have become used to the pedestal on which Crescombe placed the artist, for it felt strange that Delmore had so little presence in these hallowed halls of art; as Finley passed multiple paintings by Constable, Stubbs, Turner, never had Delmore's status as a one-hit wonder been more apparent.

Nevertheless, a few people were gathered around *Hero's Bay*, which was hanging in a corner of the gallery between a late Turner and the door to the Impressionists' room next door. Though Delmore's dark, bold seascape certainly stood out in comparison to the brighter or more realist fare displayed nearby, Finley had no doubt that what had drawn this small crowd to the painting was not its artistic merit but the mystery of its light – *Cora's* light.

Otherwise, *Hero's Bay* provoked no reaction in him – which was strange, because this was *it*, not another blurry reproduction on some tourist tat. Perhaps Finley had grown too used to seeing the same image all summer. Perhaps it was the presence of all these people, or that, here, the painting was jostling for attention with so many others. Or perhaps Ambrose Montgomery, despite his ulterior, moneymaking motive, had been right, and *Hero's Bay* really did belong in Crescombe.

Regardless, maybe it was no bad thing that Finley found the real painting a little underwhelming. Until now, he had been trying to treat his investigations into Cora Crocker as a kind of intellectual diversion – a natural offshoot of his smuggling research for Lorraine – but if he was going to entertain the possibility that something supernatural was going on, he was certain that it had started with Cora. However, if she had latched onto him in the same way she had Cynthia – and if her influence extended beyond Crescombe – surely Finley would be feeling more than mild indifference right now? *Hero's Bay* had been painted about Cora, maybe even *for* her.

Was Cynthia mistaken, then? Could the lasting effects she had described be attributed instead to fragile mental health, post-traumatic stress, a tendency to sleepwalk? But that didn't explain her *hand* . . .

Maybe he should listen to her anyway – maybe he shouldn't go back. He could return to Fiona's place for a bit, or get a train back up to Edinburgh and stay with his parents until he figured out what to do next. After all, he had already avoided Mollie's wedding. What would he be going back for?

Megan was his immediate, unchecked thought, though he disliked the idea of being buffeted from one woman to another. There was also Lorraine to consider, because it seemed a poor way to repay her hospitality, bolting before their booklet was complete – and with their relationship strained.

And what about Cora herself? If some connection did exist between them, was there any way to sever it without returning to Crescombe? It might be easier in the short term for Finley to retreat to Edinburgh and pretend none of this had ever happened, but what would be the long-term consequences of his cowardice? Not just for him, but for others, too. He, like Cynthia, would find it hard to forgive himself if another body washed up in East Crescombe – and he hadn't forgotten that his own godmother was living under that roof.

His eye lingered on the darkest, deepest parts of *Hero's Bay*, while Cynthia's words echoed in his mind: *It's like, I woke up in the sea.* If the kind of loop Dawn had described truly was playing out in Crescombe, it had cost Jacqueline Fairchild and Michelle Lei their lives – and Cynthia herself had been living something of a half-life since, in spite of her escape. Finley was under no illusions about his own swimming abilities; if he ended up in that water, he'd never survive.

Only, it wouldn't come to that, would it? Unlike his predecessors, he knew something of what – or rather, who – he was dealing with. And he wanted to know *more*. He had come this far, discovered this much; he was too invested to back out now. If he returned to Crescombe, surely it was only a matter of time before he could piece together what had happened to Cora that summer – and forewarned, Finley thought, with a final, apathetic glance up at *Hero's Bay*, was forearmed.

'I've started a new painting.'

I make a small, interested noise, but I'm not really listening. I'm trying to concentrate on committing all of this to memory: our entwined legs, your briny smell, the sensation of your fingertips stroking up and down my lower back. I need to lock it in my mind for later. You talk of your painting, your past, of anything that falls into your head as though we have endless nights to waste, but we don't. Our time together is rapidly draining away, and I will need something to sustain me after you've gone.

'It's about you.'

I lift my head, my ear warm from where it's been pressed against your bare chest. 'A portrait?'

I don't know how to feel about this. I had thought, when you started swimming here at night, you had given up trying to capture my likeness.

'Not a portrait, more . . .'

You trail off, and it's strange to see you falter. In everything else you sound so certain – even those words of love you've taken to murmuring into my skin, which I neither need nor believe. I know this is still just a game to you; a chance to pretend we're those mythical lovers whose tale consumes you, separated as they were by a similar stretch of dark water. None of this is any more real than that old story.

'I'm not sure I can explain the painting,' you tell me now, 'but you'll understand when I'm done – when you see it.'

Will I see it? Do you imagine me swishing through a London gallery, peeking at this painting from behind a lacy fan? Surely you realise how impossible that would be.

I study your face, which is so handsome it makes me ache, for some sign that you're not as naïve as you sound. But you are smiling to yourself, eyes now closed, one hand resting behind your head, as though you're still basking in the sun during one of our swimming lessons.

I replace my head on your chest, listening to your deepening breaths, the thump-thump of your heart, and just when it seems you've fallen asleep, you murmur, 'I think it might be the best thing I've ever painted.'

I hope you are right. Truly. But I sense your attention to all things is fleeting – how could it not be, when your life is rich and full? This is why you talk so easily, so idly. It might be consuming you now, this painting, but soon you will forget it for another, just as you will forget this dingy little attic room and these secret, stolen nights.

Just as you will forget me.

14

Westcliff

Being from Edinburgh, Finley was no stranger to a place being entirely taken over by festivities, but it was still jarring to return to what felt like a very different Crescombe. The promenade, which was draped in pastel-coloured bunting, was now crammed with food carts, craft stalls and fairground rides. Irresistible fried-food smells mingled with the fresh sea air, and the town's usual soundtrack of breaking waves and keening gulls had been replaced by blaring music and the happy shrieks of children being spun over the beach in giant teacups.

The Drowned Painter had set up its own beer stall by the beach – an attraction that was proving popular with the adult contingent of the many visitors that had descended upon Crescombe over the weekend. The day after his return, Finley spotted Megan among the staff serving under its bright blue marquee, her cheeks unusually pink from working in the heat.

'Oh,' she said without enthusiasm, when he reached the front of the queue, 'you're back.' Then, after wordlessly handing another customer the deposit for their pint glass, she asked Finley, 'What do you want?'

He assumed she meant to drink but, even so, this was not quite the reunion he'd hoped for. To save face, he ordered a beer, then retreated to the low wall by the beach to drink it, feeling both sheepish and disappointed. He tried to console himself that she was just busy, but the more he thought about it, the more he wondered what exactly he'd been expecting.

Still, the encounter increased his resistance to the Crescombe Art Festival, something he tried to share with Lorraine later that afternoon. They were on good terms again – helped, no doubt, by the fancy tin of biscuits he had brought her from London – and now she seemed to feel it was safe to give him more tasks, the latest being drafting an invitation for a Crockers Nest cream tea.

'I thought this festival stuff was just a few venues around the town turning into galleries for the week?' said Finley. This, at least, was what he had understood from the dark mutterings of locals.

'Well, that's how it started,' said Lorraine, frowning at the reception computer through her winged reading glasses. 'But now it's a bit bigger than that, with the regatta and whatnot . . . Do you think we should do plain or fruit scones?' she asked suddenly. Then, before Finley had a chance to answer, she turned to the stairs and bellowed, 'Martin! *Martin!*'

Within seconds, the handyman materialised, a thick coil of cables hanging from the crook of his elbow.

'Martin, I've a load of unhappy campers on my hands, because apparently the Wi-Fi doesn't work in the garden,' Lorraine wailed, in reference to all the tents and campervans that had sprung up around the guesthouse. 'Can you get it, you know, extended for the week or something?'

Briefly, Martin met Finley's sympathetic gaze. 'Um, I'm not sure that's—'

'*Try*, Martin!' Lorraine beseeched him. 'I can't have them tramping in here all day, they're doing my head in.'

As Martin departed, Lorraine removed her glasses with a sigh, and Finley noticed she had forgotten to draw on one of her eyebrows. It was quite distracting – the other looked permanently raised in suspicion – though, for the moment, he thought it kinder not to say anything.

'But this whole thing's over by Sunday, right?' he asked, as much for her sake as his own. 'After that, Crescombe goes back to normal?'

'Sunday night, technically,' said Lorraine. 'It ends with the fireworks. You know, it's all in the programme, my love ...'

She handed him one of the festival brochures – which were piled around the guesthouse, always within reach. The front cover featured a night-time shot of the other side of Crescombe, where Westcliff House was lit up from within, and the headline: Experience (Del)More in Crescombe. This was in reference to the museum extending its opening hours for the festival, in order that visitors could stand at Delmore's easel after sundown, when the murky view would most resemble the one depicted in *Hero's Bay*.

Despite his resolve in the National Gallery, Finley had felt wary about returning to his room at Crockers Nest. He'd spent the train ride back picturing cracked mirrors, mysterious bloodstains, the pages of his books ripped out and strewn across the floor ... But everything had looked exactly as he'd left it, though somebody had obviously been in to clean; that soapy, floral smell that was neither soap nor flowers was back, so perhaps it was cleaning product.

As the week drew on, Finley experienced nothing more unusual than the blowing open of the porthole window. Perhaps it was because of the festival: the guesthouse's extra visitors meant there was a great deal more noise and activity than normal, which was to say nothing of the random blasts of music, boat horns and drunken shouting that now regularly pierced the peace of East Crescombe. Or maybe, Finley thought – and despite Cynthia's insistence to the contrary – by leaving he had stretched whatever connection had existed between him and Cora Crocker to breaking point, until it had snapped like a rubber band. More likely, though, she had never been here at all.

Whatever it was, Finley was happy to remain at the guesthouse for most of the festival week, helping Lorraine and, by extension, avoiding Megan – for the more he reflected on their encounter at the beer stall, the more embarrassed he felt. By Sunday afternoon, however, his godmother finally seemed to realise how much of his time she'd taken up, and shooed him towards town, instructing, 'Go and see some art.'

As it turned out, Finley enjoyed drifting in and out of all the cafés, gift shops and other establishments that were temporarily doubling as galleries. Much of the art on display was crowd-pleasing – pretty watercolours of the town at sunset, cutesy illustrations of seals – but every so often something more striking would capture his attention, such as the old video footage of fishermen being projected at the back of the post office, or the vast driftwood sculpture that twisted and multiplied around the old bandstand, like a hydra.

In the town hall, Finley was astonished to find a black and white portrait of a smiling *Megan*. In spite of how mixed up he felt about her, he couldn't resist taking a closer look, unable to believe she had allowed somebody to take her photo and display it like this. And, sure enough, as he drew nearer, he realised that although the woman in the portrait had the same tousled blonde hair and wide-set eyes, she looked a little older, and warmer too; her smile, which displayed no gap between her front teeth, was open and unguarded.

SANDRA SALTER
(1965 – 2006)

Sandra 'Sandy' Salter was a local artist, sculptor and glassmaker. Born here in Crescombe, she attended the Falmouth School of Art before returning to her home town, where she married and remained until her tragic death by drowning at the age of just 41.

Salter specialised in 'found' art, which she would create from objects collected around our beautiful coastline. In her later years, she began to specialise in sea glass, fusing it to create dazzling new artworks. Her final collection, *Refraction*, is considered the high point of her career, and was nominated for several prizes.

Salter was a founding member of the Crescombe Art Festival, and a passionate believer that the town should nurture local talent and be recognised as a historic hub of all mediums of art. The Sandra Salter Memorial Grant is awarded annually to a local artist of great merit, and generously sponsored by The Delmore Experience.

Finley glanced around at the glimmering fusions of coloured glass suspended nearby, which were casting rainbows around the hall and looked like something magical that might hang above a merbaby's crib. With an ache, he thought of Megan – though if Sandy Salter had drowned, why had she told him her mum had died of cancer? Because it wasn't as though he had been prying, that day at the cove; Megan had offered up the information freely.

Finley read the caption again, wondering if he was imagining a slight resistance to the legacy of Delmore. There was also an uncanny echo of Delmore's demise, the drowning of this relatively young artist at the peak of her powers. The real *Hero's Bay* would have been long gone from Westcliff during Sandy Salter's lifetime, but was it ridiculous to imagine that she too had fallen victim to its supposed curse?

Finley was still ruminating on this when he entered the next exhibition space, which smelled, inexplicably, of rich, garlicky food, and he realised he'd descended through the back door of Marina's. Perhaps because its gelato stand was doing such a roaring trade on the promenade, the entirety of the restaurant's back room had been devoted to the Art Festival. It even had a gallery attendant in the form of the dark-haired waitress, Giulia, who had chatted to him and Megan over their dinner – though tonight she was more diverted by her phone.

This temporary gallery was dedicated to the ancestor Giulia had told them about that evening, the eponymous Marina Vitali, who had made a kind of pilgrimage to Crescombe after Delmore's death. As well as the photorealistic painting of grapes and bread that had previously caught Finley's attention, and the large-eyed self-portrait that, before, had been hanging above the bar, there were half a dozen other still lifes and paintings of figures, plus several landscapes, most of which looked like they had been inspired by Vitali's native Italy.

It was all extremely skilled but, no doubt informed by what he had just seen from Sandy Salter and others, Finley couldn't help but feel there wasn't any cohesion to Vitali's work. She felt like an artist who hadn't quite found her style – in that respect, she was not unlike Delmore, though, unfortunately, she had never painted her *Hero's Bay*.

'Thanks,' Finley called to Giulia, who murmured a goodbye without looking up from her phone.

He made his way towards the exit – which, enterprisingly, was through the restaurant – and outside found the queue snaking from Marina's gelato stand clogging up the promenade. The noise was immense: buskers now competed with the music of the fair and the overexcited chatter of a pair of local radio presenters being blasted over gigantic speakers. A gangly boy who was definitely underage was selling drinks from a cool box and, after paying far too much for a beer, Finley began to swig it down, too quickly.

Then he was taken by the current of the crowd, buffeted between the various stalls and entertainments – a caricaturist, a one-man band, a group of Morris dancers. He caught sight of a few familiar faces: Dawn, beckoning to the throng outside her hut; the vicar holding up a mallet after scoring surprisingly high on the strong-man game – and was that *Lorraine and Martin* on the big wheel, sharing a stick of candy floss? Finley could have stopped and waited to speak to any one of them, but in spite of this – in spite of all these people – he felt suddenly, horribly alone.

Eventually, he managed to wrestle his way to the beach wall, dropping from the promenade like a single scale from some immense, serpentine creature's hide. It was growing dark now, but the beach was hardly less busy than during the day, speckled with drinkers gathered around the smoking remains of barbecues, and children allowed to stay up late. Finley felt fuzzy – that beer had gone straight to his head – and a little disorientated. Behind him, the promenade was a glittering strip against the gloom, and this was mirrored by the stark band of gold the sunset had left over the sea, giving Finley the unnerving sensation that he was trapped between Crescombe and its reflection.

All at once, he felt full of foreboding. He shouldn't have come back here. What if he really did become trapped? What if he was trapped already? He gripped the neck of his empty beer bottle, trying to fend off his mounting unease, then felt cool fingers slide into his free hand, while a voice in his ear breathed, '*Get out of here . . .*'

Heart lurching, Finley whirled around, only to find Megan at his side, still in her Drowned Painter T-shirt, a grubby tote bag slung over one shoulder.

'*What?*' he asked, though he wasn't sure she had spoken.

She gave him a quizzical look, then tugged at his fingers, which were clasped in hers. 'I said, do you want to get out of here?'

'I—' Finley's brain was still trying to catch up with what was going on. 'All right, yeah.'

Mutely, he allowed her to pull him across the sand for a few paces, before asking, 'Where are we going?'

'I know a good spot to watch the fireworks,' she said, as though this was pre-arranged.

'Aren't you working tonight?' He tried to sound aloof, which was difficult when she was still leading him across the beach, towards West Crescombe.

'Keith took on extra people for the weekend,' she said. 'We've been really understaffed this year, it's been crap. But there's loads of us now – he won't notice I've gone.'

Finley wondered whether this explained her rudeness of the other day – and perhaps she'd registered his tone, because she had let go of his hand. He still felt a little annoyed with her, but now he was more annoyed with himself that this connection between them had been broken. As unpredictable as she could be, and as powerless as he felt in this friendship or whatever it was, Megan remained the only person in Crescombe – perhaps the only person anywhere – he genuinely wanted to spend time with.

'I need some dinner,' she announced, when they had reached the end of the beach.

This turned out to be a hot dog and a stripy pink bag of pick-and-mix sweets from a stand by the harbour. Megan wolfed down the former in seconds, then chewed and crunched contentedly on the sweets as they began to ascend the hill to Westcliff House. After Finley refused her third offer to share with the explanation that they would play havoc with his blood sugar, she accepted this with a serious nod.

'You're welcome to keep these for later, though,' she said, withdrawing three tubes of pale purple sweets from the bag and pulling a face.

Finley took them, reading, 'Parma violets . . .'

'So gross,' Megan scoffed, through a mouthful of fizzy cola bottles. 'Like eating old lady soap or something.'

Finley pulled at the ends of a packet, inhaling the smell within. Until a few weeks ago, it would have transported him back to his childhood, but now . . . This was sweeter and more synthetic, but the substance of the scent was that same smell that he hadn't been able to identify at Crockers Nest: it was *violets*.

He pictured the fragments of pressed purple flowers from the tinderbox. Those scraps were too old to have retained any scent, but the association with Cora made Finley uneasy; suddenly, it felt unlikely that, for the past few weeks, he'd simply been smelling some violet-scented air freshener or cleaning product.

Quickly, he shoved the violet sweets into the pocket of his shorts and changed the subject to one that always guaranteed a response from Megan: 'Where's Skipper?'

'In the flat with Dad. He's actually not too bad with fireworks, but just in case.'

As they proceeded up the hill, Megan expanded on Skipper's festival experience, which had apparently involved a lot of begging for food, plus trying to climb into the water at the hook-a-duck stall. The coastal path was surprisingly busy, and they overtook several people who, like them, were navigating the earthy track by the light of the temporary lanterns affixed to the fence posts. At first, Finley assumed everyone was trying to find higher, more peaceful ground for the fireworks; then he remembered this was the last night of The Delmore Experience's extended opening hours.

He wondered whether this was where Megan was leading him – perhaps she had access to some balcony or rooftop. But as they approached Westcliff House, which looked imposing in the dark, she continued to follow the path skirting the cliff until, at a spot that looked entirely unremarkable to Finley, she ducked between the rails of the fence, turned on the torch of her phone, and advised, 'Watch your step.'

Finley didn't need telling twice. Even without the beam of her phone and the glow from The Delmore Experience, he would have been able to tell by the tug of the breeze and the rumble of the water that the sea was close. He swallowed. Vertigo was not one of his principal neuroses, but that didn't mean he was keen to stumble about in the dark next to a cliff edge.

'I thought you might want to see this,' said Megan, up ahead.

Finley couldn't imagine what would have given her this idea, but he peered at where she was pointing. There was not, as he had feared, a sheer drop, but a series of grassy slopes and ledges that gradually descended to sea level.

'I think this is where Delmore would've swum from,' explained Megan. 'It's where *I* swim from, when conditions are good.' Then, correctly reading concern in Finley's silence, she added, 'Honestly, in the day, you're mostly in danger of being divebombed by gulls.'

But Delmore didn't just swim in the day, thought Finley.

It emerged that Megan intended one of the uppermost ledges for their firework-watching, where, fortunately, there was plenty of space. As they settled on the grass, and Megan withdrew from her bag a bottle of white wine she had pilfered from The Drowned Painter, Finley gazed at the inky view of the other side of Crescombe with a grudging kind of respect for Delmore. Clearly, the artist had not lacked athleticism to have swum that distance in the first place, but to have made the journey in the dark, and at the mercy of unpredictable waters ... He must have been motivated by more than just boredom, or swagger, or even lust. Finley frowned, considering something he hadn't really thought about before: what if Delmore had genuinely *loved* Cora?

After taking a sip of the stolen wine, which was sweet and too warm, Finley gestured across the water with the bottle and asked, 'Would you swim that? Right now, in the dark?'

Megan turned to him. 'Are you daring me?'

'God, no!' he said, alarmed she might suddenly dive in. 'I just—I'm trying to get my head around the fact that Delmore did.'

'Maybe he didn't?' said Megan. 'Maybe he just painted it?' But she didn't sound convinced, and Finley thought she must have a better grasp of the artist's personality than that.

'Well, let's say he did,' Finley continued. 'He wouldn't even have been able to see as much as we can now.'

His palm twingeing, Finley indicated Crockers Nest, the most easterly glow over the water, which tonight was boosted by the campers in the garden and car park. Above it was a lone light, right on top of the cliff.

'If Delmore really did follow Cora's light, like Leander followed Hero's,' he said, ignoring his hand, 'it wouldn't have been any brighter than that one up there, above Crockers Nest.'

Megan, who had been swigging at the wine, lowered the bottle. 'What light?'

'You see where the guesthouse is?' he said, circling its brightness with a finger as though pointing out a constellation. 'If you look up from it, there's a light on its own. I guess it's someone on top of the cliff – up at Crockers Point, isn't it called?' he added, remembering he had seen a light up there before – Martin's, he had thought – that night he'd walked across the dark beach.

After a pause, Megan shook her head. 'Are you messing with me or something?'

'I—' Finley faltered. 'Are *you* messing with *me*? Up there!'

He jabbed towards it, more urgently this time, and his palm throbbed in protest. But Finley continued to stare into the darkness: if anything, the light was clearer than the rest; warmer, and strangely pulsing – almost like a twinkling star. How could she not see it? It was right there. Unless ...

Bang!

He jumped as a cheer erupted around the bay, and golden sparks began raining from the sky. Finley had looked up at the fireworks automatically, and when his gaze returned to the opposite cliff, flecks of gold were imprinted over the darkness. He blinked a few times, trying to clear his vision, and as the impression of the fireworks faded he realised the light – whatever it had been – was gone.

'Here we go,' said Megan, leaning back on her elbows as two, three, four more fireworks bloomed over the water. Then, perhaps noticing that Finley was still squinting at the opposite shore, she offered him back the bottle of wine, saying, 'Hey, I'm sure you're right.'

Finley wasn't particularly reassured by this, but took a swig of wine and reclined on his own elbows, trying to focus on what he knew to be real: the fizzing colours in the sky; the constant breath of the sea; the warmth of Megan's skin against his own, where their bare knees were just touching.

Sometime later, when an especially frantic series of bangs earned a round of applause from the beach, Megan laughed. '*Oooh*,' she said, deadpan, '*ahhh*.'

Finley smiled. 'This was your idea,' he reminded her.

'Oh, it's the same every year,' she said, with a shrug. 'I don't think they ever change it up . . .'

She yawned, flopped back on the grass and untied her hair, presumably so it wasn't bunched up beneath her head. She sounded so nonchalant about it all – so over it, even – that Finley gave voice to a question he had been pondering for some time: 'Do you ever think about leaving this place?'

'I did.'

It wasn't clear whether she meant that she had actually left, or merely thought about it, and Finley once again realised that there was a lot he didn't know about Megan Salter. He wanted to ask her more – about her past, about her mum, about *everything*. But as he looked down at her, with her hair fanned out around her head and her face aglow from the flickering fireworks, all his words deserted him.

They held one another's gaze for a long time, Megan's large eyes very dark in the gloom. Then slowly, deliberately, she reached up to hook a finger around the collar of his T-shirt and draw him closer. He obeyed this gentle pull until it stopped and they both froze, a few inches of space between their noses, though it felt to Finley there was much more separating them, and she was gazing up at him from some deep watery realm.

Or perhaps he was the one submerged, because the sound of the fireworks was muffled now, no louder than popping bubbles. Everything felt smudged. How much of that wine had they drunk? And what was really going on here? Maybe he should just—

'Shh,' said Megan, touching a finger to his collarbone.

Finley blinked, confused. 'I didn't say anything,' he whispered.

'You're thinking too much,' she whispered back.

This was true – of course it was true – so before he could think anymore, Finley kissed her.

And as he shut his eyes and closed that short, airless distance between them – as he sank into the dreamy otherworld she seemed to inhabit – he abandoned more than just his persistent, pointless worries on the shore. In the absence of thought, he could *feel*: her soft mouth, her warm face, the rapid rise and fall of her chest, half wedged under his. Plus, he was more aware, perhaps than ever before, of his own body, which had turned bold and curious.

Megan gripped at his arms, urging him nearer, every so often making a small, low noise of approval or even impatience that Finley found almost overwhelming. Her breath was sugary from the sweets, sharp from the wine. He cupped her cheek with his palm, partly to stop his hands wandering elsewhere too early and partly to check that she was really here, that this was really happening. But as his fingers made contact with the side of her face, he realised her skin was wet – was she *crying*?

At once, he drew back, ready to apologise for coming on too strong – and, to his alarm, saw the side of her face was stained not with tears, but with something darker.

'What is it?' she asked, propping herself up on her elbows again.

'You're ... you're bleeding!'

'What?' Megan touched her fingertips to the side of her face, then looked at Finley's hand. 'No, *you* are ...'

She took hold of his wrist and they both stared at his palm. Finley's stomach dropped: the line on his hand seemed to have burst open, for it was dotted with beads of blood that glinted in the light of the fireworks.

'What did you do?' Megan asked.

'I—Nothing,' he said, so abruptly she drew back a little. 'It's nothing.'

'You need a bandage or something.' Megan glanced back at The Delmore Experience. 'I think there's a first aid kit at the front desk ...'

Finley didn't move. He was picturing Cynthia's bandage, with its rusty line of dried blood. He tried to push the image away. He didn't want to think about it – any of it. He wanted to go back to just feeling, to that rapturous oblivion of kissing Megan.

'How did you do it?' she asked.

'*I* didn't do it,' insisted Finley and, again, it came out snappish. 'It was—' He hesitated, forcing himself to say it: 'I think it's something to do with *her*, with Cora.'

Megan let go of his hand, her expression unreadable. But Finley was distracted by the dark blotch still staining the side of her face. He wished she would wipe it away; it looked like he had *marked* her.

In an attempt to explain, he began, 'The other day, I met this woman who once stayed at Crockers Nest ...'

'What?'

'Earlier in the week, when I went to London . . .'

'Oh, that's where you disappeared to.'

Finley rubbed his head with the back of his hand, his palm aching. Why did she keep interrupting? He was finding it hard to focus, and closed his eyes, but that only made the banging and crackling of the fireworks sound louder. He thought he could still see their lights flickering beyond his eyelids – and *what* had that light been up at Crockers Point? Why hadn't Megan been able to see it?

'I think I'd better check on Skipper.'

Finley opened his eyes, discovering she had stood up, for he was now looking at her knees.

'Megan . . .' He didn't know what he was going to say, only that this had all gone horribly wrong and, somehow, he had to save it.

'See you, Finley.'

And before he could say or do anything else, she had scrambled back up towards The Delmore Experience and disappeared into the darkness.

For a few seconds, Finley just sat there, staring numbly at his bloody palm. It wasn't fair – this wasn't his fault. *So go after her*, he told himself, furiously.

'Megan!' he called, stumbling as he got to his feet, a little woozy from the wine. '*Megan, wait!*'

He emerged from between the fence rails to see her hurrying towards Westcliff House, its lawn almost resembling a battlefield, illuminated as it was by a crescendo of explosions overhead. When she disappeared into the building, Finley followed, still calling her name. She seemed to have let herself in via a side entrance, its door covered in flaking blue paint. With his uninjured hand, Finley pushed at its iron handle, not expecting it to budge, and was surprised when it swung open to admit him.

Inside, he stepped into a long, narrow corridor, one he guessed had once been used by servants, jumping as the door slammed shut behind him. It was dark and smelled dry and dusty. Once the echo of the door had subsided, it was also unusually quiet, considering the commotion outside.

Remembering Adrian had mentioned a flat above, Finley jogged along a few passageways until he found a narrow staircase. At the top, he opened his mouth to call Megan again, then pressed his lips together, reconsidering. What was he *doing*? She had run off for a reason – and he had effectively just barged into her house.

He had to go, only now he wasn't sure of the way out. It would have helped if it hadn't been so dark, but he couldn't see a light switch – or, for that matter, any lightbulbs. And why was it so *quiet*? The soles of his trainers slapping against the stone floor sounded very loud as he tried to retrace his steps.

Then, ahead: a glow. Gratefully, he raced towards it, surprised to then find himself in Delmore's quarters. Finley recognised it from his first visit – the mahogany furniture, the botanical wallpaper – only the museum had gone all out for the festival, because it looked even more authentic than before. The rope barriers marking the path through the room had gone, several candelabra had been lit, and the surfaces – the mantlepiece, the chest of drawers, even the damask covers of the four-poster bed – were covered in clutter: letters, sketches, books. It gave the eerie impression that the artist had only recently left – or that, somewhere nearby, he was still around.

But where was everyone else? The late opening of The Delmore Experience had been heavily publicised – surely this place should be packed? Finley turned, intending to rejoin the main route through the museum, but hesitated at the doorway of the artist's studio.

He shouldn't go in. Something about this whole evening was off. Yet in the same way that he might pick at a scab or peer at a piece of roadkill, he couldn't help himself stepping over the threshold.

The reproduction of *Hero's Bay* had been moved to the easel. It loomed very large in the small corner room, more like a window than a piece of artwork. As Finley edged towards it, the candles lining the walls were causing light and shadow to dance across the surface of the canvas, so it almost looked like the seascape was moving. Only . . . Finley frowned, crept closer. *Was* it the candlelight? Because the more he stared, the more those pitchy waves seemed to swell, the more those dark clouds seemed to circle; the more the painting looked *alive*.

'What . . . ?'

As he had outside, after the first fireworks, Finley blinked hard, trying to correct his vision. But the dark sea and sky of the painting continued to writhe.

It's a screen, he told himself firmly; a clever bit of technology designed to mimic the view that had inspired Delmore; a surprise the museum had arranged for its festival visitors. But as he raised a trembling, bloody hand towards the painting and felt cold air slide beneath his fingers, he knew he would meet no resistance from either glass or canvas. This really was an impossible kind of window; now, he could hear the roar of the waves and wind beyond. And a voice:

'*Finley* . . .'

She was coming. He knew it because the scent of her was flooding his nose, his mouth, his whole mind: *violets*. And he knew it because mixed in with his fear and bewilderment, there swelled a stronger, stranger emotion; a potent mix of joy and regret, something so bittersweet he could have sobbed. He didn't understand what it was, what it meant, only that this feeling was *not his own*.

Finley tried to back away from the painting, but something icy was coiling around his wrist, like an invisible hand clasping him in place. He yelped, tried to tug himself free, but now the painting's beam – *her* beam – was burning brighter and brighter. It was an interrogation light, boring into his soul; it was a searchlight, hunting him down.

He shut his eyes, still fighting against the pull of the painting. What would happen if he was dragged right through? *They say it's cursed*, that man in the pub had said. *They say that it brings bad luck, that it brings* death...

'Finley...'

Already turned from the dazzling light, Finley dared to open his eyes, and there she was. Or at least, her outline – her long dress, her wild hair – because most of his vision was obscured by blotchy imprints of light. She was moving towards him, her hand outstretched like his, and, in spite of his terror, he wanted to reach out and touch his fingers to hers...

But he mustn't – he *mustn't*. With one monumental last effort, Finley wrenched himself free of the painting's grip and, like Perseus in the gorgon's lair, screwed shut his eyes once more, stumbling towards what he hoped was the way out.

Old William refuses to send for a doctor, says we can't afford the expense, but I think he's afraid of discovering how little time he has left. So, we all pretend we can't hear his guttural coughing, even Ma, though it goes on and on. At night, it makes me think of some ghoulish creature dragging its chains through Crockers Nest, like the stories we've spread around the town have come true.

I feel indifferent to the thought of my uncle's death. We share no blood, and though he's not a good or kind man, he's never tormented me as much as the others. Usually, he pretends I don't exist. At some point, he must have allowed me to stay here, must have honoured the promise Ma made to her dying sister that she would look after me, but I'm not sure I owe him much gratitude for that.

No, it's what will follow Old William's death that interests me. Without him, Ma and Edwin will wrestle one another for control of the family. Even as my uncle lies upstairs, coughing and coughing and coughing, they've already begun.

'The time to do it is now,' says Edwin. 'This mist is a gift, but one that won't last.'

For once, I hope he's right. I've not dared to show my light through the fog, so you, as well as the ships, have stayed away. And I miss you – *I miss you*.

Ma doesn't respond to Edwin, though she's jabbing at her darning. Usually, such a chore would fall to my nimbler fingers but, in Old William's absence, I'm huddled over his accounting book, trying to remember the letters and numbers my mother taught me. My cousins are doing nothing at all. Tom is even slumped over the kitchen tabletop, his breathing heavy.

'You can't resist this forever,' Edwin tells Ma.

'Your father said—'

But he cuts across her: 'Father's own father did it! Other Crocker generations have done it!'

And this, I think, is why he can't let this go: by taking this risk, by doing this wicked thing, my feeble, half-blind cousin will finally prove himself not just a man, but a Crocker.

'Your father's father did it at Westcliff!' Ma reminds him. 'When there was nothing there, nobody to bear witness. Crescombe has changed, boy. You might be able to keep the visitors from here with threats and ghost stories, but you can't stop them taking moonlit strolls on their own side of town.'

'That's why we'll do it here, at Crockers Point.'

Ma gapes at him. 'On our own land? Under the nose of the coastguard!'

'He's not a concern,' says Edwin, in reference to the barrels we leave on his doorstep. Then, glaring at Ma with his remaining eye, he continues, 'It'll be one time – one night. Don't we owe it to this family? We need to think to the future – because look at this shithole!' He sneers at the kitchen's cracked flagstones, its mould-spattered ceiling. 'We're already crumbling away.'

Ma's dark eyes narrow and I wonder if Edwin might feel the bite of one of her needles. This is her house, and she has her pride. Then I realise it's he who has stung her. She's proud of being a Crocker. Old William plucked her, an ungainly fisherman's daughter, from poverty and she rewarded him with strapping sons and a loyalty that's never wavered. The family fading, the family threatened . . . That won't be her legacy.

'I'll talk to your father again,' she says, then raises a hand to Edwin's objections. 'And perhaps we'll request an audience with Harcourt.'

Something spasms in Edwin's scarred cheek, but he nods. I think back to that conversation between Ma and Harcourt outside Westcliff House – does Edwin know she stood up for him that night?

'Enough, then,' she decides, bundling up her mending. 'I've got jobs for you boys, before you creep off to The Crown.'

On her way towards the door, she smacks Tom around the head, startling him awake. Grumbling, he and Bill lumber to their feet, following their brother out of the kitchen. I take my time laying down Old William's prized pen and replacing the inkwell's lid, waiting until Edwin is far ahead. But when I finally rise from the table, a hand hooks under the neck of my dress and yanks me backwards.

'Why do you smell like that?' Ma demands in my ear.

'Like what?' The front of my collar presses into my throat, and my heart flutters in panic. Like the sea? Like *you*? Though the mist has kept me from both, perhaps those scents have been absorbed into my skin.

'Like . . .' Ma pushes her nose towards my neck and inhales sharply. 'Like *flowers*.'

It's the violets, I realise, with another lurch. I thought I'd scrubbed that scent away.

'I was making a posy for my uncle's room,' I whisper, 'to freshen the air.'

It's a stupid lie. I don't even know how I thought of it, though sometimes I see fine ladies on the promenade with little baskets of flowers they've collected from the hedgerows. But I'm no lady, and Ma . . . I doubt Ma has ever picked a flower in her life.

I wait for her rebuke, but then feel her grip on the back of my collar slacken, like I'm a kitten being released from its mother's jaws. Massaging my throat, I half turn, still expecting a slap, but, to my amazement, Ma is looking down at me with watery eyes.

'Well, where is it, then?' she snaps. 'I'll take it to him.'

'I—I need to finish it.'

And before she can recover herself, or lash out at me for witnessing her emotion, I dart towards the door – though not before I see her fumble for the hem of her dirty apron and begin to dab at her eyes.

15

The Promenade

'No more fortunes,' moaned Dawn, who was reclining on the low wall between the promenade and beach. 'The festival has finished me. My inner eye is closed.'

Her outer eyes were closed too, Finley noted; screwed up against the weak sun trying to break through the cloud overhead. For the first time in a while, Dawn was wearing what Finley had come to think of as her normal clothes – her leggings, her baggy hoody – which, right now, made her look a little like someone who had set off for a run and then thought better of it.

'Erm, would you be available for a bit of advice, rather than a fortune?' he ventured.

Dawn deigned to open one eye. 'Do I have to move?'

'No,' Finley assured her, relieved not to have to squash into her stuffy little hut again.

'All right,' she said, her voice growing muffled as she buried her face in the crook of her elbow.

Finley sat beside her on the wall, following the progress of some volunteers in hi-vis jackets who were patrolling the beach with litter-picking sticks. Over the past few days, Crescombe had reverted to its sleepy seaside town status; there had been a mass exodus of visitors on Monday, as though nothing about the town could have tempted them to stay beyond the festivities, while the stalls and rides had disappeared from the promenade by midweek. Finley had watched it all being packed away as he had roamed the town centre, trying to avoid both Crockers Nest and Westcliff, yet feeling caught between the two, like a wriggling fish in a drift net.

'Is this about the ghost?' prompted Dawn, from under her arm.

'Yeah ...'

Following that night at The Delmore Experience, Finley had run out of both logical explanations and denial: he was being haunted. Maybe not by Cora's *ghost*, exactly, but by her memories, her feelings ... He shuddered, recalling that strange emotion that had surged through him when wrestling the pull of the painting. He hadn't just seen her, smelled her; in that moment, he had *been* her.

'You're still experiencing something, then?' asked Dawn. 'In Crockers Nest?'

'Yeah, and—Well, in other places too.'

'Oh?' Dawn raised her elbow to look at him. 'Where?'

Stomach churning, Finley remembered barrelling out of The Delmore Experience and through the festival crowds, half wild with fright. Then he thought of that phantom figure diving into the dark water at Crockers Beach, and even the light on the eastern cliff that only he could see.

'Just other parts of Crescombe,' he muttered vaguely.

Apparently, this was interesting enough to rouse Dawn into a sitting position on the wall, though Finley thought he'd rather she didn't look at him; it was one thing to accept he was being haunted, quite another to actually talk about it.

'I was thinking ...' he began, haltingly. 'Last time, when you talked about residual energy – I was thinking, that *is* what this feels like. But then, if it's not specific to one place ...'

'Crescombe could still count as one place,' she pointed out. 'Like I said, I believe it's especially susceptible to the supernatural, because of its shape.'

As she had the other week, Dawn traced in the air the outline of a letter C that had toppled over, and Finley remembered what she had said about energy being trapped in the town's cauldron-shaped bay. At the time, he had thought it nonsense, but now he wasn't so sure. Even if there was something in it, though, that didn't explain why that energy was still lingering with Cynthia ...

'Do you feel something is trying to communicate with you?' asked Dawn.

'I—No, I don't think so.' But then, wincing, he recalled the voice he had seemed to hear as he'd stood before that painting: *Finley* ...

'Then it's probably unlikely it's an intelligent spirit,' mused Dawn. 'If it's anything like Michelle described, it's probably still residual energy, even if there are discrepancies. Don't forget these terms, these *rules*, are made up by the living – the dead don't have to abide by them.'

Finley, who didn't find this as reassuring as perhaps she'd intended, stared out at the sea, whose greyness appeared almost gloopy today, like liquid mercury. Automatically, he began looking for Megan, but she remained as elusive as she had all week. Considering she hadn't answered any of his texts – and considering the size of Crescombe and how frequently they usually bumped into one another – Finley suspected she was actively avoiding him. And who could blame her? Of all the many ways he had humiliated himself over the years, bleeding over a girl while kissing her was right up there.

He looked down to find he was picking at a loose thread of the bandage he now had to wear on his right hand. Maybe he should tell Dawn about his wound. Maybe he should tell her everything. But, as unruffled as she was, Dawn had said she didn't mess around with the dead – and Finley didn't need to be warned that this was dangerous.

Instead, then, he braced himself to ask, 'Can it be stopped?'

Because this was why he had sought her out, wasn't it? He couldn't carry on like this. Since that night at The Delmore Experience, he'd barely been able to sleep, or eat, or do anything, other than dread whatever came next. He was so exhausted and anxious, he didn't feel like himself at all – at times, he feared he *wasn't* himself, not entirely. But if it was too late to leave Crescombe without this following him, as it had Cynthia, his only option was to try and do something about it here, now.

Dawn took her time in responding, raising her knees and tucking one ankle over the other. 'As I told you before, this isn't my area of expertise,' she said. 'There are, as far as I'm aware, various things you can do to cleanse a space of a ghost: sage, salt, a full-blown exorcism ... Apparently, one of the most effective ways is simply *asking* it to leave.'

Finley stared at her: did that really work?

'But, again, we're not exactly talking about a *ghost* here, are we?' continued Dawn. 'We're talking about *memories*. This isn't a pest problem, it's likely a recording of trauma, which, under certain circumstances, plays over and over. It's not intelligent, so you can't reason with it – trying to do so would be like bargaining with an old tape player – and it's not as though you can destroy that tape player, because in this case it's Crockers Nest, or maybe even Crescombe itself.'

Hopelessness began to seep through Finley, weighing him down like sodden clothes. 'So, there's nothing I can do?'

'That's not exactly what I said,' Dawn told him, with an almost teacher-like look. 'You can't destroy the tape player, but you might be able to record over the memory.'

'I—What?' said Finley, who was getting lost with this analogy.

'The trauma!' she cried, now seeming almost frustrated with him. 'There's a reason that memories get stuck, a root cause to it. If you can figure out what happened, it's possible you could find a way to prevent it from happening again.'

'But I thought you couldn't reason with a residual haunting?' said Finley, who still wasn't sure he was following this.

'True,' Dawn allowed, 'but you might be able to find a way of changing something here, now, in the present – something that disrupts the loop that's been playing over and over. That stops it, even.'

'And that's happened before?'

'Of course,' said Dawn, before admitting, 'Maybe not *often*, but I believe it's possible ...' She shifted on the wall, trying to find a more comfortable position. 'I once heard about a haunting up in Northumberland, back in the 50s – at least, that's when it started. It was Christmas Eve, and there was a terrible, unexpected snowstorm. This family, the Millers, were driving through it on their way back from midnight Mass, and they reached this remote crossroads where the stop sign had blown over. So they didn't stop – and they didn't make it. A vehicle was coming along the other road, a tractor or snowplough or something ...'

Dawn waved a hand to indicate she either didn't know or couldn't remember the details. Briefly, Finley wondered whether she was making this up on the spot, though that wasn't preventing him from picturing it all: the sleepy family driving through the night, carols still ringing in their ears, anticipating food and presents and warmth that, for them, would never come.

'Afterwards, there were often accidents at that crossroads, and always in the run-up to Christmas,' Dawn continued. 'Accidents that had a certain ... pattern. Those that survived them – because there *were* survivors – all said it had started to snow just beforehand, even if the weather had been mild. They all said the junction's stop sign had blown over, no matter how securely into the ground it had been fixed. And every survivor swore that, as they approached that crossroads, they had been startled by a set of headlights, which they'd swerved to avoid – that was how half of them had ended up veering off the road, or towards another vehicle. But those headlights hadn't been there, not really – or, not for a long time. They'd only appeared for a moment, only been seen by those drivers – and whatever car they'd belonged to had left no tyre tracks in the fresh snow.'

Finley shivered, though he wasn't sure if he was responding to the dark, chilly scenes she was evoking, or the undeniable overlap between this story and his own.

'The locals began to avoid that junction, especially around Christmas,' Dawn went on. 'Millers' Crossing, they started to call it, and took the long way round. Still, there were always out-of-towners who didn't know what had happened – or did, but didn't believe it would happen to them. And so it went on, for years and years.'

'Until?' Finley prompted.

'Until somebody went up there, one Christmas Eve. I forget who he was now: a survivor himself, or a relative of one of the victims – or maybe he was just a fed-up local. But he went up to Millers' Crossing in the dark, and he waited. Then, just after midnight, it started to snow, and the stop sign blew down, and he saw those headlights come speeding towards him . . . So he stepped into the road, right into the car's path, waving his arms – I think he had a torch or flares or something – and shouting "Stop!". He stood there, and he faced down those headlights until they were right on him. Dazzled, he closed his eyes, fearing the worst, then he heard the screech of brakes and felt the icy spray of the car skidding to a halt . . . When he finally dared to look again, there was nothing there: the road was empty, the snow undisturbed. But he became aware of the faint rumbling of an engine behind him, and so he turned and saw, just for a second, two red rear lights on the other side of the crossroads, disappearing into the darkness.'

Another chill prickled across Finley's back. 'And after that there were no more accidents at Millers' Crossing?' he guessed.

As Dawn shook her head, he still suspected she might have been making it all up – but maybe it didn't matter. Because he thought he now understood what she meant; how an action in the present might disrupt the looping echoes of the past.

The trouble was, in Dawn's story the source of the trauma was clear, whereas Finley still had no idea what had happened to Cora Crocker. Even if he assumed she had drowned, like Jacqueline and Michelle, it wasn't enough to simply survive; to go *on*, like that car into the night. *Cynthia* had survived, yet Cora remained – in Crescombe and in Cynthia herself. So either Dawn was wrong and it wasn't possible to alter this recording from the present, or Cora's trauma was rooted in something other than her untimely death.

Stumped, Finley gazed out to sea, where, finally, he saw her: *Megan*. She was in *Sandy Bottom*, leaving the little harbour tucked into West Crescombe, and Finley wanted to jump from the wall, run towards the shore and wave until she saw him. He wanted to apologise for bleeding on her – though, really, he knew she was avoiding him over more than just a botched kiss. Out of everybody, she was the one in whom he'd confided the most about Cora and the haunting, yet she remained cynical about . . . Well, about *all* of it. And if she didn't believe even half of what he had told her, what the hell did she think was going on with him?

To Finley's disappointment, Megan steered her boat not towards the beach, but out to sea, where she began to skirt the stretch of coastline that included The Delmore Experience. Possibly she was heading to the coves beyond Westcliff, maybe even the same one they had visited together. And as much as Finley wanted to go back to that day, as he watched her retreating form he wondered whether maybe she was right to avoid him.

Whenever he thought back on their kiss – which he did, frequently – his mind seemed to get stuck on how Megan had looked afterwards; a little dishevelled and confused, the side of her face stained with his blood. He couldn't seem to shake it, that primal, almost ritualistic image. It put him in mind of a branding, the kind an animal might be given to mark it for slaughter.

It was only a bit of blood, he told himself – yet it was forcing him to confront something he may have overlooked. In returning to Crescombe, Finley had understood he might be putting himself at risk, but he hadn't considered whether that risk extended to anyone else – except, perhaps, Lorraine. He had assumed he was on his own in this, but *was* he? The effects of the haunting, he now knew, were not exclusive to the guesthouse; what if they weren't exclusive to *him* either?

'Speaking of ghosts,' murmured Dawn.

'Huh?' Finley had almost forgotten she was there, but now saw the fortune teller was also watching Megan's progress around the bay.

'Oh – nothing.'

Dawn closed her eyes again, angling her face towards the virtually non-existent sun. Finley wanted to press her on what she had meant, but suddenly remembered the tarot card Megan had accidentally drawn, almost at this exact spot: *DEATH*.

Another chill trickled down Finley's back. But hadn't Dawn said that the cards weren't supposed to be interpreted literally? That Megan's card hadn't necessarily been about death, but about . . . What had it been? Something about change, something about letting go? He turned back to Dawn, wanting it all explained again, but instead something made him ask, 'Did you know her mum?'

'Everyone knew Sandy Salter,' said Dawn, who seemed to sense Finley's mind was on Megan.

'What was she like?'

'Vibrant.'

Finley, who had expected some kind of platitude – *a true free spirit, a talent gone too soon* – thought this a more interesting description. It seemed to suit the smiling woman whose portrait he had seen at the festival.

'And she died of cancer?' he continued, cautiously.

Dawn opened her eyes. 'Who told you that?'

'Megan did.'

'Really?' Dawn twisted around to face him, her fatigue forgotten again.

Intrigued by her apparent surprise, Finley continued, 'But at the festival, on this plaque, it said she drowned.'

Dawn inhaled, as though to speak, then seemed to think better of it. 'You should probably talk to Megan about this.'

'I don't think Megan wants to talk to me about anything.'

'Ah.'

In silence, they watched *Sandy Bottom* draw level with The Delmore Experience, until Finley thought that was the end of the discussion. Then Dawn appeared to take pity on him, because she said, 'The official story is that, yes, Sandy Salter drowned. That's what it says in her obituary and the bios accompanying her work – as you saw,' she added, as though to cover her back. 'One day, she took out her boat and just . . . didn't come back. The boat floated back to shore entirely empty. Awful,' Dawn concluded, with a shudder. 'The shock of it – you could feel it in the bones of this place.' She rapped a knuckle against the promenade wall. 'But then, of course you could: she'd spent her whole life here.'

Finley wasn't sure Dawn was speaking literally, and that Sandy Salter's death had actually been felt in Crescombe, but he was inclined to believe it. After all, was it so very different to what they had just been speaking about? To Cora, whose life – or perhaps death – had been so impactful that its memory still echoed here, almost two centuries later?

'So, what's the unofficial story?' he asked, after allowing a few respectful seconds to pass.

'Well, there isn't one, not really,' admitted Dawn. 'It's just . . . in the last few months of her life, Sandy was . . . she was fading. She'd lost a lot of weight, she'd lost a lot of energy – because before then she'd always been out and about, collecting her sea glass and so on. So if you were paying attention, it wasn't her dying that was a shock, it was *how* she died . . .' Dawn fixed him with a significant look. 'Do you see what I mean?'

Finley thought he did – and thought he understood why the once vibrant Sandy Salter might have sailed out to meet her fate, rather than wait for it to claim her. So perhaps, at the cove, Megan had been telling him the truth; perhaps she'd even told him more truth than most people knew.

'Megan took it very hard,' continued Dawn. 'I mean, obviously. She was just a young teenager at the time, and she'd always been a bit withdrawn, a bit different – she's more like her dad than people realise – but after Sandy died . . .' Dawn let out a heavy sigh. 'And then one day she just appeared in that *boat* and, well, that spooked people a bit. Still does, I think.'

'Because it was her mum's boat?' asked Finley, before realising: 'Oh, because it was *the* boat.'

'Yes – and yes,' said Dawn. 'And . . .' She fixed him with another shrewd look. 'I don't suppose you've ever seen a picture of Sandy Salter, have you?'

'Yeah, at the festival, it was . . .'

Finley trailed off, recalling his first glimpse of that black and white portrait and how, for a moment, he could have sworn he was looking at Megan. Suddenly he understood why it spooked the people of Crescombe, to see Megan criss-crossing the bay in that little boat, and even Dawn's comment on first seeing her a few minutes earlier: *speaking of ghosts . . .*

Megan was almost out of sight now. She was about to steer *Sandy Bottom* around Crescombe's westernmost tip; in a few moments, she would vanish completely. Finley knew this, but in that moment, as he watched her slow the boat to navigate the rocky coastline, he had the strangest feeling that she wouldn't make it. Maybe it was the effect of the bright but overcast day, which rendered the protruding land very stark against the smudge of sea and sky, but it looked like Megan was trying to pass some impenetrable barrier – or even a vast, ancient arm that, in an instant, might snatch her back.

The mist lifts for a night, revealing a moon so full it lends everything a pearly gleam – the waves, the rocks, the sand – like an enchantment spreading along the shore. At my window, you persuade me to sneak through the house, meeting me at the top of the cliff steps and guiding me down to our little beach. There, we slip into the glimmering shallows, abandoning our clothes on the rock. It's much easier to swim without them. I feel weightless, uninhibited, and as we reach for one another in the water, we too are aglow.

Afterwards, we remain on the sand. I bunch myself up in a blanket you carried from my room, its coarse wool scratching at my bare skin, while you recline beside me, oblivious to any chill. We shouldn't be lingering here; I should never have left my light. But the short time away from one another has made us reckless, and perhaps I sense what you are about to say as you lie there, idly coiling the ends of my hair around your fingers.

'I am to leave Crescombe.'

I've been expecting this, so I don't ask *why?* or *when?* or *what about me?* I don't say anything at all. But it still feels like a great wave has crashed over my body, knocking the breath from my lungs.

'Come with me.'

This is less expected. I turn to stare down at you, certain I've misheard. 'Come with you?'

'Yes.'

'Where?'

'I haven't really thought...' You smile, sweep a hand across the sand. 'I suppose London first, and you'll need to see the family seat in Kent. But what I'd really like is to take you abroad.'

'Abroad?'

'Yes, after we're married, perhaps as part of the bridal tour...'

You list half a dozen places you wish to show me, though I'm still caught on that word: *married*. I assumed you were asking me to leave with you as your mistress, or perhaps a servant you sometimes summon to your bedchamber.

'I don't understand,' I whisper, drawing the blanket more tightly around me, for this feels like a cruel trick.

But you are still smiling. 'Of course you don't, I'm doing this all wrong...' You sit up, prise the ring from your smallest finger, and begin to talk of love and fate and second chances, though the only words I really hear are, 'Cora, I want you to be my wife.'

I let you take my hand, though the ring hangs loose on my fourth finger, so you slip it onto my thumb instead.

'You will have a proper ring in London,' you tell me, folding my palm with your own. 'You will have anything you desire.'

Then you are kissing me, so eagerly we might have been apart for months, and for a moment I want nothing more than to fold you into this blanket, for you to press me into the sand, for us to forget everything but this. Yet I can feel the ring on my thumb, its cool weight unfamiliar, and I push you away.

'I can't.'

The hurt on your face is difficult to bear. 'You can't marry me?'

'It's not—' How can I make you understand? 'No one will accept us, no one!'

You hesitate, knowing it's true, even if you can't admit it. But you recover quickly: 'As I said, we'll go abroad! We'll start anew. I have no need of London anyway. This painting, Cora – it's the start of something for me!'

I shake my head, suspecting you're as naïve about this painting's qualities as you are about mine. 'What about your family? Do you have no need of your mother either?'

You wince. 'I'm not pretending it'll be easy . . .' I think your conviction is faltering, then you cry, 'But this is love, Cora! If we don't even try for the sake of love, what's the point in trying for anything?'

Love. You bandy that word about so carelessly, as though you are rich in it and have far too much to ever use up. As though it means nothing to you at all.

I extend a hand to your cheek, feeling the familiar contours of your face under my water-wrinkled fingers. 'I know you mean to try,' I say, tweaking that lock of your hair that is always so determined to fall into your eyes. 'But once you are back to your other life – your real life – you will see this cannot work.'

It's easy to imagine how it will go. How, at first, you will pretend to be unbothered by the whispers and stares, the disapproval from your mother. But, over time, it will bother you. It will torture you, being shunned for the sake of a coarse little creature whose novelty will be wearing thin. Until, eventually, you will see that you were wrong and everyone else was right, and you will finally fall in line with your mother's wishes, and turn your eye to someone pretty, and wealthy, and uncomplicated.

And what will become of me then? I may know little beyond Crescombe, but the fate of abandoned women is the same everywhere. Here, at least, I'm protected by the promise my mother extracted from her reluctant sister.

Frowning, you take my wrist, lowering it from your face. 'Do you really think so little of my word? So little of me?' You show me my own hand. 'This is my father's ring!'

The truth is, I think so little of myself, and of my ability to exist beyond this town.

You let go of my hand, draw back a little. Your brows are still knitted together; you're looking at me as you did when we first met, when I was a riddle to be solved.

'What would you be staying for, Cora?' you ask. 'Don't tell me you owe your family any loyalty?'

You mean the Crockers and, no, I owe them nothing. But Ma isn't the only one with a promise to keep. My father told me he would come back for me and, with his stone, I promised I would wait for him. He is what binds me to this place, not them: my true family, my blood.

When I don't reply, you ask something else: 'Do you love me?'

The question surprises me; I didn't think it mattered to you, as long as I was here.

I'm not sure I know how to love. I think I loved my mother once – and my father, for giving me the stone, and in a few minutes of conversation a lifetime of hope. And if I were somebody else, I could easily love you, fickle and foolish though you are. But I've lost so much already; I need to hold on to my heart.

If you're frustrated by my silence, you don't show it, though your expression is unusually earnest. 'I think you do love me,' you whisper, leaning back towards me to plant the softest of kisses on my cheek. 'I know you do,' you add, moving to kiss my temple, 'because I know *you*, Cora . . .'

You kiss me again and again, the tenderest of touches across my face, and it is so gentle it makes me ache. Until, this time, it's me who impatiently presses my lips against yours, and you who pulls away.

'We still have a few days,' you say. 'Think on it all. Then light your lantern, and I will come for you!'

You grin, and suddenly you are back: boyish and buoyant again, anticipating your next adventure. You kiss me one last time – a fiercer, deeper kiss I feel all the way to my toes – then stride back towards the sea.

I watch you go, and as you are swallowed by the dark water, I'm filled with foreboding. I shouldn't let you leave like this; we are making some kind of mistake. But then you dive, disappearing beneath the surface.

'Wait!' I cry, as your head bobs up a little later. '*George!*'

I've never used your name before. It feels like a sweetmeat on my tongue, sugary and soft. But you don't hear me, and slip back under.

I stagger to my feet, splashing in after you, submerging myself to my chest, my shoulders, my neck. But there I stop, teetering just in my depth. The moonlight might be enough to guide you back, but all I can see is the darkness at its edges.

So, I retreat. I drag myself out of the water, pull on my nightdress and head back towards the house – towards the life I've now chosen for myself – trying to quell the fear that I will never see you again. And it isn't until I'm halfway up the weathered steps, where I put out a hand to steady myself against the rock, that I glimpse a glint of gold, like a wink between the two of us, and I realise: I still have your ring.

16

Crockers Point

Of what avail to me that the billows are not broad that sunder us?
Is this brief span of waters less an obstacle to me?
I almost would that I were distant from you the whole world,
so that my hopes were far removed, together with my lady...

The words swam as Finley's eyes unfocused. He glanced up from the page, rubbing at his brow with his hands, and when he opened his eyes again found himself face to face with his own reflection in the dark window of the sunroom. He looked pinched, almost gaunt. Taken aback, he hoped he might look a little healthier in a true mirror, but, still – he needed to get more sleep.

For now, though, he contemplated Ovid's *Heroides* again. For the past couple of hours, he had been flicking between the copy he had bought in London and several mythology sites on his phone, revisiting the myth of Hero and Leander in the – most likely vain – hope that it might help him figure out what had happened to their nineteenth-century counterparts.

The story had been referenced and retold in many forms over the centuries, by everyone from Musaeus to Marlowe, but as far as Finley could tell, the details remained fairly consistent: the star-crossed lovers, the near impossible swim, the light in the tower, the tragic ending ... And, unusually for a tale of its kind, it was not a tragedy fated or engineered by the gods. Finley could easily appreciate why someone like Delmore had identified so strongly with it – in fact, he doubted the artist had been wildly different to the Leander of Ovid's imagination: dashing, daring, doomed.

Ovid's Hero, on the other hand, was a more inconsistent character, simultaneously encouraging Leander to make the swim and urging him to be cautious. Had Cora been the same? Had she even known the classical story Delmore was alluding to, both with his swim and in his painting?

Given what had happened to Cynthia and the others, it seemed likely that Cora had suffered a watery death, and Finley considered the possibility that Delmore's demise with *The Persephone* had led her to emulate Hero and fling herself into the sea. He wasn't sure he believed it, though – not when he pictured the scrappy-looking person from the sketch, whose gaze was fixed on some distant point, like she was seeing far beyond the moment that Delmore had drawn her. But what was the alternative? Tensing, Finley remembered Cynthia's conviction that *murder* might be at the centre of all of this ...

Whatever it was, Finley suspected he would need to find out at least the bare bones of what had happened to Cora before even considering attempting to *rerecord the tape*, as Dawn had put it. He looked back towards the dark window, towards his own strained face, wondering whether he could really do something here and now that would alter a memory of the past. It didn't seem possible – but then none of this was possible, was it? Besides, as Dawn had also said, the dead didn't have to abide by the rules of the living.

Finley's vision blurred again – he was so *tired* – and his reflection began to dissolve into the darkness behind the glass. Then he blinked, and when his eyes refocused on the window, he saw a figure behind him. With a gasp, Finley lurched around, his book toppling from his lap. But it was only Lorraine in a fluffy purple dressing gown, switching off the lamps in the neighbouring lounge.

'You're up very late,' she noted. 'I thought you were almost finished with the booklet?'

'I am,' said Finley, his heart still thumping as he bent to retrieve *Heroides* from the floor. 'This is, erm ... something else.'

He willed her not to ask him about it – and not to ask him why he was here, and not in his room, the mere thought of which made him feel morose. He'd hardly seen Lorraine over the past few days; he supposed, like everyone else, she'd been recovering from the festival. He had missed her, even her endless chores.

She tugged at one of the sunroom's gauzy curtains and said, 'Shall I close these for you?'

'Yeah, please,' said Finley, unwilling to look at his haggard reflection any longer. Then, pushing himself up from his chair, he said, 'Actually, I'll do it.'

In the end, they took a curtain each, drawing them round the sides of the extension until they met in the middle. As they pulled the two swathes of fabric together, Lorraine frowned down at Finley's hand.

'Here, what happened to you?'

Instinctively, Finley clutched his bandaged palm to his chest.

'Erm – glass,' he said, before remembering those volunteers with their litter-picking sticks and adding, 'On the beach. It's not that bad ...'

As Lorraine began to harrumph about careless tourists, Finley reflected that his hand *was*, in fact, that bad. When he changed the bandage at night, which was becoming as much a part of his bedtime routine as taking his long-lasting insulin, he was shocked by how bloody and raw it looked. And when he thought back to how Fiona had mistaken it for a scar the previous week, and the faint line it had been a few days before that, he had a horrible feeling that it was *un*healing; that he was experiencing some injury in reverse.

To his relief, Lorraine didn't press him about it, but after turning to leave the sunroom she hesitated, looked back. 'Are you all right, love?' she asked. 'Because you look a bit peaky, if you don't mind my saying ...'

Finley minded a little – but, having seen his own reflection, he supposed she had a point.

'I'm fine,' he said, tersely. 'Just . . . tired. I'm not sleeping too well.'

He considered asking her if he could move to another room – the guesthouse was all but empty now – but couldn't even start to form the words. After all, the damage was already done; no matter where he went, he was connected to that place, to *her*.

Besides, what would happen to the next person Lorraine put up there? *It's likely a recording of trauma*, Dawn had said, *which, under certain circumstances, plays over and over* . . . Until now, Finley had thought those circumstances might be the room being opened up again, or perhaps the time of year, but what if the thing that was causing all of this was . . . *him*?

The thought was new and unsettling: was there something about him that had kickstarted this cycle again? And was it something he shared with Cynthia, and Jacqueline, and Michelle? When Finley had decided to come back to Crescombe, he had been focused on how he might be different to them, but perhaps he'd been looking at it the wrong way round; perhaps, to make sense of this, he needed to understand how they were the same.

'Finley?'

'Huh?'

'Are you *sure* you're all right?'

Lorraine was now leaning against the sunroom table, her expression unusually serious. She'd taken off her make-up and, somehow, it made her look softer. Clearly, she was in Godmother Mode tonight, and Finley found he wasn't annoyed at her concern – perhaps he even welcomed it.

'Because I know it was Mollie's wedding the other weekend . . .' she continued, suddenly becoming very interested in the sleeve of her dressing gown.

'Oh, I don't care about that,' said Finley, surprised to realise this was true: since his return from London, he'd hardly thought of Mollie at all.

With the air of someone advancing with extreme caution, Lorraine continued, 'And you are . . . taking care of yourself, aren't you?'

It was almost exactly the phrasing Fiona had used the other day, which roused Finley's suspicions. 'Did Mum tell you about my diabetes?'

'Well – yes,' said Lorraine, now a little pink. 'But years ago, when you first got it. She was so worried about you.'

Again, Finley felt too weary to be annoyed with his mum, or Lorraine, or anyone. He suddenly wondered why he was still so secretive about his condition. This wasn't school: nobody was going to torment him about it anymore.

'My blood sugar's fine – it's all fine,' he sighed.

Lorraine looked a little relieved, then ventured, 'It must be a lot.'

Finley shrugged and, in an echo of what he had told Megan at the cove, said, 'You get used to it.'

'Do you, though?'

He looked up, once again struck by her sincerity – and wondering whether her disappointing marriage had honed her bullshit detector.

'You get used to all the practical stuff,' he clarified. 'The carb-counting, ordering enough insulin, planning ahead – that's all second nature now. But I'm not sure I'll ever feel the same as I did before – you know, in myself.'

He sought out his own reflection again, forgetting the dark window was now obscured by the gauzy curtain he had drawn a few minutes ago.

'Sometimes I feel like I'm not even supposed to be here,' he went on, before catching Lorraine's alarmed expression out of the corner of his eye and explaining, 'I mean, I *want* to be here, I'm not saying I don't, it's just—I'm very aware that I wouldn't be, if it wasn't for the insulin and stuff.'

He had never told anyone this before, not even Mollie. He wasn't even sure why he was telling Lorraine now, except that her questions had coincided with his being too tired to offer up any resistance. He thought she might be disturbed, or try and gloss over what he had said, but instead she reached over to give his shoulder a gentle squeeze.

'Oh, love, you can't think like that,' she said quietly. 'I expect most of us wouldn't be here without modern medicine. We all would've croaked from infections, or in childbirth, or—Hey, I had appendicitis as a teenager, that probably would've done for me.' She gripped his shoulder again, more firmly this time. 'You absolutely should be here, mister.'

Finley wanted to explain that most people weren't reminded of their own reliance on modern medicine – of their own mortality, even – in the way that he was, all day, every day. But he appreciated what she was saying and the fact that, by saying it, she had made him feel a little better.

Maybe Lorraine sensed this, because she stood up, saying, 'Well, I'm going to make myself a hot chocolate and turn in.' Then, with a glance around the sunroom and adjoining lounge, she added, 'It's quite nice when it's quiet, isn't it? I can finally hear myself think again.'

Finley smiled, though he wasn't sure how many more of his own thoughts he wanted to listen to.

'Though remind me to change that "No Vacancies" sign in the morning, will you?' Lorraine added, through a yawn. 'We'll need some more guests eventually . . .'

'I can do it now if you like?'

'Oh no, love, it's pitch black out there.'

'I don't mind,' said Finley, now eager to move – and eager to do this small thing for her.

'Well, if you're sure – there can be a hot chocolate in it for you and all.'

'Deal,' he agreed, uncapping his insulin pen in anticipation.

The security light flared as Finley stepped out of the guesthouse's front door a few minutes later, and somewhere below his feet the sea seemed to grumble in response. Perhaps Lorraine was right, he thought, as he crossed the gravel driveway; perhaps he needed to reframe his attitude. After all, he was *lucky* to live in the age of modern medicine. Maybe he needed to be less morbid about his diabetes, and a bit more positive, a bit more *seize the day* . . .

He frowned as he approached the old fence post where the 'No Vacancies' sign was dangling: why had the phrase *seize the day* popped into his head like that? Someone had said it recently, and it took him a moment to remember it had been Dawn again, back when they'd spoken in her hut. She'd been recalling her meeting with peppy Michelle Lei, who'd survived leukaemia as a child.

Finley's skin began to prickle as he flipped over the sign and, unbidden, he conjured the image of Cynthia pressing a spot just below her collarbone. *Took a knife to the shoulder*, she'd said, in that nonchalant tone – and then, later, she'd told him that Jacqueline Fairchild had been planning to get a new car, because she'd recently been in an accident . . .

Finley dropped the sign, which clattered against the fence post. Was *that* it? Had they all been susceptible to this link with the dead because they'd all had a brush with death themselves? Consciously or not, had Cynthia and Jacqueline and Michelle also felt as though they weren't supposed to be here?

Then Finley was plunged into darkness. He let out a little yelp, before realising the now-distant security light had turned itself off. His breathing slightly shallow, he waited for his eyes to adjust to the gloom, trying to get his bearings by tracing the shadowy outline of Crockers Point looming above him.

There was a light up there again, right at the edge of the cliff. Finley's skin began to tingle once more, because the glow didn't have the solid quality of a torch or phone beam. Even at this distance, it seemed to flicker.

'Marshmallows and cream?'

The security light flooded the driveway again, silhouetting Lorraine in the doorway of Crockers Nest. Finley squinted against this sudden brightness, trying to make out the smaller golden glimmer beyond it.

'Finley?' Lorraine called. 'The hot chocolate – were you wanting—?'

'Lorraine, what's that light?'

'Eh?' She began to pad across the driveway in her slippers, turning to look where he was staring. 'What light?'

'Up there, on the cliff.'

Lorraine peered up at the most easterly point of Crescombe. 'Eh?' she said again.

'It's right . . .'

But he trailed off, knowing she couldn't see it, just as Megan hadn't been able to see it on the night of the fireworks. Because it wasn't really there, was it? Not *now*, anyway . . .

'I could get my specs?' Lorraine offered. 'Maybe it's just my— Hey, where are you going?'

For Finley had started to run. He skidded past the sign now reading 'Vacancies' and vaulted over a stile to the footpath that snaked the wooded cliff behind Crockers Nest. He needed to get to that light. Because it hadn't just appeared by itself; someone was up there. No, not someone – *she* was up there.

With fumbling fingers, he switched on his phone's torch and threw himself up the path. Here, in the trees, it was no longer possible to see the light; Finley just had to hope it would still be there by the time he reached the summit. Was it part of the signal or something else? Or had he got it wrong, and the light depicted in *Hero's Bay* wasn't coming from his room after all?

His feet thumped against the earthy track, his phone trained downwards for protruding roots. Low branches scratched at his arms and legs, one even cuffing him on the side of the head, but Finley sprinted on, focused only on the dark path ahead.

After a few minutes, pain began to sear in his left side and he leaned against the nearest tree, his fingers digging into his ribs. His hand was hurting again – possibly, it had been hurting for some time – but he ignored it, attempting instead to massage his stitch away.

He thought he must be almost halfway up to Crockers Point already, judging by the shadowy view of the bay through the trees. Here, the scent of the sea was tempered by something earthier, like moss, and over the sound of his own panting Finley could hear the wind teasing at leaves and the hooting of a solitary owl. He felt acutely alert; he had never ventured into the wilderness after dark like this.

Before fear could replace the adrenaline coursing through him, Finley pushed away from the tree, ready to run again. But as he did so, his legs wobbled and the beam of his phone torch seemed to quiver and blur.

'Shit . . .'

Already knowing what he was going to see, Finley adjusted his phone in his shaking fingers and tapped it to the sensor on his arm.

'*Shit.*'

He'd taken insulin for that hot chocolate, then dashed into the night not only without drinking it, but without any supplies: no sweets, no banana, no just-in-case juice . . . How could he be so careless, so *stupid*?

He wiped his sweaty forehead, his breathing still heavy. He had to go back. Even as he thought it, though, he took a step forward, and the light glimmered into view through the trees up ahead, as mesmeric as a will-o'-the-wisp. But no, going on would be madness – suicide, even. He had to get back down the hill, and fast.

Cursing his own negligence, Finley turned, patting at his shorts, because occasionally he would find the end of a roll of sweets at the bottom of a pocket. And, miraculously, there *was* something: three little tubes of Parma violets. Finley stared at them for a moment, glowing curiously bright in the gloomy woods, before he tore off the plastic wrapping and began to cram handfuls of the pale purple sweets into his mouth.

As he broke into a jog, the sound of his own crunching loud in his ears, Finley knew this wasn't the best plan. He had no idea how much sugar the violets contained and should probably be looking it up on his phone while he sat down and recovered. But the lure of the light was too strong. He craved reaching it almost as much as his body was screaming for sugar and, as unpleasant as it was, forcing down the soapy sweets, their association with Cora only made him more determined to catch up with her.

When Finley finally emerged from the wooded path, he clutched his knees for a few seconds, chest burning, mouth dry, hand throbbing. It was windier up here, cooling the sweat that was soaking his hair and seeping through his T-shirt, and he didn't feel any woozier than he had in the clearing, so the sweets must be taking effect.

He straightened up, his gaze roving over the open field – past the pale outlines of sheep, and a small white cottage – until it reached the point where the land of East Crescombe fell away; the sheer drop into the dark sea which, tonight, was shrouded in mist. And there, at the cliff's edge, was the light – the *lantern* – being held aloft by a small, cloaked figure.

All at once, Finley's whole body felt like it was trying to turn itself inside out. He'd been expecting this – hoping for it, even – though now he was here, just a few metres away, fear was unravelling through him like never before. He needed to go back. All of his instincts were telling him to put as much distance as possible between himself and this place. But he couldn't move.

The figure was hooded, so it wasn't possible to see anything of their face, despite the glow of the lantern dangling from their hand. Nevertheless, Finley knew who this was.

'Cora?'

She gave no indication she had noticed him, though he was sure he'd spoken loudly enough to be heard above the wind. She just kept standing there, and there was something deliberate about her stance, about the way she was staring not out to Westcliff, but to the open sea. Finley thought of all the ships that would have passed up the Bristol Channel and, for the second time, wondered whether he had got it all wrong: perhaps she hadn't been signalling from her room at all.

'Cora?' he said again.

Still she didn't turn, didn't even move. Finley forced himself to take a step towards her, then another, even though each one seemed to cost him all of his courage. He felt like he was playing that playground game, grandmother's footsteps – only, what would happen when he reached her?

'Cora?'

She was close now, close enough to reach out and touch; he could see the fibres in the weave of her cloak, as tangible as his own clothes. And it seemed she could ignore him no longer because, finally, she turned her head. Finley inhaled, trying to brace himself for whatever came next ... But as the figure's hood fell back, exposing the face beneath to the lantern light, he experienced another tremor of shock.

It wasn't her. It wasn't even a woman. The person – the *phantom* – standing before him was a small, sallow man with one pale eye and a scarred, stretched hollow where the other should have been.

'You're too late,' he rasped, and began to laugh.

Finley's hand spasmed and, glancing down, he discovered it was wet with blood, the bandage completely soaked through. The other man's focus returned to the lantern, his mirth causing the scar to twist across his face like a second mouth. Finley, too, stared at the light and then, with burgeoning dread, followed its beam out to sea.

A moment ago, the water had been deserted. Now, though, a shape was emerging from the mist, a vast, narrow something that seemed to extend from the waves like Cetus or the Kraken. But it wasn't a monster, Finley realised, as he began to make out sails, a mast, a prow – it was a *ship*.

'No . . .' he whispered, because this vessel, whatever it was, was much too close.

But there was nothing he could do – it *was* too late – so, feeling sicker than he had all evening, and with the other man's laughter ringing in his ears, Finley could only stand there and stare as the ship sped towards the rocky coast of East Crescombe, guided by the lantern's glow.

There are mermaids on your ring. Before, when that band of gold was on your paint-stained hand, sliding across my skin, I never thought or cared to study its little engraving. But now I stare and stare at these water women, who remind me of the strange stories my mother used to tell me; their long tails are twisted around a shield like they mean to crush it.

Until I can return it to you, I should tuck the ring away in my tinderbox, but I don't. Like my sea stone, I keep it in my apron pocket, where I trace the outline of those mermaids with a fingertip. Or, if I'm certain I'm alone, I dare to lay down my mop or broom and slip the ring back onto my thumb, admiring the way it glints in the gloom, and I wonder: is there still time to change my mind?

'Have you heard?'

At Edwin's voice, I plunge my hand back into my pocket, heart pounding.

'Cousin?' He leaps down the last of the stairs and tramples through my sweeping. 'What's happened to you? You used to be so alert, a little mouse watching all, and now . . .' He claps in front of my face, then laughs as I jump.

'Have I heard what?' I ask, wary of his cheer.

He grins, his scarred skin pulling at the space where his eye once was. 'We're going ahead with it. Even Harcourt's in agreement, so we'll have his men as well as our own.' Edwin seems almost giddy with victory. 'What do you think of that, eh?'

I'm surprised to be asked, though perhaps I shouldn't be; Edwin knows I'm no fool.

I consider his question while, in my pocket, I work the ring off my thumb. He's right when he says the Crockers must adapt to a changing Crescombe. Otherwise, what will become of this family, who have never known anything but the sea's bounty? I feel no loyalty towards them, have no interest in helping to safeguard their future, yet I understand Edwin's reasoning and why he'd risk all our necks for this.

But it's wicked, this thing he's planning. I've grown numb to news of the occasional casualty during a run, but this? The scale of it is staggering. And it sickens me to think that, in a way, it is already done; somewhere out there is a ship whose course has been set, an oblivious crew now speeding towards their doom.

'Well?' Impatient for a response, Edwin grabs my arm, shakes me.

I force myself to look into his pale eye. 'Does it really matter what I think?'

He smiles again. 'No,' he concedes, 'not at all. But you'd better wake up, cousin.' He releases me to clap in my face again, only this time I don't flinch. 'You'll need to put those sharp eyes of yours to good use if you want to stay under this roof.'

'Ma wouldn't let you cast me out,' I say, before I can think better of it.

'Ma isn't in charge of this family!'

I want to tell him that neither is he, not as long as Old William still draws his rattling breaths, but I bite my tongue. Still, I've angered him. He jabs a finger in my face, forcing me to step back.

'You'd better play your part – you'd better do exactly what I tell you, or I'll throw you out myself. And where will you go then?' he sneers.

Again, his question surprises me, and I immediately think of you, and the places you said you would take me. It's only for a moment, but something must show in my face, because Edwin frowns.

'Where?' he demands.

'I—I don't know.'

He lunges at me again, this time grabbing my chin. '*Where?*'

Our faces are so close I can smell his putrid breath. I whimper as his fingers dig into my skin, squeezing my jaw. There's a curious strength to him that frightens me, though he's half the size of his brothers.

'My father!' I cry, because I have to say something. 'He told me he'd come back for me, that he'd take me away!'

Edwin's eye widens as he lets me go, then he begins to make a horrible, high-pitched crowing noise. At first, I think he's having some kind of fit, but when a tear starts to roll down one side of his face, I realise: he's *laughing*.

'Is that—?' He can't get the words out over his own mirth. 'Is that what you really believe?' He clutches at himself, managing to croak, 'You stupid girl, didn't she tell you? He's long gone!'

I stand perfectly still while he tries to compose himself, yet it feels like the ground has turned to water. 'Didn't who tell me what?'

'Ma!' Edwin wheezes. 'He did come back, years ago, but she told him you'd died with your whore mother.'

Suddenly, there seems to be nothing under my feet at all.

'Don't know why she bothered, really . . .' Edwin spits out the glob of mucus he's just coughed up. 'I would've let him take you. I was up there, I heard it all.' He gestures back towards the stairs. 'He was weeping and wailing and gnashing his teeth . . . They really are savages, aren't they? His kind.' Edwin grins. 'Your kind.'

I barely hear the insult. Now, even the air around me seems to be rearranging itself, and I've no idea whether I'm looking forward or back, up or down.

Edwin smirks as he remembers more: 'She told him you were buried in the churchyard, with your mother, and he went dashing off there. Stayed for days, muttering his strange language, singing his heathen songs ... He scared people. In the end, the vicar had to ask him to leave.' Edwin gives me a mocking little pat on the shoulder. 'So, I'm sorry to have to tell you this, cousin, but your father's gone – and he's never coming back.'

I shove his hand away. With a growl, Edwin tries to grab me again, but this time I'm too quick and I dart across the hallway, throw myself out of the door. I hear him start after me, shouting threats, but I don't care and I don't stop.

He won't follow me for long, but I keep running, pelting through the woods that fringe our side of the bay. The ground still seems to be shifting beneath my boots, while the trees, the houses, the whole of the town feels like it's collapsing around me. Moving is the only way to stay on my feet.

I don't know where I'm going, yet it's not a surprise when I arrive, panting, at the churchyard. I hoist myself over the back wall and stumble towards the Crocker plot, where I collapse in front of my mother's gravestone. Then I scream.

And I scream and I scream and I scream.

For now, it's all I can do. I need to release this rage, this anguish, or I will break apart from the pain of it. All this time I thought he was coming back. All these years I've waited, clinging onto his sea stone, and the hopeless promise I made to return it with him. But he's gone. He's gone, and it's all their fault.

I don't know how long I lie there, howling at the sky. But when I eventually quieten – my throat burning, my whole body shaking – I find, unexpectedly, that I'm smiling. Because Edwin thought this would defeat me. He thought it would force me to fall in with his monstrous plans. But he was wrong. I'll never forgive them for this.

For this, I'll destroy them.

To my right, a bird chirrups in the renewed hush of the churchyard. I turn to look, through clumps of heart-shaped leaves that, every spring, are dotted with violets. Was he here when they were in bloom? Did he drink in their scent, did it make him think of her? But I can't bear to imagine him in this place, singing, mourning. To know he was so close is agony.

Another wail escapes me, startling the bird from its branch. It's for him, and for my mother too – but mostly it's for me, and all the times I've been drawn here, never once realising I was lying on my own grave.

17

The Persephone

Beyond Finley's closed eyelids was a light so bright it had to be the sun. He must be at the cove again, lying on the sand with his book, having been lulled to sleep by the sound of the waves ...

'Finley?'

As he drifted back to consciousness, though, he realised he was cold, the ground beneath him hard, and the person shaking him awake didn't sound remotely like Megan. Finley's eyes snapped open. Improbably, crouched over him with a torch, was Martin.

'Are you all right?' he asked.

Finley lurched up to sitting, frantically patting his pockets, then groping at the dark ground until he located his phone lying face down in the grass. He tapped it to the sensor on his arm before exhaling in relief: those violet sweets had done their job.

Unwilling to dwell on his own recklessness, Finley's jumbled mind tried to make sense of why else he might have been lying on the ground at night and, in a rush, it came back to him: the light on the cliff, the hooded figure with the lantern, the scarred man who hadn't been Cora, that *ship* ...

'I'm fine,' he murmured.

Obviously, this was a lie. He couldn't stop shaking, and his hand was still covered in blood. But he was temporarily distracted by the worried, weather-beaten face of the handyman: what the hell was *Martin* doing here?

'I saw you from my window,' he explained, apparently sensing Finley's bewilderment. He gestured at the lone white building behind him, the old coastguard's cottage, and continued, 'Hardly anyone comes up here at this time, so I thought it was a bit strange when I heard you calling, when I saw your light ...'

'Did you see anyone else?' Finley asked urgently.

Martin shook his head, though there was something uncertain about his manner that made Finley ask, 'But ... ?'

'But it looked like you were talking to someone,' Martin mumbled, now unable to meet his eye.

'Someone who wasn't there?'

'Yeah ...'

Mortification rose through Finley, but he tried to ignore it. 'And in the sea, you didn't see any ships?'

Martin frowned. 'You mean, in the distance? Like a ferry?'

'Like one of those old-fashioned tall ships,' said Finley, wincing at how absurd it sounded, but he needed to know. 'Right there, coming straight at the coast.'

He gestured to the cliff's edge, then let his arm hang limp as he saw Martin's expression: confused, concerned. There was an uncomfortable silence before the handyman nodded, once more, towards his cottage and said, 'Look, why don't we go inside and have a brew?'

Finley had a brief vision of Martin distracting him with tea while he phoned ... Lorraine? The police? A psychiatric hospital?

'I'm fine now,' he said, forcing himself to his feet. Then, reasoning his blood sugar was stable enough to get down the hill, he continued, 'I think I'll just go back to Crockers Nest. Sorry, Martin, I just—' Finley wracked his brain for a plausible explanation of his behaviour, drew a total blank, so repeated, 'I'm fine now.'

Unsurprisingly, this didn't convince Martin, who offered to accompany Finley back to the guesthouse, and became uncharacteristically firm when he tried to resist.

As they set off into the trees, Finley found it difficult to believe he had run so far and fast in the dark. Every so often, the beam of Martin's torch illuminated a tiny violet sweet that he had dropped in his haste to get up the hill, which now marked their route like fairy-tale breadcrumbs. Finley couldn't stop looking out for them. Until now, his thoughts had felt like those sweets, scattered in the darkness, but the slow descent to Crockers Nest gave his mind the chance to collect up everything he had seen and heard and read, before – with a little thrill – Finley realised that it was all beginning to make *sense* . . .

'*Oh my Lord!*'

As soon as they triggered the security light, the front door of the guesthouse banged open and Lorraine came hurrying across the driveway, her purple dressing gown flapping.

'Finley, love, where've you *been*? What's going on? Are you all right?'

Without being given the opportunity to answer any of these questions, Finley was bundled into the guesthouse and steered towards one of the squashy green sofas in the lounge. Then Lorraine began to make a concoction at the honesty bar in the corner, which seemed to involve a little boiling water and a lot of whisky.

'Here, get this down you,' she said, offering him a mug that read, 'It's Heaven in Devon!'

'Thanks,' said Finley, taking a sip and immediately beginning to splutter – it really was a *lot* of whisky.

Once he had been thumped on the back by Martin, Finley looked up at Lorraine, saying, 'Sorry for running off like that. I needed a bit of air – you know, after our talk – and then I messed up my blood sugar . . .'

He was deliberately trying to remind her of the confidence they had just shared and, to his relief, she nodded in understanding. He didn't dare look at Martin, afraid the handyman might suddenly mention his collapse, or his gabbling about tall ships, or that he'd been trying to talk to thin air ... Finley was also aware that either one of them might notice his sodden bandage, and pulled his sleeve over his hand.

'Well, I'm just very glad you're all right,' said Lorraine, 'and that Martin—' She broke off, apparently only just noticing that the handyman was there, perched on the arm of Finley's sofa. 'Oh Martin, I'm not *dressed*!'

She made a show of pulling her fluffy purple robe tightly around her body, which Finley couldn't help but feel had the opposite effect of modesty. Not that Martin was looking: having turned roughly the same colour as the dressing gown, he was staring determinedly at his dirty shoes.

Fortunately, there was then a knock at the lounge door, and Finley was stunned to see Megan peering through one of the glass panels. Lorraine, too, looked momentarily stumped, then stopped fussing with her dressing gown and said, 'Oh yes, I called the pub, I thought you might be with her.' She beckoned to Megan. 'Come in, love!'

Megan edged over the threshold, followed by Skipper, who immediately began to sniff at the room's corners, his tail a blur.

'What's going on?' she asked.

Everyone looked at Finley, who was still too surprised by Megan's arrival to answer. He wasn't sure how he felt about her being here. On the one hand, he was highly embarrassed that Lorraine had called The Drowned Painter about him, as though he were some wayward teenager, but he couldn't deny that Megan – a little unkempt and sleepy-looking after her shift – was a thoroughly welcome sight.

'It's all fine now,' Lorraine told her, 'Finley will explain.' Then, looking between them a few times, she added, 'Come on, Martin, I'll make you a sandwich for your trouble ...'

Still staring at his shoes, Martin was chivvied out of the lounge. Left alone with Megan, Finley was suddenly very conscious that they hadn't spoken since the night of the festival fireworks. At the thought, he tugged his sleeve further over his bloody hand.

'She said you'd run off or something?' Megan prompted, taking Martin's place on the arm of Finley's sofa.

'Yeah...'

Haltingly, he began to relate the previous half-hour or so. He tried to be as honest as possible, even though he knew it would sound ridiculous, especially to someone like Megan, who didn't believe in any of this stuff. Despite her scepticism, he needed to confide in *someone*.

Halfway through his account, she crossed to the honesty bar to make herself a drink that smelled similar to his, her light eyebrows furrowed as she listened to his description of the mysterious man on the cliffs. When she returned to the sofa, she sat down beside him, which felt comforting; if nothing else, it was good to have a friend right now.

'Well,' she said, when he had finished speaking.

'Well,' he agreed.

Megan stared up at the shelves of dog-eared books and old board games, though Finley had the impression she wasn't really seeing them but turning over everything she had just heard. He fidgeted for a few seconds, and when he could bear the silence no longer, clinked his mug against hers in a toast.

Her reverie broken, Megan nodded at 'It's Heaven in Devon!' and said, 'Nice mug.'

Her own was handmade with a sea-green glaze – the kind Finley had seen for sale all over the Crescombe Art Festival.

'Yeah,' he agreed, studying the novelty item cradled between his hand and his sleeve. 'Though it should probably read something like, "I went to Devon and all I got was this lousy haunting"...'

Reluctantly, Megan laughed and, as Finley caught a rare glimpse of the gap between her front teeth, his stomach tipped, like a boat rocked by a wave. Perhaps it was the whisky, but he had the strongest urge to forget all about this conversation – to forget about *any* conversation – and instead lean over and kiss her again. Because why should he care about mysterious figures and ships and people long dead when he and she were both here, alone – *alive?*

Megan, however, seemed less easily distracted, and after gesturing at Skipper to stop investigating the room and lie down at their feet, she asked, 'What do you think it all means, then?'

'I think,' began Finley, returning to what he'd been theorising during his walk down the hill, and experiencing another thrum of excitement, 'I think it means I know why Delmore died.'

Megan's face was impassive but, somehow, he could tell he'd surprised her.

'Actually,' he added, 'I think I know why a lot of things happened that night.'

Still Megan said nothing, but after taking a sip of his hot toddy – this time managing not to splutter – Finley found he didn't need her encouragement.

'Everyone knows the Crockers were smugglers, right?' he began eagerly. 'Not just Cora's lot, but going back generations. Only, by the time Delmore was here, smuggling had become increasingly risky.' Then, ticking off each fact on the fingers of his left hand, he continued, 'The development of West Crescombe had brought loads of visitors to the area. A coastguard had been established at Crockers Point, meaning the family had had to move the signal from the beach to their own house. And, according to the vicar, import taxes were about to be lowered to such an extent that smuggling would become virtually pointless.'

'But what's this got to do with Delmore?' Megan asked.

'I'll get to that,' he assured her. Then, picking up where he'd left off, he said, 'We know the Crockers turned their hand to a bit of highway robbery a few years later – unsuccessfully, seeing as it got them deported – but what if they tried something a bit more familiar first? What if, faced with destitution, the Crockers decided to use their signal light to lure a ship towards the rocks in order to claim *all* of its cargo?'

Megan blinked at him for a few seconds, then said, 'Are you talking about *wrecking*?'

'Yes.'

She shook her head. 'But that didn't happen, not really. I mean, ships got wrecked along this coast, yes, but not on purpose. Those wrecking stories – they're exactly that: stories told for tourists.'

Finley remembered his first few days in Crescombe, when he'd felt like a gullible tourist himself. But now he knew a lot more about this town and, in an echo of Dawn, insisted, 'Those stories must have come from somewhere.'

But Megan still looked unconvinced. 'It would've been far too risky.'

'For a bunch of crooks like the Crockers? Who risked their necks anyway, every time they unloaded a ship?'

'Well, exactly – ships docked here all the time, they presumably had some kind of agreement with the Crockers,' said Megan, changing tack. 'Wrecking a ship would've been a massive betrayal ...'

'But who would've known?' asked Finley, springing up and disturbing Skipper, who had been trying to settle on his shoes. 'Nobody from the ship would've survived to talk about it – and ships were accidentally wrecked along this coast all the time, you just said so. With smuggling on its way out anyway, I think the Crockers would've felt they had very little to lose.'

Megan stared up at him, following his progress as, too agitated to keep still, he began to pace in front of the sofa, his drink sloshing in its mug.

'You're talking as if you know them,' she said, and it didn't sound like a compliment. 'Is that who you think you saw tonight, then? One of the Crockers?'

'Yes,' said Finley, choosing to ignore the word *think*.

He considered telling her about that drawing of Agnes Crocker and her sons, one of whom – *Edwin* – had been scrawny and missing an eye, but decided against it, sensing Megan's patience with all of this was already stretched thin.

'Usually, it was Cora who signalled to the ships from her room,' he said instead, 'prompting those ships to steer into the bay and dock at Crescombe Beach, where the contraband would be unloaded. But on this particular night, one of the sons took the signal light up to Crockers Point, which, in the dark, disorientated the ship's course and caused it to steer straight into the rocks.'

Megan ran her fingers along the uneven surface of her mug, where the glaze had been artfully dripped over the rim. 'I still don't understand what this has to do with Delmore,' she said, after a moment.

'Because he was swimming to Cora's room every time she signalled to those ships!' exclaimed Finley, trying to quell his frustration that Megan wasn't able – or wasn't willing – to make these connections herself.

'You don't know that for sure ...'

But Finley batted away this doubt with a wave of his sleeve. 'So Delmore, like *The Persephone*, followed the wrong light. He swam across the bay thinking—'

'Wait, you think this is about *The Persephone*?' Megan broke in. 'You think *that's* the ship that was wrecked?'

'Of course this is about *The Persephone*!' cried Finley, so loudly that Skipper gave another start. 'How many other ships were wrecked during Delmore's stay? But he didn't dash away from his card games at the hotel to save the crew – or not at first, anyway.

He was following the light on the cliff, thinking it was Cora. That's why he was out in the water that night. That's why he drowned.'

'*If* he drowned . . .' said Megan quietly.

Finley, who had been about to take a triumphant sip of his hot toddy, paused, the mug raised halfway to his mouth. 'What?'

'It's never actually been proven that Delmore drowned,' said Megan slowly, as though she wasn't sure she should be talking about this – wasn't sure she should be encouraging him. 'I mean, yes, his body washed up with all the rest, but he had this head injury that might've been from a rock or a piece of the ship, and it was probably that that killed him.'

Finley, who now remembered reading this at The Delmore Experience, wasn't sure why it mattered, exactly – was it not enough that the artist had died because he had followed the wrong light?

His confusion must have been showing on his face, because Megan continued, 'In the stories about wreckings – and again, I think they're mostly stories – it always goes that if there were any sailors, any *witnesses*, left alive, the wreckers would silence them.'

In the air, she mimed swinging an invisible weapon, like a bat. Staggered, Finley almost felt that she had struck him for real.

'So, you're saying that not only did the Crockers inadvertently lure Delmore out to sea, they quite possibly murdered him?' he said, his voice sounding distant over the thumping of his own heart.

He barely noticed Megan's reluctant nod. Piece after piece of this puzzle was falling into place, and though Finley still didn't understand exactly what had happened to Cora, he thought he now knew what he needed to do.

'I have to stop it,' he said, finally pausing in his pacing, his skin abuzz.

'Stop what?'

'All of it: Cora's death, Delmore's death, the sinking of *The Persephone* . . . It all starts with that light on the cliff, the one I saw tonight. The one I need to intercept,' he said, with a shiver of realisation as he thought back to Dawn's story, and the man who had stepped in front of those headlights at a dark crossroads on Christmas Eve.

'Sorry,' said Megan, who sounded anything but as she got to her feet, 'but what the fuck are you talking about?'

Finley stared at her, surprised by her ire — surprised she was still here, even. If she thought it was all so nonsensical, why was she even entertaining this discussion? And why was he bothering to spell it out for her when his mind was working far beyond the confines of this conversation?

'I was speaking to Dawn the other day,' he began, striving to ignore how Megan rolled her eyes at this. 'She thinks that, with this kind of haunting — a residual haunting — there might be a way to interrupt the loop of events that keeps playing over and over. There might be something you can do in the present to affect what's happened in the past.'

'But . . . but it's *happened*!' cried Megan, looking more indignant than Finley had ever seen her. '*The Persephone* sank, Delmore died — it's done, it's finished! You can't change the past, Finley!'

'It's not *changing* it, exactly, it's more like . . . Look, if you think of Crescombe as a kind of old-fashioned tape player . . .'

'*What?*'

'. . . And these memories of Cora's like a recording playing over and over . . .'

'Finley . . .'

He trailed off, realising he wasn't going to get through to her like this, not when she was looking at him like he was totally mad. Annoyed, Finley was reminded of Fiona — though, unlike his sister, Megan was from this town; she had grown up here, surrounded by these stories, by this *energy*, even. Plus, he thought, with a twinge of hurt, it was her, more than anyone else, he'd confided in this summer.

'You don't understand,' he said, frustrated. 'You haven't seen the stuff I've seen . . .'

'What stuff?'

'At The Delmore Experience,' he said, realising he hadn't yet told her this. 'On the night of the fireworks, after we—After you left. I went into Delmore's studio, and I saw the painting on the easel, and it sort of . . . *came alive.*' He shuddered at the memory of how he had been wrenched towards the dark, swirling seascape. 'And I saw *her*, this figure in the doorway, reaching out to me . . .'

He expected Megan to scoff, maybe roll her eyes again. Instead, though, she laid down her drink on a side table, turning back to him with an uncomfortable expression.

'Finley,' she said quietly, 'I think you saw *me.*'

'What?'

'I heard you from upstairs, I came down to—Well, to tell you to piss off, actually. I called your name, but you were . . . you weren't yourself.'

Finley frowned, mentally replaying the moment he had seen that figure in the doorway, who, admittedly, hadn't been much more than an outline against the brightness of the painting. 'No . . .' he said, slowly. 'It was her, she was in this long dress thing . . .'

'I was in my dressing gown?' said Megan. 'I was on my way to bed.'

Finley still wasn't sure he believed he could have made this mistake, but was unwilling to dwell on it – and unwilling to dwell on what a state Megan must have seen him in if she really had been there that night (no wonder she hadn't spoken to him since).

'That doesn't explain what happened with the painting – and where was everyone else?' he asked, suddenly remembering the eerie silence of the museum, which had allegedly been open late for the festival.

'Everyone else was outside watching the fireworks,' said Megan, as though this was obvious. 'They clear the museum for the actual display. You can ask Dad, it's something to do with security.'

Finley wanted to object, but what was the point? It didn't really matter whether or not the museum had been deserted – or even whether he had seen Megan or Cora. What mattered was how it had all *felt*, and he couldn't describe that to Megan, not when she was so determined to dismiss everything he said.

'Do you believe any of this?' he asked, a little hopelessly.

She didn't say anything, but he knew her answer – and, really, what had he expected? Hadn't she been clear, from when they had first discussed this at Crockers Beach, how she felt about the supernatural? And perhaps it was understandable, considering what he had learned about her since. He pictured her during that conversation of a few weeks back, sitting in her mum's boat: *If they could, the dead would come back for the living*, she'd said. *They wouldn't be able to stay away.*

'Look,' Megan sighed now, her manner placating, 'didn't you say you were only staying until the end of the month? Maybe, until then, you should just ... try and forget about this?'

'Why?' he snapped. 'If you don't believe it's really happening, what's the harm in it?'

'You're doing harm to *yourself*.'

She grabbed his wrist, pulling up the sleeve of his jumper and, together, they stared down at his hand. He hadn't inspected it since coming down the hill. The bandage was soaked, the blood dark and streaky where it had seeped through layers of gauze. Curiously, it didn't hurt right now – perhaps the whisky was having a numbing effect – but the sharp metallic smell emanating from the wound sent a tremor through his stomach.

'You think *I* did this?' he cried, snatching back his hand. How unhinged did she think he was?

'No, I—' Megan faltered. 'I don't know, Finley ...'

'Why are you even here?' he demanded, choosing to lean into his resentment rather than focus on how humiliating this all was.

'Because Lorraine called the pub,' said Megan, looking concerned he could have forgotten this already. 'Because she thought you might've gone there when you—'

'But why did *you* come *here*?' asked Finley. 'If I'm such a nutjob, why are you bothering with me at all?'

What did he want her to say, exactly? *Because I was worried about you?* That was probably closest to the truth but, right now, he thought he might have preferred a lie: *Because I believe you.* Even then, that wasn't what he needed to hear from her, not really. Because whatever their differences in opinion, none of it would matter if she gave him some glimmer of encouragement, of hope; if she replied, *Because I like you.*

As it was, Megan said none of these things. In the face of his anger, she seemed to be retreating. Her shoulders slackened, and any tension she had been carrying for this conversation appeared to leave her body, until it could've been the aloof, siren-like figure Finley had met at the beginning of his stay who said, in a voice that was almost bored, 'I don't know why I'm here.'

She clicked her fingers, prompting Skipper to jump up and begin bounding around her ankles. But as Megan then strode from the room without another word, the dog seemed to realise it wasn't the time for games. Finley watched them go through the glass door, his annoyance already tinged with regret, and he knew Megan wouldn't glance back. Skipper, however, cast a bewildered and rather doleful look behind him – a *what did you do?* sort of look – before trotting after her, his tail only wagging at half-speed.

In the dwindling light, Westcliff House is an immense block of gold on the horizon. Halfway up the hill towards it, I pause to catch my breath and, looking over my shoulder, I see that Crescombe too has been burnished by the dusk.

This is how I will remember it, I decide. Years from now, when I think back to where I grew up, I don't want to picture my dingy little room, or even that overgrown graveyard where another me is buried. Instead, I'll remember these rocks, that sand, those waves, and I will see it all as it is now, sprinkled with gold dust.

At the top of the hill, I dart towards the house, pressing myself against its bulk at the corner where, weeks ago, I spied on Ma and Harcourt. Where you crept up on me and tried to strike a bargain. Where you asked, *What is it you want?*

My answer now is the same as it was then, except I finally understand that it's only you who can help me escape this place. My father isn't coming back, there will be no salvation from a distant sea. Leaving with you – as your wife, or mistress, however you'll have me – is my only chance.

I start to edge along the side of the house, searching for an open window so I can find you, tell you – beg you, if necessary. Because I can't stay with them a moment longer. I can't stand Edwin's crowing, and I can't bear to be anywhere near Ma. When I think of what she did, I'm afraid of what *I* will do. Over the past few days, I've imagined crushing nightshade berries into her food, or pressing a pillow to her face while she sleeps.

So it may be a risk to put my trust in you – you, who do not love me as you say or even think you do – but I have no other choice. In comparison to a life with the Crockers, one without any hope of rescue – and one in which I will surely become as wicked as them – even the thought of you abandoning me doesn't seem so bad. If it happens, I will survive it.

Halfway along this side of the house I find a blue door, unlocked – the wealthy are so careless. I emerge into a servants' passageway, which I follow for a while, alert for the sound of voices or approaching footsteps. I need to find some stairs, because you've told me your quarters are on the first floor, though when I peep through a door into the main house to check my bearings, I'm surprised to find I recognise where I am.

It's the corridor Ma and I walked down the night of the meeting, the one lined with cabinets full of wondrous things. I know I shouldn't linger here – it's a miracle I've come this far unnoticed – but all is quiet and still, so I can't resist stepping out onto the soft patterned carpet to peer through the glass.

What are all these treasures? Some I can't even name. A stuffed bird that must have been caught on some exotic shore, its feathers like rainbows. A chest made of shiny dark wood, its contents a mystery (medicine? Tea? Tobacco?). In particular, I'm puzzled by that vast spiralling object I saw before, which looks like a giant stony ram's horn or snail shell. What *is* it? I stare, practically pressing my nose to the glass, until it starts to look like an immense staircase twisting down and down . . .

'That one's a fossil, an ammonite.'

I whirl around, horrified to discover Ambrose Montgomery himself standing right behind me. My mouth moves silently as I try to speak, to cobble together some excuse for why I'm here.

'It's the remains of some ancient creature's shell, if I've understood correctly,' he continues, studying the spiral almost as closely as I was. 'I bought it in Dorset, at a very fine seaside resort, though it's nothing to what else they've discovered there. The most monstrous, marvellous beasts . . . If only we could find such things here!'

As he chuckles to himself, I wonder what to do. He's talking to me almost as though he expected to find me here. Is he taunting me? Is he mad? Has he mistaken me for someone else?

Then, just as I'm considering simply dashing away, Montgomery looks directly at me and says, 'You've been here before, haven't you? At the meeting?'

He sounds curious rather than accusing. It doesn't put me at ease, exactly, but it makes it easier to nod, to admit, 'My name is Cora Crocker.'

'Yes,' he says, almost to himself, 'yes, I thought so – Crocker.'

Trying not to wince at that hated name, I look up at him, waiting for whatever he'll do next. He seems a little diminished from the last time I was here: thinner, more tired. Even his vivid hair and clothes look faded, like he's been left out too long in the sun.

'Miss Crocker, may I show you something?' he asks.

Without elaborating or even waiting for a response – though I can't exactly refuse – he beckons me towards his library. Cautiously, I follow, half expecting to find an angry manservant within, but it's empty. It seems much bigger than before, without all those crusty gentlemen occupying its chairs and settees, though my gaze moves to the blue chaise longue where you reclined, as though I hope to find you there still. In the corner, the portrait of Montgomery remains unfinished.

'Here,' says the man himself, motioning me to join him at his desk. 'Come.'

I do as I'm bidden, noticing that he's pulled back the cover that was here before, revealing an unpainted wooden model of a town.

At first, I take it to be an elaborate toy for some fortunate child, yet as I step closer, I realise there's something familiar about this miniature place: the incline of its land, the arrangement of its buildings, its crescent-shaped coastline . . .

'Is this Crescombe?'

'This is the *future* of Crescombe,' he corrects me.

Sure enough, though I recognise certain features – the curved promenade, the square belltower of the church – the model contains details that don't yet exist: more houses, more roads, what looks like a public garden and, of course, the landing pier.

'I had it made in Bristol – at great expense,' says Montgomery. 'Isn't it glorious?'

I don't know how to respond. It's impressive, certainly, but there's something eerie about seeing the town empty of people, and boats, and horses – even of colour.

Montgomery then explains that he's waiting for you to paint it before he requests another meeting with Harcourt and the other gentlemen. He thinks that if he presents them with this model – if they see what the town could become – they'll be more amenable to the changes he wants to bring about. 'Do you not agree, Miss Crocker?'

I look into his bright blue eyes and, again, I don't know what to tell him. He's desperate, I realise – why else would he be confiding in someone like me? – and though I want to give him some hope, I'm not sure I can.

'Crescombe's not a modern place, sir,' I tell him. 'Families like the Crockers, they'll resist any changes with everything they have, not just because they dislike the idea of progress, but because a quieter, secluded Crescombe suits . . .' I hesitate. 'It suits their way of life.'

'You mean, their smuggling?'

He's not as naïve as I thought, then. 'Yes.'

'So, what should I do?' he asks, a little helplessly.

I look at him again, reminding myself that, beyond his gaudy clothes and tufty hair, is a man of power and influence. A man who's risked a lot for this town, and who'll likely risk more to preserve his vision. I couldn't have anticipated this conversation, yet perhaps, just perhaps, it was meant to be.

I reach out to touch the miniature rendering of Crockers Nest, resisting the urge to reduce it to splinters beneath my fingers, and say, 'You should remove them.'

Then I tell him everything. How the Crockers have been smuggling for generations, unloading barrels on the beach, piling them up under the house, then moving them to Harcourt Manor. How Harcourt himself is part of it – in charge of it, even – as is half the town, which is why Montgomery will find few allies here. And I tell him how, any night now, the family and their men are planning to lure a ship towards the rocks at Crockers Point, plunder its cargo, and leave all its crew for dead.

The only thing I don't tell him is my role in all of this. I'm a coward, perhaps. But does it really matter, now I've lit my last signal?

When I'm finished, Montgomery's eyes are popping. For a while, he doesn't seem to know what to say, and simply stares between me and his miniature town. Until, at last, he whispers, 'You would share this about your own family?'

'They're not my family,' I tell him, thinking of my poor mother, and of my father who will never return here.

Montgomery nods, seems to understand, but doesn't appear to know what to do next. I want him to ring a bell, have a carriage prepared, ride to Ilfracombe or Barnstaple. I need him to alert another coastguard, or a customs officer, or a constable – some authority who can break down the doors of Crockers Nest, find all the evidence it contains, then flush out the family like rats.

Instead, he just scratches his head, making his vivid hair stand on end, and says, 'You have given me much to think about, Miss Crocker.'

I want to shake him. I've given him so much more than that; I've given him enough information to take this town for himself. All he has to do is use it.

But I don't dare say any more – I'm fortunate he didn't throw me out as soon as he saw me. So, as he turns back towards his model, his bushy eyebrows knotted in a frown, I begin to retreat from the desk.

I'm almost at the door when Montgomery says, 'He isn't here, you know.'

'Sorry?'

'George.'

It's lucky he's no longer looking at me, because I feel my face grow hot – again, he's more astute than I realised. But beneath my blush is a pang of disappointment, even panic: where are you?

'He's never here,' Montgomery continues, absently. 'As I said, I was hoping he might paint this' – he indicates the model of Crescombe – 'before he leaves. But he's been so distracted of late. At this rate I will be fortunate if he even finishes my portrait.'

I look, once more, to the painting in the corner. It's a good likeness, though now I've spoken with its sitter, I'm not sure it does him justice. His expression holds none of the thoughtfulness and vulnerability I've just seen, only pride and ambition. You've made him look a little ridiculous – a reaction, maybe, to feeling like another of his trophies this summer – and I wonder again how your new painting will depict me.

'I can tell him you called,' says Montgomery.

'Thank you, sir,' I mumble.

'Will you show yourself back out?'

Recognising this as a dismissal, I nod and slip from the room.

I should go now. While I'm still in Montgomery's good graces, I should leave this house, trust he'll tell you I was here. But I want to see more. Not just of the cabinets full of treasures, but of this place where you've spent the summer. I want to see where you've stayed, slept, sketched. I want to see where you've looked out for my light.

I hurry back past the spiralling object – the fossil – until I find the marble hallway where, last time, Ma and I came in. From there, I dart up the grand, curving staircase, and along a corridor that leads to the right. Everywhere I look, something catches my eye: an arrangement of spiky shells, the biggest I've ever seen; a collection of animals made of coloured glass; and, in a bottle no larger than my hand, a tiny, intricate ship.

I expect I could take any one of these objects for my own collection and it wouldn't even be missed. Perhaps on another day I would. Today, though, my companionable conversation with Montgomery is too recent, and I'm concentrating on moving through this unfamiliar space unseen. Here, in the heart of the house, I can hear the distant opening of a door, male laughter from downstairs and, at one point, I spy a footman hurrying along the balcony on the other side of the staircase.

I begin to peep into the grand rooms I pass, which all look the same, full of rich fabrics, gilded fixtures and useless clutter. But when I reach the quarters at the end of the corridor, I know at once that this is where you reside. Every surface is scattered with sketches: of the view, of random objects, of people either real or imagined ... Once again, I reflect on this compulsion of yours to draw anything and everything, and wonder what it would be like to have such a gift.

There are smaller clues to your presence, too, like the strands of copper-coloured hair in a brush, and that mermaid motif on a sealing stamp. Above all, it smells of you. Not any artificial aroma – though I see a bottle of that too – but your natural scent, the one even the sea can't wash away. The one I smell when I kiss you, or press my face into your neck, or lay my head against your chest. Somehow, it's fresh and deep all at once and, as I breathe it in, I try to ignore the fluttering in my chest, like a little bird is caged within my ribs.

Soon, Ma or Edwin will notice I'm gone, but perhaps that doesn't matter anymore. I lower myself onto the edge of your four-poster bed, perching on its silky golden cover. I want to lie back, stretch out; I want you to find me here, among your sketches, waiting for you ... But then I glance down at my worn woollen dress, so coarse and dull against the intricate embroidery of the cover and, ashamed, I jump back to my feet.

A beam of low sunlight falls across my sleeve, warming my arm like a comforting hand. It's shining through a doorway and, as I approach, I smell something oily with a tang of what might be turpentine. It's your studio, I realise, and though I should turn back – this feels too personal, like reading someone else's letters – I've already peered into the room, already seen what's on the easel by the window.

You've talked about the painting often, and with great passion, but I hardly even listened. I dismissed it as enthusiasm for a passing diversion. How very wrong I was. I may have little to compare it to, but the moment I see it, I know: it's extraordinary. Dark and strange and sinister, yet at the same time full of light, full of hope.

I move towards it in a trance, its pull as powerful as that of the sea itself. My gaze is darting across the canvas as I try to drink in its every detail, but then my vision blurs, and it all starts to swim together. I blink, hard, and to my surprise tears drip down my cheeks and onto the paint-splattered sheet at my feet.

Why am I crying? I tell myself it's because I'm in awe of your skill, and flair, and dedication – and of your courage, too, because never before has it been clearer what a feat it is to brave those murky waters with only my light to guide you. But it isn't just that, not really. Standing there, humbled by this scene from our story, I'm crying because it isn't possible to create something like this from apathy or duplicity. This painting is truth. Every brushstroke sings with something I've never before allowed myself to accept from you: love.

And with this realisation – this revelation – that fluttering bird within my chest is singing too. In my fear, I've kept you at arm's length, dismissed you in my mind as a shallow fool, when you are so much wiser than me, and know your heart so much better. But I see you now. You are the light, not I. You've been shining all this time, beckoning to me through the gloom, and I can't suppress it any longer, this thrill, this joy, this *love*.

I turn from the painting, my skin humming with the knowledge that the rest of my life starts today. I want to take one last look at this golden town, but your studio has grown dim, and when I approach the window I see the sun has already set.

Nevertheless, I stare out at the darkening bay, standing so close to the window that my breath fogs the glass. At first, I think it's me distorting the view, but then I understand: the mist is back. It's smudging the scene before me, rendering it more like your painting than ever, but this land is so familiar to me that even through the haze I have my bearings. I trace the shadowy curve of coast until my gaze rests upon the spot where Crockers Nest must be, and I stare at it a while, wondering whether I've already seen the last of that hateful house.

Then, as I'm watching, something happens that I've never seen before – because it shouldn't be happening, not without me – and it's so unexpected, so foreboding that my whole body starts to quake: up at Crockers Point, a light flares in the darkness, like the sudden opening of an eye.

18

The Graveyard

Cora Crocker
1822–1840

The writing was still visible, but not for long. Already, ivy was creeping back over the gravestone, threatening Finley's efforts of the other week. Soon, even this scant proof of Cora's existence would be reabsorbed into the earth.

Finley pulled at a few blades of the damp grass at the base of the stone. Was she really under here, lying inert just beneath his feet? He felt further into the greenery, his fingertips finding the cold soil beneath. He wanted to go deeper, to plunge his hands right into the earth; he had the strongest compulsion to dig and dig until he discovered something physical of this restless spirit that roamed Crescombe: her bones, her teeth, a few scraps of whatever they had buried her in.

Who *had* buried her? The Crockers, he assumed, because although he didn't imagine them to have been particularly sentimental, it had been another, more God-fearing time. Perhaps, then, this measly headstone had been their final insult to the *bastard baby* they had confined to the attic room. Or what if, Finley thought with a shudder, the Crockers had given Cora a place in their family plot out of a sense of guilt?

The crew of *The Persephone*, he remembered, were buried elsewhere, in consecrated ground at Harcourt Manor. In The Delmore

Experience, Finley had read that this churchyard had been unable to accommodate so many bodies at such short notice, but had the lord of the manor had an ulterior motive for wanting them on his own land? If, as the vicar had suggested, the Harcourts had long been in cahoots with the Crockers, had this alliance extended to the wrecking? Last night, Megan had told him the wreckers would silence any survivors, and Finley was suddenly certain that many of those bodies buried at Harcourt Manor would have the same tell-tale head wounds as Delmore.

The thought of it – of all those nameless, murdered men slung into the ground – made Finley feel unsteady, and he teetered a little where he crouched. He was so weary he might have run here, and a part of him wanted to let himself tip over, to lie back and disappear into this wet, overgrown grass. With effort, he extended a hand to support himself, and as his fingers found the cold stone of Cora's little grave, something began to surge through his chest, as urgent as nausea, the sound of it already ringing in his ears: a desperate, endless scream.

'What's the matter with you?'

Finley twisted around, overbalancing into the tangle of vegetation. The wizened figure of Seymour the vicar was glaring at him from the path. But that *scream* . . . Finley stared around at the otherwise deserted graveyard as he scrambled to his feet. Had it been her? Had it been *him*?

'What are you doing?' demanded the vicar, eyeing the gravestones behind Finley, as though expecting to find them vandalised.

'I—Nothing.'

Finley tripped as he attempted to extract himself from the undergrowth, then joined the vicar on the path.

'You don't look very well,' said Seymour, with more suspicion than sympathy.

'I'm fine.'

The vicar looked unconvinced, and Finley imagined how he must look: shaken and clammy, with soil-smeared fingers and a soggy, grubby bandage beginning to unravel from one hand. Nevertheless, the other man asked, 'How's your booklet?'

It took Finley a moment to realise what he meant. 'Oh – yeah, good,' he said, feeling little enthusiasm for the project that had occupied him these last few weeks. 'Finished, really – we're expecting copies from the printer any day.'

'Well then, you probably won't want to hear this,' sniffed the vicar, 'but I did a little more digging into your Crockers . . .'

'No, I want to hear it,' Finley assured him, craving anything that might reveal more about Cora.

'Don't get too excited,' cautioned Seymour, 'it isn't much. But I spoke with a friend who's a member of all those genealogy websites and so on, and he managed to find the last of the Crockers through the National Archives, which has a lot of information on criminal trials and convictions, including convict voyages.'

'Ah,' said Finley, trying to mask his disappointment, for the Crockers' transportation had been after Cora's time.

'Apparently Agnes Crocker and her sons were deported in 1842 on a ship called *The Shepherd*,' continued the vicar. 'My friend couldn't find out what happened to them on the other side, so either they fell into obscurity or changed their name – which wasn't unheard of,' he added. 'There was a great deal of stigma attached to arriving as a convict, as you can imagine. What's interesting, though, is that four Crockers boarded that ship at Plymouth in September – and only three arrived in Botany Bay the following January.'

'Really?' said Finley, now interested in spite of himself.

'Yes, the youngest – Edwin, I believe? – perished on the journey there. The Crocker boys had a reputation for being big and brutish, but those crossings were dangerous and conditions were appalling.

A bad case of dysentery or similar could have taken out even the strongest of men.'

And Edwin Crocker might not have been the strongest of men, thought Finley, failing to summon much sympathy for the slight, one-eyed figure he had encountered on the cliffs, luring a whole ship to its doom.

'Another interesting titbit my friend dug up was how the Crockers were finally brought to trial,' continued Seymour, who seemed to be enjoying relaying this research. 'As I think I said before, in close-knit communities like these, everyone was either part of the smuggling, or convinced through bribery or blackmail to keep quiet about it. Coastguards or customs officers usually had to catch smugglers in the act to have any hope of convicting them.

'But that's not actually what happened here,' the vicar went on. 'Instead, it seems someone rather influential started building a case against the Crockers over a couple of years, and even ended up testifying against them in court.'

'Who?' asked Finley.

'Ambrose Montgomery,' said Seymour, with a small smile.

Finley stared at him, momentarily doubting they were thinking of the same person; it seemed so unlikely that the preening, boyish figure from Delmore's unfinished portrait had brought down a family like the Crockers.

'I was surprised too,' admitted the vicar. 'I always thought he sounded like a bit of an idiot, getting himself into debt over piers and suchlike. But yes, it seems he was instrumental in getting them convicted.'

'I suppose he wanted them out of the way of his fancy seaside resort?' speculated Finley.

'Perhaps – though it's worth remembering that, around the time the Crockers were deported, Montgomery was enjoying more visitors to Crescombe than ever before, because *Hero's Bay* was still here . . .' Seymour frowned. 'But I can't really think why else he would have done it. Adrian up at the museum might have theories, I suppose?'

'Hmm,' said Finley, wondering, not for the first time, how much Montgomery had known about the last few weeks of Delmore's life.

'Anyway, that's all I have,' said the vicar, a little abruptly.

'No, that's a lot, thanks.'

'Though it would have been interesting to discover what nefarious deeds Agnes Crocker and her two eldest got up to Down Under,' mused Seymour. 'Assuming, of course, they hadn't seen the error of their ways on the journey there . . .' He tweaked the wooden cross hanging from his neck, the string of which had become twisted. 'I suppose sometimes one has to content oneself with not knowing all the answers.'

'Yeah . . .' said Finley, fearing this might also be the case for him with Cora.

As the vicar turned to go, Finley stared back towards her little grave, which was dwarfed by the larger stones around it, jutting from the greenery like shark fins. Earlier, he had felt almost compelled to come here, but now, that unplaceable scream still raw in his memory, his feet felt firmly rooted to the path.

'It's funny,' called Seymour, a little way off now, 'that such a disreputable family has the prettiest plot in the graveyard.'

Finley said nothing, but he wasn't sure this was how he would have described it: the wildest, maybe, or the most atmospheric – but the *prettiest*?

'In spring, at least,' added the vicar, his voice growing faint as he continued to shuffle back towards the church. 'It's quite a sight, actually – that whole corner is covered in violets.'

*

'Cora.'

It was a nice name. Old-fashioned, but not fussy. There was something unexpected about it too, that hard C-sound followed by the softer *aura*; it was like the crash of a wave followed by the slink of water over sand.

'Cora.' Finley tried it out again, then as a question: 'Cora?'

Was he expecting a reply? Something akin to the bang of the window, or that scraping of stone? Finley's shoulders tensed as he looked around his room, but nothing happened. All was still – the dried flowers on the mantlepiece, the little framed pictures of boats nailed to the wooden walls – and, save for the hum of the fridge and the continuous murmur of the sea down below, all was silent too.

Finley sank back onto his bed, picturing the moment the hooded figure of Edwin Crocker had brandished that lantern in the dark, and *The Persephone* emerging from the mist, set to smash against the rocky shore. He imagined, somewhere down below, the Crockers and their cohort would have been lying in wait to pull ashore the spoils of the wrecking, their bats primed for any sign of survivors ... This, Finley was now sure, was the reason Cora's spirit was still bound to Crescombe; because her cousin had lit a signal that had not only lured the crew of *The Persephone* to their deaths, but Delmore too.

You're too late, Edwin had laughed, presumably to Cora – but what if Finley wasn't? Megan was right, there was no way he could change what had happened in the past, but could he do something in the present to tweak this chilling loop, this echo of events that had already claimed at least two more lives?

This was the question that had consumed Finley for much of his last week in Crescombe. Each night, he scrambled up that slope in the dark, roaming the cliff path, both craving and dreading another sighting of that phantom figure. He wasn't even sure what he would do if he got to Edwin any earlier. Knock the lantern from his hands? Wrestle him to the ground? Even if either were possible, which Finley doubted, the hooded figure remained elusive, as did his light.

'*Cora?*'

His voice was more urgent now, because he was sick of waiting around, of letting all of this just happen to him. Some kind of connection existed between him and Cora Crocker and, for weeks, he had been shrinking from the possibility that – in some way, in some form – she was reaching out to him. But what if he reached back? What if he reached *first*?

The idea was almost unthinkable. He was a person who double-knotted his laces, hated driving on the motorway, crossed the street at even a hint of a disagreement up ahead. Having been victimised throughout his adolescence, he had since dedicated a great deal of energy to making himself feel safe – and this was decidedly unsafe territory. These were forces even someone like Dawn wouldn't go near.

But where had being who he was ever got him? It had left him heartbroken, unemployed, with a chip on his shoulder about his diabetes and his overachieving sister, and relentless feelings of inadequacy. It had, in fact, landed him right here, in this room, contemplating all these half-crazed ideas by himself.

How to reach Cora? How to trigger this series of events he needed to disrupt? Pushing himself from the bed, Finley padded over to the table, where he had left the tinderbox among clutter from his own stay: a few coins and half-eaten rolls of sweets; a ticket for The Delmore Experience and a pair of cheap sunglasses he'd already scratched; there was even that old-fashioned matchbook he'd received with the bill at Marina's, all that time ago.

Sweeping aside this debris, he began to lay out Cora's belongings instead: the shells and stones, Delmore's ring and sketch, the scraps of violets. He then dug into his pocket for the larimar stone, which he considered setting down too, but somehow it remained in his hand, where it seemed to just *fit*, in spite of the twinge from beneath his bandage.

'Cora.'

Her body, whatever had happened to it, might be gone, but these items she had collected had survived her. She had kept them for a reason, and as Finley began to study each one – picking it up, turning it over – he was aware, once again, that the last person to have touched them was likely Cora herself. In trying to bridge the gap between them, then, was one of these objects the keystone?

At the same time, though, Finley had the strongest feeling that he was missing something. Not just an idea or memory, but something more tangible, as though one of the objects from the tinderbox – something inherently *Cora* – had got lost. But that didn't make any sense; everything he'd found in it was right here.

With a growl, Finley stood up, distancing himself both from the tinderbox and from this pointless endeavour. What was he *doing*? This was so stupid – *he* was so stupid, still obsessing over this when it had already cost him his friendship with Megan, and perhaps some of his sanity too.

In a fit of frustration, he lobbed the larimar stone across the room. It hit the door to the kitchenette then bounced across the floor with a satisfying clatter. Finley then turned his attention to the other objects, knocking them off the table with a sweep of his bandaged hand. It wasn't enough: he wanted to crush each one beneath his feet, then tear off the rest of the room's wooden panelling, maybe claw at his own skin too, as Cynthia had done ... But he was too tired: not just from the lack of sleep, but of always feeling so weak, so wrong; of always feeling like he shouldn't be here.

*

The following afternoon, Finley returned from a day of roaming Crockers Point to find Lorraine waiting for him in reception. On the front desk was a cardboard box, over which she was brandishing a pair of scissors as though poised to start carving up a Sunday roast.

'It's addressed to you, so I didn't want to open it ...' she said, the scissors twitching in her fingers.

'It's fine,' Finley said, 'go ahead.'

Not needing to be told twice, Lorraine fell upon the box, hacking at its tape and then peering inside with such wonder she might have been a pirate contemplating the glittering contents of a treasure chest.

'Well, would you look at that!' She threw aside several scrunches of packing paper. 'Oh, they're gorgeous! And what about that *smell*?' She leaned over the box and inhaled.

Finley waited for her to remember he was there, and when she did, he was handed half a dozen copies of the booklet he had spent the last month writing. He felt a little underwhelmed as he flicked through the top one, although the paper looked glossy, the text and illustrations crisp, and all the pages seemed to be in the right order.

'Oh, I *love* them!' Lorraine gushed, still pulling booklets from the box. 'How clever you are, Finley! I'm going to put them in the rooms straight away ... No, no, you keep those ones,' she said, when he attempted to hand back the copies she'd pressed into his hands. 'You'll want to hold on to some, as a memento.'

After she had bustled off, Finley lowered himself into the chair behind the barrels that served as the front desk, wondering how much of a souvenir of his time in Crockers Nest these booklets really were. Admittedly, they would quieten people like Fiona, who'd assumed he'd done nothing all summer, and if any guests did bother to pick one up, they would learn a pretty thorough history of the guesthouse. Despite its focus on Crockers Nest as a hub for local smuggling activity, though, Finley didn't feel like the place represented within these pages truly reflected the one in which he had stayed this summer.

To start with, it had seemed both bad for business and in very poor taste to dwell on the apparent suicides of Jacqueline Fairchild and Michelle Lei, but he wasn't sure he had been right to omit them entirely. As far as Finley was concerned, their deaths were the biggest mystery of the guesthouse's modern era, and his not even making a passing reference to them felt a little like he had colluded in some kind of cover-up.

Then there was Delmore, who wasn't so much as mentioned in the booklet. Early on, Finley and Lorraine had agreed that trying to tenuously link the artist to Crockers Nest would look a little desperate. Now, though, given what he thought he knew – that Delmore had swum here, loved here – it felt strange that the artist had been entirely erased from the guesthouse's story.

Though not as strange as the absence of the figure who had dominated Finley's thoughts these past few weeks. Yet almost everything he knew about Cora Crocker was based on conjecture, or on feelings, dreams and visions he couldn't explain. If he had recorded only what he *knew* to be true about her – that an illegitimate baby had been born to Ellen Babbage, sister of Agnes 'Ma' Crocker, and had died young – it would have seemed so anecdotal as to be a waste of ink. But if he had written down everything he *believed* to be true about Cora – her involvement in the smuggling, her love affair with Delmore, her being the Hero of the famous painting – it would, without proof, have made him sound like a complete fantasist.

'Actually, my love, I think I'll leave a few here.' Lorraine was back, still clutching her pile of booklets. 'And you couldn't move that box somewhere, could you? I'd get Martin to do it, but he's gone home to change because ...' She suddenly became very interested in the box's tendril of packing tape. 'Well, if you really need to know, we're going out for a little dinner.'

'Oh,' said Finley, who hadn't *needed* to know this, but was amused to learn it nonetheless.

Now he looked at her, Lorraine did seem a bit dressed up, in a floaty pink and orange ensemble and lots of chunky jewellery. Her face was rather pink too, even through her make-up. Finley pictured Martin up in the old coastguard's cottage, likely fretting over what to wear, and suddenly felt inordinately fond of them both.

'You couldn't check everything's locked up before you go to bed?' asked Lorraine, still a little flushed as she handed him a bunch of keys. 'You'll be on your own tonight.'

There was a note of concern in her voice. Evidently, their heart-to-heart in the sunroom hadn't stopped her from worrying about him – though perhaps that was unsurprising, given he had then hared off into the darkness.

Now, Finley once again assured her he was fine, though the thought of the empty guesthouse made him feel melancholy. Crescombe's festival crowds were long gone, and he thought the English school holidays must be just about over because most of the families had departed too. Now, whenever he ventured into town, Finley felt conspicuous, superfluous, as though one of the tour buses still stopping off at The Delmore Experience had left him behind by accident.

It was time to leave. His open return to Edinburgh was due to expire and, really, why shouldn't he just catch a train in the next few days? The booklet was done, the guesthouse was quiet, and, as much as he wanted to patch things up with Megan, he didn't see how they could come back from their argument of the other night.

But he couldn't go yet, could he? With a glance down at his bandaged hand, Finley didn't even think it was fear trapping him here now – or not *just* fear, anyway. He had come so far, discovered so much; how could he leave when the chance to do something – to make a difference – felt so close?

As darkness began to steal over the bay, Finley checked everything was locked, just as Lorraine had asked. When he then stepped out of the sunroom doors, it was into a mizzle that immediately dampened his face and caught in his hair. He peered through the haze towards Crescombe's eastern cliff, as he had every night since he'd encountered that phantom figure – and, like every night since, he could see no light up at Crockers Point.

Deciding he would head up there regardless, Finley edged around a flowerbed and, with a yelp, leaped backwards: the hatchway of the cellar was wide open; he had almost tumbled right in. Martin must have forgotten about it – maybe he'd been distracted ahead of his date – and as Finley crouched to close the hatchway doors, he noticed, somewhere in the depths below, a faint glow.

His right hand twitched in pain, but he ignored it, still staring down into that square of darkness. The light was too faint to be coming from the cellar's overhead bulb – though it seemed unlikely Martin had left a torch down there for a second time. As Finley began to edge down the hatchway steps, it occurred to him it might be the torchlight of an *intruder* . . . Though, really, anyone who cleared out this place would probably be doing Lorraine a favour.

At the base of the steps, he yanked quickly at the light pull, intending to startle anyone who might be down here. The space flooded with brighter, whiter light, and though Finley couldn't see anyone, he was still a little spooked as all the piles of abandoned clutter appeared. Was it the thought that many of these objects must have outlasted their owners? The almost tangible weight of the house above? Or was he unnerved that the meagre lightbulb only illuminated a fraction of the space, while the rest of it seemed blotted with shadows, ones that could be crawling with spiders or rats; ones in which a figure might be watching, waiting . . .

Get a grip, Finley scolded himself, pressing his thumb against his throbbing palm. The cellar was cold, and he was aware of a faint rolling sound, which was perhaps air circulating the confined space, and reminded him of pressing his ear to a conch shell. But when he glanced around – at a few mouldering cushions, a stack of outdated phone books, an old trouser press – he could no longer see the light of the torch or whatever it was in the brighter overhead glare.

His hand was really hurting now, so he turned back to the hatchway stairs, preparing to go. But as soon as he tugged the light pull again, returning the cellar to darkness, the glow reappeared; a dim, low beam among the clutter, like a child's nightlight. Heart quickening, Finley began to step carefully through the mess towards it, now certain this was the same light he had seen before – and that it was no torch.

Was it his imagination, or was it getting brighter as he approached? *Warm*, it seemed to say, like they were playing that searching game; *getting warmer – really hot now*. It was, he realised, in the mound of broken and damaged objects he had noticed the previous time. He squinted into the glare, over the three-legged chair, the iron-marked curtain, the chipped vase, until he found its source: the lantern with the smashed glass.

Finley's burning hand gave another involuntary twitch, and though he grasped at his wrist, he was already following the direction his fingers wanted to go. The lantern was small and worn, its frame speckled with rust. It appeared to have some kind of shutter mechanism, though it was difficult to tell beneath the cracked, grimy glass, some of which had completely fallen away, leaving a line of lethal-looking shards, like jagged teeth.

As Finley's fingers closed around its handle, it was like taking the hand of someone beloved he hadn't seen in many years. The metal creaked as he straightened up again. This felt familiar; it felt *right*. Though when he held the lantern aloft, he realised that although it contained the stub of a grubby candle, it wasn't lit, and neither could he see anything to explain that ever-increasing glow.

It was dazzling now. Finley had to shield his face from it, as he would against the sun. Brighter and brighter it grew – painfully bright – until, with a little pop like a bulb blowing, it went out, and Finley was plunged back into darkness. He stood there a moment, breathing hard, the image of the lantern still burned into his mind – along with the realisation that what he'd initially assumed to be rust and dirt wasn't that at all, but a far older version of the substance he could now feel leaking through his bandage and running down his wrist, dripping onto the broken glass below.

Tonight. It's tonight. They're doing it *tonight*.

The mist and the darkness are thickening as I pelt down the hill, but that light on the opposite cliff is still streaming through the gloom. I thought I would know when it was time, that I would be the one forced to lead the ship astray. And because it's not me up there, I can't suppress that old fear that we have summoned something through our stories – that one of the spirits we've invented is now beckoning back.

I tumble down into the town, where only a sliver of dark beach is visible, for the sea is right in, grasping at Crescombe's toes. The promenade, its own lights dim in the haze, is almost deserted, though as I race along it I almost collide with a group of gentlemen spilling from the new hotel. A few call out to me, laughing, but I don't stop. I can't stop, not until I snuff out that light.

If I do, I can save all the men whose lives will be lost tonight – and I can save *you*. Because what if you see it? You told me to light my lantern, that you would come for me, and as the night deepens, even I would struggle to pinpoint the location of that beam. *It isn't me*, I want to scream, but I don't know where you are, and I'm trying not to think about what will happen if you've already slipped into that inky water ...

A little past the church, I collapse against a tree, a sharp pain in my side; I've never run so fast or far. Yet as I pause there, my breathing ragged, someone looms out of the darkness and tries to block my way. With a gasp, I dart around him, ignoring his shout of recognition, because it's only one of our men, and he won't follow – he won't leave his post. It's even reassuring, the thought of him and all the others lining the lanes, waiting: it's not yet done, I tell myself, forcing my feet onwards; there may still be time.

It's almost pitch black in the woods, and I must feel my way up to Crockers Point as though blindfolded. I know this path – I've trodden it all my life – yet still I stumble over roots and stones, still I startle from snagging branches and the rustling and snuffling all around me.

Then, up ahead, I see it: *the light*. I throw myself forward, out of the trees, clambering up the last part of open slope. The figure holding the lantern is hooded, but I know who it is. Even if I didn't recognise his size and stance, who else would dare? And though I would never have done this, the sight of him holding that light – *my* light – fills me with rage for more than just his wicked aim, and I fly towards him, intending to knock my lantern – and maybe my cousin, too – clean off the cliff.

Edwin hears me coming, his hood falling from his face as he turns. I should keep running – throw myself over with him if I have to – but something vast is looming out of the fog, and I stumble to a halt, meeting Edwin's pale eye, which is bright with triumph. Even before he opens his mouth, I know what he's going to say:

'You're too late.'

After that, everything is noise. The crash of the ship striking the rocks; sharper than thunder, deeper than gunfire. Edwin's laughter, high and harsh and wild. My own screams. Behind me too, I hear hurrying footsteps, puffing breath, a dull thud, before – just for a moment – a clang of pain rings through my skull.

And then, nothing.

*

'Now, where've you been?'

I hardly know where I am now. I've opened my eyes to darkness, and a cool, hard floorboard against my cheek. It smells of damp, though I also detect the faint, familiar scent of violets, so I must be in my room.

When I push myself up to sitting, my head is pounding. I blink, willing my eyes to adjust to the gloom. My lantern is on the floor, emitting only a faint stripe of light, for its shutter is almost completely closed. Next to it, perched on a stool, is a large, shadowy someone: *Ma*. That it's her prompts a rush of rage but, for now, I can't remember why.

'I asked you a question, girl,' she says. 'Where've you been?'

I can't remember that either. I think I was at Westcliff, and talking to Montgomery – though that can't be right, can it?

'The churchyard,' I croak, hoping to throw her by prodding at one of her oldest wounds. 'I was visiting my mother.'

'Liar.' The word is barely a whisper, but it feels like Ma is shouting. 'You've been with him.'

You. And suddenly it all comes back to me: the light, the dash through the dark, the ship. I stagger to my feet and across the room, my head throbbing. Beyond the window, there's nothing but mist, but as I wrench it open I can hear distant crashes, shouts and screams, and the slavering of the sea, like a beast being fed.

My stomach contracts. Where are you? You could swim right into this, if you haven't already ... I need to find you, stop you.

'Where do you think you're going now?'

Ma's voice is calm, which is so unsettling that halfway to the door I pause. What's she doing here? And how can she just sit so serenely after what they've done?

'I—I need to help.'

She shakes her head. 'Don't take me for a fool, girl.' The little stool creaks beneath her as she leans forward. 'You know, I watched him during that meeting at Westcliff, lounging there in his fine clothes. I saw how he stared and stared at you, drooling like a *dog*. But I wasn't worried. I didn't think he'd get anywhere near you – never dreamed he'd even try.'

My heart is juddering, though I force myself not to react: she doesn't know anything; she *can't*.

'Then I began to see a change in you,' Ma continues. 'The last few weeks, you've been ... *different*. And when you started drenching yourself in that sickly scent, I knew – no matter what nonsense you told me about gathering flowers for your uncle.'

For the first time, there's a tremor of anger in her voice and I tense, bracing myself for some physical rebuke. But, for now, she stays seated.

'Still, I convinced myself it was nothing,' she says, more evenly. 'Hoped you'd just bewitched some local boy. But then . . .' She laughs. 'Who around here would want you?'

This hurts, perhaps because it's true; the local boys just ignore me or call me names, sometimes throwing a few stones with their insults. If I came from any other family, they'd probably do worse, but nobody in this town is stupid enough to get on the wrong side of the Crockers.

'No, deep down, I knew it was far more likely you'd caught the eye of someone with more exotic, more *unnatural* tastes,' says Ma. 'Someone who probably only looked your way because he was running out of other women to bed.'

Inwardly, I wince, but I say nothing, determined not to show that her goading is getting to me. Because is this all she has – a hunch, a lucky guess? It doesn't matter anyway – nothing matters, other than finding you – so I stride towards the door and pull, wondering why I'm then surprised to find it locked.

'I've been having a look around,' Ma tells me, ignoring my rattling at the handle. 'I discovered your putrid perfume – and I was very interested to find this.'

My eyes have adjusted to the dim light now, and as I turn I can see the cylindrical outline of my tinderbox clamped between her stubby, calloused fingers. Fresh rage rushes through me: that's *mine*.

'Though, I'll admit, at first I thought it was full of junk . . .'

One by one, Ma tosses my precious objects from the tin: my shells, my stones, my feather, my robin egg – which breaks against the floor. I didn't intend to take any of it with me, but it's still a punch to my heart, her disdain for these treasures. I dig my hands deep into the pocket of my apron, reminding myself that my father's stone and your ring are still safe.

'Junk, junk, junk . . . Or so I thought' – Ma plucks something from the base of the tin – 'until I found this.'

When she unfurls the little scroll, my stomach seems to drop from my body. So much has happened since that sketch, which was just one of your many attempts to draw me. I forgot it was even in there.

'Now, who around here could've produced something like this?' Ma wonders aloud.

Even if I had an answer, my throat has turned too dry to give it. She'll have seen it all, I realise: my name, your initials, the rock just off Crockers Beach. And, sure enough, she stabs towards the sketch, hissing, 'He's been here, hasn't he? To our shore. To your bed.'

Still, I say nothing, though I glance towards the weak light of the lantern at her feet. Perhaps it's the association with you – or perhaps I just can't face Ma's disgusted expression.

'Yes, that's how you managed it, isn't it?' she says, noticing where I'm looking. 'It took me a while to work it out. You told him that light meant we were out, so that's when he came creeping across our land, into our house.'

Through my fear, I note it hasn't occurred to her that you come from the water, that you make that perilous climb in and out of my window. It's a small comfort, but perhaps it will make a difference.

'You stupid, treacherous little whore!' Finally, Ma's anger boils over. 'Do you think he'll care what you gave up for him when he leaves this place? Do you think he'll even remember you?'

A few days ago – a few hours ago – this might have affected me differently. Now, though, I've seen your painting, and the truth of it gives me courage. I lunge forward to snatch the drawing from her hands – wincing as it tears a little – then stoop to grab my lantern, which she must have brought back from Crockers Point: these are mine too.

'What are you doing?' she asks.

In my hand, the lantern is rocking from its handle, urging me on. 'Leaving.'

'With him?' Ma laughs. 'Do you really think you'll be able to hold his interest beyond Crescombe? Do you even know what happens to girls like you out there?'

As she starts to tell me, I pull at the door again, as though it might have unlocked itself. It hasn't, of course, and neither can I wrench it from its hinges, so instead I dare to take a step towards Ma and say, 'Anything's better than here.'

Something tenses in her face and, as she rises, I once again anticipate the impact of her fist or her boot. But all she does is ask, 'What have you told him about us?'

I almost laugh myself. Because this isn't about you coming here, or my virtue, or even my fate beyond this night. It's about what it's always about: protecting the family.

'He doesn't know anything,' I tell her, though, as I say it, I think of what I shared with Montgomery this evening – how I gave him every detail he could need to see them brought to justice. Now, more than ever, I hope he listened.

Heartened by the thought of this other, secret betrayal, I step back towards the door, the lantern squeaking in my hand. 'Open it.'

Ma folds her arms across her chest, tries to arrange her coarse features into a softer expression. 'No, you'll stay here, where you're safe. Because I promised my sister I would . . .'

But I don't even hear the rest of her sentence, because rage is suddenly crashing through me, and I'm shouting, 'You broke that promise when you told my father I was dead!'

Her mouth falls open. 'Who told you that?'

'Edwin.'

She grunts with annoyance, then jabs a finger towards me. 'You know nothing about your father, what kind of man he was.'

'I do,' I insist, picturing his smile as he pressed the sea stone into my hand. 'I remember him.'

'He *destroyed* her!'

At last, the full force of Ma's anger emerges, and though she still hasn't laid a finger on me, her anguished roar seems to shake the very foundations of the house. Perhaps she even surprises herself, because then she sniffs, and continues more quietly, 'Nelly was a good girl. Too good for this place, and far too good for the likes of him. Our parents didn't have much, but she was kind and pretty and could have had her pick of the men in this town. She could have married Harcourt!'

I picture the shrivelled old man from the meeting at Westcliff, who would've already been a decrepit widower eighteen years ago, and I shudder. Was that the best my mother could have hoped for?

'But then *he* came,' says Ma, 'and he was nothing – less than nothing. Born a *slave*,' she sneers, 'only freed because he saved somebody from drowning, or so he claimed. He didn't even have a proper name, just the one he chose for himself.'

'What was it?' I whisper, because if he or my mother ever told me, I've forgotten.

Ma looks as though she might keep it to herself, but then spits, '*Titus.*'

To Agnes Crocker, I expect it sounds as ridiculous as the notion of a man naming himself. But to me, it's perfect: *Titus*. It suits the man I met that day, for it feels both faraway and familiar – so perhaps I did know it, long ago.

'He came here with a ship, got himself shot by a customs officer during a landing,' Ma continues, frowning just over my head, as though she can see the scene playing out on the beach beyond my window. 'We lost men that night, but that wretch survived and, well, we couldn't just leave him bleeding out in the sand. We were honour-bound to bring him in, patch him up. And how did he repay us? By defiling one of our own – an innocent girl!'

'She loved him,' I say, because although I don't remember much of her, I remember this.

'She was a fool,' says Ma, though she doesn't contradict me. 'She was my sister, but she was a fool. He filled her head with all sorts of stories as she nursed him back to health, so of course she was awed by him, flattered by his attention. Of course she—' Ma breaks off, her expression hardening. 'When I found out, I wanted him dead. I told William to do it – I would've done it myself if they'd let me near him. But William said we had no idea who he really was, what friends he might have, so they beat him and sent him off on the next ship west . . .'

She trails off, still looking lost in the past, and though I don't have time for this tale – did you see the light? Are you on your way? – I don't want her to stop. I've never heard her speak like this before.

'Then there was *you*.' Looking back into the room, at me, Ma loads that last word with contempt. 'Perhaps, if he'd been someone else, we could've pretended you were one of mine – you could've been Edwin's twin. But look at you!' My skin crawls, not from the insult, but at the idea of *her* as my mother, of *him* as my brother. 'I wanted to leave you outside the church – or better yet, out on the cliff – but she begged and begged to keep you. She was convinced he was coming back for you both.'

'He did come back – I met him!' I cry, wondering whether Ma will give me the answer to something I've long wondered. 'Why didn't he take us away then?'

'Because she was *dying*!' Ma cries, and now the shake in her voice is more from grief than anger. 'She was too sick and you were too young to go sailing off on some godforsaken ship with a feckless savage who hadn't a farthing to his made-up name. I told him so – and a lot more besides. Until, in the end, he knew I was right, and he left, promising to come back a more honourable provider,' she adds, with another sneer.

'And he did come back again,' I say, returning to the root of this conversation. 'He came back after she'd died, and you told him I'd died too. *Why?*'

Now my voice is trembling, but if I expect her to look ashamed I'm mistaken. If anything, she looks proud.

'Because it was his fault!' she snaps. 'Nelly was never the same after she met him, not in her body and not in her mind either. He filled her head with all these impossible dreams . . . It broke her, having you, and then it broke her some more when he left. That's why she died, because of the both of you.'

This pains me as much as she intends. I want to tell her that her reasoning is skewed – *she* was the one who sent him away – but she still hasn't answered my question.

'So why not let him take me? You could have been rid of the both of us.'

Ma smiles, then seems to consider her next words. 'I don't know if he really loved my sister,' she says, her voice quietening. 'I suspect, like your artist, he simply found a trusting girl and couldn't help himself. But you . . . As soon as he knew about you, he loved you. Everything he did from then on was for you.'

I don't know why she's telling me this – why she's giving me this unexpected gift – but it fits the image of him I've had in my head all these years and a lump rises to my throat.

'So, that's why, girl,' concludes Ma, her tone flat. 'He took her from me, so I took you from him.'

It takes me a moment to understand what she's said – for it to sink in that the only reason I've been abandoned here my whole life is one woman's spite – but when I do, something breaks inside me too. I lunge forward, not even knowing what I'm going to do, only that I want to hurt her. But Ma cuffs me away, and I lurch back, the lantern swinging from my fingers.

'Besides, you've been useful, haven't you?' she says, ignoring my outburst. 'If nothing else, you've sharp eyes. Until, of course, you made the same stupid mistake as your mother—'

'So let me go,' I interrupt. I won't beg her, but neither will I stand here wasting any more time. 'If I've outlived my usefulness, let me go.'

'As I said, I made a promise to my sister . . .'

'She wouldn't want this,' I say, desperately trying to appeal to whatever's left of her heart. 'You know she wouldn't. Let me go.'

'No.'

She folds her arms again and I know that, no matter what she says or even thinks, she's keeping me here for the same reason she denied me to my father: pure, unbending spite. And I can't fight it, or her, but somehow I need to get through that door. I need to get to you.

'No, you know too much for me to let you go,' says Ma, giving me a little shove, so I stumble further back into the room.

This time, remembering my conversation with Montgomery brings me no comfort. Ma can't possibly guess that I spoke to the developer, but I fear she suspects something, because when she reaches out again it's not to push me, but to curl her fingers around my throat.

I freeze, and as her hand begins to squeeze, I'm more surprised than anything. Ma's always been cruel, but for as long as I can remember I've known about that promise and the protection it affords me: I'm her sister's child. As my throat begins to tighten under her grip, I wonder if that matters anymore – and I think Ma is wondering the same, because her expression is thoughtful, like this is some experiment and she's unsure of the outcome.

Making a decision for us both, I dig my nails into her hand, wrenching myself free. I half expect her to grab me again, but instead she flexes her fingers a few times, like almost strangling me has caused her mild discomfort.

'I'll look out for your artist tonight,' she murmurs.

I almost miss this over the sound of my own coughing. 'What?'

'There'll be all sorts happening out there – and we can't have any witnesses.'

At the unspoken threat, my insides turn to ice. But Ma is unlocking the door now – she's *leaving* – so I make one last, desperate appeal.

'Let me come,' I plead, raising the lantern still flickering beneath my hand, as though to remind her of all I've done for this family. 'Let me help, let me—'

But I can hardly hear myself over her laughter. 'Do you think me stupid? As if I'd ever trust you with anything again, you deceitful little bitch!'

She seizes the lantern from my fingers and throws it across the room, where it lands with a smash that snuffs out the tiny flame and litters the floor with broken glass. In the sudden darkness, I catch a glimpse of her raised fist, before I too am sent sprawling.

Bang!

The door slams shut: she's gone.

'Wait!'

But it's no use: I hear the clunk of the lock – that guttural, immovable sound – and then her heavy footsteps grow faint.

For a moment, I remain on the floor, dizzy from shock, from panic, and from the pain in my head and throat. From the pain somewhere else too ... I look down, gasping as I see a great shard of glass lodged in my hand. It's jutting at an angle, like those rocks on the beach, and in the gloom my blood looks very dark as it pools in my palm and begins to trickle down my wrist.

19

Hero's Bay

In the lamplight of Finley's room, the lantern was an even sorrier sight: its surfaces looked grimier, its bloodstains starker, and there were dents in its asymmetrical frame that he hadn't noticed in the cellar, suggesting it had once been struck or dropped. Its smashed glass seemed more like predatory teeth than ever, and Finley feared that if he reached between the cracked panels to light the candle end within, those spiky jaws might snap down on his hand – though in a way, he reflected, picking at the fresh bandage around his palm, they already had.

Should he light it? This, he now – somehow – understood, was what he'd been missing: the object, the *keystone*, that could bridge the gap to Cora. Though the lantern's bruised and bloodied appearance made him hesitate, teetering between unexpected courage and a more familiar sense of self-preservation. Did he really want to venture any further into the traumatic events of that summer? But then, he thought, already reaching for the matchbook from Marina's – how could he *not*?

After the scrape and flare of the match, Finley examined the tiny flame quivering next to his fingers, tempted to shake it straight out again. But he guided it towards the lantern, wincing as his injured hand passed all that broken glass, and cajoled it towards the stump of wax. At first, he thought it wasn't going to work: the ancient, long-dormant wick hissed and crackled at being disturbed, while an acrid smell of burning dust filled Finley's nostrils. Then, just as he was considering looking for a more modern candle – or perhaps taking this as a sign that he should leave well alone – the flame caught, and the lantern was suddenly alight.

Finley set it down on the table, next to Cora's tinderbox, whose objects he'd returned after his fit of temper the previous day. Then he backed away, partly to give himself room to blow out the match, for its flame was nipping at his fingers, but also because the lantern's light was blazing again – much more so than seemed natural. As he squinted at it, Finley became aware of the soapy smell of violets filling the room, mingling with the smoky aroma of the match. Before, without warning, Cora's tinderbox flew off the table, its contents spilling across the floor – only this time, Finley hadn't touched it.

He stared at the scattered objects, his breathing hard and fast. There was a strange new tightness to his throat, as though it were bruised – something was clicking every time he tried to swallow. Then, before his pulse had even slowed, the lantern rolled off the table too, clunking against the floor, its light disappearing just as the bulb of Finley's bedside lamp popped and went out.

I did it, Finley told himself in the dark, half in wonder, half in horror. He had reached back, had triggered these echoes of the past, setting it all in motion again, and now . . . Now he had to intercept that false light.

Only, when he crossed to the door and tugged at the handle, it was locked.

Finley tried again, knowing he had merely kicked it closed behind him when he'd come up here with the lantern. The door rattled in its frame – just as it had the other week, seemingly of its own accord – but it didn't open, not even when Finley grabbed the crocheted seagull and tried to work its key into the lock.

'Hello?'

Even as he called, he knew it was pointless. Crockers Nest was empty: all the guests had gone, and Lorraine was out with Martin. His nerve wavering, Finley realised there was nobody to help him – and nobody who could have trapped him, either; if someone had locked this door from the other side, they had done it long, long ago.

Creak...

Finley froze, confused, for the slow, grating noise had sounded like an opening door and the one in front of him still wouldn't budge. Then he turned where he stood, forcing himself to stare towards the porthole window – and its latch, which was moving downwards.

A puff of shock escaped him, which seemed to empty his mouth of all moisture, and his eyes bulged in the gloom as he tried to make sense of what he was seeing. He had long ago accepted that the window wasn't being blown open by the wind, but for this to be actually happening here, in front of him like this; to see it being unlatched as though by some invisible hand ...

'Cora?' he whispered.

The window began to open, the circle of darkness beyond making it look like a mouth widening in shock – or in a scream. Heart crashing, Finley pressed himself against the door at his back, willing it to unlock, willing himself right through it, all the while inhaling that cloying scent of violets, which was now so potent he could taste it.

Thunk!

He jumped as the window latch clunked against the neighbouring wall, though it was the same sound that had woken him all summer. Wind was whipping through the room now, nudging Cora's sketch further across the floor, and with it came not just the sound of the sea, but the distant shouts and crashes of another night. So that even before Finley took a stumbling step forward, then another, compelled towards that window as though a fishing line was hooked onto to his ribs, he already knew: once again, he was too late.

My lantern is broken.

It's all I can think about, even as I pull the shard of glass from my palm, drop it to the floor and bundle up my apron against the wound: my ruined, blood-spattered lantern.

Perhaps it's shock – in this moment, everything else is too big to feel – but that lantern was mine. With it, I summoned ships; with it, I summoned *you*. And now, because of Edwin, because of Ma, it is tainted and shattered.

Should I try and light it again? If you saw my cousin's signal – if you're already in the water – maybe I could guide you here, away from the worst of it. But as I crawl towards my tinderbox, trying to navigate my way through fragments of glass to find my flint and steel, I pause. Because what if you *didn't* see Edwin's light? Mine could draw you right into this, when perhaps you could simply wake up tomorrow and discover, along with everyone else on your side of town, what we have done.

Where are you?

I've never feared for your life like this before. I had an idea of what you risked, in following my light, but I didn't truly understand until I saw your painting – nor did I want to, before I looked into my own heart. But to love you is to see you clearly, as a brilliant but vulnerable man. One who won't just face the sea tonight – which, though capricious, strikes without malice – but the Crockers.

It's unbearable enough, the idea of your life being snuffed out, but to be the cause of your demise ... How will I stand it? Perhaps, then, it would be a relief to feel Ma's fingers around my throat again. *If you're gone, I'll have nothing left to live for.*

I sway where I'm crouching, lightheaded. The wad of apron in my hand is now soaked through, and it looks like I'm clutching a bloody heart. In the gloom, I survey my scattered treasures: the robin egg is smashed, as are a few of the shells, and the jay feather completely crumpled. With my good hand I begin to pick up anything that remains intact – the pebbles, the sea glass, even the pressed violets – and drop them back into the tinderbox.

It's not a lot to show for a life. Maybe Ma was right, and this is all just junk – though when I dig between the folds of my sodden apron I withdraw my two genuine treasures: the stone and the ring. I turn them over in my left hand a few times, diverted by the clacking sound they make as they knock together, like a pair of dice. Only, there's no point in throwing them. No good fortune awaits me now. The men who gave me these trinkets are gone, or soon to be, so I drop them into the tin with everything else.

The last thing I replace is that treacherous sketch. I wish I could go back to that day, that morning you drew me at Crockers Beach. I wish I could warn myself what was to come – though I knew, didn't I? I might have underestimated the depth of your feelings for me, but I never imagined this would end well.

Even now, I'm surprised by how you depicted me: proud, poised, a little wild. I've never thought of myself like that, but I'm beginning to trust your judgement above my own. So, even after I've rolled up the sketch and staggered up to slide the tinderbox back into the wall – for I won't let the Crockers find this again – that image is still lingering in my mind. It's reminding me: *I'm still here.*

I'm not even really trapped, I realise, turning to stare at the open window. All this time, I've been waiting around to be freed – by my father, by you – but the only person truly stopping me from leaving Crockers Nest has been myself.

Well, no longer. I take a step towards the window, then another, feeling stronger in spite of my raw hand. It's time to hold on to all that hope you've given me, all that daring you've shown me. It's time to roll my own dice.

Because perhaps, if I can save myself, I can also save you.

Finley blinked, summoned back to himself by a cold pressure lining the left side of his face, which turned out to be one of the flimsy safety bars of the porthole window. He drew back, but only a little. How had he got here? The last few minutes were a dream: at the time, they had felt vivid, but now, as he tried to recall any detail, it all faded away.

He reached out to tug at that left bar, which came away easily from the old window frame, just as he had known it would. He held it in his good hand for a few seconds; it was surprisingly light, like a relay baton. But there was no one to pass it to – he was at the finish line now – so he let the bar go, hearing it clang as it hit the roof below.

An increasingly muffled part of his brain was telling him to slam shut the window, to barricade himself in the bathroom if necessary. But his body seemed to be moving of its own will – or rather, of *her* will – because now he was wrenching at the other safety bar and tossing it too into the night.

Was this how it had been for the others? He leaned out of the window, his eyes stinging as he stared into the haze, and he thought of Jacqueline, and Michelle, and Cynthia. He had assumed this part would be more violent, more of a struggle, but, for him at least, it felt closer to relief. That tiny part of his mind might be shouting at him to stop, but it was stifled by something he hadn't realised until now: he *wanted* this.

Finley had tried to convince himself that he was compelled by an unquenchable curiosity, or a need to sever the dangerous bond between himself and Cora, or even a selfless desire to protect others from the same fate, but it was more than that. As he hoisted himself up onto the window frame, his thoughts growing dim, he decided he might as well admit it to himself: he longed to play the hero. He needed to find out whether he was different, even special, in comparison to those who had gone – and perished – before him. Whatever lay ahead, he would emulate those shining figures from myth that he had idolised as a boy, back in the days when storybook heroics had felt possible; before he grew up, before he grew cautious, before his own body turned against him.

For as long as I can remember, I've stood at this window almost every night, but never before have I dared to venture through it. I wouldn't even have thought to try, before you came here and made everything feel possible. Now, as I clamber up into that suspended circle, one hand gripping at the rotted frame, the other bandaged up in a strip of torn apron, I feel a jolt of exhilaration: *I'm leaving*.

When my legs are dangling over the edge, I hold my breath and jump. I land with a thump on the roof below, my knees knocking against the tiles, my hand burning as I plant both palms to steady myself. Still, the damp night air is energising, and it feels like a victory to even get this far.

Below, someone is barking orders – Bill, I think – and I can just make out a few figures, hazy in the mist. Towards the lane, too, there are voices, and the snorting and pawing of horses. I flatten myself against the roof, my heart ticking. Usually, it's quieter here, with everyone down at Crescombe Beach, but tonight . . . Tonight, they must be crawling all over the rocky shoreline, scavenging.

My route into town is blocked. Even if there was time to run back there and raise the alarm – to try and save some of the men that were on that ship – I couldn't sneak down that crowded lane undetected. Instead, I must focus on saving just one man – and to do that, I need to get down to the water.

I scramble down the side of Crockers Nest, grazing my knees and elbows, tearing my dress, the bloody cloth loosening from my hand. In the mist, it's surprisingly easy to slip past Bill and the others – I'm just a cat or a fox, flitting through the dark – but when I reach the top of the cliff steps, my stomach squirms.

Every morning, in the sunlight, I clamber down here without a second thought. Even the other night, guided by the bright moon and your reassuring hand, it didn't seem so difficult. But now I can barely see two steps ahead, and I know that one false move will send me hurtling towards the rocks below, or plunging into the growling water. How did you climb this in the dark, night after night? And how did I ever think you could be driven by anything but love?

I take one step, then another, these small movements costing me more courage than I ever dreamed I possessed. But I will brave this for you, as you have braved it for me, time and time again. Because perhaps, if I reach Crockers Beach, I will find you there, emerging from the water as you did for our lessons. I try to picture it as I force my feet down a few more steps, but I can't. Perhaps you are already dead, I think, gripped by sudden panic; you're already gone, and it's my fault, because you saw that light and you *knew* – I love you.

I can't go any further. The thought of your death has pinned me here, the wind tugging at my hair and the hem of my dress. I press my back against the rock, as though to carry the whole of the cliff on my shoulders, because I'm dizzy again, and trembling so violently I feel I've lost control of my body. Here, closer to the seething water, I can hear it all – the shrieks, the crashes – and I close my eyes, childishly willing myself anywhere but here.

I don't know how long I stand like this, only that eventually my short, shallow breaths begin to deepen, mimicking the endless rhythm of the water below. It reminds me of our lessons again, of how you taught me to float, and as I think back to those shining mornings, I tell myself: I will swim with you again.

And with this glimpse into a possible future – with this *hope* – my body seems to unstick from the rock. I manage to hobble a little further down the steps, and as I do, I push aside all my old doubts and distrust, and finally allow myself to imagine what a life with you might be like. If I marry you, I will be safe. I will be loved. I will be far away from here.

I begin to move faster down the steps, and my mind too is racing as I strain against the limits of my own imagination. We will travel. We will go to places where I will be accepted as your wife, and I will finally see the world beyond Crescombe. We will go further than England, further than Europe, further than even you have journeyed before. Perhaps, together, we could even find my father.

I'm hurrying now, my body turned towards the narrow path ahead – towards my fate, which no longer seems dark and treacherous. The mist has mottled the sky, making it look more like your painting than ever, and I can almost see your light blazing through the gloom, beckoning me not just to you, but towards all our tomorrows . . .

Crack!

The sudden noise of something splintering apart sends me skidding, and I overbalance, half sprawling over the ledge. Desperately, I grip onto a lumpy step, its edges crushing my stomach, my legs flailing over the water far below. But I'm slipping, and as much as I kick and strain, I can't pull myself back up. I don't have the strength, the skill – I don't even have both my hands, because I can't feel my right any longer. The strip of apron has unwound, and as I finally lose my hold on the step, all I can see is my crude bandage fluttering in the night air, like a bloodied white flag urging me to surrender.

*

Finley experienced the next few minutes in disjointed fragments, like an old radio tuning in and out: his hands and knees grazing roof tiles; a moment's pause at the top of the cliff steps; and an almighty crack, which he seemed to remember, rather than actually hear.

It was only when he crashed through the surface of the water with a force that rattled all his teeth that everything seemed to converge again. Down, down he plunged, into the cold, into the dark, and although some optimistic instinct compelled him to try and kick back towards the sky, he had lost all sense of where it might be. His body was contorted, his limbs tangled; like clothes in a washing machine, he was being relentlessly spun and soaked until every part of him felt upside down, inside out.

A brief respite occurred as an undercurrent swelled beneath him, pushing him towards the water's crust. As he was flung back up into the night, Finley gasped for air, his eyes and nose and ears stinging as he attempted to stay afloat. Blearily, he could see the lights of Crockers Nest, just make out the shadowy mass of cliff from which he had tumbled ... But the sea's mercy was fleeting, and when he tried to throw himself towards the shore, a wave snatched at him, dragging him away, and back under.

So it continued for the next few seconds, or minutes, or hours: repeatedly, he was wrenched into icy darkness, churned up and disorientated, then spat out again, each time further from the shore. No matter how much he struggled – no matter how hard he attempted to propel himself back towards land – it was all in vain. If he had been able to think, his only thought would have been that he had no others: now, he was just a fleshy lump of primal panic; he was prey, being toyed with by this monstrous creature before he was devoured.

Then, all at once, the beast grew bored. Finley felt the water's grip encircle him, tighten and, with a lurch, he was sucked deeper, deeper, deeper ...

*

As I'm pulled under, all I can think about is floating.

I feared you might stay down there, you once told me, wrenching me upright when I held my face too long in the water. Back then, you might have been right to fear it. There have been times that I've craved that oblivion.

But now, more than ever, I need to live – not a half-life in this town, but a shared life beyond it, with you. If only I'd accepted your love earlier, or understood my own heart sooner. If only I'd been braver, less guarded. If only.

I can't see. I'm so cold. I feel like I'm shrinking, being twisted and reshaped for whatever comes next. I think I might be halfway there already—

But I won't go any further. I won't. Not tonight, not like this.

Not without you.

You, you, you.

You.

There was nothing Finley could do now. It was over. He was done. And with this realisation came relief – not because he wanted to die, but because it felt good to know, one way or the other, how this ended.

It felt good to think, too, because his mind seemed to be working again. It was oddly peaceful down here, and memories began to float around his head like shiny bubbles, rising from both his recent and distant past, before popping into nothing: being offered a lollipop if he let his mum ease a splinter from his finger; tripping on his own gown at graduation; Megan calling him *brave*; searching through The Book Bothy's crowded key ring; lying back on a holiday house bunkbed and pressing his toes between the slats above, just as Fiona was drifting off to sleep . . . Strangely, though a dozen different people were drifting through his mind, he could almost feel his twin here, curled up at his side as she had in the hospital that night. She was going to be furious with him for dying.

Was this how it had felt for Cora? For Jacqueline and Michelle? It now seemed the epitome of arrogance that Finley had ever thought himself different from them, as having some extra skill or virtue that might prevent history from repeating itself yet again. In the end, he was nothing more than that card he'd plucked from the tarot deck: the fool.

Down and down he sank, his lungs screaming for air, the rest of him as pliant as a puppet. It was so dark. Had he closed his eyes? He blinked once, twice, but the blackness seemed to be inside his head now, leaking across his vision . . .

Until, overhead, there was a flare of golden light.

Finley jerked in the water – but of course, this was it, wasn't it? This was *the* light. Inwardly, he laughed, because against the murky deep, it almost looked like *Hero's Bay* – so perhaps Delmore had had a premonition after all.

And with this thought, a figure burst from the beam. Silhouetted against a storm of bubbles, they dived towards him, plunging through the water with a superhuman grace. In the gloom, Finley tried to focus on what he was seeing. An angel? Some kind of mermaid? But no, that didn't make sense: *he* was the creature from the deep now . . .

You.

The figure was close, and as Finley began dipping in and out of darkness, he became aware of a pressure under his arms, urging him upwards. A part of him didn't want to go – this felt like being shaken awake just as he was drifting off to the most delicious sleep – but that grip was insistent, painfully so, and Finley didn't have the strength to resist the pressure to his armpits, wrenching him up and up and . . .

'Fuck!'

Finley might have thought this an atypical exclamation for an ethereal being, but as he broke through the surface of the water he was far more concerned with gulping down sweet, cold air. The sea was still lashing at him, trying to drag him back under, and though his rescuer was half lying beneath him, just about keeping him afloat, he was completely disorientated. Not least because he was being dazzled by that beam of light – which, he now realised, was the torch tied to the front of *Sandy Bottom*.

'Fuck!' Megan shouted again, right in his ear. Then, 'Hold this!'

Finley felt something being bundled into his hands, and looked down to find he was clutching at a bright orange lifebuoy attached to the boat by a rope. Megan then slipped from beneath him, and Finley barely had a chance to mourn her solid, reassuring presence before he found himself being shoved towards *Sandy Bottom*.

'Get in!'

Finley stared up at the three metal rungs that served as the boat's steps – which, oddly, were not unlike the so-called safety bars on his window – and balked at the effort it would take to pull himself up. But it seemed he had little choice, because Megan began pushing and elbowing any part of him she could reach, until Finley collapsed into the hull of the boat.

Panting, he lay back against the wet wood, and had a brief impression of a dark sky heavy with mist before a dripping Megan appeared above him, her expression a mixture of anger and alarm.

You're alive.

'Of course *I'm* alive,' Megan snapped.

Confused, Finley pressed a hand to his throbbing forehead (he hadn't spoken, had he?) and pushed himself up, still staring at Megan. Drenched, shivering and crabby-looking though she was, the sight of her was miraculous.

He wanted to check she was real, to anchor himself to her, because this was all so uncanny – her, the mist, the rescue – maybe, in reality, his now-vacated body was still somewhere under the water. So he reached out, their gazes locked on one another as his shaking fingers found the side of her face, where he smoothed back a few loose strands of her wet hair.

You're here.

Finley felt a change the moment he touched her. He hadn't taken his eyes off Megan, but he was aware of the haze around them shifting, dispersing. Something about him was clearer too; like in the aftermath of a cold, he felt like he could smell and taste and *breathe* properly again. He felt, for the first time since arriving here – perhaps for the first time in years – like himself.

Then the boat bucked, sending them both sprawling.

'We need to go,' said Megan, glancing up at the now star-speckled sky. 'We're miles from the shore . . .'

She moved away and, moments later, Finley heard the wheeze of the boat's temperamental engine, and felt the vessel begin to bump fitfully over the waves. He heaved himself onto one of the seats – which was difficult, because he was still half tangled in the lifebuoy's rope – and as he stared at the shadowy outline of East Crescombe in the distance, he tried to take stock of how he felt. Exhausted, mostly, and otherwise very wet and cold – but in addition to all of that were symptoms he couldn't entirely attribute to the shock of a near drowning: sweatiness, dizziness, tingly lips . . .

It was so typical that Finley began to laugh, and he didn't need his phone, which he must have left back in his room, to tell him that all the exertion and adrenaline of the last few minutes had sent his blood sugar plummeting. Besides, what could he do about it here, in the middle of the sea? In spite of Megan's efforts tonight, there was a good chance he wasn't going to make it back to shore.

'Hey?'

Finley turned and, despite the darkness and the rumble of the boat's engine, he became aware of something rolling over the hull towards him. He stopped it with a foot, picked it up: it was a bottle of lemonade.

'Thought you might need that,' said Megan, before returning to patting the boat's spluttering engine, as though soothing a distressed animal.

She spoke as though it was nothing at all – and to her, Finley supposed it wasn't. But as he unscrewed the lid and began to glug down the bottle's syrupy contents, he imagined her throwing it into the boat before she had set off, almost as an afterthought. However casually she'd considered it, that decision meant she had likely saved his life twice over.

Once Finley had gulped down half the lemonade, he paused, lowering the bottle. It was one of the fancy drinks from the museum's café – the same kind that Megan had brought on their picnic. He could just make out the artist's self-portrait on the label, though the condensation had caused the image to wrinkle, and Delmore's handsome face was now distorted almost beyond recognition.

The boat bumped against a particularly powerful wave, causing Finley's already chattering teeth to knock together, and he glanced up to find East Crescombe much closer than before – from here, it was even possible to discern the rangy outline of Crockers Nest. Though he wasn't about to relax just yet: *Sandy Bottom* was still emitting frequent gasps and coughs, and Finley wasn't sure Megan's muttered encouragement or her firm knocks to its engine were enough to sustain the boat for long.

When, somehow, they did come within touching distance of the shore, Finley saw they had another problem: there was nowhere to dock. The tide was still right in, so Crockers Beach was completely submerged, and the whipping waves rendered the rest of the rocky coastline far too treacherous to approach. As they bobbed there, so near yet so far to salvation, it also wasn't lost on Finley that this was the place that had felled *The Persephone*, a far bigger and stronger vessel than *Sandy Bottom*.

With a grunt of frustration, Megan cajoled the struggling boat further into the bay. Finley assumed they were heading to Crescombe Beach's wide stretch of sand, and wondered whether they would make it that far. However, Megan guided the boat to a spot roughly halfway along the eastern shoreline, parallel to the coastal footpath. There, the water was a little calmer, and a rusty mooring ring attached to the rock suggested that – historically, at least – other boats had docked here.

As soon as they were close enough, Finley leaped for the shore, anxious for Megan not to have to shove him to safety this time. He landed in an untidy heap, his skin prickling from the branches and thorns he'd disturbed, then staggered to his feet to reach back for Megan. She gripped at his fingers with one hand, clutching the boat rope in the other as she joined him on the overgrown shore.

At the other end of this leash, *Sandy Bottom* was rearing up in the waves. Worried that Megan would be pulled into the water, Finley hurried to help her, but she must have already lost her grip, for in an instant the rope had slipped away.

'No!'

Her voice was unusually high, like a child's, as she groped at the air where the rope had been. But it was too late – *Sandy Bottom* had already been snatched by the sea. With another cry, Megan scrambled forward, teetering at the water's edge, and something about the tension in her body sent a jolt of warning through Finley: *she was going to dive in.*

Without stopping to think about it, he lurched forward, flinging out his arms to secure her like a straitjacket. She was almost as tall as him, and might have been able to throw him off – only, before she could try, *Sandy Bottom* went smashing into the neighbouring rock.

'Oh no, no, no ...'

As Megan whimpered, Finley tightened his grip on her, but she wasn't straining to reach the water anymore. Her whole body had slackened, and if it hadn't been for her gasps of grief, he might have feared she'd fainted. She sank towards the ground, Finley going with her, and together they collapsed in the scrubby earth, unable to do anything but watch as the waves continued to dash Sandy Salter's boat against the rocks, breaking its bulk into splinters that were already being carried out to sea.

Aside from the unlocked door, Finley found his room exactly as he had left it. The window was wide open, its safety bars gone. The broken lantern was lying on the floor, its light long extinguished. Cora's belongings were still strewn nearby. Yet it all felt altered – it felt empty.

He too felt different. Woozy and wobbly-legged though he was, his mood was oddly euphoric. Elation was fizzing through him, as sweet and sharp and effervescent as the bubbles in that lemonade. It felt like a release, and a loss, and above all like that word that had been echoing around his head since they had struggled to shore: *alive, alive, alive.*

He turned to Megan, intending to ask whether the room felt changed to her, before remembering she had never been up here. He wasn't even sure why she was here now. They had only exchanged a few words since emerging from the dark footpath into the guesthouse, their sodden shoes squelching against its fluffy, recently laid carpet. Perhaps, as his rescuer, she simply wanted to see the job through to its end, to check he wasn't going to get himself into any more trouble. Or maybe, he thought, with a rush of guilt, she was preparing to have a go at him; for endangering himself, for endangering her, for inadvertently destroying her mum's boat . . .

In the room's artificial light, Megan looked paler and smaller than usual. How had she hoisted him from that churning water? How had she even found him? He thought her heroics might be catching up with her now; gone was her mettle, even her annoyance, and, like him, she couldn't seem to stop shaking.

'You okay?' he asked.

She nodded and, despite evidence to the contrary, Finley believed her. Because there was also something *charged* about her as she stood there, wide-eyed and trembling. Finley recognised it because he could feel it too. Most likely, they were both in shock, but still ... Perhaps there was also a kind of triumph, in cheating death.

They stared at one another for a few moments: what now?

'Tea,' Finley decided, mostly to give himself something to do.

After closing the porthole window, he spent a minute or so fiddling about in the kitchenette: filling the kettle, searching for clean mugs, checking his blood sugar – which, remarkably, was now fairly normal. His hand, he noticed, was also better. At some point, he had lost his bandage, and the wound beneath had reverted to its early scar-like appearance. It didn't even hurt anymore.

He was just lamenting that he didn't have any whisky to take the edge off the shock when, behind him, Megan spoke for the first time since they had arrived at Crockers Nest:

'Finley.'

He turned in time to see – without warning, without ceremony – Megan pull her sodden T-shirt over her head. She dropped it to the floor, then proceeded to wriggle out of her shorts, too, while Finley, who was still clutching two empty mugs, stared, too stunned to look away; her mismatched underwear was also completely soaked, and left very little to the imagination. Still, though most of his body seemed to have stopped working, his brain was racing at twice its usual speed as he tried to rationalise what was going on (naturally, she should want to take off her wet clothes; it was good she felt comfortable enough to do so in his presence; should he fetch her a towel, or perhaps offer her the first shower?).

You're thinking too much, he reminded himself – and, guided almost as much by the exhilaration still bubbling through him as by the nearly naked sight of her, Finley set down the mugs, strode across the room and pulled her into a kiss.

For the second time that evening, Megan swayed in his arms, though these circumstances felt a lot more promising. Especially as, moments later, she was tugging up the hem of *his* T-shirt, then slipping her clammy hands into his to lead him towards the bed. They left two trails of watery footprints in their wake, which stopped as they cocooned themselves in the stripy covers, by which point Finley didn't need to stop kissing her to check: this was *happening*.

Clumsily at first, their eager mouths bumping together in the darkness, their shaking fingers struggling to peel off what remained of their clothes. But by the time the forgotten kettle had given a distant click, they had shifted back towards something resembling their leisurely passion under the fireworks. In the heat of their makeshift nest, their shivers turned sweeter as they revelled in exploring one another, Finley intoxicated not just by Megan herself – by the tautness and softness of her body, by the briny taste of her warming skin – but also the fervour with which she seemed to want him (*him!*). Until they were not so much clinging survivors of a shipwreck, but floating pieces of sea-drift; untethered, unhurried, tangled by an unexpected tide.

20

Crescombe

Finley was unsurprised to wake up alone. Aside from the two unused mugs by the sink and some very rumpled bedsheets, there was little evidence that he had spent the night in anyone's company but his own. At some point in the early hours, Megan must have gathered up her wet clothes, like a selkie reclaiming her sealskin, and returned to the water.

Although it wasn't just Megan's absence Finley could feel as he drifted back to consciousness, his whole body aching – presumably more from the exertions of the first half of the night. Possibly the one part of him that didn't hurt was his hand, and when Finley held it above his face he saw that his palm was completely healed. More than healed, in fact, because now there wasn't even the faintest trace of a scar. It was as though the wound had never existed.

Cora's gone, he thought, and in addition to his immense relief and satisfaction, there was a little sadness too. Even aside from his unmarked hand, he had known something had changed the moment he'd touched Megan in the boat last night – and he knew it now from the porthole window, which this morning remained shut, as definitive as a full stop.

He had done it, then – or rather, *Megan* had done it. Because this was her victory, wasn't it? Not only had she hoisted Finley from the water, but in doing so she had disrupted that loop of events – she had rerecorded the memory. *You're here*, Finley had heard himself say, but in that moment he and Cora had been perceiving different rescuers. He now understood that it wouldn't have been enough to survive on his own, like Cynthia – and neither had Cora's unfinished business involved avenging herself on the Crockers, or some futile attempt to save those poor souls aboard *The Persephone*. In the end, all she had wanted – all she had *needed* – was Delmore.

Finley flexed his right hand a few times, marvelling at how unblemished it was, while his thoughts lingered on Cynthia. How was she feeling this morning? He would message her to ask, but for the moment he pictured her returning from her night shift and feeling, like him, unexpectedly calm. He hoped so, anyway. She had lived with this far longer than him – was it too much to imagine that she might be able to sleep at night, or stop that incessant scratching? That perhaps she could even walk right into the National Gallery, stand before *Hero's Bay*, and feel absolutely—

Finley bolted upright in bed, ignoring the creaks of protest from his exhausted body: he had just realised something – something so *obvious* he had no idea how he hadn't seen it before . . . Only, he had to double-check. He needed to go back to The Delmore Experience one last time.

Suddenly energised, he clambered out of bed and dragged himself into the shower, before heading out into Crescombe. He was now so accustomed to the route that he walked much of it automatically, feeling for the latch on the other side of the footpath gate, stooping under the low branches of a hazel tree, hopping over the wobbliest stone of the steps that led down to the main beach. The tide was out – Crescombe had puffed out its chest this morning – and Finley took off his shoes to walk across wet sand pockmarked by tiny bubbles.

I could stay here, he thought, after taking a quick detour to one of the promenade's kiosks for a bacon roll. He could ask Lorraine if he could remain at Crockers Nest for the foreseeable, or look into renting a flat elsewhere in town. He could get a proper job, either at the guesthouse or a café or somewhere like The Delmore Experience. Maybe one day he could even open his own bookshop here; Crescombe, he felt, could use a bookshop.

But by the time he was halfway across the beach, reservations had started to creep in. Crescombe was about as far away from his parents as it was possible to be while still in Britain – and not even very close to Fiona. He also didn't feel particularly enthused by the prospect of a Crescombe winter, which he suspected would be bleak, even for someone from Scotland. More than anything, though, Finley felt he was done here. Staying wouldn't give him any more insight into what he wanted to do – what he wanted to *be*. Yet perhaps, he thought, remembering how enviously he had gazed on that route of Delmore's grand tour, his time here had made him open to possibilities that, before now, he'd been too cautious to consider.

As it was mid-morning, The Delmore Experience was teeming with tourists. Most were either thronging around the café or queuing for the studio on the first floor, and Finley, too, hurried through the rooms covering the artist's life before Crescombe. The Delmore who had inhabited those places felt different to the one Finley had discovered these past few weeks, almost as though the town had remade him – and *unmade* him, Finley supposed.

Instead, he headed to the gallery containing *Hero's Bay*. Like Crescombe, the painting didn't look the same as it had at the start of the summer. Previously, Finley had enjoyed it as a casual appreciator of art, but now every detail, every brushstroke seemed infused with significance. Conversely, though – and like his room back at Crockers Nest – the painting now felt dormant, and standing before it was like experiencing that thick silence after a background noise that hadn't fully registered finally stopped.

Finley wasn't sure how long he remained there, lost in the light and shadow of this image that would probably be imprinted on his mind for the rest of his life. Every once in a while, he was vaguely aware of the gallery's other visitors filing in and out around him, and even caught snatches of their conversations as they looked for missing members of their groups and wondered where the nearest toilets were. But, somehow, when he heard a particular set of footsteps to his left – their tread light yet purposeful – he sensed immediately that it was Megan, and finally tore his gaze from the painting.

'Hey,' he said.

'Hey.'

They shared a shy smile that Finley thought might be the only acknowledgement that anything out of the ordinary had happened between them the previous night, though his heart hitched at the sight of her. She was leaning against the empty doorframe of the gallery with her arms folded, her hands concealed by the long sleeves of a thin grey jumper, her blonde hair, which looked unusually dry, hanging over her shoulder in a messy plait.

Megan offered no explanation for finding him there – perhaps she had spotted him arriving at the gallery, or coming up the hill, or maybe she had simply known that, after what had occurred the night before, this was where he would be. She seemed to be waiting for him to speak and, after his gaze had flicked back towards the painting, Finley decided to voice the theory that had led him here.

'Did you know that this is the real *Hero's Bay*?' he said. 'The original, the one painted by Delmore himself?'

Megan said nothing, her expression inscrutable. Which was a little disappointing, because Finley had been hoping to surprise her into more of a response. Nevertheless, he decided to persevere.

'It's been bothering me a while, the effect this painting has had on me, when supposedly it's just a copy,' he said, staring up at the seascape again. 'I've been assuming the reason it sent me so strange was because of Cora – that I was experiencing some memory of her reacting to this image that was all about her, all about *them*. But then, why did I feel nothing when I went to see what's allegedly the real *Hero's Bay* in London?'

Still, Megan remained silent, though Finley noticed she'd unfolded her arms.

'I think I've figured out what happened,' he said, confident he had her attention. 'It's well documented, right, that Ambrose Montgomery was reluctant to hand over *Hero's Bay* to Lady Delphine Delmore after her son's death? Your dad told me they'd had a public falling-out about it. Obviously, she wanted her late son's final, brilliant painting, but Montgomery needed to hold on to it because it had already become famous around here, and therefore a nice little earner for him – especially considering he was spiralling into debt because of his overly ambitious plans to develop Crescombe.'

He paused, and Megan inclined her head in a tiny nod.

'Eventually, Montgomery backed down and agreed to part with the painting – or so he *said*,' continued Finley, who was quite enjoying himself. 'Because what I reckon he actually did was hire someone to replicate *Hero's Bay*. Crescombe was crawling with artists at the time, and one in particular had a talent for mimicry – *and* she would have been cheap because she was a woman.'

In his mind's eye, Finley saw the owlish self-portrait that presided over the bar in Marina's, like a reigning monarch, and was pleased to reflect that this story – which had so far been floating around his head only in fragments – really did fit together.

'So Marina Vitali recreated *Hero's Bay*,' he said, 'and Montgomery handed over that copy, the fake, to Lady Delphine, who had never seen the original so wouldn't have known the difference. He probably assumed the grieving dowager would keep it to herself, or at worst put it on display in her private residence. But that's not what she did. She was desperate to secure her son's artistic legacy, so the painting eventually ended up in the National Gallery, where its mystery and Delmore's early death caused its fame to skyrocket ...'

He trailed off as a couple of elderly women strolled into the gallery, arm in arm. But they seemed more interested in their own gossipy conversation, and only gave the painting a cursory glance before they passed through the other doorway.

'And then Montgomery must've had an issue,' said Finley, once the women had left. 'He had the genuine *Hero's Bay*, but couldn't *say* it was the genuine *Hero's Bay* because he'd be accused of fraud – not to mention betraying his dear friend, Lady Delphine. So, he had to keep quiet. He had to sit on this artwork that was taking off in value, while his own money dwindled – and it did dwindle, because not only were his plans for Crescombe proving too ambitious, but the Vitalis got wind of what was going on and started blackmailing him into keeping the secret.' Finley glanced towards the Montgomery Gallery, where he had seen those inexplicable regular payments from the developer to the Italian restauranteurs. 'And eventually, it all caught up with him,' Finley concluded. 'Montgomery took his own life a few years later, hugely in debt – yet in possession of an almost invaluable painting that could have totally transformed his fortunes.'

For a long time, neither he nor Megan said anything, merely stared at *Hero's Bay* – the real *Hero's Bay* – though Finley was also picturing the once vibrant figure of Ambrose Montgomery as he appeared in the next gallery, immortalised and slightly ridiculed in an unfinished painting.

'My mum had a similar theory,' Megan said at last.

Somehow, this didn't surprise Finley. 'Is it just a theory?' he asked her daughter now. 'Nobody – your dad, perhaps – has ever investigated it?'

Megan shook her head and, again, Finley could believe it. In fact, he thought he understood something Ambrose Montgomery had never been able to grasp: this was a town that eschewed publicity, modernity, change.

Still, it was staggering to think that that famous image in the coffee table books and on the tea towels might not have been painted by Delmore at all, but by a young woman fleeing the effects of war, forced to start again in a new country. Delmore's original painting was, to Finley at least, the more vibrant of the two – the result, perhaps, of an artist driven by pure passion, rather than one practically painting by numbers, albeit extremely skilfully. But that didn't mean any of this felt fair on Marina Vitali. Like Cora Crocker, she had played a crucial part in the story of *Hero's Bay*, and yet both women had been almost entirely lost to history.

'Are you going to tell anyone else?' Megan asked, her tone so detached it was difficult to know how bothered she was by the idea.

Finley hadn't really considered this, but found himself shaking his head. He was no art historian or journalist – and what an ordeal it would be, to prove something for which there was so little evidence. Again, pursuing this would make him akin to someone like Montgomery, trying to force this resistant town into change. Finley pictured the vegetation already reclaiming Cora's gravestone, and even that watermark blooming across the parish records, and thought he now understood another of this town's most fundamental principles: Crescombe kept its secrets.

Without really agreeing to do so, Finley and Megan left the gallery, following the back route through the old house that Finley had taken on the night of the festival fireworks. Before they reached the door, Megan paused to whistle over her shoulder and, seconds later, heralded by the clicking of claws on stone, Skipper bombed out of the gloom, almost knocking them both over in his eagerness to greet them.

Together, they emerged into sunlight, the wide semi-circle of Crescombe Beach gleaming like a golden smile. Skipper immediately found a patch of long grass to sniff and roll about in, while Megan led Finley to the fencing fringing the cliff, where the daylight offered a clear view down onto the tufty ledges where they'd shared their first kiss – and where Delmore had once descended into inky water to swim over to Crockers Nest.

Struck all over again by the magnitude of what had happened the previous night, Finley asked, 'How did you find me? How did you even know I'd be out there?'

'I saw your light,' said Megan, and Finley remembered the unnatural brightness of Cora's lantern, before everything had gone suddenly dark. 'I thought something might be up, so I went out to check.'

Her tone was matter-of-fact, as though this were an entirely logical reason to head out to sea in an unreliable boat in the middle of the night.

'You stopped it, you know,' he told her. 'In being there, in pulling me out of the sea, you—' He broke off, doubting she would appreciate talk of *loops* and *rerecordings*, so simply repeated, 'You stopped it.'

'Hmm,' she said.

This was likely the best he was going to get from her: it wasn't an acknowledgement of the haunting, exactly, but nor was it a denial. It was frustrating, because she had *been* there, in that shifting mist; she must have sensed something of what he had. And, in the early hours of this morning, when he'd finally been drifting off to sleep, Megan still curled up next to him on the narrow bed, one of the last things he'd been aware of was her examining his hand, fiddling with his fingers so she could press her lips to his palm . . .

'Well, you were the one who figured it all out,' she said now.

Surprised, Finley's instinct was to deny this unexpected compliment, to instead credit all the people who had helped him: Dawn, Cynthia, the vicar, Megan's own father, even those Delmore obsessives online. But, for once, he ignored his natural inclination towards self-effacement: 'Yeah, I guess I did.'

The effort it cost to say this had him digging for the reassuringly smooth surface of the larimar stone in his pocket, but instead he discovered something else – something he had deliberately brought to The Delmore Experience.

'Do you want this?' he asked Megan, showing her Delmore's ring.

She raised a pale eyebrow. 'Look, Finley, last night was fun, but there's no need to make an honest woman out of me or anything.'

He laughed, as pleased by her acknowledgement of what had happened between them as he was by her joke. Because it *had* been fun, hadn't it? Just as it had been comforting, and emboldening, and *enlightening* ...

'Erm,' he said, trying to remember what they'd been talking about, before handing her the ring – and the responsibility of what to do with it. 'You can throw it in the sea if you like,' he said. 'Or you can give it to your dad – I guess he'll be able to get it verified. Or you can keep it,' Finley added, for already Megan had slid the band onto her thumb, just as she had in the pub. He smiled. 'It suits you.'

He was referring less to the way it looked on her and more its mermaid engraving. He hoped she would keep it – she deserved it. After the part she had, quite literally, played in the events of the previous night, it felt right that she should have something of Delmore's.

Megan continued to examine the ring for a while, before she dropped her hand to pick at a piece of lichen on the nearest fence post, and said, 'You don't have to leave.'

Her tone was entirely neutral. It sounded like a statement of fact – one she was only airing in case the possibility that he could remain in Crescombe hadn't occurred to him. Nevertheless, Finley was touched. Tempted.

'You don't have to stay,' he replied, directing this statement of fact to the horizon.

'I know,' she said, surprising him again by adding, 'I won't. I'd like to see a bit more of the world – well, a bit more of the sea.'

At this, Finley's imagination began to construct an unlikely yet irresistible scenario in which he was on a beach somewhere very far-flung and exciting, and appearing from the sparkling, sun-kissed sea was Megan in *Sandy Bottom* . . . Before, with a wrench of guilt, he remembered the vessel now only existed in fragments.

'I'm really sorry about your boat,' he blurted out.

Megan shrugged. 'Wasn't really my boat.'

This might have been true, but her response was a far cry from her raw grief of the night before. Was she putting on a brave face? He didn't think so – Megan was nothing if not sincere – so perhaps, in the short time that had elapsed since *Sandy Bottom*'s demise, she had come to terms with its loss.

Still, he thought he should offer her something for the vessel that had saved his life (how much did boats cost?). Before he could, however, she gave him a thumbs up, Delmore's ring glimmering, and said, 'Maybe I'll pawn this for a new one.'

He laughed again, almost certain she was joking – though, as always, it was difficult to tell.

Skipper, who had evidently grown bored with rolling about in the grass, then reappeared, prodding at Megan's legs with his nose.

'Yeah, yeah, we're going . . .' she said, scratching his glossy head.

Finley felt a flutter of panic: was this the moment of their parting already? What should he do? What should he say?

'See you on another sea?' Megan suggested.

'Yeah,' he agreed, reflecting that perhaps his fantasy hadn't been so outlandish after all. 'See you on another sea.'

He craved a moment of contact, something to mark the end of whatever this had been between them. But he held back, fearful of being brushed off, and instead decided to emulate her usual exit strategy by walking away.

'Finley?'

He had only gone a few paces when she called him, and he'd barely had the chance to turn around before she had thrown her arms around his neck, her body thumping against his with a force that was almost Skipper-like. Immediately, Finley hugged her back, holding her as tightly as he dared, breathing in the coconutty aroma of her soap or shampoo.

They stood there for a long time, and somehow it felt just as intimate as the previous night. They might only have met a few weeks earlier, but she had been his confidante, his companion, she had saved his life – and perhaps he had even saved her a little too. So, while it was impossible to know whether they could have sustained this beyond Crescombe, beyond even the summer, it didn't really matter; here, now, they had been exactly what they needed one another to be.

When they finally disentangled themselves, it was a gradual breaking apart, one in which fingers held on to sleeves until the last possible moment, and somehow ended in the touching of their foreheads, like a kiss of a different kind.

'Bye,' Megan whispered.

'Bye.'

This time, they both walked away, she taking the path that continued around Westcliff, while he prepared to head back towards Crescombe and, eventually, Crockers Nest. Though before the hill dipped, he couldn't resist turning back, just once. Megan was already a distant figure on the cliff, her loosening hair streaming in the breeze, the black dog bounding at her heels. And as Finley gazed after her, silhouetted as she was by endless, shining sea, he realised that, of course, he *had* had something the haunting's other victims had not: he'd had her.

*

The tide was still out by the time Finley returned to East Crescombe. So before he went back to Crockers Nest – before he started looking up train times, and packing, and saying goodbye to Lorraine – he headed down the cliff steps for a last look at the water.

He descended carefully, his disjointed memories of the previous night still raw, though he knew he wouldn't fall today. In fact, when he reached the point where he – and Cora, and the others – must have slipped, it was quite irritating how serene the sea looked below, its silver-blue surface only lightly wrinkled by ripples. Considering how dark and monstrous the water had been the night before, this composed façade felt disingenuous, even a little mocking.

Perhaps this was why, when he reached Crockers Beach, Finley stepped up onto the Nessie-shaped rock, in a futile, Canute-like attempt to gain some status over the water. It was, he realised with a pang, the exact spot he had first met Megan – and where Delmore had drawn Cora, almost two centuries earlier. It was an amazing thought: whatever Finley did or didn't know about her, Cora Crocker had been real, had been right here, her feet where his were now, on this rock – which, save for a few more limpets and strands of seaweed, was still exactly the same.

The more tangible evidence of Cora's existence was now scattered. The ring was with Megan, and Finley had replaced the tinderbox in its hidey hole in the wall, along with the now dormant lantern, which had felt too significant an object to throw away or even return to the clutter of the cellar. He had decided to hold on to the sketch, at least for the time being. Somehow, knowing what he did, he felt he owed it to Cora to retain her image, to remember her – plus, it was bleakly amusing to think that, like Montgomery, he was in possession of a valuable artwork he'd never be able to sell.

That only left the larimar stone. Looking down, Finley realised he had already withdrawn it from his pocket and was pressing it between his fingers, its shape familiar, soothing. He was tempted to keep it. Because Dawn had been right – about many things, but especially this: it was an excellent worry stone.

Yet Cora's talisman seemed to belong here in the same way that she and Delmore did – in the same way that *Hero's Bay* did – and it felt wrong to take it with him, especially when he wasn't sure he had any more need of it. So Finley raised his arm and, as hard as he could, threw the larimar stone away – glimpsing, for a second, its electric blue arc across the sky, like the streak of a kingfisher, before it plopped into the water, and was gone.

Now, the sea will decide its fate.

Maybe it will wash up in a child's bucket by the end of the week. Maybe it will drop into some sunken cave or wreck, or be dragged right to the very bottom of the ocean.

Or maybe – for the sea doesn't forget – over the course of tens or hundreds or thousands of years, that little stone will travel all the way back to the clear, warm waters from where it came; a promise fulfilled on a faraway shore.

Acknowledgements

Recently, I had the revelation that I'm a bit of a Lorraine, and this book was my Crockers Nest; a big, ambitious project I entered into with great enthusiasm and frequently ended up in a flap about. Thank goodness, then, that I too have been able to rely on the expertise and kindness of so many brilliant people.

First, I want to say a huge thank you to all the readers, authors and book bloggers who got behind my debut novel, *The Lost Storyteller*, as well as the immense support I received from booksellers, especially in my home city of Edinburgh (may your bookshops fare better than The Book Bothy!). I was also staggered by how many friends and family members got in touch, bought a copy, or sent a picture of the book in some far-flung destination; thank you – it meant the absolute world.

I first pitched *The Haunting of Hero's Bay* in deepest, darkest lockdown on a Zoom call to two exceptional women: my then editor, Sara Nisha Adams, and my then agent, Jo Unwin. I'm so sad to no longer be working with you both, but so grateful for what we achieved together – and that it was such *fun* (that fairy tale treasure hunt!). Thank you for being such an important part of this book's story – and, indeed, my own.

I'd also like to thank my wonderful new editor, Lucy Stewart, for taking on a far messier manuscript than I would have liked, for helping me figure out what kind of story I was trying to tell, and in particular for pointing out that *really obvious* solution to the plot hole I'd been tripping over for weeks. Thank you also to Jake Carr, Ella Young, Kallie Townsend, Natalie Chen and the whole team at Hodder & Stoughton for taking such good care of me.

I'm grateful to every single one of my friends for enduring all my *moaning* about this book, but special thanks must go to Flo Vincent for her early encouragement when the story was so new and unformed; to my first readers, Kirsty Mackay and Joe Murray, for important notes on tarot etiquette and the correct way to address a baron, but mostly for keeping me smiling and (just about) sane during final edits; and to Helen Patuck, for gallantly driving me and my ten-month-old baby around North Devon in a hastily borrowed campervan when I suddenly decided I needed to return to the captivating stretch of coast that inspired this novel.

Above all, I want to thank Joely Badger, my companion in make-believe ever since, aged fifteen, we sat next to one another in Art and started dreaming up stories. It's such a joy that we're still doing this now – even if these days our discussions have to be scheduled around our children's bedtimes or shouted across soft play centres. I'd also like to mention Joely's beloved dog, Buffy, who accompanied us on countless plot walks, yawned through hours of late-night story-planning and even came to the launch of my first book; she was so loved, and is much missed.

Thank you to my amazing parents, who support me in all the big, important ways, but in countless small ones too, like casually enquiring whether my book is in stock at every bookshop they pass, or coming to my events and asking questions they already know the answers to. I'm also hugely thankful to my (sort of) mother-in-law, Bing, for keeping my children happy and my house tidy while I sneak off to write – just stop smuggling in so many treats, please.

I have so many reasons to thank my partner, Chaz: for solo parenting before big deadlines, for having a sensible job that actually pays the bills, for allowing me to use his type 1 diabetes in this story ... But mostly I'm grateful that I have at my side the sort of man I think we need to see more of, both in fiction and in real life; I'll never admit this to your face, but you're a bit of a hero.

And finally, thank you to my daughters, Lia and Phoebe. When I first envisioned this book, long before you were born, I couldn't have predicted that the writing of it would coincide with your learning to swim. Watching how boldly and gleefully you have taken to the water reminded me why I wanted to tell this story in the first place, and – like everything you do – makes me feel prouder and more inspired than you'll ever know.